The CLOISTERS

The WHITE CHAPEL

The WEEPING TOWER

ARD

WATFORD

TREES

# CARRY ON

# CARRY ON

## THE RISE AND FALL OF SIMON SNOW

# RAINBOW ROWELL

MACMILLAN

First published in the US 2015 by St. Martin's Press

First published in the UK 2015 by Macmillan Children's Books
an imprint of Pan Macmillan
20 New Wharf Road, London N1 9RR
Associated companies throughout the world
www.panmacmillan.com

ISBN 978-1-4472-9890-8

1 3 5 7 9 8 6 4 2

A CIP catalogue record for this book is available from
the British Library.

Designed by Anna Gorovoy
Printed and bound by CPI Group (UK) Ltd, Croydon CR0 4YY

*For Laddie and Rosey—*
*May you fight your own battles*
*and forge your own wings*

MAGIC SEPARATES US FROM THE WORLD; LET NOTHING SEPARATE US FROM EACH OTHER

# BOOK ONE

# 1

## SIMON

I walk to the bus station by myself.

There's always a fuss over my paperwork when I leave. All summer long, we're not even allowed to walk to Tescos without a chaperone and permission from the Queen—then, in the autumn, I just sign myself out of the children's home and go.

"He goes to a *special* school," one of the office ladies explains to the other when I leave. They're sitting in a Plexiglas box, and I slide my papers back to her through a slot in the wall. "It's a school for dire offenders," she whispers.

The other woman doesn't even look up.

It's like this every September, even though I'm never in the same care home twice.

The Mage fetched me for school himself the first time, when I was 11. But the next year, he told me I could make it to Watford on my own. *"You've slain a dragon, Simon. Surely you can manage a long walk and a few buses."*

I hadn't meant to slay that dragon. It wouldn't have hurt me, I don't think. (I still dream about it sometimes. The way the fire consumed it from the inside out, like a cigarette burn eating a piece of paper.)

I get to the bus station, then eat a mint Aero while I wait for my first bus. There's another bus after that. Then a train.

Once I'm settled on the train, I try to sleep with my bag in my lap and my feet propped up on the seat across from me—but a man a few rows back won't stop watching me. I feel his eyes crawling up my neck.

Could just be a pervert. Or police.

Or it could be a bonety hunter who knows about one of the prices on my head. . . . ("It's *boun*ty hunter," I said to Penelope the first time we fought one. "No—*bone*ty hunter," she replied. "Short for 'bone-teeth'; that's what they get to keep if they catch you.")

I change carriages and don't bother trying to sleep again. The closer I get to Watford, the more restless I feel. Every year, I think about jumping from the train and spelling myself the rest of the way to school, even if it puts me in a coma.

I could cast a **Hurry up** on the train, but that's a chancy spell at the best of times, and my first few spells of the school year are always especially dicey. I'm supposed to practise during the summer—small, predictable spells when no one's looking. Like turning on night-lights. Or changing apples to oranges.

"Spell your buttons and laces closed," Miss Possibelf suggested. "That sort of thing."

"I only ever wear one button," I told her, then blushed when she looked down at my jeans.

"Then use your magic for household chores," she said. "Wash the dishes. Polish the silver."

I didn't bother telling Miss Possibelf that my summer meals are served on disposable plates and that I eat with plastic cutlery (forks and spoons, never knives).

I also didn't bother to practise my magic this summer.

It's boring. And pointless. And it's not like it *helps*. Practising doesn't make me a better magician; it just sets me off. . . .

Nobody knows why my magic is the way it is. Why it goes off like a bomb instead of flowing through me like a fucking stream or however it works for everybody else.

"I don't know," Penelope said when I asked her how magic feels for her. "I suppose it feels like a well inside me. So deep that I can't see or even imagine the bottom. But instead of sending down buckets, I just think about drawing it up. And then it's there for me—as much as I need, as long as I stay focused."

Penelope always stays focused. Plus, she's powerful.

Agatha isn't. Not as, anyway. And Agatha doesn't like to talk about her magic.

But once, at Christmas, I kept Agatha up until she was tired and stupid, and she told me that casting a spell felt like flexing a muscle and keeping it flexed. "Like *croisé devant*," she said. "You know?"

I shook my head.

She was lying on a wolfskin rug in front of the fire, all curled up like a pretty kitten. "It's ballet," she said. "It's like I just hold position as long as I can."

Baz told me that for him, it's like lighting a match. Or pulling a trigger.

He hadn't meant to tell me that. It was when we were fighting the chimera in the woods during our fifth year. It had us cornered, and Baz wasn't powerful enough to fight it alone. (The *Mage* isn't powerful enough to fight a chimera alone.)

"Do it, Snow!" Baz shouted at me. "Do it. Fucking unleash. Now."

"I can't," I tried to tell him. "It doesn't work like that."

"It bloody well does."

"I can't just turn it on," I said.

"*Try.*"

"I *can't,* damn it." I was waving my sword around—I was pretty good with a sword already at 15—but the chimera wasn't corporeal. (Which is my rough luck, pretty much always. As soon as you start carrying a sword, all your enemies turn out mist and gossamer.)

"Close your eyes and light a match," Baz told me. We were both trying to hide behind a rock. Baz was casting spells one after another; he was practically singing them.

"What?"

"That's what my mother used to say," he said. "Light a match inside your heart, then blow on the tinder."

It's always fire with Baz. I can't believe he hasn't incinerated me yet. Or burned me at the stake.

He used to like to threaten me with a Viking's funeral, back when we were third years. "Do you know what that is, Snow? A flaming pyre, set adrift on the sea. We could do yours in Blackpool, so all your chavvy Normal friends can come."

"Sod off," I'd say, and try to ignore him.

I've never even had any Normal friends, chavvy or otherwise.

Everyone in the Normal world steers clear of me if they can. Penelope says they sense my power and instinctively shy away. Like dogs who won't make eye contact with their masters. (Not that I'm anyone's master—that's not what I mean.)

Anyway, it works the opposite with magicians. They love the smell of magic; I have to try hard to make them hate me.

Unless they're Baz. He's immune. Maybe he's built up a tolerance to my magic, having shared a room with me every term for seven years.

That night that we were fighting the chimera, Baz kept yelling at me until I went off.

We both woke up a few hours later in a blackened pit. The boulder we'd been hiding behind was dust, and the chimera was vapour. Or maybe it was just gone.

Baz was sure I'd singed off his eyebrows, but he looked fine to me—not a hair out of place.

Typical.

# 2

## SIMON

I don't let myself think about Watford over the summers.

After my first year there, when I was 11—I spent the whole summer thinking about it. Thinking about everyone I'd met at school—Penelope, Agatha, the Mage. About the towers and the grounds. The teas. The puddings. The *magic*. The fact that *I* was magic.

I made myself sick thinking about the Watford School of Magicks—daydreaming about it—until it started to feel like nothing more than a daydream. Just another fantasy to make the time pass.

Like when I used to dream about becoming a footballer someday—or that my parents, my real parents, were going to come back for me. . . .

My dad would be a footballer. And my mum would be some posh model type. And they'd explain how they'd had to give me up because they were too young for a baby, and because his career was on the line. *"But we always missed you, Simon,"* they'd say. *"We've been looking for you."* And then they'd take me away to live in their mansion.

Footballer mansion . . . Magickal boarding school . . .

They both seem like crap in the light of day. (Especially

when you wake up in a room with seven other discards.)

That first summer, I'd beaten the memory of Watford to a bloody pulp by the time my bus fare and papers showed up in the autumn, along with a note from the Mage himself. . . .

*Real.* It was all real.

So, the *next* summer, after my second year at Watford, I didn't let myself think about magic at all. For months. I just shut myself off from it. I didn't miss it, I didn't wish for it.

I decided to let the World of Mages come back to me like a big surprise present come September, if it was going to. (And it *did* come back. It always has, so far.)

The Mage used to say that maybe someday he'd let me spend summers at Watford—or maybe even spend them with him, wherever he goes all summer.

But then he decided I was better off spending part of every year with the Normals. To stay close to the language and to keep my wits about me: *"Let hardship sharpen your blade, Simon."*

I thought he meant my actual blade, the Sword of Mages. Eventually I figured out that he meant me.

*I'm* the blade. The Mage's sword. And I'm not sure if these summers in children's homes make me any sharper. . . . But they do make me hungrier. They make me crave Watford like, I don't know, like life itself.

Baz and his side—all the old, rich families—they don't believe that anyone can understand magic the way that they do. They think they're the only ones who can be trusted with it.

But no one *loves* magic like I do.

None of the other magicians—none of my classmates, none of their parents—know what it's like to live without magic.

Only I know.

And I'll do anything to make sure it's always here for me to come home to.

⋆

I *try* not to think about Watford when I'm away—but it was almost impossible this summer.

After everything that happened last year, I couldn't believe the Mage would even pay attention to something like the end of term. Who interrupts a war to send the kids home for summer holidays?

Besides, I'm *not* a kid anymore. Legally, I could have left care at 16. I could've got my own flat somewhere. Maybe in London. (I could afford it. I have an entire bag of leprechaun's gold—a big, duffel-sized bag, and it only disappears if you try to give it to other magicians.)

But the Mage sent me off to a new children's home, just like he always does. Still moving me around like a pea under shells after all these years. Like I'd be safe there. Like the Humdrum couldn't just summon me, or whatever it was he did to me and Penelope at the end of last term.

"He can *summon* you?" Penny demanded as soon as we got away from him. "Across a body of water? That isn't possible, Simon. There's no precedent for that."

"Next time he summons me like a half-arsed squirrel demon," I said, "I'll tell him so!"

Penelope had been unlucky enough to be holding my arm when I was snatched, so she'd been snatched right along with me. Her quick thinking is the only reason either of us escaped.

"Simon," she said that day, when we were finally on a train back to Watford. "This is serious."

"Siegfried and fucking Roy, Penny, I know that it's serious. He's got my number. *I* don't even have my number, but the Humdrum's got it down."

"How can we still know so little about him," she fumed. "He's so . . ."

"Insidious," I said. " 'The Insidious Humdrum' and all that."

"Stop teasing, Simon. This is *serious.*"

"I know, Penny."

When we got back to Watford, the Mage heard us out and made sure we weren't hurt, but then he sent us on our way. Just . . . sent us home.

It didn't make any sense.

So, *of course,* I spent this whole summer thinking about Watford. About everything that happened and everything that *could* happen and everything that's at stake . . . I stewed on it.

But I still didn't let myself dwell on any of the *good* things, you know? It's the good things that'll drive you mad with missing them.

I keep a list—of all the things I miss most—and I'm not allowed to touch it in my head until I'm about an hour from Watford. Then I run through the list one by one. It's sort of like easing yourself into cold water. But the opposite of that, I suppose—easing yourself into something really good, so the shock of it doesn't overwhelm you.

I started making my list, my good things list, when I was 11, and I should probably cross a few things off, but that's harder than you'd think.

Anyway, I'm about an hour from school now, so I mentally take out my list and press my forehead against the train window.

**Things I miss most about Watford:**

No. 1—Sour cherry scones

I'd never had cherry scones before Watford. Just raisin ones— and more often plain, and always something that came from the shop, then got left in an oven too long.

At Watford, there are fresh-baked cherry scones for

breakfast every day if you want them. And again in the afternoon with tea. We have tea in the dining hall after our lessons, before clubs and football and homework.

I always have tea with Penelope and Agatha, and I'm the only one of us who ever eats the scones. "Dinner is in two hours, Simon," Agatha will tsk at me, even after all these years. Once Penelope tried to calculate how many scones I've eaten since we started at Watford, but she got bored before she got to the answer.

I just can't pass the scones up if they're there. They're soft and light and a little bit salty. Sometimes I dream about them.


## No. 2—Penelope

This spot on the list used to belong to "roast beef." But a few years back, I decided to limit myself to one food item. Otherwise the list turns into the food song from *Oliver!*, and I get so hungry, my stomach cramps.

I should maybe rank Agatha higher than Penelope; Agatha *is* my girlfriend. But Penelope made the list first. She befriended me in my first week at school, during our Magic Words lesson.

I didn't know what to make of her when we met—a chubby little girl with light brown skin and bright red hair. She was wearing pointy spectacles, the kind you'd wear if you were going as a witch to a fancy dress party, and there was a giant purple ring weighing down her right hand. She was trying to help me with an assignment, and I think I was just staring at her.

"I know you're Simon Snow," she said. "My mum told me you'd be here. She says you're really powerful, probably more powerful than me. I'm Penelope Bunce."

"I didn't know someone like you could be named Penelope,"

I said. Stupidly. (Everything I said that year was stupid.)

She wrinkled her nose. "What should 'someone like me' be named?"

"I don't know." I *didn't* know. Other girls I'd met who looked like her were named Saanvi or Aditi—and they definitely weren't ginger. "Saanvi?"

"Someone like me can be named anything," Penelope said.

"Oh," I said. "Right, sorry."

"And we can do whatever we want with our hair." She turned back to the assignment, flipping her red ponytail. "It's impolite to stare, you know, even at your friends."

"*Are* we friends?" I asked her. More surprised than anything else.

"I'm helping you with your lesson, aren't I?"

She was. She'd just helped me shrink a football to the size of a marble.

"I thought you were helping me because I'm thick," I said.

"Everyone's thick," she replied. "I'm helping you because I like you."

It turned out she'd accidentally turned her hair that colour, trying out a new spell—but she wore it red all of first year. The next year, she tried blue.

Penelope's mum is Indian, and her dad is English— actually, they're both English; the Indian side of her family has been in London for ages. She told me later that her parents had told her to steer clear of me at school. "My mum said that nobody really knew where you came from. And that you might be dangerous."

"Why didn't you listen to her?" I asked.

"Because nobody knew where you came from, Simon! And you might be dangerous!"

"You have the *worst* survival instincts."

"Also, I felt sorry for you," she said. "You were holding your wand backwards."

I miss Penny every summer, even when I tell myself not to. The Mage says no one can write to me or call me over the holidays, but Penny still finds ways to send messages: Once she possessed the old man down at the shop, the one who forgets to put in his teeth—she talked right through him. It was nice to hear from her and everything, but it was so disturbing that I asked her not to do it again, unless there was an emergency.

### No. 3—The football pitch

I don't get to play football as much as I used to. I'm not good enough to play on the school team, plus I'm always caught up in some scheme or drama, or out on a mission for the Mage. (You can't reliably tend a goal when the bloody Humdrum could summon you anytime it strikes his fancy.)

But I do get to play. And it's a perfect pitch: Lovely grass. The only flat part of the grounds. Nice, shady trees nearby that you can sit under and watch the matches . . .

Baz plays for our school. Of course. The tosser.

He's the same on the field as he is everywhere else. Strong. Graceful. Fucking ruthless.

### No. 4—My school uniform

I put this on the list when I was 11. You have to understand, when I got my first uniform, it was the first time I'd ever had clothes that fit me properly, the first time I'd ever worn a blazer and tie. I felt tall all of a sudden, and posh. Until Baz walked into our room, much taller than me—and posher than everyone.

There are eight years at Watford. First and second years wear striped blazers—two shades of purple and two shades of green—with dark grey trousers, green jumpers, and red ties.

You have to wear a boater on the grounds up until your sixth year—which is really just a test to see if your **Stay put** is strong enough to keep a hat on. (Penny always spelled mine on for me. If I did it myself, I'd end up sleeping in the damn thing.)

There's a brand-new uniform waiting for me every autumn when I get to our room. It'll be laid out on my bed, clean and pressed and perfectly fitted, no matter how I've changed or grown.

The upper years—that's me now—wear green blazers with white piping. Plus red jumpers if we want them. Capes are optional, too; I've never worn one, they make me feel like a tit, but Penny likes them. Says she feels like Stevie Nicks.

I like the uniform. I like knowing what I'm going to wear every day. I don't know what I'll wear next year, when I'm done with Watford. . . .

I thought I might join the Mage's Men. They've got their own uniforms—sort of Robin Hood meets MI6. But the Mage says that's not my path.

That's how he talks to me. *"It's not your path, Simon. Your destiny lies elsewhere."*

He wants me to stand apart from everyone else. Separate training. Special lessons. I don't think he'd even let me go to school at Watford if he weren't the headmaster there—and if he didn't think it was the safest place for me.

If I asked the Mage what I should wear after Watford, he'd probably kit me out like a superhero. . . .

I'm not asking anybody what I wear when I leave. I'm 18. I'll dress myself.

Or Penny will help.

## No. 5—My room

I should say "our room," but I don't miss the sharing-with-Baz part of it.

You get your room and your roommate assignment at Watford as a first year, and then you never move. You never have to pack up your things or take down your posters.

Sharing a room with someone who wants to kill me, who's wanted to kill me since we were *11*, has been . . . Well, it's been rubbish, hasn't it?

But maybe the Crucible felt bad about casting Baz and me together (not literally; I don't *think* the Crucible's sentient) because we've got the best room at Watford.

We live in Mummers House, on the edge of school grounds. It's a four-and-a-half-storey building, stone, and our room is at the very top, in a sort of turret that looks out over the moat. The turret's too small for more than one room, but it's bigger than the other student rooms. And it used to be staff accommodation, so we have our own en suite.

Baz is actually a fairly decent person to share a bathroom with. He's in there all morning, but he's clean; and he doesn't like me to touch his stuff, so he keeps it all out of the way. Penelope says our bathroom smells like cedar and bergamot, and that's got to be Baz because it definitely isn't me.

I'd tell you how Penny manages to get into our room—girls are banned from the boys' houses and vice versa—but I still don't know. I think it might be her ring. I saw her use it once to unseal a cave, so anything's possible.

## No. 6—The Mage

I put the Mage on this list when I was 11, too. And there've been plenty of times when I thought I should take him off.

Like in our sixth year, when he practically ignored me. Every time I tried to talk to him, he told me he was in the middle of something important.

He still tells me that sometimes. I get it. He's the headmaster. And he's more than that—he's the head of the Coven, so technically, he's in charge of the whole World of Mages. And it's not like he's my dad. He's not my anything. . . .

But he's the closest thing I've got to anything.

The Mage is the one who first came to me in the Normal world and explained to me (or tried to explain to me) who I am. He still looks out for me, sometimes when I don't even realize it. And when he does have time for me, to really talk to me, that's when I feel the most grounded. I fight better when he's around. I think better. It's like, when he's there, I almost buy into what he's always told me—that I'm the most powerful magician the World of Mages has ever known.

And that all that power is a *good* thing, or at least that it will be someday. That I'll get my shit together eventually and solve more problems than I cause.

The Mage is also the only one who's allowed to contact me over the summer.

And he always remembers my birthday in June.


**No. 7—Magic**

Not *my* magic, necessarily. That's always with me and, honestly, not something I can take much comfort in.

What I miss, when I'm away from Watford, is just *being* around magic. Casual, ambient magic. People casting spells in the hallway and during lessons. Somebody sending a plate of sausages down the dinner table like it's bouncing on wires.

The World of Mages isn't actually a world. We don't have

cities. Or even neighbourhoods. Magicians have always lived among mundanity. It's safer that way, according to Penelope's mum; it keeps us from drifting too far from the rest of the world.

The fairies did that, she says. Got tired of dealing with everybody else, wandered into the woods for a few centuries, then couldn't find their way back.

The only place magicians live together, unless they're related, is at Watford. There are a few magickal social clubs and parties, annual gatherings—that sort of thing. But Watford is the only place where we're together all the time. Which is why everyone's been pairing off like crazy in the last couple years. If you don't meet your spouse at Watford, Penny says, you could end up alone—or going on singles tours of Magickal Britain when you're 32.

I don't know what Penny's even worried about; she's had a boyfriend in America since our fourth year. (He was an exchange student at Watford.) Micah plays baseball, and he has a face so symmetrical, you could summon a demon on it. They video-chat when she's home, and when she's at school, he writes to her almost every day.

"Yes," she tells me, "but he's *American.* They don't think about marriage the way we do. He might dump me for some pretty Normal he meets at Yale. Mum says that's where our magic is going—bleeding out through ill-considered American marriages."

Penny quotes her mum as much as I quote Penny.

They're both being paranoid. Micah's a solid bloke. He'll marry Penelope—and then he'll want to take her home with him. *That's* what we should all be worried about.

Anyway . . .

Magic. I miss magic when I'm away.

When I'm by myself, magic is something personal. My burden, my secret.

But at Watford, magic is just the air that we breathe. It's what makes me a part of something bigger, not the thing that sets me apart.

## No. 8—Ebb and the goats

I started helping out Ebb the goatherd during my second year at Watford. And for a while, hanging out with the goats was pretty much my favourite thing. (Which Baz had a field day with.) Ebb's the nicest person at Watford. Younger than the teachers. And surprisingly powerful for somebody who decided to spend her life taking care of goats.

"What does being powerful have to do with anything?" Ebb'll say. "People who're tall aren't forced to pay thrashcanball."

"You mean basketball?" (Living at Watford means Ebb's a bit out of touch.)

"Same difference. I'm no soldier. Don't see why I should have to fight for a living just because I can throw a punch."

The Mage says we're all soldiers, every one of us with an ounce of magic. That's what's dangerous about the old ways, he says—magicians just went about their merry way, doing whatever they felt like doing, treating magic like a toy or an entitlement, not something they had to protect.

Ebb doesn't use a dog with the goats. Just her staff. I've seen her turn the whole herd with a wave of her hand. She'd started teaching me—how to pull the goats back one by one; how to make them all feel at once like they'd gone too far. She even let me help with the birthing one spring. . . .

I don't have much time to spend with Ebb anymore.

But I leave her and the goats on my list of things to miss. Just so that I can stop for a minute to think about them.

## No. 9—The Wavering Wood

I should take this one off the list.

Fuck the Wavering Wood.


## No. 10—Agatha

Maybe I should take Agatha off my list, too.


I'm getting close to Watford now. I'll be at the station in a few minutes. Someone will have come down from the school to fetch me. . . .

I used to save Agatha for last. I'd go all summer without thinking about her, then wait until I was almost to Watford before I'd let her back into my head. That way I wouldn't spend the whole summer convincing myself that she was too good to be true.

But now . . . I don't know, maybe Agatha *is* too good to be true, at least for me.

Last term, just before Penny and I got snatched by the Humdrum, I saw Agatha with Baz in the Wavering Wood. I suppose I'd sensed before that there might be something between them, but I never believed she'd betray me like that—that she'd cross *that* line.

There was no time to talk to Agatha after I saw her with Baz—I was too busy getting kidnapped, then escaping. And then I couldn't talk to her over the summer, because I can't talk to anybody. And now, I don't know . . . I don't know what Agatha is to me.

I'm not even sure whether I've missed her.

# 3

## SIMON

When I get to the station, there's no one to meet me. No one I know, anyway—there's a bored-looking taxi driver who's written *Snow* on a piece of cardboard.

"That's me," I say. He looks dubious. I don't look much like a public school toff, especially when I'm not in uniform. My hair's too short—I shave it every year at the end of term—and my trainers are cheap, and I don't look *bored* enough; I can't keep my eyes still.

"That's me," I say again. A bit thuggishly. "Do you want to see my ID?"

He sighs and drops the sign. "If you want to get dropped off in the middle of nowhere, mate, I'm not going to argue with you."

I get in the back of the taxi and sling my bag down on the seat next to me. The driver starts the engine and turns on the radio. I close my eyes; I get sick in the back of cars on good days, and today isn't a good day—I'm nervous, and all I've had to eat is a chocolate bar and a bag of cheese-and-onion crisps.

Almost there now.

This is the last time I'll be doing this. Coming back to

Watford in autumn. I'll still come back, but not like this, not like I'm coming home.

"Candle in the Wind" comes on the radio, and the driver sings along.

**Candle in the wind** is a dangerous spell. The boys at school say you can use it to give yourself more, you know, *stamina*. But if you emphasize the wrong syllable, you'll end up starting a fire you can't put out. An actual fire. I'd never try it, even if I had call for it; I've never been good with double entendres.

The car hits a pothole, and I lurch forward, catching myself on the seat in front of me.

"Belt up," the driver snaps.

I do, taking a look around. We're already out of the city and into the countryside. I swallow and stretch my shoulders back.

The taxi driver goes back to singing, louder now—*"never knowing who to turn to"*—like he's really getting into the song. I think about telling *him* to belt up.

We hit another pothole, and my head nearly bangs against the ceiling. We're on a dirt road. This isn't the usual way to Watford.

I glance up at the driver, in the mirror. There's something wrong—his skin is a deep green, and his lips are red as fresh meat.

Then I look at him, as he is, sitting in front of me. He's just a cabbie. Gnarled teeth, smashed nose. Singing Elton John.

Then back at the mirror: Green skin. Red lips. Handsome as a pop star. *Goblin.*

I don't wait to see what he's up to. I hold my hand over my hip and start murmuring the incantation for the Sword of Mages. It's an invisible weapon—more than invisible, really; it's not even there until you say the magic words.

The goblin hears me casting, and our eyes meet in the

mirror. He grins and reaches into his jacket.

If Baz were here, I'm sure he'd make a list of all the spells I could use in this moment. There's probably something in French that would do nicely. But as soon as my sword appears in my hand, I grit my teeth and slash it across the front seat, taking off the goblin's turning head—and the headrest, too. *Voilà.*

He keeps driving for a second; then the steering wheel goes wild. Thank magic there's no barrier between us—I unbuckle my seat belt and dive over the seat (and the place where the goblin's head used to be) to grab the wheel. His foot must still be on the gas: We're already off the road and accelerating.

I try to steer us back, but I don't actually know how to drive. I jerk the wheel to the left, and the side of the taxi slams into a wooden fence. The airbag goes off in my face, and I go flying backwards, the car still smashing into something, probably more fence. I never thought I'd die like *this*. . . .

The taxi comes to a stop before I come up with a way to save myself.

I'm half on the floor, and I've hit my head on the window, then the seat. When I eventually tell Penny about all this, I'm skipping the part where I took off my safety belt.

I stretch my arm up over my head and pull the door handle. The door opens, and I fall out of the taxi onto my back in the grass. It looks like we've gone though the fence and spun out into a field. The engine is still running. I climb to my feet, groaning, then reach into the driver's window and turn it off.

It's a spectacle in there. Blood all over the airbag. And the body. And me.

I go through the goblin's jacket, but don't find anything besides a packet of gum and a carpet knife. This doesn't feel like the Humdrum's work—there's no itchy sign of him in the air. I take a deep breath to make sure.

Probably just another revenge run, then. The goblins have been after me ever since I helped the Coven drive them out of Essex. (They were gobbling up drunk people in club bathrooms, and the Mage was worried about losing regional slang.) I think the goblin who successfully offs me gets to be king.

This one won't be getting a crown. My blade's stuck in the seat next to him, so I yank it out and let it disappear back into my hip. Then I remember my bag and grab that, too, wiping blood on my grey trackie bottoms before I open the bag to fish out my wand. I can't just leave this mess here, and I don't think it's worth saving anything for evidence.

I hold my wand over the taxi and feel my magic scramble up to my skin. "Work with me here," I whisper. ***"Out, out, damned spot!"***

I've seen Penelope use that spell to get rid of unspeakable things. But all it does for me is clean some blood off my trousers. I guess that's something.

The magic is building up in my arm—so thick, my fingers are shaking. "Come on," I say, pointing. ***"Take it away!"***

Sparks fly out of my wand and fingertips.

"Fuck me, come *on* . . ." I shake out my wrist and point again. I notice the goblin's head lying in the grass near my feet, back to its true green again. Goblins are handsome devils. (But most devils are fairly fit.) "I suppose you ate the cabbie," I say, kicking the head back towards the car. My arm feels like it's burning.

***"Into thin air!"*** I shout.

I feel a hot rush from the ground to my fingertips, and the taxi disappears. And the head disappears. And the fence disappears. And the road . . .

*

An hour later, sweaty and still covered in dried goblin blood and that dust that comes out of airbags, I finally see the school buildings up ahead of me. (It was only a patch of that dirt road that disappeared, and it wasn't much of a road to start with. I just had to make my way back to the main road, then follow it here.)

All the Normals think Watford is an ultraexclusive boarding school. Which I guess it is. The grounds are coated in glamours. Ebb told me once that we keep casting new spells on the school as we develop them. So there's layer upon layer of protection. If you're a Normal, all the magic burns your eyes.

I walk up to the tall iron gate—THE WATFORD SCHOOL is spelled out on the top—and rest my hand on the bars to let them feel my magic.

That used to be all it took. The gates would swing open for anyone who was a magician. There's even an inscription about it on the crossbar—MAGIC SEPARATES US FROM THE WORLD; LET NOTHING SEPARATE US FROM EACH OTHER.

"It's a nice thought," the Mage said when he appealed to the Coven for stiffer defences, "but let's not take security orders from a six-hundred-year-old gate. I don't expect people who come to my house to obey whatever's cross-stitched on the throw pillows."

I was at that Coven meeting, with Penelope and Agatha. (The Mage had wanted us there to show what was at stake. *"The children! The future of our world!"*) I didn't listen to the whole debate. My mind wandered off, thinking about where the Mage really lived and whether I'd ever be invited there. It was hard to picture him with a house, let alone throw pillows. He has rooms at Watford, but he's gone for weeks at a time. When I was younger, I thought the Mage lived in the woods when he was away, eating nuts and berries and sleeping in badger dens.

Security at the Watford gate and along the outer wall has got stiffer every year.

One of the Mage's Men—Penelope's brother, Premal—is stationed just inside today. He's probably pissed off about the assignment. The rest of the Mage's team'll be up in his office, planning the next offensive, and Premal's down here, checking in first years. He steps in front of me.

"All right, Prem?"

"Looks like I should be asking *you* that question. . . ."

I look down at my bloody T-shirt. "Goblin," I say.

Premal nods and points his wand at me, murmuring a cleaning spell. He's just as powerful as Penny. He can practically cast spells under his breath.

I hate it when people cast cleaning spells on me; it makes me feel like a child. "Thanks," I say anyway, and start to walk past him.

Premal stops me with his arm. "Just a minute there," he says, raising his wand up to my forehead. "Special measures today. The Mage says the Humdrum's walking around with your face."

I flinch, but try not to pull away from his wand. "I thought that was supposed to be a secret."

"Right," he said. "A secret that people like me need to know if we're going to protect you."

"If I were the Humdrum," I say, "I could've already eaten you by now."

"Maybe that's what the Mage has in mind," Premal says. "At least then we'd know for sure it was him." He drops his wand. "You're clear. Go ahead."

"Is Penelope here?"

He shrugs. "I'm not my sister's keeper."

For a second, I think he's saying it with emphasis, with magic, casting a spell—but he turns away from me and leans against the gate.

There's no one out on the Great Lawn. I must be one of the first students back. I start to run, just because I can, upsetting a huddle of swallows hidden in the grass. They blow up around me, twittering, and I keep running. Over the Lawn, over the drawbridge, past another wall, through the second and third set of gates.

Watford has been here since the 1500s. It's set up like a walled city—fields and woods outside the walls, buildings and courtyards inside. At night, the drawbridge comes up, and nothing gets past the moat and the inner gates.

I don't stop running till I'm up at the top of Mummers House, falling against my door. I pull out the Sword of Mages and use it to nick the pad of my thumb, pressing it into the stone. There's a spell for this, to reintroduce myself to the room after so many months away—but blood is quicker and surer, and Baz isn't around to smell it. I stick my thumb in my mouth and push the door open, grinning.

My room. It'll be our room again in a few days, but for now it's mine. I walk over to the windows and crank one open. The fresh air smells even sweeter now that I'm inside. I open the other window, still sucking on my thumb, and watch the dust motes swirl in the breeze and the sunlight, then fall back on my bed.

The mattress is old—stuffed with feathers and preserved with spells—and I sink in. *Merlin.* Merlin and Morgan and Methuselah, it's good to be back. It's always so good to be back.

The first time I came back to Watford, my second year, I climbed right into my bed and cried like a baby. I was still crying when Baz came in. *"Why are you* already *weeping?"* he snarled. *"You're ruining my plans to push you to tears."*

I close my eyes now and take in as much air as I can:

Feathers. Dust. Lavender.

Water, from the moat.

Plus that slightly acrid smell that Baz says is the merwolves. (Don't get Baz started on the merwolves; sometimes he leans out our window and spits into the moat, just to spite them.)

If he were here already, I'd hardly smell anything over his posh soap. . . . I take a deep breath now, trying to catch a hint of cedar.

There's a rattle at the door, and I jump to my feet, holding my hand over my hip and calling again for the Sword of Mages. That's three times already today; maybe I should just leave it out. The incantation is the only spell I always get right, perhaps because it's not like other spells. It's more of a pledge: *"In justice. In courage. In defence of the weak. In the face of the mighty. Through magic and wisdom and good."*

It doesn't *have* to appear.

The Sword of Mages is mine, but it belongs to no one. It doesn't come unless it trusts you.

The hilt materializes in my grip, and I swing the sword up to my shoulder just as Penelope pushes the door open.

I let the sword drop. "You shouldn't be able to do that," I say.

She shrugs and falls onto Baz's bed.

I can feel myself smiling. "You shouldn't even be able to get past the front door."

Penelope shrugs again and pushes Baz's pillow up under her head.

"If Baz finds out you touched his bed," I say. "He's going to kill you."

"Let him try."

I twist my wrist just so, and the sword disappears.

"You look a fright," she says.

"Ran into a goblin on the way in."

"Can't they just *vote* on their next king?" Her voice is light, but I can tell she's sizing me up. The last time she saw me, I was a bundle of spells and rags. The last time I saw Penny, everything was falling apart. . . .

We'd just escaped the Humdrum, fled back to Watford, and burst into the White Chapel in the middle of the end-of-year ceremony—poor Elspeth was accepting an award for eight years of perfect attendance. I was still bleeding (from my pores, no one knew why). Penny was crying. Her family was there—because everybody's families were there—and her mum started screaming at the Mage. *"Look at them—this is your fault!"* And then Premal got between them and started screaming back. People thought the Humdrum must be right behind Penny and me, and were running from the Chapel with their wands out. It was my typical end-of-year chaos times *a hundred,* and it felt worse than just chaotic. It felt like the end.

Then Penelope's mum spelled their whole family away, even Premal. (Probably just to their car, but it was still really dramatic.)

I haven't talked to Penny since.

Part of me wants to grab her right now and pat her down head to toe, just to make sure she's whole—but Penny hates scenes as much as her mum loves them. *"Don't say hello, Simon,"* she's told me. *"Because then we'll have to say good-bye, and I can't stand good-byes."*

My uniform is laid out at the end of my bed, and I start

putting it away, piece by piece. New grey trousers. New green-and-purple striped tie . . .

Penelope sighs loudly behind me. I walk back to my bed and flop down, facing her, trying not to smile from ear to ear.

Her face is twisted into a pout.

"What can possibly have got under your skin already?" I ask.

"*Trixie*," she huffs. Trixie's her roommate. Penny says she'd trade Trixie for a dozen evil, plotting vampires. In a heartbeat.

"What's she done?"

"Come back."

"You were expecting otherwise?"

Penny adjusts Baz's pillow. "Every year, she comes back more manic than she was the year before. First she turned her hair into a dandelion puff, then she cried when the wind blew it away."

I giggle. "In Trixie's defence," I say, "she *is* half pixie. And most pixies are a little manic."

"Oh, and doesn't she know it. I swear she uses it as an excuse. I can't survive another year with her. I can't be trusted not to spell her head into a dandelion and blow."

I swallow another laugh and try hard not to beam at her. Great snakes, it's good to see her. "It's your last year," I say. "You'll make it."

Penny's eyes get serious. "It's *our* last year," she says. "Guess what you'll be doing next summer. . . ."

"What?"

"Hanging out with me."

I let my grin free. "Hunting the Humdrum?"

"Fuck the Humdrum," she says.

We both laugh, and I kind of grimace, because the

Humdrum looks just like me—an 11-year-old version of me. (If Penny hadn't seen him, too, I'd think I'd hallucinated the whole thing.)

I shudder.

Penny sees it. "You're too thin," she says.

"It's the tracksuit."

"Change, then." She already has. She's wearing her grey pleated uniform skirt and a red jumper. "Go on," she says, "it's almost teatime."

I smile again and jump up off the bed, grabbing a pair of jeans and a purple sweatshirt that says WATFORD LACROSSE. (Agatha plays.)

Penny grabs my arm when I walk past Baz's bed on the way to the bathroom. "It's good to see you," she whispers.

I smile. Again. Penny makes my cheeks hurt. "Don't make a scene," I whisper back.

# 4

## PENELOPE

Too thin. He looks too thin.

And something worse . . . scraped.

Simon always looks better after a few months of Watford's roast beef. (And Yorkshire pudding and tea with too much milk. And fatty sausages. And butter-scone sandwiches.) He's broad-shouldered and broad-nosed, and when he gets too thin, his skin just hangs off his cheekbones.

I'm used to seeing him thin like this, every autumn. But this time, today, it's worse.

His face looks chapped. His eyes are lined with red, and the skin around them looks rough and patchy. His hands are red, too, and when he clenches his fists, the knuckles go white.

Even his smile is awful. Too big and red for his face.

I can't look him in the eye. I grab his sleeve when he comes close, and I'm relieved when he keeps walking. If he didn't, I might not let go. I might grab him and hold him and spell us both as far away from Watford as possible. We could come back after it's all over. Let the Mage and the Pitches and the Humdrum and everyone else fight the wars they seem to have their hearts set on.

Simon and I could get a flat in Anchorage. Or Casablanca. Or Prague.

I'd read and write. He'd sleep and eat. And we'd both live to see the far end of 19. Maybe even 20.

I'd do it. I'd take him away—if I didn't believe he was the only one who could make a difference here.

If I stole Simon and kept him safe . . .

I'm not sure there'd be a World of Mages to come back to.

# 5

## SIMON

We practically have the dining hall to ourselves.

Penelope sits on the table with her feet on a chair. (Because she likes to pretend she doesn't care.)

There are a few younger kids, first and second years, at the other side of the hall, having tea with their parents. I notice them, children and adults, all trying to get a look at me. The kids'll get used to me after a few weeks, but this'll be their parents' only chance to get an eyeful.

Most magicians know who I am. Most of them knew I was coming before I knew myself; there's a prophecy about me—a few prophecies, actually—about a superpowerful magician who'll come along and fix everything.

*And one will come to end us.*
*And one will bring his fall.*
*Let the greatest power of powers reign,*
*May it save us all.*

The Greatest Mage. The Chosen One. The Power of Powers.

It still feels strange believing that that bloke's supposed to be me. But I can't deny it, either. I mean, nobody else has power like mine. I can't always control it or direct it, but it's there.

I think when I showed up at Watford, people had sort of given up on the old prophecies. Or wondered if the Greatest Mage had come and gone without anybody ever noticing.

I don't think *anybody* expected the Chosen One to come from the Normal world—from mundanity.

A mage has never been born to Normals.

But I must have been, because magicians don't give up their kids. There's no such thing as magickal orphans, Penny says. Magic is too precious.

The Mage didn't tell me all that, when he first came to get me. I didn't know that I was the first Normal to get magic, or the most powerful magician anyone had heard of. Or that plenty of magicians—especially the Mage's enemies— thought he was making me up, some sort of political sleight of hand. A Trojan 11-year-old with baggy jeans and a shaved head.

When I first got to Watford, some of the Old Families wanted me to make the rounds, to meet everyone who mattered, so they could check me out in person. Kick my tyres. But the Mage wasn't having any of it. He says most magicians are so caught up in their own petty plots and power struggles that they lose sight of the big picture. *"I won't see you become anyone's pawn, Simon."*

I'm glad now that he was so protective. It'd be nice to know more magicians and to feel more a part of a community, but I've made my own friends—and I made them when we were young, when none of them were overly fussed about my Great Destiny.

If anything, my celebrity status has been a liability for making friends at Watford. Everybody knows that things tend to explode around me. (Though no *people* have exploded yet—that's something.)

I ignore the staring from the other tables and help Penelope get our tea.

Even though we go to an exclusive boarding school—with its own cathedral and moat—nobody's spoiled at Watford. We do our own cleaning and, after our fourth year, our own laundry. We're allowed to use magic for chores, but I usually don't. Cook Pritchard does the cooking, with a few helpers, and we all take turns serving at mealtimes. On weekends, it's help yourself.

Penelope gets us a plate of cheese sandwiches and a mountain of warm scones, and I tear through half a block of butter. (I eat my scones with big slabs of it, so the butter melts on the outside but keeps a cold bite in the middle.) Penny's watching me like I'm mildly disgusting, but also like she's missed me.

"Tell me about your summer," I say between swallows.

"It was good," she says. "Really good."

"Yeah?" Crumbs fly out of my mouth.

"My dad and I went to Chicago. He did some research at a lab there, and Micah and I helped." She loosens up as soon as she mentions her boyfriend's name. "Micah's Spanish is amazing. He taught me so many new spells—I think if I study the language more, I'll be able to cast them like a native."

"How is he?"

Penelope blushes and takes a bite of sandwich so she doesn't have to answer right away. It's only been a few months since I saw her last, but she looks different. More grown up.

Girls don't have to wear skirts at Watford, but both Penelope and Agatha like to. Penny wears short pleated ones, usually with knee-high argyle socks in the school colours. Her shoes are the black sort with buckles, like Alice wears in Wonderland.

Penny's always looked younger than she is—everything about her is round and girlish, she has chubby cheeks and thick legs and dimples in her knees—and the uniform makes her seem even younger.

But still . . . she's changed this summer. She's starting to look like a woman in little girl's clothes.

"Micah's good," she says finally, pushing her dark hair behind her ears. "It's the most time we've spent together since he was here."

"So the thrill isn't gone?"

She laughs. "No. If anything, it felt . . . real. For the first time."

I don't know what to say, so I try to smile at her.

"Ugh," she says, "close your mouth."

I do.

"But what about you?" Penny asks. I can tell she's been waiting to interrogate me and can't wait any longer. She glances around us and leans forward. "Can you tell me what happened?"

"What happened when?"

"This summer."

I shrug. "Nothing happened."

She sits back, sighing. "Simon, it's not my fault that I went to America. I tried to stay."

"No," I say. "I mean there's *nothing to tell*. You left. Everyone left. I went back in care. Liverpool, this time."

"You mean, the Mage just . . . sent you away? After everything?" Penelope looks confused. I don't blame her.

I'd just escaped a kidnapping, and the first thing the Mage did was send me packing.

I thought, when Penny and I told the Mage what

had happened, that he'd want to go after the Humdrum immediately. We knew where the monster was; we finally knew what he looked like!

The Humdrum has been attacking Watford as long as I've been here. He sends dark creatures. He hides from us. He leaves a trail of dead spots in the magickal atmosphere. And finally, we had a *lead*.

I wanted to find him. I wanted to punish him. I wanted to end this, once and for all, fighting at the Mage's side.

Penelope clears her throat. I must look as lost as I feel. "Have you talked to Agatha?" she asks.

"Agatha?" I butter another scone. They've cooled off, and the butter doesn't melt. Penny holds up her right hand, and the large purple stone on her finger glints in the sunlight—
**"Some like it hot!"**

It's a waste of magic. She's constantly wasting magic on me. The butter melts into the now-steaming scone, and I bounce it from hand to hand. "You know Agatha's not allowed to talk to me over the summer."

"I thought maybe she'd find a way this time," Penelope says. "Special measures, to try to explain herself."

I give up on the too-hot scone and drop it on my plate. "She wouldn't disobey the Mage. Or her parents."

Penny just watches me. Agatha is her friend, too, but Penelope's much more judgemental of her than I am. It's not my job to judge Agatha; it's my job to be her boyfriend.

Penny sighs and looks away, kicking at the chair. "So that's it? Nothing? No progress? Just another summer? What are we supposed to do now?"

Normally I'm the one kicking things, but I've been kicking walls—and anyone who looked at me wrong—all summer. I shrug. "Go back to school, I guess."

✤

Penelope's avoiding her room.

She says Trixie's girlfriend came back early, too, and they don't have any personal boundaries. "Did I tell you Trixie got her ears pierced this summer? She wears big noisy bells right in the pointy parts."

Sometimes I think Penny's Trixie diatribes are borderline speciesist. I tell her so.

"Easy for you to say," she says, all stretched out on Baz's bed again. "You don't live with a pixie."

"I live with a vampire!" I argue.

"Unconfirmed."

"Are you saying you don't think Baz is a vampire?"

"I know he's a vampire," she says. "But it's still unconfirmed. We've never actually seen him drink blood."

I'm sitting on the window ledge and leaning out a bit over the moat, holding on to the latch of the swung-open pane. I scoff: "We've seen him covered in blood. We've found piles of shrivelled-up rats with fang marks down in the Catacombs. . . . I've told you that his cheeks get really full when he has a nightmare? Like his mouth is filling up with extra teeth?"

"Circumstantial evidence," Penny says. "And I still don't know why you'd creep up on a vampire who has night terrors."

"I live with him! I have to keep my wits about me."

She rolls her eyes. "Baz'll never hurt you in your room."

She's right. He can't. Our rooms are spelled against betrayal—the Roommate's Anathema. If Baz does anything to physically hurt me inside our room, he'll be cast out of the school. Agatha's dad, Dr. Wellbelove, says it happened once when he was in school. Some kid punched his roommate, then got sucked out through a window and landed outside the school gate. It wouldn't open for him again ever.

You get warnings when you're young: For the first two years, if you try to hit or hurt your roommate, your hands go stiff and cold. I threw a book at Baz once in our first year, and it took three days for my hand to thaw out.

Baz has never violated the Anathema. Not even when we were kids.

"Who knows what he's capable of in his sleep," I say.

"You do," Penny says, "as much as you watch him."

"I live with a dark creature—I'm right to be paranoid!"

"I'd trade my pixie for your vampire any day of the week. There's no anathema to keep someone from being lethally irritating."

Penny and I go back to the dining hall to get dinner—baked sweet potatoes and sausages and hard white rolls—then bring it all back to my room. We never get to hang out like this when Baz is around. He'd turn Penny in.

It feels like a party. Just the two of us, nothing to do. No one to hide from or fight. Penelope says it'll be like this someday when we get a flat together. . . . But that's not going to happen. She's going to go to America as soon as the war is over. Maybe even before that.

And I'll get a place with Agatha.

Agatha and I will work through whatever this is; we always do. We make sense together. We'll probably get married after school—that's when Agatha's parents got married. I know she wants a place in the country. . . . I can't afford anything like that, but she has money, and she'll find a job that makes her happy. And her dad'll help me find work if I ask him.

It's nice to think about that: living long enough to have to figure out what to do with myself.

As soon as Penelope's done with her dinner, she brushes off her hands. "Right," she says.

I groan. "Not yet."

"What do you mean, 'not yet'?"

"I mean, not yet with the strategizing. We just got here. I'm still settling in."

She looks around the room. "What's to settle, Simon? You already unpacked your two pairs of trackie bottoms."

"I'm enjoying the peace and quiet." I reach for her plate and start to finish off her sausages.

"There's no peace," she says. "Just quiet. It makes me nervous. We need a plan."

"There *is* peace. Baz isn't here yet, and look"—I wave her fork around—"there's nothing attacking us."

"Says the man who just thrashed a goblin. *Simon,*" she says, "just because we've been checked out for two months doesn't mean the war took a break."

I groan again. "You sound like the Mage," I say with my mouth full.

"I still can't believe he ignored you all summer."

"He's probably too busy with 'the war.'"

Penny sighs and folds her hands. She's waiting for me to be reasonable.

I'm going to make her wait.

*The war.*

There's no point talking about *the war.* It'll get here soon enough. It isn't even one war: It's two or three of them—the civil war that's brewing, the hostilities with the dark creatures that have always been there, the whatever it is with the Humdrum— and it will all find its way to my door eventually. . . .

"Right," Penny repeats. And I must look miserable, because next she says, "I guess the war will still be there tomorrow."

I clean her plate, and Penny makes herself comfortable on Baz's bed, and I don't even nag her about it. I lie back on my own bed, listening to her talk about aeroplanes and American supermarkets and Micah's big family.

She falls asleep in the middle of telling me about a song she's heard, a song she thinks will be a spell someday, though I can't think of any use for "Call me maybe."

"Penelope?" She doesn't answer. I lean off my bed and swing my pillow at her legs—that's how close the beds are; Baz wouldn't even have to get out of his to kill me. Or vice versa, I guess. "*Penny.*"

"What?" she says into Baz's pillow.

"You have to go back to your room."

"Don't want to."

"You have to. The Mage'll suspend you if you get caught in here."

"Let him. I could use the free time."

I get out of bed and stand over her. Her dark hair is spread out over the pillowcase, and her glasses are smashed into her cheek. Her skirt has hiked up, and her bare thigh looks plump and smooth.

I pinch her. She jumps up.

"Come on," I say, "I'll walk you."

Penny straightens her glasses and untwists her shirt. "No. I don't want you to see how I get past the wards."

"Because that's not something you'd want to share with your best friend?"

"Because it's fun watching you try to figure it out."

I open my door and peek down the staircase. I don't see or hear anyone. "Fine," I say, holding the door open. "Good-night."

Penny walks past me. "Good-night, Simon. See you tomorrow."

I grin. I can't help it—it's so good to be back. "See you tomorrow."

As soon as I'm alone, I change into my school pyjamas—Baz brings his from home, but I like the school ones. I don't sleep in pyjamas when I'm at the juvenile centres, I never have. It makes me feel, I don't know—vulnerable. I change and crawl into bed, sighing.

These nights at Watford, before Baz gets here, are the only nights in my life when I actually sleep.

I don't know what time it is when I wake up. The room is dark, and there's a shaft of moonlight slicing across my bed.

I think I see a woman standing by the window, and at first I think it's Penny. Then the figure shifts, and I think it's Baz.

Then I decide I'm dreaming and fall back into sleep.

# 6

## LUCY

I have so much I want to tell you.
   But time is short.
   And my voice doesn't carry.

# 7

## SIMON

The sun is just rising when I hear my door creak open. I pull the blankets up over my head. "Go away," I say, expecting Penny to start talking at me anyway. She's good at immediately making me forget how much I missed her over the summer.

Someone clears his throat.

I open my eyes and see the Mage standing just inside the door, looking amused—at least on the surface. There's something darker underneath.

"Sir." I sit up. "Sorry."

"Don't apologize, Simon. You must not have heard me knock."

"No . . . Let me just, I'll just, um . . . get dressed."

"Don't trouble yourself," he says, walking to the window, giving Baz's bed a wide berth—even the Mage is afraid of vampires. Though he wouldn't use the word "afraid." He'd say something like "cautious" or "prudent."

"I'm sorry I wasn't here to welcome you back yesterday," he says. "How was your journey?"

I push the covers off and sit at the edge of my bed. I'm still in my pyjamas, but at least I'm sitting up. "Fine," I say. "I mean, I suppose . . . not exactly fine. My taxi driver was a goblin."

"Another goblin?" He turns from the window to me, hands clasped behind his back. "Persistent, aren't they. Was it alone?"

"Yes, sir. Tried to scarper off with me."

He shakes his head. "They never think to come in pairs. What spell did you use?"

"Used my blade, sir." I bite at my lip.

"Fine," he says.

"And **Into thin air** to clean it up."

The Mage raises his eyebrow. "Excellent, Simon." He looks down at my pyjamas and bare feet, then seems to study my face. "What about this summer? Anything to report? Anything unusual?"

"I would have contacted you, sir." (I *can* contact him, if I need to. I have his mobile number. Also, I could send a bird.)

The Mage nods. "Good." He looks at me for a few more seconds, then turns back to the window, like he's observed everything about me that he needs to. The sunlight catches in his thick brown hair, and for a minute, he looks even more like a swashbuckler than usual.

He's in uniform: dark green canvas leggings, tall leather boots, a green tunic with straps and small pockets—with a sword hanging in a woven scabbard from his tooled belt. Unlike mine, his blade is fully visible.

Penny's mum, Professor Bunce, says that previous mages wore a ceremonial cowl and cape. And that other headmasters wore robes and mortarboards. The Mage, she says, has created his own uniform. She calls it a costume.

I think Professor Bunce must hate the Mage more than anyone who isn't actually his enemy. The only time I ever hear Penny's dad talk out loud is when her mum gets going on the Mage; he'll put his hand on her arm and say, *"Now, Mitali . . ."* And then she'll say, *"I apologize, Simon, I know the Mage is your foster father. . . ."*

But he isn't, not really. The Mage has never presented himself to me that way. As family. He's always treated me as an ally—even when I was a little kid. The very first time he brought me to Watford, he sat me down in his office and told me everything. About the Insidious Humdrum. About the missing magic. About the holes in the atmosphere like dead spots.

I was still trying to get it through my head that magic was *real*, and there he was telling me that something was killing it—eating it, ending it—and that only I could help:

*"You're too young to hear this, Simon. Eleven is too young. But it isn't fair to keep any of this from you any longer. The Insidious Humdrum is the greatest threat the World of Mages has ever faced. He's powerful, he's pervasive. Fighting him is like fighting off sleep when you're long past the edge of exhaustion.*

*"But fight him we must. We want to protect you; I vow to do so with my life. But you must learn, Simon, as soon as possible, how best to protect yourself.*

*"He is our greatest threat. And you are our greatest hope."*

I was too stunned to respond or to ask any questions. Too young. I just wanted to see the Mage do that trick again, the one where he made a map roll out all by itself.

I spent that first year at Watford telling myself that I was dreaming. And the next year telling myself that I wasn't . . .

I'd already been attacked by ogres, shattered a circle of standing stones, and grown five inches before I thought to ask the real question:

*Why me?*

Why did *I* have to fight the Humdrum?

The Mage has answered that question a dozen different ways over the years:

*Because I was chosen. Because I was prophesied. Because the Humdrum won't leave me alone.*

But none of those are real answers. Penelope has given me the only answer that I know what to do with. . . .

*"Because you can, Simon. And someone has to."*

The Mage is watching something out my window. I think about inviting him to sit down. Then I try to remember whether I've ever *seen* him sit down.

I shift my weight, and the bed creaks. He turns to me, looking troubled.

"Sir?"

"Simon."

"The Humdrum—did you find him? What have I missed?"

The Mage rubs his chin in the notch between his thumb and forefinger, then jerks his head quickly from side to side. "Nothing. We're no closer to finding him, and other matters have needed my immediate attention."

"How could anything be more important than the Humdrum?" I blurt out.

"Not more important," he says. "Just more pressing. It's the Old Families—they're testing me." He balls his right hand into a fist. "Half of Wales has stopped tithing. The Pitches are paying three members of the Coven to stay away from meetings, so we don't have quorum. And there have been skirmishes up and down the road to London all summer long."

"Skirmishes?"

"Traps, tussles. Tests—they're all tests, Simon. You know the Old Families would seize the reins if they thought for a moment I was distracted. They'd roll back everything we've accomplished."

"Do they think they can fight the Humdrum without us?"

"I think they're so shortsighted," he says, looking over at me, "that they don't care. They just want power, and they want it now."

"Well, I don't care about them," I say. "If the Humdrum takes our magic, we won't have anything to scrap over. We should be fighting the Humdrum."

"And we *will*," he says, "when the time is right. When we know how to beat him. But until then, my first priority is keeping you safe. Simon . . ." He folds his arms. "I've been consulting with the other members of the Coven, with those I can trust. We think maybe our efforts to protect you have backfired. Despite the spells and surveillance, the Humdrum seems to have the best luck getting to you when you're here, at Watford. He spirited you away in June without triggering any of our defences."

It's embarrassing to hear him say this. It feels like *I'm* the one failing, not the Mage or the protection spells. I'm supposed to be the only one who can fight the Humdrum. But I finally got a chance to face him, and the most I could do was run away. I don't think I'd have managed even that without Penelope.

The Mage clenches his jaw. He has one of those chins that flattens out in the middle—with a sharp dimple, like he was nicked by a knife. I'm dead jealous of it. "We've decided," he says slowly, "that you would be safer somewhere other than Watford."

I'm not sure what he's getting at. "Sir?"

"The Coven has secured a place for you. And a private tutor. I can't talk about the details now—but I'll take you there myself. We'll leave soon; I need to be back by nightfall."

"You want me to leave Watford?"

He narrows his eyes. The Mage hates to repeat himself. "Yes. You won't need to pack much. Your boots and your cloak, any artefacts you want to keep—"

"Sir, I can't leave Watford. Our lessons start this week."

He cocks his head. "Simon. You're not a child. There's nothing more for you to learn at Watford."

Maybe he's right. I'm a hopeless student; it's not like this year is going to make or break me, but still . . . "I can't leave Watford. It's my last year."

The Mage rubs his beard. His eyes narrow to slits.

"I just can't," I say again. I try to think of why not, but all that comes to me is *no*. I can't leave Watford. I've been waiting all summer to get here. I've been waiting my whole life. I'm always either at Watford or wishing I was at Watford, and next year that will change—it has to—but *not yet*. "No," I say. "I can't."

"Simon"—his voice is stern—"this isn't a *suggestion*. Your life is at stake. And the entire World of Mages is depending on you."

I feel like arguing that point: *Baz* isn't depending on me. None of the magicians who stand with the House of Pitch believe I'm their saviour. . . .

I grind my teeth so tight, I can practically feel the shape of them. I shake my head.

The Mage frowns down at me like I'm a child who's refusing to listen. "Hasn't it ever occurred to you, Simon, that the Humdrum attacks you only when you're here?"

"Has it just now occurred to you?" I swallow. "Sir," I add too late.

"I don't understand this!" he says, raising his voice. "You've never questioned my decisions before."

"You've never asked me to leave Watford before!"

His face is hard. "Simon, we're at war. Do I need to remind you of that?"

"No, sir."

"And we all make sacrifices at wartime."

"But we've *always* been at war," I say. "As long as I've been here. We can't just stop living because we're at war."

"Can't we?" He's finally lost his temper. He jerks his hand back down to the hilt of his sword. "Look at me, Simon. Have you ever known me to indulge myself with a normal life? Where is my wife? My children? Where's my house in the country with my cosy chair and a fat cocker spaniel to bring me my slippers? When do I go on holiday? When do I take a break? When do I do *anything* other than prepare for the battle ahead? We don't get to ignore our responsibilities because we're bored with them."

My head drops down like he's shoved it. "I'm not bored," I mutter.

"Speak up."

I lift my head. "I'm not bored, sir."

Our eyes meet.

"Get dressed. Gather your things. . . ."

I feel every muscle in my body grab. Every joint lock. "No."

I *can't*. I just got here. And this summer was the worst summer yet. I held on because I was coming to Watford at the end of it, but I can't hold on any longer. I don't have it in me. My reserves are empty, and the Mage won't even tell me where he wants me to go—and what about Penny? And Agatha?

I'm shaking my head. I hear the Mage take in a sharp breath, and when I look up, there's a haze of red between us.

*Fuck. No.*

He steps away from me. "Simon," he says. His wand is out. ***"Stay cool!"***

I fumble for my own wand and start running through spells. ***"Keep it together! Suck it up! Steady on! Hold fast!"*** But spells take magic, and drawing on my magic right now just draws it to the surface—the red between us thickens. I close my eyes and try to disappear. To think of nothing at all. I fall back on the bed, and my wand bounces onto the floor.

When I can focus again, the Mage is leaning over me, his hand on my forehead. Something is smoking—I think it's my sheets. "I'm sorry," I whisper. "I didn't mean—"

"I know," he says, but he still looks scared. He pushes my hair up off my forehead with one hand, then brushes his knuckles down my cheek.

"Please don't make me leave," I beg.

The Mage looks in my eyes, and through them. I can see him deliberating—then relenting. "I'll talk to the Coven," he says. "Perhaps we still have time. . . ." He purses his lips together. He has a pencil-thin moustache, just above his lips; Baz and Agatha both like to make fun of it. "But it isn't just *your* safety we're concerned with, Simon. . . ."

He's still leaning over me. I feel like there's nothing to breathe between us but smoke.

"I'll talk to the Coven," he says. He squeezes my shoulder and stands. "Do you need the nurse?"

"No, sir."

"You'll call for me if something changes. Or if you see anything strange—any signs of the Humdrum, or anything . . . out of the ordinary."

I nod.

The Mage strides out of the room, his palm resting on the

hilt of his sword—that means he's thinking—and closes the door firmly behind him.

I roll around and make sure that my bed isn't actually burning, then collapse back into sleep.

# 8

## LUCY

And the fog is so thick.

# 9

## SIMON

Penny's sitting at my desk when I wake up again. She's reading a book as thick as her arm. "It's past noon," she says. "You've become an absolute sluggard in foster care; I'm writing a letter to *The Telegraph*."

"You can't just let yourself into my room without knocking," I say, sitting up and rubbing my eyes. "Even if you do have a magickal key."

"It's not a key, and I *did* knock. You sleep like a corpse."

I walk past her to the bathroom, and she sniffs, then closes her book. "Simon. Did you go off?"

"Sort of. It's a long story."

"Were you *attacked*?"

"No," I shut the door to the bathroom and raise my voice: "I'll tell you later." Penny's going to flip her shit when I tell her the Mage wants to send me away.

I look in the mirror and try to decide whether to shower. My hair's matted to my head on one side and standing up on top—I always break into a sweat when I lose control like that. I feel grimy all over. I examine my chin in the mirror, hoping I need a shave, but I don't; I never really do. I'd grow a moustache just like the Mage's if I could, and I wouldn't care at all if Baz took the piss.

I strip off my shirt and give the gold cross around my neck a rub. I'm not religious—it's a talisman. Been passed down in Agatha's family for years, a ward against vampires. It was black and tarnished when Dr. Wellbelove gave it to me, but I've rubbed it gold. Sometimes I chew on it. (Which is probably a bad thing to do to a mediaeval relic.) I don't really need to wear it all summer, but once you get used to wearing an anti-vampire necklace, it seems stupid to take it off.

All the other kids in care always think I'm religious. (And they think I smoke a pack a day, because I always sort of smell like smoke.)

I look at the mirror again. Penny's right. I'm too thin. My ribs stick out. You can see the muscles in my stomach, and not because I'm ripped—because I haven't really eaten for three months. Also I've got moles all over my body, which make me look poxed even when I'm *not* suffering from malnutrition.

"I'm taking a shower!" I shout.

"Hurry—we'll miss lunch!" I hear Penny moving around the room while I climb into the shower; then she's talking to me again from just outside the door: "Agatha's back."

I turn on the water.

"Simon, did you hear me? Agatha's back!"

I heard her.


What's the etiquette for talking to your girlfriend after three months, when the last time you saw her, she was holding hands with your nemesis? (Both hands. Facing each other. Like they were about to break into song.)

Things had got dodgy with Agatha last year even before I saw her with Baz in the Wood. She'd been distant and quiet, and when I was injured in March (someone tampered with my wand), she just rolled her eyes. Like I'd brought it on myself.

Agatha's the only girl I've ever dated. We've been together for three years now, since we were 15. But I wanted her long before that. I've wanted her since the first time I saw her—walking across the Great Lawn, her long pale hair rippling in the wind. I remember seeing her and thinking that I'd never seen anything so beautiful. And that if you were that beautiful, that graceful, nothing could ever really touch you. It would be like being a lion or a unicorn. Nobody could really touch you, because you wouldn't even be on the *same plane* as everyone else.

Even sitting next to Agatha makes you feel sort of untouchable. Exalted. It's like sitting in the sun.

So imagine how it feels to date her—like you're carrying that light around with you all the time.

There's a picture of us together from the last winter solstice. She's in a long white dress, and her mother plaited mistletoe into her milky gold hair. I'm wearing white, too. I felt naff, but in the photo—well, I look fine. Standing next to Agatha, wearing a suit her father lent me . . . I actually look like I'm who I'm supposed to be.

The dining hall is half full today. The term starts tomorrow. People are sitting on tables and standing in loose circles, catching up.

Lunch is ham and cheese rolls. Penelope grabs a plate of butter for me, and I smile. I'd eat butter with a spoon if it were acceptable. (I did it anyway, my first year, whenever I was the first one down to breakfast.)

I scan the room for Agatha but don't see her. She must not be at lunch. I can't believe she'd be in the dining hall and not sit at our table, even considering everything.

Rhys and Gareth, the boys who live in the room under mine, are sitting at our table already, at the far end.

"All right, Simon?" Rhys says. Gareth is shouting at someone across the hall.

"All right, fellas?" I answer.

Rhys nods at Penny. Penelope has never had time for most of our classmates, so they don't really have time for her. It would bother me if everyone ignored me like that, but she seems to appreciate the lack of distractions.

Sometimes when I'm walking through the dining hall, just saying hello to people, she'll drag me by my sleeve to hurry me up.

"You have too many friends," she'll say.

"I'm pretty sure that's not possible. And, anyway, I wouldn't call them all 'friends.'"

"There are only so many hours in the day, Simon. Two, three people—that's all any of us have time for."

"There are more people than that in your immediate family, Penny."

"I know. It's a struggle."

Once, I started listing off all the people that I truly cared about. When I got to number seven, Penelope told me I either needed to whittle down my list or stop making friends immediately. "My mother says you should never have more people in your life than you could defend from a hungry rakshasa."

"I don't know what that is," I told her, "but I'm not worried; I'm good in a fight."

I like having people. Close ones like Penny and Agatha and the Mage and Ebb the goatherd and Miss Possibelf and Dr. Wellbelove. And just friendly ones like Rhys and Gareth. If

I followed Penny's rules, I'd never find enough people for a football match.

She waves halfheartedly at the boys, then sits between me and them, turning towards me to close off our conversation. "I saw Agatha with her parents," she says, "earlier, in the Cloisters."

The Cloisters is the oldest and largest girls' house, a long low building at the other side of the grounds. It only has one door, and all the windows are made up of tiny panes of glass. (The school must have been mega-paranoid when it started letting girls in back in the 1600s.)

"You saw who?" I ask.

*"Agatha."*

"Oh."

"I can go get her if you want," she offers.

"Since when do you pass notes for me?"

"I thought you might not want to talk to her for the first time in front of everyone," she says. "After what happened."

I shrug. "It'll be fine. Agatha and I are fine."

Penny looks surprised, then dubious; then she shakes her head, giving up. "Anyway," she says, tearing off a piece of her sandwich, "we should track down the Mage after lunch."

"Why?"

"'Why?' Are you playing dumb today because you think I'll find it cute?"

"Yes?"

She rolls her eyes. "We need to track down the Mage and make him tell us what's been going on all summer. What he's found out about the Humdrum."

"He hasn't found out anything. I already talked to him."

She stops mid-bite. "When?"

"He came to my room this morning."

"And when were you going to tell me this?"

I shrug again, licking butter off my thumb. "When you gave me a chance."

Penny rolls her eyes again. (Penny rolls her eyes a lot.) "He didn't have anything to say?"

"Not about the Humdrum. He—" I look down at my plate, then quickly around us. "—he says the Old Families are causing trouble."

She nods. "My mum says they're trying to organize a vote of no confidence against him."

"Can they do that?"

"They're trying. And there've been duels all summer. Premal's friend Sam got into it with one of the Grimm cousins after a wedding, and now he's on trial."

"Who is?"

"The Grimm."

"For what?"

"Forbidden spells," she says. "Banned words."

"The Mage thinks I should go," I say.

"What? Go where?"

"He thinks I should leave Watford."

Penny's eyes are big. "To fight the Humdrum?"

"No." I shake my head. "To just . . . go. He thinks I'd be safer somewhere else. He thinks everyone here would be safer if I left."

Her eyes keep getting bigger. "Where would you go, Simon?"

"He didn't say. Some secret place."

"Like a hideout?" she asks.

"I guess."

"But what about school?"

"He doesn't think that's important right now."

Penny snorts. She thinks the Mage undervalues education

at the best of times. Especially the classics. When he dropped the linguistics programme, she wrote a stern letter to the faculty board. "So he wants you to do what?"

"Go away. Stay safe. Train."

She folds her arms. "On a mountain. With ninjas. Like Batman."

I laugh, but she doesn't laugh with me. She leans forward. "You can't just leave, Simon. He can't stash you in a hole your whole life."

"I'm not going," I say. "I told him no."

She pulls her chin back. "You told him *no*?"

"I . . . well, I can't just leave Watford. It's our last year, isn't it."

"I agree—you told him *no*?"

"I told him I didn't want to! I don't want to hide and wait for the Humdrum to find me. That doesn't feel like a plan."

"And what did the Mage say?"

"Not much. I got upset and started to—"

"*I knew it*. Your room smelled like a campfire. Oh my word! You *went off* on the Mage?"

"No. I pulled back."

"*Really?*" She looks impressed. "Well done, Simon."

"I think I scared him, though."

"It'd scare me, too."

"Penny, I . . ."

"What?"

"Do you think he's right?"

"I just said I didn't."

"No. About . . . me being a danger to Watford. A danger to—" I look over at the first year tables. They've all skipped sandwiches and are eating big bowls of jam roly-poly. "—everyone."

Penny starts tearing at her sandwich again. "Of course not."

"*Penelope.*"

She sighs. "You pulled back, didn't you? This morning? When have you ever hurt anyone but yourself?"

"Smoke and mirrors, Penny—should I make a list? I'll start with the decapitations. I'll start with *yesterday.*"

"Those were battles, and they don't count."

"I think they count."

She folds her arms again. "They count *differently.*"

"It's not even just that," I say. "It's . . . I'm a target, aren't I? The Humdrum only attacks me when I'm at Watford, and he only attacks Watford when I'm here."

"That's not your fault."

"So?"

"Well, you can't help that."

"I can," I say. "I could go away."

"*No.*"

"Compelling argument, Pen." I spread butter on my third ham and cheese roll. My hands are shaking.

"No. Simon. You can't just go away. You shouldn't. Look, if you're a target, then I'm the most at risk. I spend the most time with you."

"*I know.*"

"No, I mean, look at me—I'm fine."

I look at her.

"I'm *fine,* Simon. Even Baz is fine, and he's constantly stuck with you."

"I feel like you're glossing over all the times you've nearly died just because you were with me. The Humdrum kidnapped me a few months ago, and you got dragged along."

"Thank Morgana I did."

She's looking in my eyes, so I try not look away. Sometimes I'm glad Penny wears glasses; her eye contact is so fierce, it's good to have a buffer.

"I told the Mage no," I repeat.

"Good." she says. "Keep telling him."

*"Nan!"* A little girl's shout tears through our conversation, and I'm already whispering the incantation to summon my blade. Across the hall, the girl—a second or third year—is running towards a shimmery figure at the door.

"Oh . . . ," Penelope says, awed.

The figure fades in and out, like Princess Leia's hologram. When the girl reaches it—it looks like an older woman in a white trouser suit—it kneels down and catches her. They huddle together in the archway. Then the figure fades out completely. The girl stands, shaking, and a few of her friends run to her, jumping up and down.

"So cool," Penelope says. She turns to me and sees my blade. "Great snakes, Simon, put that away."

I keep it up. "What *was* that?"

"You don't know?"

*"Penelope."*

"She got a Visiting. Lucky kid."

"What?" I sheathe the blade. "What kind of visiting?"

"Simon, the *Veil* is lifting. I know you know about this. We studied it in Magickal History."

I make a face and sit down again, trying to decide whether I'm done with my lunch.

"*'And on the Twentieth Turn,'*" Penny says, "*'when the year wanes, and night and day sit in peace across the table— the Veil will lift. And any who have light to cast may cross it, though they may not tarry. Greet them with joy and with trust, for their mouths, though dead, speak truth.'*"

She's using her quoting voice, so I know it's from some ancient text or another.

"You're not helping," I say.

"The Veil is lifting," she says again. "Every twenty years, dead people can talk to the living if they have something that really needs to be said."

"Oh . . . ," I say, "I guess maybe I have heard of that—I thought it was a myth."

"One would think, after seven years, you'd stop saying that out loud."

"Well, how am I supposed to know? There isn't a book, is there? *All the Magickal Things that Are Actually True and All the Ones that Are Bollocks, Just Like You Thought.*"

"You're the *only* magician who wasn't raised with magic. You're the only one who would read a book like that."

"Father Christmas isn't real," I say, "but the Tooth Fairy is. There's no rhyme or reason to this stuff."

"Well, the Veil is totally real," Penny says. "It's what keeps souls from walking."

"But it's lifting now?" I feel like getting my sword out again.

"The autumnal equinox is coming," she says, "when day and night are the same length. The Veil thins, then lifts—sort of like fog. And people come back to tell us things."

"All of us?"

"I wish. People only come back if they have something important to say. Something true. It's like they come back to testify."

"That sounds . . . dramatic."

"My mother says her aunt came back twenty years ago to tell them about a hidden treasure. Mum's kind of hoping she'll come back again this time to tell us more."

"What kind of treasure?"

"Books."

"Of course." I decide to finish my sandwich. And Penny's boiled egg.

"But sometimes," she says, "it's scandalous. People come back to reveal affairs. Murders. The theory is, you have a better shot of crossing over if your message serves justice."

"How can anyone know that?"

"It's just a theory," Penny says. "But if Aunt Beryl comes to me, I'm going to ask her as much as I can before she fades out again."

I look back across the hall. "I wonder what that girl's granny told her."

Penny laughs and stacks her dishes. "Probably her secret toffee recipe."

"So these Visitors . . . they're not zombies?" It doesn't hurt to be sure about these things.

"No, Simon. They're harmless. Unless you're afraid of the truth."

# 10

## THE MAGE

I should make him go. I could.

He's not a child anymore, but he would still take an order.

*I promised to take care of him.*

How do you keep a promise like that? To take care of a child, when the child is the greatest power you know . . .

And what does it *mean* to take care of power? Do you use it? Conserve it? Keep it out of the wrong hands?

I'd thought I could be of more help to Simon, especially by now. Help him come into his power. Help him take *hold* of it.

There must be a spell for him. . . . Magic words that would fortify him. A ritual that would make the power itself manageable. I haven't found it yet, but that doesn't mean that it isn't out there. That it doesn't exist!

And if I do find it . . .

Is it enough to stabilize his power, if I can't stabilize the boy?

This isn't in the prophecies; there's nothing about headstrong children.

I could hide Simon from the Humdrum itself.

I could hide him from everything he isn't ready to face.

I could—*I should!* I should order him to go away—he'd still do it. He'd still listen to me.

But what if he didn't. . . .

*Simon Snow, would I lose you completely?*

# 11

## LUCY

Hear me.

He was the first of his family at Watford, the first with enough power to get past the trials. He came all by himself, all the way from Wales, on the train.

David.

We called him Davy. (Well, some of us just called him daft.)

And he didn't have any friends—I don't think he ever had any friends. I don't even think *I* was his friend, not at first.

I was just the only one listening.

"World of Mages," he'd say. "What world, I ask you—*what world?* This isn't a school; schools educate people—*schools lift people up*—do you understand me?"

"*I'm* getting an education," I said.

"You are, aren't you?" His blue eyes glinted. There was always a fire in his eyes. "You get power. You get the secret password. Because your father had it, and your grandfather. You're in the club."

"So are you, Davy."

"Only because I was too powerful for them to deny me."

"Right," I said. "So now you're in the club."

"Lucky me."

"I can't tell if you mean that. . . ."

"Lucky me," he said. "Unlucky everyone else. This place isn't about sharing knowledge. It's about keeping knowledge in the hands of the rich."

"You mean, the most powerful."

"Same difference," he spat. He always spat. His eyes were always glinting, and his mouth was always spitting.

"So you don't want to be here?" I asked.

"Did you know that the Church used to give services in Latin, because they didn't trust the congregation with God's word?"

"Are you talking about Christianity? I don't know anything about Christianity."

"Why are *we* here, Lucy? When so many others are refused?"

"Because we're the most powerful. It's important for us to learn how to manage and use our magic."

"Is it that important? Wouldn't it be *more important* to teach the least powerful? To help them make the most of what they *do* have? Should we teach only poets to read?"

"I don't understand what you want. You're *here*, Davy. At Watford."

"I'm here. And maybe if I meet the right people—if I bow and scrape before every Pitch and Grimm, they'll teach me the trickiest spells. They'll give me a seat at the table. And then I can spend my life as they do, making sure that no one else takes it from me."

"That's not what I'm going to do with my magic."

He stopped spitting for a second to squint at me: "What are you going to do, Lucy?"

"See the world."

"The World of Mages?"

"No, *the world.*"

I have so much to tell you.

But time is short. And the Veil is thick.

And it takes magic to speak, a soul full of it.

# 12

## SIMON

As it happens, I *am* alone when I see Agatha.

I'm lying out on the Lawn, thinking about the first time I got here—the grass was so nice that I didn't think we were allowed to walk on it.

Agatha's wearing jeans and a gauzy white shirt, and she comes up the hill towards me slowly blocking the sun, so there's a halo for just a second around her blond hair.

She smiles, but I can tell she's nervous. I wonder if she's been looking for me. I sit up, and she sits down on the ground next to me.

"Hey," I say.

"Hello, Simon."

"How was your summer?"

She gives me a look like she can't believe how lame that question is, but also like she's kind of relieved to make small talk. "Good," she says, "quiet."

"Did you travel?" I ask.

"Only for events."

Agatha's a show jumper. Competitively. I think she wants to jump for Great Britain someday. Or maybe ride? I know jack-all about horses. She tried to get me on a horse once, and I chickened out.

"*Simon, you can't be scared of this horse. You've slain dragons.*"

"*Well, I'm not afraid to slay it, am I? You want me to ride it.*"

"Any luck?" I ask now.

"Some," she says. "Mostly skill."

"Ah." I nod my head. "Right. Sorry."

I sort of hate to talk to Agatha about horse stuff—and not because I'm afraid of them. It's just one more thing I'll never get right. All that posh crap. Regattas and galas and, I don't know, polo matches. Agatha's mum has hats that look like wedding cakes.

It's too much. I've got enough to deal with, trying to figure out what it means to be a magician—I'll never pass as to the manner born.

Maybe Agatha would be better off with Baz after all. . . .

If he weren't evil.

I must look like I'm fuming, because she clears her throat uncomfortably. "Do you want me to go?"

"No," I say. "No. I'm glad to see you."

"You haven't actually looked at me," she says.

So I look at her.

She's beautiful.

And I want her. I want everything to be fine.

"Look, Simon. I know you saw—"

I cut her off. "I didn't see anything."

"Well, I saw *you*," she says. Her voice sharpens: "And Penelope, and—"

I cut her off again. "No, I mean . . ." I'm not doing this right. "I *did* see you. In the Wood. And I saw . . . him. But it's all right. I know you wouldn't—well, I know you *wouldn't*, Agatha. And it doesn't matter, anyway. It was months ago."

Her eyes are wide and confused.

Agatha has lovely brown eyes. Almost golden. And lovely long eyelashes. And the skin around her eyes sparkles like she's a fairy. (She's not a fairy. Fairies who can speak with magic are welcome at Watford, if they can find it, but none have ever chosen to attend.)

"But, Simon, we have to . . . I mean, shouldn't we *talk* about this?"

"I'd rather just move on," I say. "It's not important. And it's just—Agatha, it's so good to see you." I reach for her hand.

She lets me take it. "It's good to see you, too, Simon."

I smile.

She almost smiles back.

# 13

## AGATHA

It is good to see him, it's *always* good to see him.

It's always such a relief.

I think about it sometimes, what it will be like the time that he doesn't come back.

*Someday Simon isn't going to come back.*

Everyone knows it—I think even the Mage knows it. (Penelope knows, but she doesn't believe.)

It's just . . . It's *impossible* for him to live through this. Too many people want him dead. Too many things worse than people. Dark things. Creatures. Whatever the Insidious Humdrum is. They all want him gone, and he can't keep surviving; there've been too many close calls.

Nobody's that strong.

Nobody's that lucky.

Someday he won't come back, and I'll be one of the first people they tell. I've thought it out because I know that however I react, it won't be enough.

Simon's the Chosen One. And he chose me. And even though I love him—we grew up together, he spends every Christmas at my house, I *do* love him—it isn't enough. Whatever I feel isn't enough; it won't *be* enough, when I lose him.

What if it's like that time our collie got hit by a car? I cried, but only because I knew I was supposed to, not because I couldn't help it. . . .

I used to think that maybe I was holding back my feelings for Simon as some sort of self-defence. Like, to protect myself from the pain of losing him, the pain of maybe losing everything—because, if Simon goes, what hope do any of us have?

(What hope *do* we have? Simon isn't the solution to our problems; he's just a stay of execution.)

But it isn't that—it isn't self-defence.

I just don't love Simon enough.

I don't love him the right way.

Maybe I don't have that sort of love in me—maybe I'm defective.

And if that's the case, I may as well stand by Simon, shouldn't I? If that's where he wants me? If that's where everyone expects me to be?

If it's the only place I can make any difference?

# 14

## SIMON

I spend an hour or so with Agatha, but we don't say much. I don't tell her about the Mage.

(What if Agatha agreed with the Mage? What if she wanted me to go, too? I'd want *her* to go, if she were in danger at Watford. Hell, she *is* in danger here. Because of me.)

When I get back to my room, Penny's there already, sprawled out with a book on Baz's bed.

"So you and Agatha talked?" she asks.

"We talked."

"Did she explain? About Baz?"

"I told her not to."

Penny sets down her book. "You don't want to know why your girlfriend was snogging your sworn enemy?"

"I don't know about 'sworn,'" I say. "I've never taken an oath."

"I'm pretty sure Baz has."

"Anyway, they weren't snogging."

Penny shakes her head. "If I caught Micah holding hands with Baz, I'd want an explanation."

"So would I."

"*Simon.*"

"Penny. Of course you'd want an explanation. That's you. You like to demand explanations and then tell everyone why their explanations are crap."

"I do not."

"You *do*. But I—look, I just don't care. It's behind us. Agatha and I are fine."

"I wonder if it's behind Baz."

"Fuck Baz, he'll do whatever he can to get to me."

And he'll start just as soon as he shows up. Which could be anytime . . .

Almost everyone else is here already. Nobody wants to miss the welcome-back picnic on the Great Lawn tonight. It's always a big to-do. Games. Fireworks. Spectacle magic.

Maybe Baz will miss the picnic; he's never missed it before, but it's a nice thought.

Penny and I meet Agatha out on the Lawn.

I don't see Baz, but there are so many people, it'd be easy for him to avoid me if he wanted. (Baz normally makes *sure* that I see him.)

The littluns are already playing games and eating cake, some of them wearing their Watford uniforms for the first time. Hats sliding off, ties crooked. There are races and singing. I get a bit choked up during the school song; there's this line about *"those golden years at Watford / those glowing, magickal years"*—and it makes me think again about how this is *it*. Every day I have this year will be the last day like it.

Last back-to-school picnic.

Last first day back.

I make a pig of myself, but Penny and Agatha don't mind, and the egg and cress sandwiches are to die for. Plus roast chicken. Pork pie. Spice cakes with sour lemon frosting. And jugs of cold milk and raspberry cordial.

I keep bracing for Baz to show up and ruin everything. I keep looking over my shoulder. (Maybe this is part of his plan—to ruin my night by making me wonder how he's going to ruin it.) I think Agatha is worried about seeing him, too.

One thing I'm *not* worried about is the Humdrum attacking. He sent flying monkeys to attack the picnic at the start of our fourth year, and the Humdrum never tries the same thing twice. (I guess he could send something *other* than flying monkeys. . . . )

After the sun sets, the littluns all head back to their rooms, and the seventh and eighth years stay out on the Lawn. The three of us find a spot, and Penny spells her jacket into a green blanket for us to lie on. Which Agatha says is a waste of magic when there are perfectly good blankets just inside. "Your jacket is going to get grass stains," she says.

"It's already green," Penelope dismisses her.

It's a warm night, and Penelope and Agatha are both good at astronomy. We lie on our backs, and they point out the stars. "I should get my crystal ball and tell your fortunes," Penelope says, and Agatha and I both groan.

"I'll save you the trouble," I say. "You're going to see me bathed in blood, but you won't be able to tell whose it is. And you'll see Agatha looking beautiful and swathed in light."

Penelope pouts, but not for long. The night is too good for pouting. I find Agatha's hand in the blanket, and when I squeeze, she squeezes back.

This day, this night, it all feels so right. Magickally right. Like a portent. (I didn't used to believe in portents—I'm not superstitious. But then we did a unit on them in Magickal Science, and Penny said not believing in portents was like not believing in beans on toast.)

After an hour or so, someone crosses the Veil, right out onto the Lawn. It's somebody's dead sister; she's come back to tell him that it wasn't his fault—

I put my blade away on my own this time, without Penny telling me to.

"It's amazing," she says. "Two Visitings in one day, and the Veil is just beginning to open. . . ."

When the ghost leaves, everybody starts hugging each other. (I think the seventh years have been passing around dandelion wine and Bacardi Breezers. But the three of us aren't class monitors, so it's not our problem.) Somebody starts singing the school song again, and we join in. Agatha sings, even though she's self-conscious about her voice.

I'm happy.

I'm *really* happy.

I'm home.

I wake up a few hours later, and I think Baz must be back.

I can't see him—I can't see anything—but there's *someone* in the room with me.

"Penny?"

Maybe it's the Mage again. Or the Humdrum! Or that thing I dreamt I saw by the window last night, which I'm only now remembering . . .

I've never been attacked in my room before—this would be a first.

I sit up and turn on the lights without trying. That happens sometimes, with small spells, when I'm stressed. It's not supposed to. Penny thinks it might be like telepathy, skipping the words to get straight to the goal.

I still don't see anything, though I think I hear a rustling sound and a sort of moaning. The windows are both open. I get up and look outside, then close them. I check under the beds. I risk an ***"Olly olly oxen free!"***—then a ***"Come out, come out, wherever you are!"*** that sends all my clothes flying out of the wardrobe. I'll put them away tomorrow.

I go back to bed, shivering. It's cold. And I still don't feel alone.

# 15

## SIMON

Baz isn't in our room when I wake up.

I look for him in the dining hall at breakfast, but he's not there either.

His name is called during my first lesson—Greek with the Minotaur. (Our teacher's name is Professor Minos; we call him the Minotaur because he's half-man, half-bull.)

He calls out Baz's name four times. "Tyrannus Pitch? Tyrannus Basilton Grimm-Pitch?"

Agatha and I look around the room, then at each other.

Baz is supposed to be in Political Science with me, too. Penny makes me take Political Science; she thinks I might end up a leader someday after I beat the Humdrum.

I'd be happy to spend my days helping Ebb herd goats if I live through the Humdrum, but Political Science is interesting enough, so I take it every year.

Baz always takes it, too. Probably because he expects to reclaim the throne someday . . .

Baz's family used to run everything before the Mage came to power.

Magicians don't have kings and queens, but the Pitches

are the nearest thing we have to a royal family—they probably would have crowned themselves at some point if they'd ever expected anyone to challenge their authority.

Baz's mum was the headmistress at Watford before the Mage, which made her the most important person in magic. (There's a hall near the Mage's office with portraits of previous headmasters; it's like a Pitch family tree.) It was actually her death that changed everything—that brought the Mage to power.

When the Humdrum killed Headmistress Pitch by sending vampires into Watford, everyone saw that the World of Mages *had* to change. We couldn't just keep on as we were, letting the Humdrum and the dark creatures pick us off one by one.

We had to get organized.

We had to think about defence.

The Mage was elected Mage, head of the Coven, in an emergency session, and he was also made Watford's interim headmaster. (That's technically still his title.) He immediately started his reforms.

Whether he's been successful or not depends on who you ask. . . .

The Humdrum's still out there.

But nobody's died on school grounds since the Mage took over. And I'm still alive, so I guess I'm inclined to say he's doing a good job.

A few years ago, we had to write essays for Poli Sci about the Mage's ascendancy. Baz's practically called for revolt. (Which took bottle, I thought. Demanding that your headmaster step down in the text of a school assignment.)

Baz has always played a strange game: publicly expressing his family's politics—which are basically "Down with the

Mage! Peacefully and legally!"—like he has nothing to hide, while his family leads an actual covert, dangerous war against us.

If you ask the Pitches why they hate the Mage, they start talking about "the old ways" and "our magickal heritage" and "intellectual freedom."

But everyone knows they just want to be in charge again. They want Watford to go back to the way it used to be—a place for only the most rich and the most powerful.

The Mage *eliminated* school fees when he took over, and threw out the oral presentations and power trials to get in. Literally anyone who can speak with magic can attend Watford now, no matter their strength or skill—even if they're half troll on their mother's side or more mermaid than mage. The school had to build another hall of residence, Fraternity House, just to make room for everybody.

*"Can't be too picky with cannon fodder"* is Baz's take on the reforms.

He just hates being treated like another student, instead of the heir apparent. If his mother were still headmistress, he'd probably get his own room and whatever else he wanted. . . .

I shouldn't think like that. It's awful that his mum died. Just because I've never had parents doesn't mean I can't understand how much it would hurt to lose one.

Baz doesn't show up to Political Science, so I keep an eye on his best friend, Niall, instead. Niall doesn't flinch when Baz's name is called, but he looks over at me, like he's trying to say he knows I'm onto them and that he gives exactly zero fucks.

I corner Niall after our lesson: "Where is he?"

"Your dick? Haven't seen it. Have you asked Ebb?"

(Honestly. I'm not sure why goatherds take such crap for being perverts. Cowboys seem to get off scot-free.)

"Where's Baz?" I say.

Niall tries to get past me, but I'm impossible to get past if I make the effort. It's not that I'm big—I'm just bold. And when people look at me, they tend to see everything I've killed before.

Niall stops and hikes his bag up on his shoulder. He's a pale, weedy boy with brown eyes that he spells a muddy blue. Waste of magic. He sneers: "What's it to you, Snow?"

"He's my roommate."

"I'd think you'd be enjoying the solitude."

"I am."

"So?"

I step out of Niall's way. "If he's planning something, I'll find out," I say. "I always do."

"So noted."

"I mean it!" I shout after him.

"Your sincerity is also noted!"

By dinner, I'm so antsy that I'm tearing my Yorkshire pudding to shreds while I eat. (Yorkshire pudding. Roast beef. Gravy. It's what we have for dinner every year on the first day of the term. I'll never forget my first Watford dinner—my eyes nearly popped out when Cook Pritchard brought out the trays of roast beef. I didn't care if magic was real at that moment. Because roast beef and Yorkshire pudding are fucking real as rain.)

"He might just be on holiday or something," Penny says.

"Why would he still be on holiday?"

"His family travels," Agatha offers.

*Oh, really?* I want to say. *Is that what you talk about alone in the woods? Your shared love of travel?* I rip off a chunk of bread and knock over my milk. Penny winces.

"He wouldn't miss school," I say, picking up my glass. Penny spells the milk away. "He cares too much about school."

Nobody argues with me. Baz has always ranked first in our class. Penny used to give him a run for his money, but being my sidekick eventually affected her grades. *"I'm not your sidekick,"* she likes to say. *"I'm your dread companion."*

"Maybe," she suggests now, "his family has decided to stop pretending that we're all at peace. Eighth year is optional anyway. In the old days, lots of people left after seventh. Maybe the Pitches have decided to get serious."

"Go to the mattresses," I say.

"Exactly."

"Against the Mage and me? Or the Humdrum?"

"I don't know," Penny says. "I always thought the Pitches would just sit back and watch both sides destroy each other."

"Thanks."

"You know what I mean, Simon—the Old Families don't want the Humdrum to win. But they don't mind him beating the Mage down. They'll wait to attack when they think the Mage is weak."

"When they think *I'm* weak."

"Same difference."

Agatha is staring over at the table where Baz usually sits. Niall and Dev, another of Baz's friends—his cousin or something—are sitting next to each other, talking with their heads close.

"I don't think Baz dropped out," she says.

Penny, sitting across from us, leans into Agatha's line

of sight. "Do you know something? What did Baz tell you?"

Agatha looks down at her plate. "He didn't tell me anything."

"He must have told you something," Penny says. "You talked to him last."

I clench my teeth. *"Penelope,"* I say without unclenching them.

"I don't care if you two have agreed to move on." She waves her hand at Agatha and me. "This is important. Agatha, you know Baz better than any of us. What did he tell you?"

"She doesn't know him better than I do," I argue. "I live with him."

"Fine, Simon, what did he tell *you*?"

"Nothing to make me think he'd drop out of school and miss a whole year of making me miserable!"

"He doesn't even have to be here to do that," Agatha mutters.

This pisses me off, even though I was thinking the same thing myself, just yesterday.

"I'm done," I say. "I'm going up to my room. To enjoy the solitude."

Penny sighs. "Calm down, Simon. Don't punish us just because you're feeling confused. *We* haven't done anything." She glances over at Agatha and tilts her head. "Well, *I* haven't. . . ."

Agatha stands up, too. "I've got homework."

We walk together to the door, then she turns off for the Cloisters.

"Agatha!" I call out.

But I don't say it until she's too far away to hear.

⚜

I have the room to myself, and I can't even enjoy it, because Baz's empty bed just seems sinister now.

I summon the Sword of Mages and practise my form on his side of the room. He hates that.

# 16

## SIMON

Baz isn't at breakfast the next morning. Or the next.

He isn't in class.

The football team starts practising, and someone else takes his place.

After a week, the teachers stop saying his name when they take attendance.

I trail Niall and Dev for a few days, but they don't seem to have Baz hidden away in a barn. . . .

I know I should be happy about Baz being gone—it's what I've always said I wanted, to be free of him—but it seems so . . . *wrong*. People don't just disappear like this.

Baz wouldn't.

Baz is . . . indelible. He's a human grease stain. (Mostly human.)

Three weeks into the term, I still find myself walking by the pitch, expecting to see him at football practice, and when I don't, I take a hard turn out into the hills behind the school.

I hear Ebb shout at me before I see her. "Hiya, Simon—ahoy!"

She's sitting above me a ways in the grass, with a goat curled up in her lap.

Ebb spends most of her time out in the hills when the weather is good. Sometimes she lets the goats roam the school grounds—she says they take care of weeds and predatory plants. The predatory plants at Watford will actually take you down if they get a chance; they're magic. The goats aren't, though. I asked Ebb once if the magic hurts the goats when they eat it. "They're goats, Simon," she said. "They can eat anything."

When I get closer, I see that Ebb's eyes are red. She wipes them with the sleeve of her jumper. It's an old Watford school jumper, faded from red to pink and stained brown around the neck and wrists.

If it were anybody else, I'd worry. But Ebb is kind of a weeper. She's like Eeyore if Eeyore hung out with goats all the time instead of letting Pooh and Piglet cheer him up.

It gets on Penelope's nerves, all the crying, but I don't mind. The thing about Ebb is, she never tells anybody else to keep their chin up or look on the bright side. It's very comforting.

I flop down next to her in the grass and run my hand down the goat's back.

"What're you doing up here?" Ebb asks. "Shouldn't you be at football practice?"

"I'm not on the team."

She scratches the goat behind its ears. "Since when do ya let that stop you?"

"I . . ."

Ebb sniffs.

"Are you okay?" I ask.

"Ach. Sure." She shakes her head, and her hair flies out around her ears. It's dirty and blond and always cut in a sharp line above her jaw and across her forehead. "Just the time of year," she says.

"Autumn?"

"Back to school. Reminds me of my own school days. You can't go back, Simon, you can never go back. . . ." She rubs her nose on her cuff again, then rubs her cuff into the goat's fur.

I don't point out that Ebb's never really left Watford. I don't want to make fun of her—it seems like a pretty sweet deal to me. Spending your whole life here.

"Not everyone came back," I say.

Her face falls. "Did we lose someone?"

Ebb's brother died when they were young. It's one of the reasons she's so melancholy; she never got over it. I don't want to set her off again. . . .

"No," I say. "I mean—Baz. Basil didn't come back."

"Ah," she says. "Young Master Pitch. Surely he'll be back. His mother did so value education."

"That's what I said!"

"Well, you know him best," she says.

"That's what I said, too!"

Ebb nods and pets the goat. "To think you used to be at each other's throats."

"We're still at each other's throats."

She looks up at me doubtfully. She has narrow blue eyes, bright blue—brighter somehow because her face is so dirty.

"Ebb," I insist, "he tried to kill me."

"Not successfully." She shrugs. "Not recently."

"He's tried to kill me three times! That I know of! It doesn't actually matter whether it worked."

"It matters a bit," she says. " 'Sides, how old was he the first time, eleven? Twelve? That hardly counts."

"It counts with me," I say.

"Does it."

I huff. "Yes. Ebb. It does. He hated me before he even met me."

"Exactly," she says.

"Exactly!"

"I'm just saying—been a long time since I had to spell you two apart."

"Well, there's no point in throwing down all the time," I say. "Doesn't get us anywhere. And it hurts. I suspect we're saving up."

"For what?" she asks.

"The end."

"The end of school?"

"The end of the end," I say. "The big fight."

"So you were saving it, and then he didn't come back for it?"

"Exactly!"

"Well, I wouldn't lose hope," Ebb says. "I think he'll be back. His mother always valued a good education. I miss her this time a'year. . . ."

She wipes her eyes on her sleeve. I sigh. Sometimes, with Ebb, you're better off just enjoying the silence. And the goats.

Three weeks pass. Four, five, six.

I stop looking for Baz anywhere where he's supposed to be.

Whenever I hear someone on the stairs outside our room now, I know it's Penny. I even let her spend the night sometimes and sleep in his bed; there doesn't seem to be any immediate danger of Baz bursting in and lighting her on fire for it. (The Roommate's Anathema doesn't prevent you from hurting anyone *else* in your room.)

I hassle Niall a few more times, but he doesn't even hint that he knows where Baz is. If anything, it seems like Niall's hoping that I'll turn up some answers.

I feel like I should talk to the Mage about it. About Baz. But I don't *want* to talk to the Mage. I'm afraid he might still be planning to send me away.

Penny says it's pointless to avoid him. "It's not like you'll fall off the Mage's radar."

But maybe I have. . . . And that bothers me, too.

The Mage is always gone a lot, but he's hardly been at Watford at all this term. And whenever he is here, he's surrounded by his Men.

Normally, he'd be checking on me. Calling me to his office. Giving me assignments, asking for help. Sometimes I think the Mage actually needs my help—he can trust me better than anyone—but sometimes I think he's just testing me. To see what I'm made of. To keep me in order.

I'm sitting in class one day when I see the Mage walking alone towards the Weeping Tower. As soon as class ends, I make for the Tower.

It's a tall, red brick building—one of the oldest at Watford, almost as old as the Chapel. It's called the Weeping Tower because there are vines that grow in every summer and creep from the top down—and because the building has started to sag forward over the years, almost like it's slumping in grief. Ebb says not to worry about it falling; the spells are still strong.

The dining hall is on the ground floor of the Tower, the whole ground floor, and then above that are classrooms and meeting rooms and summoning chambers; the Mage's office and sanctum are at the very top.

He comes and goes as he needs to. The Mage has the whole magickal world to keep track of—in the UK, anyway—and hunting the Humdrum takes up a lot of his time.

The Humdrum doesn't just attack me. That isn't even the

worst of it. (If it were, the other magicians probably would have thrown me to him by now.)

When the Humdrum first showed up, almost twenty years ago, holes began appearing in the magickal atmosphere. It seems like he (it?) can suck the magic out of a place, probably to use against us.

If you go to one of these dead spots, it's like stepping into a room without air. There's just nothing there for you, no magic—even I run dry.

Most magicians can't take it. They're so used to magic, to feeling magic, that they go spare without it. That's how the monster got its name. One of the first magicians to encounter the holes said they were like an *insidious humdrum, a mundanity that creeps into your very soul.*

The dead spots stay dead. You get *your* magic back if you leave, but the magic never comes back to that place.

Magicians have had to leave their homes because the Humdrum has pulled the magic out from underneath them.

It'd be a disaster if the Humdrum ever came to Watford.

So far, he usually sends someone else—or some*thing* else, some dark creature—in after me.

It's easy for the Humdrum to find allies. Every dark creature in this world and its neighbours would love to see the mages fall. The vampires, the werewolves, the demons and banshees, the Manticorps, the *goblins*—they all resent us. We can control magic, and they can't. Plus we keep them in check. If the dark things had their way, the Normal world would be chaos. They'd treat regular people like livestock. We—magicians—need the Normals to live their normal lives, relatively unaffected by magic. Our spells depend on them being able to speak freely.

That explains why the dark creatures hate us.

But I still don't know why the Humdrum has targeted

*me,* specifically. Because I'm the most powerful magician, I suppose. Because I'm the biggest threat.

The Mage says that he himself followed my power like a beacon when it was time to bring me to Watford.

Maybe that's how the Humdrum finds me, too.

I take a winding staircase to the top of the Weeping Tower, where it opens up into a round foyer. The school seal is laid out in marble tile on the floor and polished till it looks wet. And the domed ceiling has a mural of Merlin himself calling magic up through his hands into the sky, his mouth open. He kind of looks like the guy who hosts *QI.*

There are two doors. The Mage's office is behind the tall, arched door on the left. And his sanctum, his rooms, is behind the smaller door on the right.

I knock on his office door first—no one answers. I consider knocking on the door to his rooms, but that feels too intimate. Maybe I'll just leave him a note.

I open the door to the Mage's office—it's warded, but the wards are set to welcome me—then I walk in slowly, just in case I'm disturbing him. . . .

It's dark. The curtains are drawn. The walls are normally lined with books, but a bunch have been taken down, and they're piled in stacks around the desk.

I don't turn on the light. I wish I'd brought some paper or something—I don't want to scrounge around the Mage's desk. It's not the sort of desk that has Post-it notes and a WHILE YOU WERE OUT pad.

I pick up a heavy fountain pen. There're a few sheets of paper on his desk, lists of dates, and I turn one over and write:

> *Sir, I'd like to talk to you when you have a moment.*
> *About everything. About my roommate.*

And then I add:

*(T. Basilton Grimm-Pitch.)*

And then I wish I hadn't, because of course the Mage knows who my roommate is, and now it sort of looks like I've signed it. So then I *do* sign it:

*Simon*

"Simon," someone says, and I startle, dropping the pen.

Miss Possibelf is standing in the doorway, but doesn't step inside the office.

Miss Possibelf is our Magic Words teacher, and the dean of students. She's my favourite teacher. She's not exactly friendly, but I think she genuinely cares, and she seems more human sometimes than the Mage. (Even though she's not exactly human, I don't think. . . . ) She's much more likely to notice if you're feeling sick or miserable, or if your thumb is hanging on by a thread.

"Miss Possibelf," I say. "The Mage isn't in."

"I see that—do you have business here?"

"I thought he might be here. There were a few things I was going to talk to him about."

"He was here this morning, but he's left again." Miss Possibelf is tall and broad, with a thick silver plait hanging down her back. She's impossibly graceful, and impossibly eloquent, and if she's talking to you directly, her voice kind of tickles your ears. "You could talk to me," she says.

She still doesn't come in—she must not have permission to cross the wards.

"Well," I say. "It's partly about Baz. Basil. He hasn't come back to school."

"I've noticed," she says.

"Do you know if he's coming back?"

She looks down at her wand, a walking stick, and moves the handle in a circle. "I'm not sure."

"Have you talked to his parents?" I ask.

She looks up at me. "That's confidential."

I nod and kick the side of the Mage's desk—then realize what I'm doing and take a step away from it, tangling my fingers into the front of my hair.

Miss Possibelf clears her throat prettily; even across the room, it sends a buzz up the back of my neck.

"I *can* tell you," she says, "that it's school policy to contact a student's parents when a child doesn't return for the term. . . ."

"So you have talked to the Pitches?"

She narrows her dark brown eyes. "What do you hope to learn, Simon?"

I drop my hand in frustration. "The truth. Is he gone? Is he sick? Has the war started?"

"The truth . . ."

I keep waiting for her to blink. Even magicians blink.

"The truth," she says, "is that I don't have answers to any of those questions. His parents have been contacted. They were aware that he wasn't in school, but they didn't elaborate. Mr. Pitch is of legal age—like you, technically an adult. If he doesn't attend this school, I'm not responsible for his welfare."

"But you can't just ignore it when a student doesn't come back to school! What if he's planning something?"

"Then that's a concern for the Coven, not for the dean of students."

"If Baz is off organizing an insurgency," I press, "that's all of our concern."

She watches me. I push my jaw forward and stand my ground. (This is my standard move when I don't know what else to do.) (Because if there's one thing I'm good at . . . )

Miss Possibelf closes her eyes, but still not like she needs to blink—it's more like she's giving in. *Good.*

She looks back up at me. "Simon, I care about you, and I've always been honest with you. Listen to me—I don't *know* where Basilton is. Maybe he is off planning something awful; I hope not, for his sake and yours. All I do know is that when I talked to his father, he seemed unsurprised and ill at ease; he knew that his son wasn't here, and he didn't seem happy. Honestly, Simon? He sounded like a man at the end of his rope."

I puff a breath out hard through my nose and nod my head.

"That's all I know," she says. "I'll tell you if I learn more, if I'm able."

I nod again.

"Now, perhaps you should go to lunch."

"Thank you, Miss Possibelf."

As I move past her in the doorway, she tries to pat my arm—but I keep walking, and it's awkward. I hear the heavy oak door close behind us.

I don't go to lunch. I go for a walk that turns into a run that turns into me hacking away at a tree on the edge of the woods.

I can't believe that my blade comes when I call for it.

# 17

## SIMON

I stop looking for Baz anywhere where he's supposed to be. . . .

But I don't stop looking for him.

I take walks in the Wavering Wood at night. Penny sees the look on my face and doesn't try to join me. Agatha's always off doing schoolwork; she must be buckling down this year—maybe her dad's promised her a new horse or something.

I used to love the Wood, I used to find it calming.

I realize after a few nights that I'm not just walking aimlessly; I'm covering the Wood like I'm sweeping it. Like we swept it that year that Elspeth disappeared—all of us holding hands, walking side by side, marking off parcels as we moved through them. I'm marking off parcels in my head now, casting for light and waving my blade back and forth to clear branches. I'll mow the whole fucking forest down if I go on like this.

I don't find anything. And I frighten the sprites. And a dryad comes out to tell me that I'm basically a one-man walking woodland apocalypse.

"What do you seek?" the nymph asks, hovering over the ground even though I've already told her that it gives me the creeps. She's got hair like moss, and she's dressed like one of those manga girls with the Victorian boots and the umbrellas.

"Baz," I say. "My roommate."

"The dead one? With the pretty eyes?"

"Yes." *Is* Baz dead? I've never thought of him that way. I mean, he is a vampire, I guess. "Wait, are you saying he's dead? Like, really dead?"

"All the bloodeaters are dead."

"Have you actually seen him eat blood?"

She stares at me. My sword is stuck in the ground beside my feet.

"What do you seek, Chosen One?" She sounds irritated now. She lets her green brolly rest on her shoulder.

"My roommate. Baz. The bloodeater."

"He's not here," she says.

"Are you sure?"

"More sure than you."

I sigh and dig my sword deeper into the ground. "Well, I'm not sure at all."

"You're burning up goodwill here, magician."

"How many times do I have to save the Wood to win you people over?"

"There's no use saving it if you're just going to hack it down."

"I'm looking. For my roommate."

"Your enemy," she counters. She has grey-brown skin, ridged and rippled like bark, and her eyes glow like those mushrooms that grow deep in the woods.

"It doesn't matter what he is," I say, "you know who I'm talking about—how can you be sure he isn't here?"

The dryad tilts her head back, like she's listening to the trees behind her. Her every move sounds like a breeze blowing through branches.

"He isn't here," she says. "Unless he's hiding."

"Well, of course he's hiding! He's hiding bloody somewhere."

"If *we* can't see him here, magician, neither will you."

I pick up my sword and sheathe it at my hip. "But you'll tell me if you hear anything?"

"Probably not."

"You're impossible."

"I'm improbable."

"This is important," I say. "A very dangerous person is missing."

"Not dangerous to me," she hisses. "Not dangerous to my sisters. We don't bleed. We don't play petty games of more and most."

"Perhaps you've forgotten that Pitch is the House of Fire." I gesture to the woods behind her, all of it flammable.

Her head snaps up. Her smile creaks down. She switches her umbrella to her other shoulder. *"Fine."*

"Fine?"

"If we see your handsome bloodeater, we'll tell him you're looking for him."

"Not. Helping."

"We'll tell the golden one, then."

"The golden one . . . Am I the golden one?"

She scrunches her nose and shakes her mossy hair. Flowers bloom in it.

"Who, then?"

"Your golden one. His golden one. Your pistil and stigma."

"Pistol . . . Do you mean Agatha?"

"Sister golden hair."

"You'll tell Agatha if you see Baz?"

"Yes." Her umbrella twirls. "We find her peaceful."

I sigh and rub the back of my hand into my forehead. "I've

saved you at least three times. This whole forest. You know that, yeah?"

"What do you *seek,* Chosen One?"

"Nothing." I throw my hands in the air and turn to leave, kicking at the nearest sapling. "Nothing!"

Nothing good ever happens in the Wavering Wood.

I walk the Wood.

I walk the fields.

I cover the school grounds between classes, poking through empty buildings, opening long-closed doors.

Sometimes Watford seems as big on the inside as the walled grounds and the outer lands combined.

There are secret rooms. Secret hallways. Entirely hidden wings that only reveal themselves if you know the right spell or have the right artefact.

There's an extra storey between the second and third floors of the Cloisters. (Penny calls it "bonus content.") It's an echo of the floor above it. All the same things happen there, a day later.

There's a moat below the moat.

And warrens in the hills.

There are three hidden gates, and I've only got one of them to open.

Sometimes it feels like I've spent my whole life looking for the map or key that would make Watford—the whole World of Mages—make sense.

But all I ever find are pieces of the puzzle. It's like I'm in a dark room, and I only ever have enough light to see one corner of it at a time.

I spent most of my fifth year wandering the Catacombs below the White Chapel, searching for Baz. The Chapel's at the centre of Watford; it's the oldest building. No one knows whether Watford started as a school or something else. Maybe a magic abbey. Or a mages' settlement—that's what I'd like to believe. Imagine it, a walled town with magicians living together, practically out in the open. A magickal community.

The Catacombs sit beneath the Chapel and beyond it. There are probably lots of ways down, but I only know of one.

In our fifth year, I kept seeing Baz slip off towards the Chapel after dinner. I thought it must be some plot—a conspiracy.

I'd follow him to the Chapel, through the high, arched, never-locked front doors . . . Back behind the altar, behind the sanctuary and the Poets Corner . . . Through the secret door, and down into the Catacombs.

The Catacombs are properly creepy. Agatha would never go down there with me, and Penelope only went with me at first, when she still believed Baz might be up to something.

She stopped after a few months. She stopped going to Baz's football matches with me, too. And stopped waiting with me in the hallway outside the balcony where Baz takes violin lessons.

But I couldn't give it up. Not when all my clues were just starting to come together . . .

The blood on Baz's cuffs. The fact that he could see in the dark. (He'd come back to our room at night and dress for bed without ever turning on the light.) Then I found a pile of dead rats in the Chapel basement, all pinched and used, like squeezed-up lemons.

I was alone when I finally confronted him. Deep in the Catacombs, inside the Children's Tomb. *Le Tombeau des Enfants.* Baz was sitting in the corner, skulls stacked along the walls around him.

"You found me," he said.

I already had my blade out. "I knew I would."

"Now what?" He didn't even stand. Just brushed some dust off his grey trousers and leaned back against the bones.

"Now you tell me what you're up to," I said.

He laughed at that. Baz was always laughing at me that year, but it came out flatter than usual. There were torches staining the grey room orange, but his skin was still chalky and white.

I adjusted my stance, spreading my feet below my hips, squaring my shoulders.

"They died in a plague," he said.

"Who?"

Baz raised his hand—I flinched back.

He cocked an eyebrow and swept his arm in a flourish at the room around us. "Them," he said. *Les enfants.*" A lock of black hair fell over his forehead.

"Is that why you're here? To track down a plague?"

Baz stared at me. He was 16, we both were, but he made me feel 5. He's always made me feel like a child, like I'll never catch up to him. Like he was born knowing everything about the World of Mages—it's *his* world. It's in his DNA.

"Yes, Snow," he said. "I'm here to find a plague. I'm going to put it in a steaming beaker and infect all of Metropolis."

I gripped my blade.

He looked bored.

"What are you doing down here?" I demanded, swinging the sword in the air.

"Sitting," he said.

"*No.* None of that. I've finally caught you, after all these months—you're going to tell me what you're up to."

"Most of the students died," he said.

"Stop it. Stop distracting me."

"They sent the well ones home. My great-great-uncle was the headmaster; he stayed to help nurse the sick and dying. His

skull is down here, too. Maybe you could help me look for it—
I'm told I share his aristocratic brow."

"I'm not listening."

"Magic didn't help them," Baz said.

I clenched my jaw.

"They didn't have a spell for the plague yet," he went on.
"There weren't any words that had enough power, the right
kind of power."

I stepped forward. "What are you doing here?"

He started singing to himself. *"Ring around the rosie / a
pocket full of posies . . ."*

"Answer me, Baz."

*"Ashes, ashes . . ."*

I swung my sword into the pile of bones beside him, sending
skulls rattling and rolling.

He sneered and sat up, catching the skulls with his wand—
**"As you were!"** They turned in the air and rolled back into
place.

"Show some respect, Snow," he said sharply, then slumped
and leaned back again. "What do you want from me?"

"I want to know what you're up to."

"This is what I'm up to."

"Sitting in a fucking tomb with a bunch of bones."

"They're not just bones. They're *students*. And teachers.
Everyone who dies at Watford is entombed down here."

"So?"

"*So?*" he repeated.

I growled.

"Look, Snow . . ." He got to his feet. He was taller than
me—he's always been taller than me. Even after the summer
when I grew three inches, I swear that jammy bastard grew
four. "You've been following me," he said, "looking for me.

And now you've found me. It's not my fault if you still haven't found what you're looking for."

"I know what you are," I snarled.

His eyes locked onto mine. "Your roommate?"

I shook my head and squeezed the hilt of my sword.

Baz stepped into my reach. "Tell me," he spat.

I couldn't.

"Tell me, Snow." He stepped even closer. *What am I?*"

I growled again and raised the blade an inch. "Vampire!" I shouted. He must have felt the force of my breath on his face.

He started giggling. "Really? You think I'm a *vampire*? Well, Aleister Crowley, what are you going to do about *that*?"

He slipped a flask out of his jacket and took a swig. I didn't know that he'd been drinking—my sword dipped. I tried to remind myself to stay battle ready, and pulled it up again.

"Stake through the heart?" he asked, falling back into the corner and resting an arm on a pile of skulls. "Beheading, perhaps? That only works if you keep my head separate from my body, and even then I could still walk; my body won't stop until it finds my head. . . . Better go with fire, Snow, it's the only solution."

I wanted to just slice him in two. Right then and there. Fucking finally.

But I kept thinking of Penelope. *"How do you know he's a vampire, Simon? Have you seen him drink blood? Has he threatened you? Has he tried to put you in his thrall?"*

Maybe he had. Maybe that's why I'd been following Baz around for six months.

And now I had him.

"Do something," he teased. "Save the day, Snow. Or the night. Quick, before I . . . Hmm . . . what horrible thing shall I do? It's too late for everyone down here—there's just *you* to hurt, isn't there? And I don't think I'm in the mood to suck your blood. What if I accidentally Turned you? Then I'd be stuck with your pious face forever." Baz shook his head and took another pull at his flask. "I don't think undeath would improve you, Snow. It would just ruin your complexion." He giggled again. Mirthlessly. And closed his eyes like he was exhausted.

He probably was. I was. We'd been playing cat and mouse in the Catacombs every night for weeks.

I dropped my sword but kept it unsheathed, then stepped out of my stance. "I don't have to do anything," I said. "I know what you are. Now I just have to wait for you to make a mistake."

He winced without opening his eyes. "Really, Snow? That's your plan? Wait for me to kill someone? You're the worst Chosen One who's ever been chosen."

"Fuck off," I said. Which always means I've lost an argument. I started backing out of the tomb. I needed to talk this through with Penelope; I needed to regroup.

"If I'd known it was this easy to get rid of you," Baz called after me, "I would've let you catch up with me weeks ago!"

I headed for the surface, hoping that he couldn't turn into a bat and fly after me. (Penny said that was a myth. But still.)

I could hear him singing, even after I'd been walking for ten minutes. *"Ashes, ashes—we all fall down."*


I haven't been back to the Catacombs since that night. . . .

I wait until I'm fairly sure everyone is in bed, hopefully asleep—then I sneak down to the White Chapel.

Two busts guard the secret door in the Poets Corner—the most famous of the modern mage poets, Carroll and Seuss.

I've got some nylon rope, and I tie one end around Theodor's neck.

The door itself, a panel in the wall, is always locked, and there isn't any key. But all you have to do to open it is possess a genuine desire to enter. Most people simply don't.

The door swings open for me. And closes behind me. The air is immediately colder. I light a wall torch and choose my first path.

Down in the winding tunnels of the Catacombs, I use every revealing spell I know, and every finding spell. *(**"Come out, come out, wherever you are! It's show time! Scooby-Dooby-Doo, where are you!"**)* I call for Baz by his full name—that makes a spell harder to resist.

Magic words are tricky. Sometimes to reveal something hidden, you have to use the language of the time it was stashed away. And sometimes an old phrase stops working when the rest of the world is sick of saying it.

I've never been good with words.

That's partly why I'm such a useless magician.

*"Words are very powerful,"* Miss Possibelf said during our first Magic Words lesson. No one else was paying attention; she wasn't saying anything they didn't already know. But I was trying to commit it all to memory.

*"And they become more powerful,"* she went on, *"the more that they're said and read and written, in specific, consistent combinations.*

*"The key to casting a spell is tapping into that power. Not just saying the words, but summoning their meaning."*

Which means you have to have a good vocabulary to do magic. And you have to be able to think on your feet. And be brave enough to speak up. And have an ear for a solid turn of phrase.

And you have to actually *understand* what you're saying—how the words translate into magic.

You can't just wave your wand and repeat whatever you've heard somebody saying down on the street corner; that's a good way to accidentally separate someone from their bollocks.

None of it comes naturally to me. Words. Language. Speaking.

I don't remember when I learned to talk, but I know they tried to send me to specialists. Apparently, that can happen to kids in care, or kids with parents who never talk to them—they just don't learn how.

I used to see a counsellor and a speech therapist. *"Use your words, Simon."* I got so bloody sick of hearing that. It was so much easier to just take what I wanted instead of asking for it. Or thump whoever was hurting me, even if they thumped me right back.

I barely spoke the first month I was at Watford. It was easy not to; no one else around here shuts up.

Miss Possibelf and a few of the other teachers noticed and started giving me private lessons. Talking-out-loud lessons. Sometimes the Mage would sit in on these, rubbing his beard and staring out the window. *"Use your words!"*—I imagined myself shouting at him. And then I imagined him telling me that it was a mistake to bring me here.

Anyway, I'm still not good with words, and I'm shit with my wand, so I get by with memorization. And sincerity—that helps, believe it or not. When in doubt, I just do whatever Penny tells me to.

I work my way carefully through the Catacombs, doing my level best with the spells I can make work for me.

I find hidden doorways inside hidden doorways. I find a treasure chest that's snoring deeply. I find a painting of a girl with blond hair and tears pouring down her cheeks, actually pouring, like a GIF carved into the wall. A younger me would have stayed to figure out her story. A younger me would have turned this into an adventure.

I keep looking for Baz.

Or a clue.

Every night I turn back when I get to the end of my rope.

# 18

## LUCY

Do you know these walls are a thousand years old?

There are spirits moving through them who speak languages no one is left to understand. But it doesn't matter, I guess. Nobody hears them.

The walls are the same as when I walked them. The Chapel. The Tower. The drawbridge.

The wolves are new. The fish-beasts. Where did Davy find them, I wonder? What spell did he cast to bring them here? And what does he think they'll prevent?

"Paranoid," Mit always said. "He thinks everyone's out to get him."

"I think a few people might actually be out to get him," I argued.

"Only because he's such a spiteful git," she said.

"He cares too much."

"About himself? Agreed."

"About everything," I said. "He can't let any of it go."

"You've been listening to him for too long, Lucy."

"I feel sorry for him. . . . And if you'd listen to him, you'd realize that he's making sense. Why *can't* pixies and centaurs with mage heritage come to Watford? And why did my brother have to stay home? Just because he isn't powerful?"

"Your brother's an idiot," she said. "All he cares about is Def Leppard."

"You know how much it hurt my mother when he was rejected. He has a wand, and he doesn't even know how to use it. My parents almost got a divorce over it."

"I know." Mitali softened. "I'm sorry. But the school's only so big. It can't take everyone."

"We could make it bigger, Davy says so. Or we could build a new school. Imagine that—schools all over the country for anyone with magic."

She frowned. "But the point of Watford is that it's the best. The best education for the best magicians."

"*Is* that the point of Watford? Then Davy's right. It is elitist."

Mit sighed.

"Davy says we're getting weaker," I said. "As a society. That the wild, dark things will wipe us from the earth and let it reclaim our magic."

"Does he tell you that they live under your bed?"

"I'm being serious," I said.

"I know," she said sadly. "I wish you weren't. What does Davy expect you to do? What does he expect from any of us?"

I leaned towards her and whispered my answer—*"Revolution."*

I've been wandering.

Trying to find my way to you.

The walls are the same. And the Chapel. And the Tower.

The neckties are thinner. The skirts are shorter. But the colours are the same. . . .

I can't help but feel proud of Davy now—you'll think that's funny coming from me, but I can't *help* but feel proud of him.

He managed it. His revolution.

He opened these doors to every child blessed with magic.

# 19

## SIMON

It's almost Halloween before I finally talk to the Mage.

He calls for me himself. A robin flies into Greek and drops a note onto my desk. The Mage often has a bird or two flapping around him. Robins, mostly. And wrens and sparrows. (Like Snow White.) He'd rather cast **A little bird told me** than use his mobile.

When class is over, I head towards an outbuilding at the far end of the grounds, up against the outer wall. There are stables back there that have been turned into a garage and barracks.

His Men are outside—Penny says she'd like the Mage's Men better if there were a few women among them— and they're gathered around a big green truck I've never seen before, something like a military truck with canvas walls. One of them is holding a metal box. They're taking turns reaching for it and watching their hands pass right through.

"Simon," the Mage says, stepping out of the garage. He puts his arm around my shoulder and leads me away from the truck. "Here you are."

"I would have come right away, sir, but I was in class. And

the Minotaur said you would have sent a larger bird if it were an emergency."

The Mage frowns. "The spell doesn't work with larger birds."

"I know, sir. I'm sorry. He wouldn't listen."

"Well." He claps my shoulder. "It wasn't an emergency. I just wanted to see you. To check on you. Miss Possibelf told me about the attack, the bugs—she said it was the Humdrum."

Flibbertigibbets. In Magic Words class. A whole swarm of them. I'd never even *seen* a swarm of flibbertigibbets before.

We call them bugs because they're about the size of bumblebees, but flibbertigibbets are more like birds. One can kill a dog or a goat or a gryphon. Two or three can take down a magician. They burrow into your ears and buzz so loud, you can't think. First you lose your mind—and then they get to your brain, and you lose everything else.

Flibbertigibbets don't attack people, not usually. But they came in through the classroom window last week and surrounded me like a chattering orange cloud. The worst part was that dry, sucking feeling that always accompanies the Humdrum's attacks.

Everybody else in the class ran.

"It felt like the Humdrum, sir. But why would he send flibbertigibbets? They're hardly a threat."

"Not for you, certainly." The Mage rubs his beard. "Maybe he just wants to remind us that he's out there. What'd you hit them with?"

**"Dead in the air."**

"Well done, Simon."

"I . . . I think I killed some other things, too. Ebb found pheasants in the field. And Rhys had a budgie. . . ."

The Mage glances at the robin flitting above his shoulder,

then squeezes my arm. "You did what you had to. And no one was hurt. Did you see the nurse?"

"I'm fine, sir." I step closer. "Sir. I was hoping—I mean. Have you made any progress? With the Humdrum? I see the Men coming and going. But I don't—I could help. Penelope and me. We could help."

His hand slips from my shoulder, and he rests it on his hip. "There's nothing to report on that front. No breakthroughs, no attacks. Just the constant widening of the holes. I almost wish the Humdrum *would* show his face again"—I shudder at the memory of that face; the Mage goes on—"to remind these backwards fools what we're really up against."

I look over his shoulder at the truck. The Men have been carrying boxes past us the whole time we've been talking.

"Sir, did you get my note?"

He narrows his eyes. "About the missing Pitch boy."

"About my roommate. He still hasn't come back."

The Mage rubs his beard with the back of his leather glove. "You're right to be concerned, I think. The Old Families are closing ranks, calling their sons home, bolting their gates. They're readying to make a move against us."

"Their sons?"

He starts rattling off names—boys I know, but not well. Sixth, seventh, and eighth years.

"But surely," I say, "the Families know that the Humdrum will finish us if we don't stand together. He's more powerful than ever."

"Perhaps that's part of their plan," the Mage says. "I've stopped trying to figure these people out. They care more for their own wealth and power than for our world. Sometimes I think they'd sacrifice anything to see me fall. . . ."

"How can I help, sir?"

"By being careful, Simon." He puts his hand on my arm again and turns to face me. "I'm leaving again in a few hours. But I was hoping, in the light of this new attack, that I could convince you to heed my words. *Leave here, Simon.* Let me take you to the haven I spoke of—it's the farthest I can put you from danger."

I take a step back. "But it was just flibbertigibbets, sir."

"This time."

"No. *Sir.* I told you . . . I'm fine here. I'm perfectly safe."

"You're never safe!" he says, and he says it so fiercely, it almost seems like a threat. "Safety, stability—it's an illusion. It's a false god, Simon. It's clinging to a sinking raft instead of learning to swim."

"Then I may as *well* stay here!" I say. Too loudly. One of the Mage's Men, Stephen, looks up at me. My voice drops: "If nowhere is safe, I may as well stay here. With my friends. Or I may as well fight—*I could help you.*"

We lock eyes, and I see his fill with disappointment and pity. "I know you could, Simon. But the situation is very delicate right now. . . ."

He doesn't have to finish. I know what he means.

The Mage doesn't need a bomb.

You don't send bombs on reconnaissance missions or invite them to strategy meetings. You wait until you've run out of options, then you drop them.

I nod my head.

Then I turn away from him, walking back towards the heart of the grounds.

I can feel his Men watching me. They're all just a year or two older than I am. I hate that they think they're even older—that they feel so important. I hate the dark green breeches they wear, and the gold stars on their sleeves.

"Simon!" the Mage shouts.

I flatten my expression, then turn back.

He's holding up a hand to shield his eyes from the sun. He gives me a rare smile. A small one. "The Humdrum may be more powerful than ever, but you're more powerful than ever, too. Remember that."

I nod and watch him walk back to the garage.

I'm late to meet Penelope.

# 20

## PENELOPE

We're studying out in the hills, even though it's cold, because Simon doesn't like to practise where anyone can see him.

He's got his grey duffle coat on, and a green-on-green striped school scarf, and I should have worn trousers because the wind is blowing right through my grey tights.

It's nearly Samhain—the Veil will close soon, and Aunt Beryl hasn't shown a whisker.

***"It is what it is!"*** Simon says, pointing his wand at a small rock sitting on a tree stump. The rock shivers, then collapses into a pile of dust. "I can't tell if the spell's working," he says, "or if I'm just destroying things."

Every eighth-year student is tasked with creating a new spell by the end of the year—with finding a new twist in the language that's gained power or an old one that's been overlooked, and then figuring out how to apply it.

The best new spells are practical and enduring. Catchphrases are usually crap; mundane people get tired of saying them, then move on. (Spells go bad that way, expire just as we get the hang of them.) Songs are dicey for the same reason.

Almost never does a Watford student actually create a spell that takes hold.

But my mother was only a seventh year when she worked out **The lady's not for turning**—and it's still an incredibly useful spell in combat, especially for women. (Which Mum's a bit ashamed of, I think. To have a spell taught in the Mage's Offence workshops.)

Simon's been trying a new phrase every week since the beginning of term. His heart's not in it, and I don't really blame him. Even tried-and-true spells hiccup in his wand. And sometimes when he casts metaphors, they go viciously literal. Like when he cast **Hair of the dog** on Agatha during sixth year to help her get over a hangover, and instead covered her with dog hair. I think that's the last time Simon pointed his wand at a person. And the last time Agatha had a drink.

He brushes the rubble off the stump and sits down, shoving his wand in his pocket. "Baz isn't the only one missing."

"What do you mean?" I point my wand at some chess pieces I've set on the ground. ***"The game is on!"***

The bishop falls over.

I try again. ***"The game is afoot!"***

Nothing happens.

"This phrase has got to be good for something," I say. "It's Shakespeare *plus* Sherlock Holmes."

"The Mage told me that the Old Families have been pulling their sons out of school," Simon says. "Two seventh-year boys didn't come back. And Marcus, Baz's cousin, is gone. He's only a sixth year."

"Which one is Marcus?"

"Fit. Blond streaks in his hair. Midfielder."

I shrug and stoop to pick up the chess pieces. I'm being fairly literal myself at the moment, because I've tried everything else with this phrase. I feel like it could be a good beginning spell—a catalyst. . . . "Is it just boys who haven't come back?" I ask.

"Huh," Simon says. "Dunno. The Mage didn't say."

"He's such a sexist." I shake my head. "Marcus—is he the one who got trapped in a dumbwaiter our fourth year?"

"Yeah."

"That one's joined the other side, eh? Well, I'm shaking in my boots."

"The Mage thinks the Families are getting ready for some big strike."

"What does he want us to do about it?"

"He doesn't," Simon says.

I slip the chess pieces in my pocket. "What do you mean?"

"Well, he still wants me to leave—"

I must frown, because Simon raises his eyebrows and says, "I *know*, Penny—I'm not going anywhere. But if I stay here, then he wants me to lie low. He wants *us* to lie low. He says his Men are working on it, and it's delicate."

"Hmm." I sit next to Simon on the tree stump. I have to admit, I sort of love the idea of lying low—of letting the Mage get up to his mad business without us for once. But I don't like to be *told* to lie low. Neither does Simon. "Do you think Baz is with these other boys?" I ask.

"Makes sense, doesn't it?"

I don't say anything. I really, really hate to talk to Simon about Baz. It's like talking to the Mad Hatter about tea. I hate to encourage him.

He knocks some bark off the stump with the back of his heel.

I lean into him, because I'm cold and he's always warm. And because I like to remind him that I'm not afraid of him.

"It makes sense," he says.

# 21

## THE MAGE

Books. Artefacts. Enchanted jewellery. Enchanted furniture. Monkeys' paws, rabbits' legs, gnomes' gnoses . . .

We take it all. Even if I know it's useless to me.

This exercise has more than one aim. It's good to remind the Old Families that I'm still running this show.

This school.

This realm.

And there's not one of them who could do better.

They call me a failure because the Humdrum still drums on, stealing our magic, scrubbing our land clear—but who among them could pose a threat?

Maybe Natasha Grimm-Pitch could have put the Humdrum in his place—but she's long gone, and none of her friends and relatives have even a fraction of her talent.

I send my Men to take my enemies' treasures, to raid their libraries. I show them that even a red-faced child in my uniform has more power than they do in this new world. I show them what their names are worth—nothing.

But still . . .

I don't find what I need. I don't find any real answers—I still can't *fix* him.

The Greatest Mage is our only hope now.

But our greatest mage is fundamentally flawed. Cracked. Broken.

Simon Snow is that mage; I know it.

Nothing like him has ever walked our earth.

But Simon Snow—my Simon—still can't bear his power. He still can't control it. He's the only vessel big enough to hold it, but he is *cracked*. He is *compromised*. He is . . .

Just a boy.

There must be a way—a spell, a charm, a token—that can help him. We are mages! The only magickal creatures who can wield and *shape* power. Somewhere in our world, there is an answer for Simon. (A ritual. A recipe. A rhyme.)

This isn't how prophecies work. . . .

This isn't how stories unfold. . . .

Incompletely.

If there's a crack in Simon, then there's a way to mend him. And I will find it.

# 22

## SIMON

I'm failing Greek, I think. And I'm lost in Political Science.

Agatha and I get into a fight about going to her house for half-term break: I don't want to leave Watford, and I don't think she actually wants me to go home with her. But she wants me to want to. Or something.

I stop wearing my cross and put it in a box under my bed. . . .

My neck feels lighter, but my head feels full of stones. It would help if I could *sleep,* but I can't, and I don't really have to—I can just sort of get by, on catnaps and magic.

I keep having to kick Penny out of my room, so she doesn't catch on to how I'm spending my nights.

"But nobody's using Baz's bed," she argues.

"Nobody's using *your* bed," I say.

"Trixie and Keris push the beds together when I'm not there—there's probably pixie dust everywhere."

"Not my problem, Penny."

"All my problems are your problems, Simon."

"Why?"

"Because all of *your* problems are my problems!"

"Go to your room."

"Simon, please."

"Go. You'll get expelled."

"Only if I get caught."

*"Go."*

When Penny finally leaves, so do I.

I give up on the Catacombs and start haunting the ramparts instead.

I don't really expect to find Baz up here—where would he hide? But at least I feel like I'll see him coming.

Plus I like the wind. And the stars. I never get to see stars over the summer; no matter which city I end up in, there are always too many lights.

There's a watchtower out there with a little nook inside, with a bench and a roof. I watch the Mage's Men coming and going all night in their military truck. Sometimes I fall asleep.

"You look tired," Penny says at breakfast. (Fried eggs. Fried mushrooms. Baked beans and black pudding.) "Also—" She leans over the table. "—there's a leaf in your hair."

"Hmmm." I keep shovelling in my breakfast. There'll be time for second helpings before lessons, if I hurry.

Penny reaches for my hair again, then glances at Agatha and pulls her hand back. Agatha's always been jealous of Penny and me, no matter how many times I tell her it's not like that. (It's *really* not like that.)

But Agatha seems to be ignoring us both. Again. Still. We haven't spent any time alone since our argument. Honestly, it's been a relief. It's one fewer person asking me if I'm okay. I put my hand on her leg and squeeze, and she turns to me, smiling with the bottom half of her face.

"Right," Penny says. "We're meeting tonight in Simon's room. After dinner."

"Meeting about what?" I ask.

"Strategy!" Penny whispers.

Agatha wakes up. "Strategy about what?"

"About everything," Penelope says. "About the Humdrum. About the Old Families. About what the Mage's Men are really up to. I'm tired of lying low—don't you feel like we're being left out?"

"No," Agatha says. "I feel like we should be grateful for some peace."

Penny sighs. "That's what I thought, too—but I'm worried that we're being lulled. Intentionally lulled."

Agatha shakes her head. "You're worried that someone *wants* us to be happy and comfortable."

"Yes!" Penelope says, stabbing the air with her fork.

"Perish the thought," Agatha says.

"We should be in on the plan," Penelope says. "Whatever it is. We've always been in on the plan—even when we were kids. And we're adults now. Why is the Mage sidelining us?"

"You think the Mage is lulling us?" Agatha asks. "Or is the Humdrum doing it? Or maybe Baz?" She's being sarcastic, but Penny either doesn't notice or pretends not to.

"*Yes,*" Penny says, and stabs the air again, like she's making sure that it's dead. "All of the above!"

I wait for Agatha to argue some more, but she just shakes her head—shakes her cornsilk hair—and scoops some egg onto her toast.

She doesn't look happy *or* comfortable. She's frowning, and her eyes are pinched, and I don't think she's wearing makeup.

"You look tired," I say, feeling bad that I'm just now noticing.

She leans against me for a moment, then sits straight again. "I'm fine, Simon."

"You both look tired," Penny declares. "Maybe you have post-traumatic stress disorder. Maybe you're not *used* to this much peace and quiet."

I squeeze Agatha's leg again, then get up to get us some more eggs and toast and mushrooms.

*"Lulled,"* I hear Penny saying.

# 23

## PENELOPE

It was a murder of crows getting them both up here, and Agatha's still complaining:

"Penelope, this is a *boys'* house. We'll be *expelled.*"

"Well, the damage is done," I say, sitting at Simon's desk. "You're as likely to get caught leaving now as leaving later, so you may as well stay."

"You won't get caught," Simon says, flopping down on his bed. "Penny sneaks up here all the time."

Agatha is *not* happy to hear that. (I ignore her; if she's moronic enough to believe that Simon and I have romantic feelings for each other after all these years, I'm not wasting my time talking her out of it.) She deliberately sits as far as she can from both of us, even though that means sitting on Baz's bed.

Then she realizes what she's done, and looks like she wants to stand up again. Her eyes dart around the room, as if Baz himself might walk out of the bathroom. Simon looks just as paranoid.

*Honestly.* The pair of them.

"I still don't know why we're having this meeting," Agatha says.

"To pool our knowledge," I say, looking around the room

for materials. "This would be so much easier if we had a blackboard. . . ."

I raise my wand and cast a *"See what I mean!"* then start writing in the air—*What We Know:*

"Nothing," Agatha says. "Meeting adjourned."

I ignore her. "The way I see it, there are three things we always have to worry about."

*1.*, I write, *The Humdrum.* "What do we know about the Humdrum?"

"That he looks like me," Simon says, trying to go along with me. Agatha doesn't look surprised by this information; Simon must have told her what happened. "And that he wants something from me," Simon continues. "That he comes after me."

"And we know that he's been quiet," I say. "Nothing but flibbertigibbets since June."

Agatha folds her arms. "But the Humdrum's still out there eating magic, isn't he?"

"Yes," I acknowledge. "But not as much. I saw my dad on the weekend, and he said the holes are spreading much more slowly than usual." I add this to my notes in the air.

"We don't know that he eats it," Simon says. "We don't know *what* the Humdrum does with the magic."

"Sticking to what we do know . . . ," I say, and write, *2. The War with the Old Families.*

"I wouldn't call it a 'war,'" Agatha says.

"But there have been skirmishes, yeah?" Simon says. "And duels."

Agatha huffs. "Well, you can't walk into someone's house and demand to go through their attic without expecting a few duels."

Simon and I both turn to look at her. "What do you mean?" I ask.

"The Mage," Agatha says. "I heard Mother talking to a friend from the club. He's been raiding magicians' houses, looking for dark magic."

This is all news to me. "Has he raided your house?"

"He wouldn't," Agatha says. "My father's on the Coven."

"What sort of dark magic?" Simon asks.

"Probably anything that can be used as a weapon," Agatha says.

"Anything *can* be used as a weapon," Simon says.

I add to my notes: *Raids, dark magic, duels.*

"And we know that the Old Families have kept some of their sons from Watford," Simon adds.

"Which could just be coincidence," I say. "We should do some legwork—maybe the missing boys just went to university."

"Or maybe they're tired of being treated like villains," Agatha says.

"Or maybe," Simon says, "they're joining an army."

I add to my notes: *Pitch allies leaving school.*

Simon's getting jumpy. "What about Baz?"

Agatha runs her hand along the mattress.

"We'll get there," I say. "Let's stay focused on what we know."

He keeps pushing. "Miss Possibelf thinks he's missing. She said his dad sounded scared."

I sigh and add a third column: *3. Baz.* But there's nothing to write underneath it.

"I still don't think it's *a war*," Agatha insists. "It's just politics, just like in the Normal world. The Mage has power, and the Old Families want it back. They'll bitch and moan and cut deals and throw parties—"

"It's not just politics." Simon leans towards her, pointing. "It's right and wrong."

Agatha rolls her eyes. "But that's what the other side says, too."

"Is that what Baz says?" he asks.

I try to cut in. *"Simon."*

"It's not just politics," he says again. "It's right. And wrong. It's our *lives*. If the Old Families had their way, I wouldn't even be here. They wouldn't have let me into Watford."

"But that wasn't personal, Simon," Agatha says. "It's because you're a Normal."

"How am I a Normal?" He throws his hands in the air. "I'm the most powerful magician anyone knows about."

"You know what I mean," Agatha says, and she's being sincere, I think. "There's never been a Normal at Watford."

She's right, but I wonder who she's parroting.

"I was prophesied," Simon says, and it sounds so pathetically defensive, I try to think of a way to change the subject.

Simon *was* prophesied.

Or someone was. Over and over.

The most powerful magician ever to walk the earth was coming, and he (or she) was supposed to get here just when the World of Mages needed him most.

And Simon *did*.

The Humdrum was eating our magic, the Mage and the Old Families were at each other's throats—and then Simon arrived. He came into his power and lit up the magickal firmament like an electrical storm.

Most magicians can remember exactly where they were that day. (I can't. But I was only 11.) My mum was giving a lecture. She said it felt like touching a raw wire and feeling the electricity shake you from the inside. Raw, scalding, scorching magic . . .

Which is still how Simon's magic feels. I've never told him

so, but it's awful. Just standing near him when he goes off is like taking a shock. Your muscles are tired afterwards, and your hair smells like smoke.

Sometimes Simon's power seduces other magicians; they can feel it, and they want to be closer. But anyone who's actually been close to Simon is long past feeling seduced.

Once, he went off while protecting Agatha and me from a clan of worsegers—like badgers, but worse—and Agatha twitched and ticced for a week. She told Simon she had the flu, so he wouldn't feel bad. Agatha's less tolerant of his power than I am; it might be because she has less of her own. It might be that their magic is incompatible.

That can happen sometimes, even when two people are in love. There's an old story, a romantic tragedy, about two lovers whose magic drove each other mad. . . .

I don't think Simon and Agatha are in love.

But it isn't my job to tell them so. (And also I've already tried.)

Anyway, Mum says that when the Mage brought Simon back to Watford, it was like he was calling bluff on the whole World of Mages. *Here's that saviour you've been talking about for a thousand years.*

Even the people who didn't believe it couldn't say so out loud. And nobody could deny Simon's power.

They *did* try to keep him out of Watford. The Mage had to make Simon his heir to get him into school—and to have him entered into the Book of Magic.

There are still a lot of people who don't accept Simon, even among the Mage's allies. *"It takes more than magic to make a mage,"* is what Baz has always said.

It sounds like classist nonsense, but in a way, it's true:

The unicorns have magic. The vampires have some. Dragons,

numpties, ne'er-do-wolves—they all have magic.

But you're not a magician unless you can *control* magic, unless you can speak its language. And Simon . . . Well. Simon.

He gets up now and walks over to the window, opening it wide and sitting on the ledge. His wand is in his way, so he pulls it out of his back pocket and tosses it on his bed.

*No. 4,* I write in the air, *The Mage.*

"So we know the Mage's Men are raiding . . . ," I say. "And, Simon, didn't you say they were unloading things back in the stables? We could sniff around back there."

He ignores me, staring out the window.

"Agatha," I say, "what else have you heard at home?"

"I don't know," she says, frowning and fiddling with her skirt. "Father's had lots of emergency Coven meetings. Mother says they can't meet at our house anymore. She thinks our Normal neighbours are getting suspicious."

"All right," I say, "maybe we should move on to questions now—what *don't* we know?"

I start a new column in the air, but Agatha stands up and starts walking out. "I really need to study."

I try to stop her—"Agatha, wait, you'll get caught if you leave by yourself!"—but she's already closing the door.

Simon exhales loudly and runs his hands through his hair, making it stand up in curly bronze chunks. "I'm going for a walk," he says, marching towards the door, leaving his wand on his bed.

Part of me wishes he were following her, but I don't think he is.

I sigh, then sit down on his bed and look at our meagre lists. Before I leave, I blow my words out the window with a ***"Clear the air!"***

# 24

## AGATHA

I don't know what I'm hoping for.

That he'll see me standing at the wall, my hair whipping in the wind and my dress billowing out around me . . .

And that, what?

That it will mean something to him?

That he'll see me up here, waiting for him on the ramparts, and really *see* me for the first time—*There's the answer,* he'll think. And he'll unfasten my ribbons and tie them around his arm, or his thigh. And, Morgana, what would that even mean?

Something.

Something *new.*

I know that Basil, I don't know . . . *thinks* about me. Or at least thought about me. That he used to watch me. Especially when I was with Simon.

I know that he hated what Simon and I have. And wanted it. That he'd do anything to get between us.

Baz was always there, cutting in at every dance. Teasing me away from Simon, then just teasing me. Disappearing. Sneaking away.

I played along sometimes—maybe I should be grateful that Baz never called my bluff.

Because maybe it wasn't a bluff. Maybe I *would* walk away with Baz. I followed him into the Wood that day; I still don't know what I was thinking.

I mean, I *know* who Baz is. I know what he is.

I can't break up with Simon for a Tory vampire—my parents would disown me. And I don't even know what that would entail. Would I have to be evil? Slip poison into people's drinks? Cast dark spells? Or would it just be sitting next to a different boy at a different table . . . Being beautiful on another side of the room.

I'd be gold to his black. Both of us pale as snow.

Maybe I wouldn't have to be evil—but Baz wouldn't expect me to be good, always so *good.*

And maybe I'd live forever.

I walk the ramparts at night in a white dress and a knee-length woven cloak. The weather's turning. I feel the roses in my cheeks.

Maybe he'll see me up here before I see him.

Maybe he'll want me.

And I'll know what I want, too.

# 25

## LUCY

I keep trying.
    I keep calling.
    I know this is your place.

# 26

## SIMON

At first, when I see her standing along the ramparts, I think she's a ghost. A Visiting.

She's pale and wearing a flowy white dress, and her white hair is unbound and flying around her head. . . . But everybody else has come through the Veil wearing whatever it is they died in—not stereotypical ghost clothes.

I don't recognize the white lady on the ramparts as Agatha until she startles and turns to me. She must have heard me summon my blade. I immediately stow it when I see that it's her.

"Oh," I say. "Hey. I thought you were studying."

I don't feel angry with her anymore. Now that we're standing out in the cool air, and I've had time to clear my head.

"I *was* studying," she says. "Then I felt like taking a walk."

"Me, too." I'm lying again.

I swear I don't normally lie and keep secrets from my friends like this. It's just—I can't tell them I'm out here looking for Baz. I mean, I never want to talk to Agatha about Baz, for obvious reasons, and Penelope just doesn't want to hear it.

After our fifth year, Penny decided I wasn't allowed to talk about Baz, unless he presents *a clear and present danger—*

"You can't just whinge about him every time he gets on your nerves, Simon. That would mean nonstop whinging."

"Why can't I?" I asked. "You complain about your roommate."

"Not constantly."

"Constantly enough."

"How about this—you can talk to me about Baz when he presents a clear and present danger. And, beyond that: up to but no more than ten per cent of our total conversation."

"I'm not going to do maths every time I talk to you about Baz."

"Then err on the side of not whinging about him constantly."

She still has no patience for it, even though I was completely right about Baz that year—he *was* up to something. Even beyond his usual skulking around, being a vampire.

That spring, Baz tried to steal my voice. That's the worst thing you can do to a magician—maybe worse than murder; a magician can't do magic without words. (Not usually, anyway.)

It happened out on the Lawn: I'd spotted Baz sneaking out over the drawbridge at dusk, and went after him. I followed him as far as the main gates, and then he stopped and turned to me, all casual, with his hands in his pockets—like he'd known I was behind him the whole time.

I was just about to start something with him when Philippa ran up behind me, calling, "Hiya, Simon!" in her squeaky little voice. But as soon as she said my name, she couldn't stop. She squeaked monstrously, like a lifetime of words were being ripped from her.

I know Baz did it.

I know he did *something*.

I saw it in his eyes when Philippa went mute.

Philippa got sent away. The Mage told me that she'd get her voice back, that it wasn't permanent, but she never came back to Watford.

I wonder if Baz still feels guilty. I wonder if he ever did.

Now he's gone, too.

When I notice Agatha again, she's trembling. I unbutton my grey duffle coat, sliding the horn buttons through the cord loops. "Here," I say, sliding it off.

"No," she says. "I'm fine."

I hold it out to her anyway.

"No, it's okay. No—*Simon.* Keep your coat."

My arms drop. It doesn't seem right to put the coat back on, so I fold it over one arm.

I don't know what else to say.

This is already the most time that Agatha and I have been alone since the start of the term. I haven't even kissed her since we've been back. I should probably kiss her. . . .

I reach out and take her hand—but I must move too quickly, because she seems surprised. Her hand jerks open, and something falls out. I kneel, picking it up before it blows away.

It's a handkerchief.

I know that it's Baz's handkerchief before I even see his initials embroidered in the corner, next to the Pitch coat of arms (flames, the moon, three falcons).

I know it's his because he's the only person I've ever met who carries old-fashioned handkerchiefs. He dropped one on my bed, sarcastically, when we were in first year, the first time he made me cry.

Agatha tries to pull the linen from my hand, but I don't let go. I snap it away from her.

"What is this?" I ask, holding it up. (We both know what it

is.) "Are you—are you *waiting* for him? Are you meeting him here? Is he coming?"

Her eyes are wide and glossy. "No. Of course not."

"How can you say 'of course not' when you're up here, obviously thinking about him, holding his handkerchief?"

She folds her arms. "You don't know what I'm thinking about."

"You're right, I don't, Agatha. *I really don't.* Is this where you come every night? When you tell us you're studying?"

"Simon . . ."

**"Answer me!"** It comes out an order. It comes out drenched in magic, which shouldn't even be possible—because those aren't magic words, that isn't a spell. The spell for forcing honesty is **The truth, the whole truth, and nothing but the truth**—but I've never used it; it's an advanced spell, and a restricted one. Still, I see the compulsion in Agatha's face. "No," I say, pushing magic into my voice. **"You don't have to!"**

Her face falls from compulsion to disgust. She backs away from me.

"I didn't mean to do that," I say. "*Agatha.* I didn't. But you—" I throw my arms up. "—what are you doing here?"

"What if I *am* waiting for Baz?" she spits out, like she knows it will shock me stupid. It does.

"Why would you?"

She turns to the stone wall. "I don't know, Simon."

"*Are* you waiting for him?"

The wind is in her hair, making it lash out behind her. "No," she says. "Not waiting. I've no reason to believe he's coming."

"But you want him to."

She shrugs.

"What's wrong with you, Agatha?" I'm trying to control my

temper now. "He's a monster. An actual monster."

"We're all monsters," she says.

She means that *I* am.

I try to tamp down the anger coiling up my legs. "Did you cheat on me? With Baz? Are you with *him* now?"

"*No.*"

"Do you want to be?"

She sighs, and leans forward on the rough stones. "I don't know."

"Don't you want to say anything else to me? Like, 'I'm sorry'? Don't you want to fix this?"

She looks back at me, over her shoulder. "Fix what, Simon—our relationship?" She turns to face me again. "What is our relationship? Is it just me being there when you need a date to the ball? And crying for joy every time you come back from the dead? Because I'll still do that for you. I can still do all that. Even if we're not together."

Her perfect pink chin is thrust forward and quivering. Her arms are still crossed.

"You're my girl, Agatha," I say.

"No. Penelope's your girl."

"You're my—"

Her arms fall. "What Simon, what am I?"

I knot my hands in my hair and gnash my teeth. "You're my future!"

Agatha's face is contorted and wet with tears. Still lovely, though. "Am I supposed to want that?" she asks.

"*I* want it."

"You just want a happy ending."

"Merlin, Agatha, don't you?"

"No! I don't! I want to be someone's *right now*, Simon, not their happily ever after. I don't want to be the prize at the end.

The thing you get if you beat all the bosses."

"You're twisting everything. You're making it ugly."

She shrugs again. "Maybe."

"Agatha . . ." I hold my hand out to her. The one that isn't holding Baz's handkerchief. "We can fix this."

"Probably," she says. "But I don't want to."

I can't think of what more to say.

Agatha can't leave me. She can't leave me *for him*. Oh, he'd love that—he'd love to have that over me. Damn it all, he isn't even here to have that over me.

"I love you, Agatha," I say, believing that might work. Those words are practically magic in themselves. I say them again: "I *love* you."

Agatha closes her eyes against the sight of me. She turns her face away. "I love you, too, Simon. I think that's why I went along with this for so long."

"You don't mean that," I say.

"I do," she says. "Please don't fight me."

"You can't leave me for *him*."

She looks back at me one more time. "I'm not leaving you for Baz, Simon. He's gone. I just don't want to be with you anymore. I don't want to ride off into the sunset with you. . . . That's not my happy anything."

I don't argue with her.

I don't stay out on the ramparts.

My cheeks are hot and itchy, and that's always a bad sign.

I rush past Agatha to the stairs, and run down them so quickly that I miss a few and keep leaping down to the next landing.

And then I'm just sort of floating down the stairs. Falling without actually falling.

I've never done that before, and it's weird.

I make a note to tell Penny, then a note not to tell her, but I run towards the Cloisters anyway because I don't want to go back to my empty room, and the drawbridge is up, and I don't know where else to go.

I stand under Penny's window and think about how I could just call her if the Mage hadn't banned mobile phones at Watford two years ago.

I still feel hot.

I try to shake some of the magic off, and a few sparks catch on the dry leaves beneath me. I stamp them out.

I wonder if Agatha is still up on the ramparts—I can't believe she'd say what she said. For a moment, I wonder if she's been possessed. But her eyes weren't all black. (Were her eyes all black? It was too dark to see.)

She can't leave me like this. She can't *leave* me.

We were settled. We were sorted.

We were endgame. (If I get an endgame.) (You *have* to pretend that you get an endgame. You have to carry on like you will; otherwise, you can't carry on at all.)

Agatha's parents like me. They might even love me. Her dad calls me "son." Not like *"I think of you as my son,"* but like, *"How are you, son?"* Like I'm *a* son. The sort of guy who could be someone's son.

And her mother says I'm handsome. That's really all her mum ever says to me. *"Don't you look handsome, Simon."*

What would she say to Baz? *"Don't you look handsome, Basil. Please don't slaughter my family with your hideous fangs."*

Agatha's father, Dr. Wellbelove, hates the Pitches. He says they're cruel and elitist. That they tried to keep his grandfather out of Watford because of a lisp.

Fucking hell, I can't—I just. I can't.

I lean back against a tree and put my hands on my thighs,

letting my head fall forward and my magic course through me. When I look down at my legs, it's like I've got no boundary. Like I'm blurred at the edges.

I have to fix this. With Agatha.

I'll say whatever she wants me to say.

I'll kill Baz, so that he isn't an option.

I'll tell her, I'll change her mind—*how can she say that there's no such thing as happy endings?* That's all I've ever been working towards. The happy ending is when things are going to begin for me.

I *have* to fix this.

"All right there, Simon?" It's Rhys. He's coming up along the path from the library in his wheelchair.

I look up. "All right. Hiya." I'm not all right. My face is flushed, and I think I'm crying. Do my edges look blurred to him? He hurries past me.

I let Rhys get a head start, then follow him back to Mummers House.

I should sleep this off. . . .

I'll make sure that I power down—that I'm not going to set my bed on fire—then I'll sleep it off.

And tomorrow, I'll fix it.

# 27

## SIMON

I'm not sleeping this time when I hear the noises.

I'm just lying in my bed, thinking about Baz.

What did he say to Agatha? What did he promise?

Maybe he didn't have to say anything. Maybe he just had to be himself. Smarter than I am. Better looking. Wealthier. Fucking horsier—he could go to all her events and wear the right suit and the right shoes. He'd know which necktie went with which month of the year.

If he weren't a vampire, Baz'd be bloody perfect.

*Bloody* perfect. I roll over and press my face into my pillow.

There's a creaking then, and a cold wind. I try to ignore it. I've been taken in by this feeling before. *There's no one here.* No one at the window, no one at the door. The cold creeps up under my bedclothes, and I pull up the blankets, rolling onto my back—

And see a woman standing at the end of my bed.

I recognize her. It's the same person who was standing at the window that night. And I recognize her as a Visitor now; I've seen enough of them. She's come from behind the Veil.

*"You're not him,"* she says to me. Her voice is cold—actually

cold, like it starts in my bones and icily flushes up through my skin—and woeful.

I want to summon my sword, but I don't. "Who are you?" I say.

"*I keep coming. This is* his *place. This is where I'm called. But there's only you here. . . .*"

She's tall and wearing formal robes, like a solicitor's or a professor's, and her dark hair is pulled up into a thick bun. Even though she's translucent, I can see that her robes are red, that her skin is dark olive, and her eyes are grey. I recognize her from her portrait outside the Mage's office—

Natasha Pitch, Watford's last headmistress.

"*Where is he?*" she asks. "*Where is my son?*"

"I don't know," I answer.

"*Did you hurt him?*"

"No."

"*You can't lie to the dead.*"

"I don't want to."

She looks over at his empty bed, and her sadness is so potent that in that moment, I'd do anything to get him back for her. (I'd do anything to bring him back.)

"*The Veil is closing. It will be twenty years before I can see my son again.*" She turns back to me and pushes forward. She's starting to fade. They all fade; Penelope says they can't stay long, two minutes tops.

"*You'll have to do.*"

"Do what?" She's so cold, I can't stand having her this close to me.

She reaches out and takes my shoulders—her hands like ice, her breath a painful chill on my face.

"*Tell my son,*" she says fiercely. "*Tell him that my killer walks—Nicodemus knows. Tell Basilton to find Nico and bring me peace. Do you understand?"*

"Yes," I say. "Find Nico. . . ."

*"Nicodemus. Tell him."*

"I will," I say. "I'll tell him."

Her face falls. *"My son,"* she says, cold tears gathering in her eyes. *"Give him this."* She leans forward and presses a kiss into my temple. No one has ever kissed me there. No one has ever kissed me anywhere but on my mouth.

*"My son,"* she says, and it sounds like a whisper, but I think it's a shout—I think she's just fading now.

I lie in bed, trembling, after she's gone. The room is so cold. I should build a fire, but I don't want to open my eyes.

I must fall sleep, because the cold wakes me again, a fresh wave of it, deep in the night. It hangs like a cloud of chill over my bed, then seeps into me, touching me, cradling me.

*"My son, my son,"* I hear.

There's no figure this time, just this everywhere cold. And the voice is higher and thinner, a wail on the wind.

*"My son, my son. My rosebud boy. I never would have left you. He told me we were stars."*

"I'll tell him," I say. I shout it—"I'll tell him!"

I just want her to go away.

*"Simon, Simon . . . my rosebud boy."*

I close my eyes and pull up my blankets. But the cold is on me, it's in me. "I'll tell him!"

If Baz ever comes back, I will.

# 28

## SIMON

I can't wait to get out of my room in the morning. I run out the door with my tie hanging around my neck and my jumper thrown over my shoulder.

I have no plans to come back. Ever. There's no room for me in there with all the ghosts. Let Baz's mum hang out with his empty bed; I'm tired of staring at it.

I have to tell Penny what happened. She'll be disappointed that I didn't drill the ghost with questions. *"Sorry about your missing son, Mrs. Pitch, but since Baz isn't here, we may as well use this time to advance magickal science...."*

Penny's already got tea and toast at our table when I get there. I grab a plate of kippers with scrambled eggs.

"We need to talk," I say, dropping into a chair across from her.

"Good," she says. "I thought you were going to make me beat it out of you."

"You know already? How do you know?"

"Well, I know *something* happened. Agatha's sitting alone, and she won't even look at me."

"Agatha?" I look up. Agatha's sitting by herself on the other side of the dining hall, reading a book while she eats her cereal.

"So?" Penny asks. "Is this about me sleeping in your room? Because I can talk to her about that."

"No," I say. "No . . . we broke up."

Penny's about to take a bite of toast, but she pulls it back. "You broke up? Why?"

"I don't know. I think she's in love with Baz." That reminds me. I'm wearing the same trousers as yesterday. I reach into the pocket and feel his handkerchief.

"Oh," Penelope says. "I guess I can see that. I mean—"

I push my face forward. "You can *see* that? How can you see that? My girlfriend falling in love with my sworn enemy? My girlfriend, who's good, falling in love with my enemy, who's completely evil?"

"Well, your relationship has had better . . . years, Simon. You and Agatha both seemed like you were just going through the motions."

"And 'the motions' include cheating on me with Baz?"

"*Did* she cheat on you?"

"I don't know."

Penny sighs. Like she feels sorry for me. She's unbearably patronizing sometimes. "Agatha's not really in love with Baz. She's just looking for something that sticks. It's romantic to be in love with a dead vampire."

"*Dead?*"

"You know what I mean," Penny says. "Missing. Seriously missing."

Was Baz dead? Wouldn't his mother know if he were? Wouldn't she have seen him behind the Veil? Maybe death is a big place. (It would have to be.) Maybe she's been looking for Baz here because she hasn't seen him yet on the other side.

I jab at my eggs a few times, then drop my fork.

In all of this, I've never seriously considered that Baz might be dead. Hiding, yes—plotting. Maybe even kidnapped or hurting, but . . . not dead.

He promised to make my life miserable.

When the doors to the dining hall fly open, it's almost like I'm making it happen, like I've summoned it. Cold air pours into the room. It's bright outside, in the courtyard, and at first, all we can see is the outline of a person.

This has happened so many times since school started that no one is scared now, not even the littluns.

When the figure steps forward, I recognize him at once.

Tall. Black hair swept back from his forehead. Lips curled up in a sneer . . . I know that face as well as my own.

Baz.

I stand up too quickly, knocking my chair over. Across the room, a mug falls to the floor and shatters—I glance over and see that Agatha is standing, too.

Baz steps towards us.

*Baz.*

# BOOK TWO

# 29

## BAZ

It's unnecessarily grandiose to use an **Open Sesame** on the doors, but I do it anyway because I know everyone will be in the dining hall, and I may as well make an entrance.

I wanted it this way. I wanted to be the only person who got to break the news that I'm back.

Snow is the first to react—leaps to his feet, sends furniture flying. It's work not to roll my eyes. (It's a bit of work not to stare at him. He's thin. And drawn. Normally, he'd be back to clobbering weight by now.)

Dev and Niall, bless them, act like I've arrived eight minutes late to breakfast, instead of eight weeks. Dev nudges Niall, and Niall gives me a bored once-over, then moves the teapot away from my spot, which they've left empty. Good men.

I walk over to the serving table and make up a plate. I pretend I'm not ferociously hungry. (I feel like I'll always be hungry now.)

Snow is still standing. His meddling sidekick is yanking on his sleeve, trying to get him to sit down. He should listen to her. Wait, what's this? . . . Where's Wellbelove in this pretty tableau?

I scan the room without turning my head. There she is,

sitting on the other side of the room—trouble in paradise?—staring at me. They're all staring at me. But I can tell Wellbelove expects something extra from me, so I give it to her. A long, cool look. Let her make what she wants of that; she will anyway.

I settle down at the table, and Dev pours me a cup of tea.

"Baz," he says, smirking.

"Gentlemen," I say. "What have I missed?"

# 30

## BAZ

Snow stands again when I walk into our Greek classroom. I take my seat without looking his way. "Enough, Snow, I'm not the Queen."

He doesn't reply—he must still be working up to a bluster.

Snow blusters like no one else. *But! I! I mean! Um! It's just!* It's no wonder he can never spit out a spell.

The Minotaur folds his arms and snorts when he sees me. "Mr. Pitch," he says. "I see you've decided to join us."

"I have, sir."

"We'll have to discuss your plans to catch up."

"Of course, sir. Though I think you'll find I'm still quite ahead of the class; my mother always insisted on summer work in Greek and Latin." It's good to mention my mother with the older teachers. They all still remember her—I can see their heads start to dip into a bow.

The Minotaur worked on the grounds when my mother was headmistress; creatures weren't allowed on staff then. I dare him to hold that against me.

I dare them fucking all.

"We shall see," he says, narrowing his cow eyes.

I'm not lying. Greek won't be a problem for me—and

I'll be fine in Latin, Magic Words and Elocution. Political Science could be a bear, depending on how much they've covered. Same for History and Astrology.

I'm going to have to break my back to get to first again, and I can't imagine Coach Mac will let me back on the football team. . . .

They might all cut me some slack if I told them I'd been kidnapped.

I am never telling *anyone* I was kidnapped.

Kidnapped. And by fucking numpties, no less.

Numpties are like trolls, but even more hideous. They're big and stupid, and they're always cold. They go around wrapped in blankets and dressing gowns if they have them, and if they don't, they cover themselves in leaves and mud and old newspapers. They usually live under bridges. Because they *like* to live under bridges. And they're just smart enough to hit you over the head with a club and drag you back to their hovel, if there's something in it for them.

Aunt Fiona was appalled when she found me in the numpty den. She berated me all the way home, and all the way back to Watford. She made me sit in the back seat of her MG. (A '67. Glorious.) *"The front seat is for people who've never been kidnapped by bloody numpties. Jesus Christ, Baz."* (Aunt Fiona likes to swear like a Normal. She thinks she's punk.)

I could tell she was half disgusted with me, half relieved that I was still alive.

I'd been stuck under that bridge for six weeks, in a coffin—and I don't even think the numpties were *trying* to torture me. I think they thought that was humane treatment for a vampire. So to speak. They even brought me blood. (I decided not to think about where they got it.) They did *not* bring food. Most people don't realize that vampires need both. Most people know fuck-all about vampires. . . .

*I* know fuck-all about vampires. It's not like I got an instruction pamphlet when I was bitten.

The numpties kept me in the coffin for six weeks, and every day or so, they threw in some blood. (In a thirty-two-ounce plastic cup with a bendy straw.) I can go without food longer than regular people, but I was pretty ruined by the time Fiona got there.

Fortunately, my aunt is an utter badass. She laid waste to the numpties before she found my coffin; then she bombarded me with healing magic. ***"Early to bed and early to rise!"*** she kept whispering. And ***"Get well soon!"***

(It reminded me of the day I was Turned—Fiona and my father both hitting me with healing magic that mended the bite marks and bruises but didn't touch the changes already churning inside me.)

I was still weak when Fiona helped me out of the coffin.

"All right?" she asked.

"Hungry. Thirsty."

She kicked a dead numpty—they look like giant stones when they die, great heaps of mud and grey matter—"Can you drink one of these?"

I sneered. "No." Numpty blood is swampy and brackish, definitely nonpotable. Which is probably why someone sent them after me.

"I'll take you to McDonald's," she said.

"Take me to school."

Fiona bought me three Big Macs, and I swallowed the first one in two bites—it came right back up. She pulled the car over to let me heave at the side of the road. "You're a wreck, Basil. I'm taking you home."

"It's September, take me to school."

"It's October, I'm taking you home to rest."

"It's October? Take me to school, Fiona. Now." I wiped my mouth on my shirt. I was still in my tennis whites—the numpties had nabbed me outside the club; my clothes were stained in every way imaginable and newly vomited on.

Fiona shook her head. "School doesn't matter now, boyo. We're in the middle of a war."

"We're always in the middle of a war. Take me back to Watford—I'll be damned if Penelope Bunce finishes our last year at the top of the class."

"Baz, everything is different now. You've been kidnapped. And held for ransom."

I leaned on her car. "Is that why the numpties didn't kill me? Because you paid the ransom?"

"Fuck no, Pitches have never paid ransoms, and we're not starting now."

"I'm the only living heir!"

"That's just what your father said. He wanted to pay up. I told him I knew my sister had scraped bottom when she married a Grimm, but I wasn't letting him have any more of our pride. No offence, Basil." She handed me another Big Mac—"Try again. Slower."

I took a bite. "Why'd they kidnap me?" I asked through three layers of bun and two all-beef patties.

"They said they wanted money. Then they wanted wands."

"What would numpties want with wands?"

"They wouldn't! The question is who hired them. Or who won them over . . . I don't know how you get a numpty to do your bidding; maybe you just bring them hot water bottles. They kept calling us from your mobile, until it died. Your dad thinks they took you, and then tried to figure out later what to do with you. But it all smells like the Mage to me. It's not enough that he's laid us low; he wants everything that's ever made us powerful."

"You think *the Mage* had me kidnapped? The headmaster of my school?"

"I think the Mage is capable of anything," she said. "Don't you?"

I did think so. But Fiona blames everything on the Mage. So it's hard to take her seriously, even after she's just murdered someone to save your life.

Mostly, at that moment, I was thinking about lying down.

"Oh," Fiona said. "Here." She fished my wand—polished ivory with a leather hilt—out of her giant handbag and stuck it in my shorts pocket. I pulled it out. "So," she said. "Obviously, you are *not* going back to that school, right into that bastard's clutches."

"I am so."

*"Basilton."* Full name, all three syllables.

"He's not going to bother me at school," I argued, "not with everyone watching."

"Baz, we have to get serious. He's attacked our family *again*, directly."

"I am serious. I'm more valuable as a spy than a soldier, anyway—that's what the Families have always said."

"That's what we said when you were a child. You're a man now."

"I'm a *student*," I said. "What do you think my mother would say if she knew you were pulling me out of school?"

Fiona huffed and shook her head. We were still standing at the side of the road. She opened the car door for me. "Get in, you manipulative cur."

"Only if you take me back to Watford."

"I'm taking you home first. Your father and Daphne want to see you."

"And then to Watford."

She pulled me towards the car. "Jesus. Yes. If you still want to go."

Of course I still wanted to go to Watford . . .

. . . once I'd seen my father. Once my stepmother had wept over me. Once I'd slept for twelve hours under a new barrage of healing spells.

I stayed in bed a fortnight.

They all tried to talk me into staying longer.

Even Vera, my old nanny was brought in to apply some guilt. (Vera's a Normal. She rationalizes all our strangeness by pretending we're in the Mafia. Father spells her innocent whenever it gets to be too much for her.)

But after two weeks, I got up out of bed, packed my bags, and went and sat in the front seat of Fiona's car.

"I'll steal it if I have to!" I shouted up the drive. "Or I'll steal a bus!"

There was no way that I wasn't going back to school— this is my last year. Last year in the tower. Last year on the pitch. Last year to torment Snow before our antagonism turns into something more permanent and less entertaining.

My last year at Watford, the last place I saw my mother . . .

I was damn well going back.

Aunt Fiona stomped out in her heavy black Doc Martens boots (clichéd) and opened my door. "Back seat," she said. "Front seat's for people who haven't been kidnapped by fucking numpties."

*

I can feel Snow staring at me all through Greek—actually *feel* it. He's so worked up, his magic is leaking out all over the place.

Sometimes when he gets like this, I'm tempted to pull him aside. *"Deep breaths now, Snow. Let it go. Some of it. Before you start another fire. Whatever it is you're worried about, this won't help."*

I never do, though. Pull him aside. Or talk him down. Instead I just poke him until he goes off.

That's what Snow does best. He doesn't plan or strike—he just *goes off,* and when he does, he takes down everything in his path.

He's half a fucking numpty himself. The Mage gives him mittens and blankets, and Snow goes off in whatever direction the Mage points him in. I've seen it. I've probably seen it more than anyone but Bunce. . . .

The way Snow starts to blur and shimmer. Like a jet engine. The way sparks pop and flare in his aura. The light reflects in his hair, and his pupils contract until his eyes are thick blue. He's usually holding his sword, so that's where the flame starts—whipping around his hands and wrists, licking up the blade. It makes him mental. His brain blinks out, I think, about the time he starts swinging. Eventually the power pours off him in waves. Flattening, blackening waves. It's more power than the rest of us ever have access to. More power than we can imagine. Spilling out of him like he's a cup left under a waterfall.

I've seen it happen close up, standing right at his side. If Snow knows you're there, he shields you. I don't know how he does it, I don't even know *why.* It's just like him, really, to use what little control he has to protect other people.

The Minotaur is droning now. Conjugating verbs I've known since I was 11.

I can feel Snow's eyes on the back of my head. I can smell his magic. Smoky. Sticky. Like green wood in a campfire. The people sitting around us are getting stupid and drunk from it. I watch Bunce try to shake it off—she's glaring at him. He's glaring at me.

I turn my head just enough to let him see my lip curl.

# 31

## SIMON

I go back to our room as soon as lessons are over for the day, but Baz isn't there. His clothes are in his wardrobe. His bed is made. His bottles and tubes are back on the bathroom counter.

I open the windows even though it's freezing out; I've been overheating all day. Penelope practically had to hold me down at breakfast. I wanted to rush over to Baz and demand to know where he'd been. I wanted—I think I just wanted to make sure it was really him. I mean . . . It's obviously him.

Baz is back.

Baz is *alive*. Or as alive as he gets.

He looked awful today, even paler than usual. He's thinner than usual, too, and there's something off about the way he's moving—a drag. Like he's got stones of different weights tied to each limb.

I just want to run him down and knock him over and figure it all out. What's wrong with him. Where he's been . . .

I wait in our room until dinner, but Baz doesn't come back. Then he ignores me in the dining hall.

He ignores Agatha, too. (She's staring at him as much as I am—but I don't think she's as worried that he might have come back to kill her.) She's sitting alone at a table, and I can't decide whether that makes me sad or angry. Whether Agatha herself makes me sad or angry. Or even what I'm supposed to be feeling about her. I can't *think* right now.

"I was thinking we could study in the library tonight," Penny says at dinner, as if I'm not literally fuming.

"I'm gonna have to talk to him sometime," I say.

"No, you aren't," she says. "When do the two of you ever talk, anyway?"

"I'm gonna have to face him."

She leans over her cottage pie. "That's what I'm worried about, Simon. You need to cool down first."

"I'm cool."

"Simon. You're never cool."

"That hurts, Penny."

"It shouldn't. It's one of the reasons I love you."

"I just—I need to know where he's been. . . ."

"Well, he's not going to *tell* you."

"Maybe he'll tell me something without meaning to, in the process of not telling me. What is he even *up* to? He looks like he's been in some American terror prison."

"Maybe he's been sick."

Curses, I never thought of that either. Every scenario I thought up had Baz hidden away, plotting somewhere. Maybe he was sick *and* plotting. . . .

"No matter what the truth is," Penny says, "it won't help to pick a fight with him."

"I won't."

"Simon, you do. Every year. As soon as you see him. And I just think that maybe you *shouldn't* this time. Something's happening. Something bigger than Baz. The Mage has practically disappeared, and Premal has been on some secret assignment for weeks—my mum says he's stopped returning her texts."

"Is she worried about him?"

"She's always worried about Premal."

"Are you worried about him?"

Penny looks down. "Yeah."

"I'm sorry—should we try to find him?"

She looks back up at me sternly. "Mum says no. She says we need to wait and pay attention. I think she and Dad are asking around, covertly, and she doesn't want us drawing a lot of attention to them. Which is why you need to cool down. Just—keep your eyes open. Observe. Don't knock over any furniture or kill anything."

"You always say that," I sigh. "But then when it's us or them, you want me to kill something."

"I never want you to *kill,* Simon."

"I never feel like I have a choice."

"I know." She smiles at me. Sadly. "Don't kill Baz tonight."

"I won't."

But I'm probably gonna have to kill him someday, and we both know it.

Penelope lets me go back to my room after dinner, and she doesn't try to follow—she's stuck with Trixie and her girlfriend now that Baz is back in town. "Gay people have an unfair advantage!" she complains.

"Only when it comes to visiting their roommates," I say.

She's decent enough not to argue.

I'm nervous when I get to the top of the stairs. I still don't know what I'm going to say to him. *"Nothing,"* I hear Penny say in my head. *"Do your schoolwork, go to bed."*

As if it's ever that easy.

Sharing a room with the person you hate most is like sharing a room with a siren. (The kind on police cars, not the kind who try to entrap you when you cross the English Channel.) You can't ignore that person, and you never get used to them. It never stops being painful.

Baz and I have spent seven years grimacing and growling at each other. (Him grimacing, me growling.) We both stay away from our room as much as we can when we know the other is there, and when we can't avoid each other, we do our best not to make eye contact. I don't talk *to* him. I don't talk *in front* of him. I never let him see anything that he might take back to his bitch aunt, Fiona.

I try not to call women bitches, but Baz's aunt Fiona once spelled my feet into the dirt. I know it was her; I heard her say, **"Stand your ground!"**

And twice I've caught her trying to sneak into the Mage's office. *"It's my sister's office,"* she said. *"I just like to visit it sometimes."*

She might have been telling the truth. Or she might have been trying to depose the Mage.

And that's the problem with all the Pitches and their allies—it's impossible to tell when they're up to something and when they're just being people.

There've been years when I thought maybe I could figure out their plan if I just paid enough attention to Baz. (Fifth year.) And years when I decided that living with him was painful enough, that I couldn't keep tabs on him, as well. (Last year.)

In the early days, there wasn't any strategy or decision. Just the two of us scuffling in the halls and kicking the shit out of each other two or three times a year.

I used to beg the Mage for a new roommate, but that's not how it works. The Crucible cast Baz and me together on the very first day of school.

All the first years are cast that way. The Mage builds a fire in the courtyard, the upper years help, and the littluns stand in a circle around it. The Mage sets the Crucible—it's an actual crucible, maybe the oldest thing at Watford—in the middle of the fire and says the incantation; then everyone waits for the iron inside to melt.

It's the strangest feeling when the magic starts to work on you. I was worried that it *wouldn't* work on me—because I was an outsider. All the other kids started moving towards each other, and I still didn't feel anything. I thought about faking it, but I didn't want to get caught and booted out.

And then I *did* feel the magic, like a hook in my stomach.

I stumbled forward and looked around, and Baz was walking towards me. Looking so cool. Like he was coming my way because he wanted to, not because there was a mystical magnet in his gut.

The magic doesn't stop until you and your new roommate shake hands—I held my hand out to Baz immediately. But he just stood there for as long as he could stand it. I don't know how he resisted the pull; I felt like my intestines were going to burst out and wrap around him.

"Snow," he said.

"Yeah," I said, waggling my hand. "Here."

"The Mage's Heir."

I nodded, but I didn't even know what that meant back then. The Mage made me his heir so I'd have a place at Watford. That's also why I have his sword. It's a historic weapon—it used to be given to the Mage's Heir, back when the title of Mage was passed through families instead of appointed by the Coven.

The Mage gave me a wand, too—bone with wooden handle, it was his father's—so I'd have my own magickal instrument. You have to have magic in you, and a way to get it out of you; that's the basic requirement for Watford and the basic requirement to be a magician. Every magician inherits some family artefact. Baz has a wand, like me; all the Pitches are wandworkers. But Penny has a ring. And Gareth has a belt buckle. (It's really inconvenient—he has to thrust his pelvis forward whenever he wants to cast a spell. He seems to think it's cheeky, but no one else does.)

Penelope thinks my hand-me-down wand is part of the reason my spellwork is such shit—my wand isn't bound to me by blood. It doesn't know what to do with me. After seven years in the World of Mages, I still reach for my sword first; I know it'll come when I call. My wand comes, but then, half the time, it plays dead.

The first time I asked the Mage for a new roommate was a few months after Baz and I started living together. The Mage wouldn't hear of it—though he knew who Baz was, and knew better than I did that the Pitches are snakes and traitors.

"Being matched with your roommate is a sacred tradition at Watford," he said. His voice was gentle but firm. "The Crucible cast you together, Simon. You're to watch out for each other, to know each other as well as brothers."

"Yeah, but, sir . . ." I was sitting in that giant leather chair up in his office, the one with three horns attached to the top. "The Crucible must have made a mistake. My roommate's a complete wanker. He might even be evil. Last week, someone spelled my laptop closed, and I *know* it was him. He was practically cackling."

The Mage just sat on his desk, stroking his beard. "The Crucible cast you together, Simon. You're meant to watch out for him."

He kept giving me the same answer until I gave up asking.

He even said no the time there was *proof* that Baz had tried to feed me to a chimera.

Baz *admitted* it, then argued that the fact that he'd failed was punishment enough. And the Mage agreed with him!

Sometimes the Mage doesn't make any sense to me. . . .

It was only in the last few years that I realized the Mage makes me stay with Baz to keep Baz under his thumb. Which means, I hope—I *think*—that the Mage trusts me. He thinks I'm up for the job.

I decide to take a shower and shave while Baz is still gone. I only nick myself twice, which is better than usual. When I get out, wearing flannel pyjama bottoms and a towel around my neck, Baz is by his bed, unpacking his schoolbag.

His head whips up, and his face is all twisted. He looks like I've already laid into him.

"What are you doing?" he snarls through his teeth.

"Taking a shower. What's your problem?"

"You," he says, throwing his bag down. "Always you."

"Hello, Baz. Welcome back."

He looks away from me. "Where's your necklace?" His voice is low.

"My what?"

I can't see his whole face, but it looks like his jaw is working. *"Your cross."*

My hand flies to my throat and then to the cuts on my chin. My cross. I took it off weeks ago.

I hurry over to my bed and dig it out, but I don't put it on. Instead I walk around Baz and stand in his space until he has to look at me. He does. His teeth are clenched, and his head is tipped back and to the side, like he's just *waiting* for me to make the first move.

I hold the cross out with both hands. I want him to

acknowledge what it is, what it means. Then I lift it up over my head and let it settle gently around my neck. My eyes are locked on Baz's, and he doesn't look away, though his nostrils flare.

When the cross is around my neck again, his eyelids dip, and he squares his shoulders.

"Where have you been?" I ask.

His eyes flick back up to mine. "None. Of your. *Business.*"

I feel my magic surge and try to shove it down. "You look like shit, you know."

He looks even worse now that I can see him up close. There's a grey film over him—even over his eyes, which are always grey.

Baz's eyes are usually the kind of grey that happens when you mix dark blue and dark green together. Deep-water grey. Today they're the colour of wet pavement.

He huffs a laugh. "Thank you, Snow. You're looking rough and weedy yourself."

I am, and it's his fault. How was I supposed to eat and sleep, knowing he was out there, plotting against me? And now he's here, and if he's not going to tell me anything useful, I might as well throttle him for putting me through it.

Or . . . I could do my homework.

I'll just do my homework.

I try. I sit at my desk, and Baz sits on his bed. And eventually he leaves without saying anything, and I know that he's going down to the Catacombs to hunt rats. Or to the Wood to hunt squirrels.

And I know that once he killed and drained a merwolf, but I don't know why—its body washed up onto the edge of the moat. (I hate the merwolves almost as much as Baz does. They're not intelligent, I don't think, but they're still evil.)

I go to bed after Baz leaves, but I don't go to sleep. He's only been back a day, and I already feel like I need to know where he is at every moment. It's fifth year all over again.

When he finally does come back to our room, smelling like dust and decay, I close my eyes.

That's when I remember about his mum.

# 32

## BAZ

I almost went up to the Mage's office tonight.

Just to get my aunt Fiona off my back as soon as possible.

She lectured me all the way to Watford. She thinks the Mage is going to make another move soon. She thinks he's looking for something specific. Apparently, he's been visiting—raiding—all the Old Families' homes for the last two months. Just rolls up in his Range Rover (1981, Warwick green—lovely) and drinks their tea while his merry Men go through their libraries with finding spells.

"The Mage says one of us is working with the Humdrum," Fiona said, "that there's nothing to hide so long as we have nothing to hide."

She didn't have to tell me that there's plenty to hide at our place. We're not working with the Humdrum—why would any magician work with the Humdrum?—but our house is full of banned books and dark objects. Even some of our cookbooks are banned. (Though it's been centuries, at least, since the Pitches ate fairies.) (You can't even *find* fairies anymore.) (And it isn't because we ate them all.)

Fiona doesn't live with us. She has a flat in London and dates Normals. Journalists and drummers. *"I'm not a race traitor,"* she'll say. *"I'd never* marry *one."* I think she dates them because they don't seem real. I think it's all because of my mother.

Father says Fiona thought my mother hung the moon. (To hear my father talk about her, my mother may have *actually* hung the moon. Or maybe it was hung for her pleasure.)

Fiona was apprenticing with an herbalist in Beijing when my mother died. She came home for the funeral and never went back. She stayed with my dad until he got remarried, then moved to London. Now my aunt lives on family money and magic, and lives to avenge her sister.

It's a bad fit.

Fiona is smart—and powerful—but my mother was the chess player in the family. My mother was groomed for greatness. (That's what everyone says.)

Fiona is vindictive. She's impatient. And sometimes she just wants to rage against the machine—even if she's not exactly sure where the machine is or how to properly rage at it.

Her grand plan for uncovering the Mage's plot is to send me sneaking up to his office. She's obsessed with the Mage's office; it was my mother's office, and I think Fiona thinks she can steal it back from him.

"Sneak into his office and do what?" I asked her.

"Look around."

"What do you expect me to find?"

"Well, I don't know, do I? He must be leaving a trail somewhere. Check his computer."

"He's never even there to use his computer," I said. "He probably keeps everything on his phone."

"Then steal his phone."

*"You* steal his phone," I said. "I've got homework."

She said she'd be meeting soon with the Old Families—a

consortium made up of everyone who got left behind in the Mage's revolution.

(My father goes to these meetings, too, but his heart's not in it. He'd rather talk about magickal livestock and archival seed stock. The Grimms are farmers. My mother must have been sick in love to marry him.)

After my mother died, anyone who had the courage to stand up to the Mage's military coup was quickly forced off the Coven. No one from the Old Families has had a seat for the last decade—even though most of the Mage's reforms are aimed at us:

Banned books, banned phrases. Rules about when we can meet and where. Taxes to cover all the Mage's initiatives; most notably to pay for every faun bastard and centaur cousin, and every pathetic excuse for a magician in the Realm to attend Watford. The World of Mages never had taxes before. Taxes were for Normals; we had standards instead.

You can't blame the Old Families for striking back at the Mage however we can.

Anyway, I told Fiona that I'd do it. That I'd go up to the Mage's office and look around, even if it was pointless.

"Take something," she said, gripping her steering wheel.

I was in the back seat, so I could see only a slice of her face in the rearview mirror. "Take what?"

She shrugged. "Doesn't matter. Take something."

"I'm not a thief," I said.

"It's not thieving—that office is *hers*, it's yours. Take something for me."

"All right," I said.

I almost always go along with Fiona in the end. The way she misses my mother keeps her alive for me.

❖

But tonight I'm too tired to do Fiona's bidding.

And too jumpy. I can't shake the feeling that I'm being followed—that whoever it was who paid the numpties to take me will try again.

By the time I'm done in thc Catacombs, it feels like I'm dragging my own corpse up the tower steps to our room.

Snow's asleep when I come in.

Normally I shower in the mornings, and he showers at night.

We've got the dance all worked out, after so many years. Moving around the room without touching or talking or looking at each other. (Or at least not looking at each other while the other is paying attention.)

But there are cobwebs in my hair tonight, and I was so thirsty that I got blood under my nails when I fed.

That hasn't happened since I was 14, not since I was just getting the hang of this. I can usually drain a polo pony without staining my lips.

I move around the room quietly. As much as I enjoy disturbing Snow, tonight I just need to clean off and get some sleep.

I never should've tried to make it through a full day of classes. My leg's gone numb, and my head is killing me. Maybe it's good that Coach Mac won't take me back on the team, if I can't even manage seven hours in a desk. (He looked sad when I showed up at practice. And suspicious. He said I was on probation.)

I take a quick, quiet shower, and when I climb into bed, I feel every bone in my body groan happily.

Crowley, I missed this bed. Even though it's dusty and lumpy, with goose quills that sneak through the ticking and poke you.

My bedroom at home is enormous. All the furniture at home is hundreds of years old, and I'm not allowed to hang anything up or move anything around because it's all registered with the National Trust. Every few years or so, the local paper comes in and does an article.

My bed there is heavy and draped, and if you look close, you'll find forty-two gargoyles carved into the trim. There used to be a step stool at the head because the bed was too tall for me to climb into by myself.

This bed, at Watford, is more mine than that one ever was.

I roll over onto my side, facing Snow. He's sleeping, so it doesn't matter if I stare at him. Which I do. Even though I know it doesn't do me any good.

Snow sleeps in a knot: his legs pulled up and his fists drawn in, shoulders hunched high, head tucked low, and his hair a crush of curls on the pillowcase. What little moonlight there is catches on his tawny skin.

There was no light with the numpties. Just one endless night of pain and noise and blood.

I'm at least half dead, I think. I mean, just normally, when I'm walking around and feeling good—I'm at least half gone.

When I was in that coffin, I pushed myself closer.

I let myself slip away. . . .

Just to stay *sane*. Just to get *through* it.

And when I felt myself slipping too far, I held on to the one thing I'm always sure of—

Blue eyes.

Bronze curls.

The fact that Simon Snow is the most powerful magician alive. That nothing can hurt him, not even me.

That Simon Snow is *alive*.

And I'm hopelessly in love with him.

# 33

## BAZ

The operative word there is "hopeless."

That was evident the moment I realized I'd be the one who was most miserable if I ever succeeded in doing Snow in.

It dawned on me during our fifth year. When Snow followed me around like a dog tied to my ankle. When he wouldn't give me a *single* moment of solace to sort through my feelings—or try to wank them away. (Which I eventually tried that summer. To no avail.)

I wish I'd never figured it out. That I love him.

It's only ever been a torment.

Sharing a room with the person you want most is like sharing a room with an open fire.

He's constantly drawing you in. And you're constantly stepping too close. And you know it's not good—that there is no good—that there's absolutely nothing that can ever come of it.

But you do it anyway.

And then . . .

Well. Then you burn.

Snow says I'm obsessed with fire. I'd argue that's an inevitable side effect of being flammable.

I mean, I guess everyone's flammable, ultimately—but vampires are oily rags. We're flash paper.

The cruel joke of it is that I come from a long line of fire magicians—two long lines, the Grimms and the Pitches. I'm brilliant with fire. As long as I don't get too close.

No . . .

The cruel joke of it is that Simon Snow smells like smoke.

Snow whimpers—he's plagued by nightmares, we both are—and rolls onto his back, one arm reaching for a moment before he lets it fall over his head. His ridiculous curls tumble back onto the pillow. Snow wears his hair short on the back and on the sides, but the top is a thatch of loose curls. Golden brown. It's dark now, but I can still see the colour.

I know his skin, too. Another shade of gold, the fairest. Snow never tans, but there are freckles on his shoulders, and moles scattered all over his back and chest, his arms and legs. Three moles on his right cheek, two below his left ear, one over his left eye.

It doesn't do me any good to know all this.

But I'm not sure it makes it any worse either. I'm not sure it could *get* any worse.

The windows are open; Snow sleeps with them open all year long unless I throw a snit about it. It's easier to sleep with extra blankets on my bed than to complain. I've got used to the weight of them against me.

I'm tired. And full. I can feel the blood sloshing around in my stomach—it's probably going to wake me up to piss.

Snow moans again, and tosses back onto his side.

I'm home. Finally.

I fall asleep.

# 34

Snow doesn't give a shit about waking *me* up.

He likes to be the first person down to breakfast, Chomsky knows why. It's 6 A.M., and he's already banging around our room like a cow who accidentally wandered up here.

The windows are still open, and the sunlight is pouring in. I'm fine in sunlight—that's another myth. But I don't like it. It stings a bit, especially first thing in the morning. Snow suspects, I think, and is constantly opening the curtains.

I guess we used to fight more about stuff like this.

And then I almost killed him, and squabbling over the curtains suddenly felt ridiculous.

Snow will tell you I tried to kill him our third year. With the chimera. But I was only trying to scare him that day—I wanted to see him wet his pants and cry. Instead he went off like an H-bomb.

He also says I tried to throw him down a flight of stairs the next year. Really, we were fighting at the top of the staircase, and I got in a lucky punch that sent him flying. Then, when my aunt Fiona asked me if I'd pushed Simon Snow down a flight of stairs, I said, "Fuck yes I did."

But the next year, fifth year, I actually did try to take Snow down.

I hated him so much that spring. I hated the sight of him—I hated what the sight of him did to me.

When Fiona told me she'd found a way to "take the Mage's Heir out of our way," I was more than willing to help. She gave me the pocket recorder, an ancient thing with an actual tape, and warned me not to speak when it was on; she made me swear on my mother's grave.

I don't know what I was expecting to happen. . . . I felt like I was in a spy movie, standing by the gates and pushing the button in my pocket the moment I could see Snow start to lose his temper.

Maybe I thought I was entrapping him. . . .

Maybe I did think it would hurt him—or kill him.

Maybe I didn't think anything *could* kill him.

Then came Philippa bloody Stainton running across the lawn to embarrass herself. (She wouldn't leave Snow alone that year, even though he clearly wasn't interested.) The recorder swallowed up her voice in one horrible squeak, like a mouse being sucked up in a Hoover. I hit stop as soon as I heard her. . . . It was too late.

Snow knew I did it, but he couldn't prove anything. And no one else could either—I hadn't touched my wand. I hadn't said a word.

Aunt Fiona was hardly bothered by the mistake. *"Philippa Stainton—she's not one of ours, is she?"*

I remember handing the recorder back to my aunt, thinking of the magic she must have poured into it. Wondering where she got that much magic.

"Don't look so glum, Basil," Fiona said, taking it from me. "We'll get him next time."

A few days later, in Magic Words, Miss Possibelf assured us all that Philippa would be fine. But she never came back to Watford.

I'll never forget Philippa's face when her voice ran out.

I'll never forget Snow's.

That's the last time I tried to hurt him. Permanently.

I throw curses at Snow. I harass him. I *think* about killing him all the time, and someday I'll have to try—but until then, what's the point?

I'm going to lose.

On that day. When Snow and I actually have to fight each other.

I might be immortal. (Maybe. I don't know whom to ask.) But I'm the kind of immortal you can still cut down or light on fire.

Snow is . . . something else.

When he goes off, he's more of an element than a magician. I don't think our side will ever put him out or contain him, but I know—I *know*—that I have to do my part.

We're at war.

The Humdrum may have killed my mother, but the Mage will drive my whole family out of magic. Just to make an example of us. He's already taken our influence. Drained our coffers. Blackened our name. We're all just waiting for the day he takes the nuclear option—

*Snow* is the nuclear option. With Snow tucked in his belt, the Mage is omnipotent. He can make us do anything. . . . He can make us go away.

I can't let that happen.

This is my world, the World of Mages. I have to do my part to fight for it. Even if I know I'm going to lose.

Snow is standing in front of his wardrobe now, trying to find a clean shirt. He stretches one arm over his head, and I watch the muscles shifting in his shoulders.

All I do is lose.

I sit up and throw my covers off. Snow startles and grabs a shirt.

"Forget that I'm here?" I ask. I stride over to my wardrobe and lay my trousers and shirt over my arm. I don't know why Snow lingers over his clothes like he has big decisions to make. He wears his uniform every day, even on the weekend.

When I close my wardrobe door, he's staring at me. He looks unsettled. I'm not sure what I've done to unsettle him, but I sneer anyway, just to drive it home.

I get dressed in the bathroom. Snow and I have never dressed in front of each other; it's an extension of our mutual paranoia. And thank snakes for that—my life is painful enough.

When I'm dressed and ready and back in our room, Snow is still standing near his bed, shirt on but not buttoned, tie hanging round his neck. His hair actually looks worse than it did when he woke up, like he's been tearing his hands through the curls.

He freezes and looks up at me.

"What's wrong, Snow? Cat got your tongue?"

He flinches. **Cat got your tongue** is a wicked spell, and I used it against him twice when we were third years.

"Baz," he clears his throat. "I—"

"Am a disgrace to magic?"

He rolls his eyes. "I—"

"Spit it out, Snow. You'd think you were trying to cast a spell. *Are* you? Next time, use your wand, it helps."

He ransacks his hair again with one hand. "Could you just—?"

There's nothing remarkable about Snow's eyes. They're a standard size and shape. A little pouchy. And his eyelashes are stubby and dark brown. His eyes aren't even a remarkable colour. Just blue. Not cornflower. Not navy. Not shot with hazel or violet.

He blinks them at me. Stammering. I feel myself blushing. (Crowley, that's how much blood I drank last night—I'm capable of blushing.)

"No," I say, and pick up my books. "I *just* couldn't."

I'm out the door. Down the steps.

I hear Snow snarling behind me.

When he comes down to breakfast, his tie is still hanging. Bunce frowns and yanks on one end. He drops his scone and wipes his hand on his trousers before tying it. He looks up at me then, but I'm already looking away.

# 35

## SIMON

Penelope wants to eat lunch out on the Lawn. It's a warm day, she says, and the ground is dry, and we might not have another chance to picnic like this until spring.

I think she just wants to keep me away from Baz and Agatha—they've been playing games with each other all week. Taking turns staring across the dining hall, then quickly looking away. Baz always looks at me, too, to make sure I'm watching.

Everyone's still gossiping about where he's been. The most popular rumours are "dark coming-of-age ceremony that left him too marked up to be in public" and "Ibiza."

"My mother's coming to take me into town tonight," Penny says. We're sitting against a giant, twisting yew tree, looking out at the Lawn in slightly different directions. "We're going to dinner," she says. "Want to come?"

"That's okay, thanks."

"We could go to that ramen place you like. My mum's buying."

I shake my head. "Feels like I need to keep tabs on Baz," I say. "I still don't have a clue where he's been."

Penny sighs but doesn't argue. She stares out onto the

brown lawn. "I miss the Visitings. They were so magickal. . . ."

I laugh.

"You know what I mean," she says. "Aunt Beryl came back to my mum, and I missed it."

"What'd she say?"

"The same thing she said last time! *Stop looking for my books. There's nothing in there for the likes of you.*'"

"Wait, she came back to tell you *not* to find her books?"

"She was a scholar like Mum and Dad. She doesn't think anyone's smart enough to touch her research."

"I can't believe your relative came back just to insult you."

"Mum says she always knew Aunt Beryl would take her bad attitude to hell with her."

"Do the ghosts ever show up at the wrong place?"

"I think of them more as souls—"

"Souls, then. Do they ever get lost?"

"I'm not sure." Penny turns to face me, holding out a slice of Battenberg cake. I take it. "I know you can confuse them," she says. "You can try to hide their target. Like, if you're worried a soul might come back and tell your secret—you can try to hide the living person who might get Visited. There've even been murders. If I kill you, you can't get a Visitor; ergo, you can't hear or tell my secret."

"So the Visitors can get mixed-up. . . ."

"Yeah, they just show up where they think someone is supposed to be. Like a real person would. Madam Bellamy said she'd seen her husband lurking at the back of her classroom a few times before he actually came through the Veil."

*Just like I saw Baz's mum at the window. . . .*

I should tell Penny what happened. I always tell Penny what happened.

"Come on," she says, standing and brushing dead grass off the backs of her thighs. "We'll be late to class."

She holds her hand over the napkins and clingfilm, and spins her wrist. ***A place for everything, and everything in its place!*** They disappear.

"Waste of magic," I say out of habit, picking up our satchels.

Penny rolls her eyes. "I'm so tired of hearing that. We're *supposed* to use magic. What are we saving it for?"

"So it's there if we need it."

"I know the official answer, Simon—thanks. In America, they think that you become more powerful the more magic you use."

"Just like fossil fuels."

Penny glances over at me, then snorts.

"Don't look so surprised," I say. "I know about fossil fuels."

Baz is in half my lessons. There are only fifty kids in our year; there have been terms in the past when he and I've had every lesson together, all day long.

We usually sit as far apart as possible, but today in Elocution, Madam Bellamy has us push all the desks out of the way and work in pairs. Baz ends up right behind me.

Madam Bellamy hasn't been the same since her Visiting; it's like—well, like she's just seen a ghost. She keeps making us do practical work while she wanders around the room, looking lost.

At this point, eighth year, we're past all the basic Elocution stuff—speaking out, hitting consonants, projection. It's all nuance now. How to give spells more power by saying them with fire and intent. How pausing just before a key word can focus a spell.

Gareth's my partner today. And most days. He's terrible at Elocution. He still drones his spells out like he's reading from a cue card. They work, but they land like lead balloons. If Gareth levitates something, it jerks; if he transforms something, it looks like it's happening in cheap stop-motion animation.

Penelope says Gareth's painful to watch—and not just because of his ridiculous magic belt buckle.

Baz says Gareth wouldn't have even got into Watford in the old days.

Baz's elocution is flawless. In four languages. (Though I suppose I'm just taking his word on that when it comes to French and Greek and Latin.) I can hear him behind me, rattling off cooling spells and warming spells one after another. I feel the change in the air on the back of my neck.

"Slow down, Mr. Pitch," Madam Bellamy says. "No need to waste magic."

I hear the irritation in Baz's voice as he starts shooting the spells out even faster.

Sometimes it's disturbing how much Baz and Penelope have in common. I've mentioned it to her before—"*And*," I said, "your families both hate the Mage."

"My family is nothing like the Pitches!" she argued. "They're speciesist and racist. Baz probably doesn't even think *I* should be at Watford."

"Is he racist?" I ask. "Isn't he a race? His mum looks sort of Spanish or Arabic in her painting."

"Arabic is a language, Simon. And everyone is a race. And Baz is the whitest person I've ever seen."

"Only because he's a vampire," I said.

Damn it all, I have to tell Baz about his mum. Or I have to tell Penny about Baz's mum. . . . Or maybe even the Mage. If it wasn't the Humdrum who had Baz's mother killed, who *was* it?

I can't keep a secret this big. I don't have room for it.

Penny sneaks up to my room before she leaves that night with her mum. She's stupidly brave—it's the only stupid thing about her—and I swear it gets worse when we go too long between emergencies. I'm tempted to slam the door when I see that it's her.

"Baz will turn you in if he catches you in our tower," I say. "And you *will* get suspended."

She waves her hand, dismissively. "He's out by the pitch, watching the team practise. Pitch on the pitch."

She shoves at the door, and I stop her. "Someone else will turn you in, then."

"Nah. All the boys in our year are scared of me. They think I'll turn them into frogs."

"Is there a spell for that?"

"Yes, but it's enormously draining, and I'd have to kiss them to turn them back."

I sigh and let go of the door, peeking down the stairs while Penelope slips past me into my room.

"I'm just here to talk you into coming with me," she says.

"Not gonna work."

"Come on, Simon. My mum won't lecture me so much if you're around."

"She'll lecture me instead." I sit down on my bed. I've got a few books spread out there. And some old documents from the library.

"Right. It's a shared burden—hey, are you reading *The Magickal Record*?"

*The Record* is the closest thing magicians have to a

newspaper. It keeps track of births and deaths, magickal bonds and laws, plus minutes from every Coven meeting. I snuck a few bound volumes from the early 2000s out of the library. "Yep," I say, "I've heard it's fascinating."

"You heard that from me," she says, "and I know you weren't listening. Why are you reading *The Magickal Record*?"

I look up from the books. "Have you ever heard of a magician called 'Nico' or 'Nicodemus'?"

"Like, in history?"

"No. I don't know—maybe. Just anybody. Maybe a politician or someone who was on the Coven? Or a professor?"

She's leaning against my bed. "Is this for the Mage? Are you on a mission?"

"No." I shake my head. "No, I haven't even seen him. I was—it's about Baz." Penny rolls her eyes. "I was thinking about his mum," I say, "something I heard, that maybe she had an enemy."

"The Pitches have always had more enemies than friends."

"Right. Anyway, it's probably not important."

Penny isn't that interested, but I've asked a question, so she tries to answer it. "An enemy named Nico . . ." But then something in her coat pocket chimes. Her eyes get big, and she jabs her hand in her pocket.

I feel my eyes get big, too. "Do you have a *phone*?"

"Simon—"

"Penelope, you can't have a mobile at Watford!"

She folds her arms. "I don't see why not."

"Because of the rules. They're a security risk."

She frowns and pulls out the phone—a white iPhone, a new one. "My parents feel better if I carry it."

"How does that even work in here?" I ask. "There're supposed to be spells. . . ."

Penelope's checking her texts. "My mum magicked it. She's here now, at the gates—" She looks up. "—Please come with us."

"Your mum would make a terrifying supervillain."

Penny grins. "Come to dinner, Simon."

I shake my head again. "No, I want to look this stuff over before Baz comes back."

Finally she gives in, and runs down the tower stairs like she doesn't give a fig about getting caught. I go to the window to see if I can spot Baz out on the pitch.

# 36

## PENELOPE

My mum insisted on me having a mobile after what happened with the Humdrum.

For a few weeks this summer, she was saying I couldn't come back to Watford at all, and my dad didn't even try to talk her down. I think maybe he felt responsible. Like he should have figured the Humdrum out by now.

Dad spent the whole month of June in his lab, not even coming out to eat. Mum made his favourite biryani and left steaming plates of it outside his door.

"That madman!" Mum kept ranting. "Sending children to fight the Humdrum!"

"The Mage didn't send us," I tried telling her. "The Humdrum *took* us." But that just made her angrier. I thought she'd want to work out how the Humdrum had done it. (It's impossible to steal someone like that, to port them that far. The magic required . . . Even Simon doesn't have enough.) But Mum refused to approach it intellectually.

It made me really glad that she doesn't know the details of every other scrape Simon and I have got ourselves into—and got ourselves out of, I should add. We deserve some credit for that.

Mum probably would have cooled down sooner, if it weren't for the nightmares. . . .

I didn't scream when it actually happened:

One minute, Simon and I were in the Wavering Wood, gaping at Baz and Agatha—me holding Simon's arm. And the next minute, we were in a clearing in Lancashire. Simon recognized it—he lived in a home there when he was a kid, near Pendle Hill. There's this big sound sculpture that looks like a tornado, and I thought at first that the noise was the Humdrum.

I could already feel that we were in one of his dead spots.

Dad studies dead spots, so I've been to loads of them. They're the holes in the magickal atmosphere that started appearing when the Humdrum did. Stepping into a dead spot is like losing a sense. Like opening your mouth and realizing you can't make any noise. Most magicians can't handle it. They start to lose their shit immediately. But Dad told me he's never had as much magic as most magicians, so it isn't as terrifying for him to think of losing it.

So Simon and I show up in this clearing, and I can feel straight away it's a dead spot—but it's *more* than that. It's worse. There's this weird whistling on the wind, and everything's dry, so dry and hot.

*Maybe it's not a dead spot,* I thought, *maybe it's a* dying *spot.*

"Lancashire," Simon said to himself.

And then—the Humdrum was there.

And I knew it was the Humdrum because he was the source of everything. Like the way you know that the sun is what makes the day bright. All the heat and dryness were coming from him. Or sucking towards him.

And neither of us, Simon or me, cried out or tried to run, because we were too much in shock: There was the Humdrum—

*and he looked just like Simon.* Just like Simon when I first met him. Eleven years old, in grotty jeans and an old T-shirt. The Humdrum was even bouncing that red rubber ball that Simon never put down our first year.

The kid bounced the ball at Simon, and Simon caught it. Then Simon started screaming at the Humdrum, "Stop it! Stop it! Show yourself, you coward—show yourself!"

It was so hot, and so dry, and it felt like the life was getting sucked out of us, sucked right up through our skin.

Both of us had felt it before during the Humdrum's attacks—that sandy, dry suck. We knew what he felt like, we recognized him. But we'd never seen the Humdrum before. (Now I wonder if that was the first time the Humdrum was *able* to show himself.)

Simon was sure the Humdrum was wearing his face just to taunt him. He kept howling at it to show its real face.

But the Humdrum just laughed. Like a little kid. The way little kids laugh once they've got started, and they can't stop.

(I can't really say why I think so or what it means, but I don't think that the Humdrum appeared that way as a mean joke. I think that's his true form. That he looks like Simon.)

The suck was too much. I looked down at my arm, and there was yellow fluid and blood starting to seep through my pores.

Simon was shouting. The Humdrum was laughing.

I reached out and took the ball from Simon and threw it down the hill.

The Humdrum stopped laughing then—and immediately darted after the ball. The second he turned away from us, the sucking stopped.

I fell over.

Simon picked me up and threw me over his shoulder (which

is pretty amazing, considering I weigh as much as he does). He pushed forward like a Royal Marine, and as soon as he was out of the dead spot, he shifted me around to the front—and big bony wings burst out of his back. *Sort-of* wings. Misshapen and overly feathered, with too many joints . . .

There's no spell for that. There are no words. Simon just said, *"I wish I could fly!"* and he made the words magic.

(I haven't told anyone that part. Magicians aren't genies; we don't run on wishes. If anyone knew that Simon could do that, they'd have him burnt at the stake.)

We were both hurt, so I tried to cast healing spells. I kept thinking that the Humdrum would haul us back as soon as he found his ball. But maybe that wasn't the sort of trick he could manage twice in one day.

Simon flew as far as he could with me clinging to him—stuck to him with spells and fading fast. Then I think he realized how mad we looked and landed near a town.

We were going to take a train, but Simon couldn't get his wings to retract. Because they weren't *wings.* They were bones and feathers and magic—and will.

This is what my nightmares are about:

Hiding in a ditch along the side of the road. Simon's exhausted. And I'm crying. And I'm trying to gather the wings up and push them into his back, so that we can walk into town and catch a train. The wings are falling apart in my hands. Simon's bleeding.

In my nightmares, I can't remember the right spell. . . .

But I remembered it that day. It's a spell for scared children, for sweeping away practical jokes and flights of fancy. I pressed my hand into Simon's back and choked out, *"Nonsense!"*

The wings disintegrated into clumps of dust and gore on his shoulders.

Simon picked someone's pocket at the train station, so we could buy tickets. We slept on the train, leaning against each other. And when we got back to Watford, it was in the middle of the end-of-year ceremony, and Mum and Dad were there, and they dragged me home.

They almost didn't let me come back to school this autumn— they tried to talk me into staying in America. Mum and I yelled at each other, and we haven't really talked properly since.

I told my parents I couldn't miss my last year. But we all knew that what I really meant was that I wouldn't let Simon come back without me.

I said I'd walk back to Watford, that I'd find a way to fly.

Now they make me carry a mobile phone.

# 37

## AGATHA

Watford is a quiet place if you're not dating Simon Snow—and if you've spent so many years with Simon Snow that you never bothered making other friends.

I don't have a roommate. The roommate the Crucible gave me, Philippa, got sick our fifth year and went home.

Simon said Baz did something to her. Dad said she had sudden, traumatic laryngitis—"a tragedy for a magician."

"That would be a tragedy for *anyone*," I said. "Normals talk, too."

I don't really miss Philippa. She was dead jealous that Simon liked me. And she laughed at my spellwork. Plus she always painted her nails without opening a window.

I do have friends, real friends, back home, but I'm not allowed to tell them about Watford. I'm not even *able* to tell them—Dad spelled me mum after he caught me complaining to my best friend, Minty, about my wand.

*"I just said it was a hassle carrying it everywhere! I didn't tell her it was magic!"*

*"Oh for snakes' sake, Agatha,"* Dad said.

My mother was livid. *"You have to do it, Welby."*

So Dad levelled his wand at me: ***"Ix-nay on the atford-Way!"***

It's a serious spell. Only members of the Coven are allowed to use it. But I suppose it was a serious situation: If you tell Normals about magic, they all have to be tracked down and scoured. And if that's not possible, you have to move away.

Now Minty (we met in primary school, that's actually her first name, isn't it lush?) thinks I go to a super-religious boarding school that doesn't allow the Internet. Which is all true, as far as I'm concerned.

Magic *is* a religion.

But there's no such thing as not believing—or only going through the motions on Easter and Christmas. Your whole life has to revolve around magic all the time. If you're born with magic, you're stuck with it, and you're stuck with other magicians, and you're stuck with wars that never end because people don't even know when they started.

I don't talk like this to my parents.

Or to Simon and Penny.

Ix-nay on my ue-feelings-tray.


Baz is walking by himself across the courtyard. We haven't talked since he's been back.

We've never really talked, I guess. Even that time in the Wood. Simon burst in before we could get anywhere, and then Simon burst out again.

(Just when you think you're having a scene without Simon, he drops in to remind you that everyone else is a supporting character in his catastrophe.)

As soon as Simon and Penny disappeared that day, Baz dropped my hands. *"What the fuck just happened to Snow?"*

Those were his last words to me.

But he does still watch me in the dining hall. It makes Simon mental. This morning, Simon got fed up and slammed his fork down, and when I looked over at Baz, he winked.

I hurry to catch up with him now. The sun is setting, and it's making his grey skin look almost warm. I know it's setting my hair on fire.

"Basil," I say coolly, smiling like his name's a secret.

He turns his head slightly to see me. "Wellbelove." He sounds tired.

"We haven't talked since you've been back," I say.

"Did we talk before that?"

I decide to be bold. "Not as much as I'd like."

He sighs. "Crowley, Wellbelove, there must be a better way to get your parents' attention."

"What?"

"Nothing," he says, walking ahead.

"Baz, I thought—I thought you might need someone to talk to."

"Nope, I'm good."

"But—"

He stops and sighs, rubbing his eyes. "Look . . . Agatha. We both know that whatever you and Snow are squabbling about, you'll soon work it out and be back to your golden destiny. Don't complicate it."

"But we're not—"

Baz has started walking again. He's limping a little. Maybe that's why he isn't playing football. I keep following him.

"Maybe I don't want a golden destiny," I say.

"When you figure out how to sidestep destiny, let me know." He's walking as fast as he can with his limp, and I decide not to run to keep up with him. That would look appalling.

"Maybe I want something more interesting!" I call out.

"I'm not more interesting!" he shouts back, without turning

his head. "I'm just *wrong* for you. Learn the difference."

I bite down on my bottom lip and try not to cross my arms like a 6-year-old.

How does he know he's wrong for me?

Why does everyone else think they know where I belong?

# 38

## BAZ

Snow has been staring at me all day—for weeks now—and I'm just really not up for it. Maybe Aunt Fiona was right; I should have stayed home longer and rested up. I feel like complete shit.

Like I can't get full, and I can't get warm—and last night, I had some sort of attack in the Catacombs. It's so fucking dark down there. And even though I can see in the dark, I felt like I was back in that stupid numpty coffin.

I couldn't stay underground any longer. I caught six rats, banged their heads on the floor, tied their tails in a knot, then brought them back upstairs and drained them in the courtyard under the stars. May as well have sent an engraved announcement to the whole school, telling them I'm a vampire. A vampire who's afraid of the dark, for Crowley's sake.

I threw the rat carcasses to the merwolves. (They're worse than rats. I'd drain every one of them if the taste didn't stay in my mouth for weeks. Gamy *and* fishy.)

Then I slept like the dead for nine hours, and it still wasn't enough. I've been asleep on my feet since lunch, and I can't exactly go up to my room to take a nap. Snow would probably sit across from me and watch.

He's been following me everywhere since I got back. He hasn't been this persistent since our fifth year—he even followed me to the boys' toilet yesterday and pretended he just needed to wash his hands.

I don't have the strength for it.

I feel 15 again, like I'm going to give in if he gets too close— kiss him or bite him. The only reason I got through that year was that I couldn't decide which of those options would finally put me out of my misery.

Probably Snow himself would put me out of my misery if I tried either one.

Those were my fifth-year fantasies: kisses and blood and Snow ridding the world of me.

I watched the football practice this afternoon, just for an excuse to sit down, then slipped away from the team when everyone else headed for dinner.

Wellbelove catches me in the courtyard and tries to suck me into her maiden-fair drama, but I haven't got time for the pain. I heard Miss Possibelf say that the Mage is coming back to Watford tomorrow—and I still haven't snuck up to his office. (Probably because it's an idiotic idea.) But if I go up there and take something, it will at least get Fiona off my back for a while.

I haul myself to the Weeping Tower, and skip the spiral staircase to take the staff lift up to the very top.

I walk past the door to the headmaster's rooms. When my mother was headmistress, I lived with her here. I was just a toddler. Father would come in most weekends, and we'd all go back to the house in Hampshire every summer.

My mother used to let me play in her office while she worked. She'd come get me from the nursery, and I'd spread my Lego bricks out on her rug.

When I get to the headmaster's office, the door opens easily for me—the Mage never took down the wards my mother cast to let me in. I can get in his rooms, too. (I snuck in once and found myself puking in his toilet.) Fiona would have me inspecting his chambers every night, but I've told her we have to save that trick until we really need it. Until we can use it. And not just to leave steaming bags of shit in his bed.

*"Furthermore, Fiona, I'm not shitting in a bag."*

*"I'll do the shitting, you knob; it can be my shit."*

My stomach clenches when I walk into the office. When I see my mother's desk. It's dark in here—the curtains are drawn—so I light a fire in my palm and hold it out in front of me.

It terrifies my stepmother when I do this. *"Basilton, don't. You're flammable."*

But bringing fire is as easy for me as breathing; it hardly takes any magic, and I always feel utterly in control. I can make it twist through my fingers like a snake. *"Just like Natasha,"* my father always says. *"He's got more fire than a demon."*

(Though Father did draw a hard line when he caught me smoking cigarettes in the carriage house. *"For Crowley's sake, Baz, you are flammable."*)

The headmaster's office looks exactly the same as it did when I played here. You'd think the Mage would have thrown all my mother's things out and hung up Che Guevara posters—but he didn't.

There's dust on his chair. On my mother's chair. And thick dust on the computer keyboard—I don't think he even uses it. He's not the sitting, typing type, the Mage. He's always stalking around or swinging a sword, or doing something to justify his Robin Hood costume.

I open his top drawer with my wand. Nothing here . . . Dried-up office supplies. A phone charger.

My mother kept tea in this drawer, and mint Aero bars and clove drops. I lean in to see if I can smell them—I can smell things other people can't. (I can smell things *no* people can.) (Because I'm not a person.)

The drawer smells like wood and leather. The room smells like leather and steel and the forest, like the Mage himself. I open the other drawers with my hand. There aren't any booby traps. There's nothing personal at all. I'm not even sure what to take for Fiona. A book, maybe.

I hold my flame up to the bookshelves and think about blowing, just setting the whole room on fire. But then I notice that the books are all out of order. Obviously out of order. Stacked, instead of set on their shelves—some of them lying in piles on the floor. I feel like putting them back, sorting them by subject the way my mother used to. (I was always allowed to touch her books. I was allowed to read any book, as long as I put it back in its place and promised to ask if something confused or frightened me.)

Maybe I should take advantage of the fact that the books are out of order: No one will notice if one goes missing—or several. I reach for one with a dragon embossed on the spine; the dragon's mouth is open, and fire spews out forming the title: *Flames and Blazes—The Art of Burning*.

A shaft of light widens on the shelf before me, and I jerk around, sending the book sailing, pages flapping. Something flies out as the book hits the floor.

Snow is standing in the doorway. "What are you doing here?" he demands. His blade is already out.

I've seen that sword in action enough, you'd think I'd be terrified—but instead it's reassuring. I've dealt with this, with Snow, before.

I must truly be exhausted, because I tell him the truth:

"Looking for one of my mother's books."

"You're not supposed to be in here," he says, both hands on his sword.

I hold my light higher and step away from the shelves. "I'm not hurting anything. I just want a book."

"Why?" He looks down at the book lying between us and rushes forward, abandoning his stance to beat me to it. I lean back against the shelves and swing one ankle over the other. Snow's crouching over the book. He probably thinks it's a clue, the thing that will blow my conspiracy wide open.

He stands again, staring at a small piece of paper in his hand. He looks upset. "Here," he says softly, holding it out to me. "I'm . . . sorry."

I take the paper, a photograph, and he watches me. I'm tempted to shove it in my pocket and look at it later, but curiosity gets the best of me, and I hold it up. . . .

It's me.

Down in the crèche, I think. (Watford used to have a staff nursery and day school; it's where the vampires struck.)

I'm just a baby in this photo. Three or four years old, wearing soft grey dungarees with bloomer bottoms, and white leather boots. My skin is the shocking thing: a stark reddish gold against my white collared shirt and white socks. I'm smiling at the camera, and someone's holding my fingers—

I recognize my mother's wedding ring. I recognize her thick, rough hand.

And then I can *remember* her hand. Resting on my leg when she wanted me to be still. Holding her wand precisely in the air. Slipping into her desk drawer to get a sweet and popping it into her mouth.

*"Your hands are scratchy,"* I'd say when she cupped one around my cheek.

*"They're fire-holders' hands,"* she'd say. *"Flame throwers'."*

My mother's hands scuffing my cheek. Tucking my hair behind my ears.

My mother's hands held aloft—setting the air of the nursery on fire while a chalk-skinned monster buried his teeth in my throat.

"Baz . . . ," Snow says. He's picked up the book and is holding it out to me.

I take it.

"I need to tell you something," he says.

"What?" Since when do Snow and I have anything to tell each other?

"I need to talk to you."

I raise my chin. "Talk, then."

"Not here." He sheathes his blade. "We're not supposed to be here, and . . . what I have to tell you is sort of private."

For a moment—not even a moment, a split second—I imagine him saying, *"The truth is, I'm desperately attracted to you."* And then I imagine myself spitting in his face. And then I imagine licking it off his cheek and kissing him. (Because I'm disturbed. Ask anyone.)

I ***"Make a wish!"*** the flame out of my hand, tuck the photo into the book, and the book under my arm. "Lucky for us," I say, "we have our own suite at the top of a turret. Private enough for you?"

He nods, embarrassed, and gestures for me to walk ahead of him. "Just come on," he says.

I do.

# 39

## SIMON

I'd just caught my enemy red-handed, breaking into the Mage's office. I could have got him expelled for this. *Finally.*

And instead I gave him the thing he came to steal, then asked him if we could have some alone time—all because of a baby picture.

But the look on Baz's face in that picture . . . Smiling just because he was happy, with cheeks like red apples.

And the look on his face when he saw it. Like someone blew a horn and all his walls crumbled.

We walk back to our room, and it's awkward; we don't have any experience walking with each other, even though we're usually headed in the same direction. We keep our distance on the stairs, then move even farther away as we cross the courtyards. I keep wanting to get my sword back out.

Baz has worked himself up to a full-on strop by the time we get to our room. He slams the door shut behind us, sets the book on his bed, then crosses his arms. "Fine, Snow. We're alone. Whatever you have to say—say it."

I cross my arms, too. "All right," I say, "just . . . sit down, okay?"

"Why should I sit down?"

"Because you're making me uncomfortable."

"Good," he says. "You should be glad I'm not making you bleed."

"For Christ's sake," I say. I only swear like a Normal when I'm at my wit's end. "Could you just calm down? This is important."

Baz shakes his head, exasperated, but sits at the end of his bed, frowning at me. He has these droopy dog eyes that always look like they're peeking out from under his eyelids, even when his eyes are wide open. And his lips naturally turn down at the corners. It's like his face was designed for pouting.

I walk over to my book bag and pull out a notebook. I wrote down as much as I could the day after Baz's mum came to see me; I thought I was writing it all down to share with the Mage.

I sit on my bed, facing him, and he reluctantly shifts to sit across from me.

"All right," I say, "look. I don't want to tell you this. I don't even know if I should. But it's your mum, and I don't think it's right to keep it from you."

"What about my mother?" His arms unfold, and he leans forward, grabbing at my notebook.

I whip the notebook away. "I'm telling you, okay? Just listen."

His eyes narrow.

I'm stupidly flustered. "When you were gone—you were gone when the Veil lifted."

He guesses it immediately—his nostrils flare, and his eyes go a little wild—he's so fucking smart, I don't know how I'm ever going to get the best of him.

"My mother . . . ," he says.

"She was looking for you. She kept coming back. Here. Where were you that she couldn't find you?"

"My mother came through the Veil?"

"Yeah. She said she was called here, to our room, that *this* was your place. And she was pretty hacked off that you weren't here. Wanted to know whether I'd hurt you."

"She talked to you?"

"Yeah. I mean—*yes.*" I run my hands through my hair. "She came looking for you and scared the living shit out of me, asking if I'd hurt you. And then she said that the Veil was closing. . . ." I look down at my notebook.

Baz grabs it from me, scanning the page hungrily, then hurls it back at my chest. "You write like an animal. What did she say?"

"She said that . . ." My voice falters. "That her killer walks. That you should find Nicodemus and bring her peace."

"Bring her peace?"

I don't know what more to say. His face is in agony.

"But she *killed* the vampires," he says.

"I know."

"Does she mean the Humdrum?"

"I don't know."

"Tell me again."

I look back down at my notes. "Her killer walks, but Nicodemus knows. Find Nicodemus and bring her peace."

"Who's Nicodemus?" Baz demands. Fierce and imperious, just like his mother.

"She didn't say."

"What else?" he asks. "Was there anything else?"

"Well . . . she kissed me." My hand jerks up, and I brush my fingertips over my forehead. "She told me it was for you, to give to you."

He clenches his fists at his sides. "Then what?"

"Then she left," I say. "She came back one more time, that same night, the last night before the Veil fell"—Baz looks like he wants to choke me—"and she was different, sadder, like she was crying." I look down at my notes. "And I couldn't see her that time, but she said, '*My son, my rosebud boy.*' She said that a few times, I think. And then she called me by my name and said she never would have left you. And then: '*He said we were stars.*'"

"Who said? Nicodemus?"

"I guess, I don't know."

Baz squeezes his fists tight, and his voice comes out of him in a tight roar. "Who. *The fuck.* Is Nicodemus."

"I don't know," I say. "I thought *you'd* know."

He gets off the bed and starts prowling about the room. "My mother came back. She came back to see me. And you talked to her instead. Unbelievable."

"Well, where *were* you? Why couldn't she find you?"

"I was indisposed! It's none of your business!"

"Well, I hope your secret trip was worth it!" I shout. "Because your mother came for you! She came and she came and she came—and you were off planning your hopeless rebellion!"

He stops pacing, then charges towards me, his hands reaching for my neck. And I'm more scared for him than I am for myself, even though I know he wants to kill me. Because if he touches me, he'll be cast out. The Anathema.

I jump to my feet and catch his wrists. They're cold. "Baz, you don't want to hurt me. Do you." He strains against my grip. He's panting with rage. "You don't want to *hurt* me," I say, trying to push him back. "Isn't that right? I'm sorry. Look at me, *I'm sorry.*"

His grey eyes focus, and he steps back, snatching his arms away. We both glance around the room, waiting for the Anathema to kick in.

There's a knock at the door, and we both jump.

"Simon?" I hear Penny say.

Baz arches an eyebrow, and I can practically hear him thinking, *Interesting.* I shove past him and open the door. "Penny, what're you—?"

She's been crying. She starts again—*"Simon"*—and rushes into my arms. I slowly put my arms around her and look up at Baz, waiting for him to raise the alarm.

He shakes his head, like it's all too much for him. "I'll leave you alone," he says, sliding past us out the door. I hate to think of how he'll use this against Penelope, or me—but right now I've got Penny sobbing into my shirt.

"Hey," I say, patting her back. I'm not good at hugging, she knows that, but she must not care right now. "Hey, what's wrong?"

She pulls back and wipes her face on her sleeve. She's still wearing her coat. "My mum . . ." Her face is all crumpled. She wipes it on her sleeve again.

"Is she okay?"

"She's not hurt—nobody's hurt. But she told me that Premal came yesterday." Penny's talking too fast, and still crying. "He came for the Mage with two more of his Men, and they wanted to search our house."

"What? Why?"

"The Mage sent them. Premal said it was a routine search for banned magic, but Mum said there's no such thing as a routine search, and she'd be damned to Slough before she let the Mage treat her like she was an enemy of the state. And then Premal said it wasn't *a request.* And Mum said they could come back with an order from the Coven"— Penny's shaking in my arms—"and Prem said that we're at war, and that the Mage is *the Mage,* and what did Mum have to hide, anyway? And Mum said that *wasn't the point.* The point was civil liberties, and freedom, and not having your 20-year-old son showing up at your house like Rolf in *The Sound of Music.* And I'm sure Premal was humiliated and not acting like himself—or maybe just acting *more* like his tosser self than usual—because he said he'd be back, and that Mum had better change her mind. And Mum said he could come back as a Nazi and a fascist, but not as her son." Penny's voice breaks again, and she covers her face in her arms, elbowing me in the chin.

I pull my head back and hold on to her shoulders. "Hey," I say, "I'm sure this is just something that got out of hand. We'll talk to the Mage."

She jerks away from me. "Simon—no. You can't talk to him about this."

"Pen. It's the Mage. He's not going to hurt your family. He knows you're good."

She shakes her head. "My mum made me promise not to tell you, Simon."

"No secrets," I say, suddenly defensive. "We have a pact."

"I know! That's why I'm here, but you cannot tell the Mage. My mother's scared, and my mother doesn't *get* scared."

"Why didn't she just let them search the house?"

"Why *should* she?"

"Because," I say, "if the Mage is doing this, he has a reason. He doesn't just hassle people. He doesn't have time for that."

"But . . . what if they found something?"

"At your house? They wouldn't."

"They might," she says. "You know my mum. *'Information wants to be free.' 'There's no such thing as a bad thought.'* Our library is practically as big as Watford's and better stocked. If you wanted to find something dangerous in there, I'm sure you could."

"But the Mage doesn't *want* to hurt your family."

"Who *does* he want to hurt, Simon?"

"People who want to hurt us!" I say. I practically shout it. "People who want to hurt me!"

Penny folds her arms and looks at me. She's mostly stopped crying. "The Mage isn't perfect. He's not always right."

"No one is. But we have to trust him. He's doing his best." As soon as I say it, I feel a pound of guilt settle in my stomach. I should have told the Mage about the ghost. I should have told Penny. I should have told them *both* before I told Baz. I could be spying for the wrong side.

"I need to think about this," Penny says. "It's not my secret to tell—or *yours.*"

"All right," I agree.

"All right." A few more tears well up on her, and she shakes her head again. "I should go. I can't believe Baz hasn't come back with the house master yet. They probably think he's lying—"

"I don't think he's snitching on you."

She huffs. "Of course he is. I don't care. I have bigger worries."

"Stay for a bit," I say. If she stays, I'll tell her about Baz's mum.

"No. We can talk about this tomorrow. I just needed to tell you."

"Your family will be safe," I say. "You don't have to worry about it. I promise."

Penelope looks unconvinced, and I half expect her to point out how worthless my words have been so far. But she just nods and tells me she'll see me at breakfast.

# 40

## BAZ

I could watch Bunce swing for this.

(I didn't think it was possible for anyone to get past the residence hall's gender barriers. Trust Bunce to find a way. She's incessantly fiendish.)

But I don't even care.

I find my way down to the Catacombs and hunt mindlessly.

My mother's tomb is here. I hate to think that she might be watching me. Can souls see through the Veil? Does she know I've become one of them?

I wonder sometimes what would have happened if she'd lived.

I was the only child in the nursery who was Turned that day. The vampires might have taken me with them if my mother hadn't stopped them.

My father came for me as soon as he heard. And he and Fiona did everything they could to heal me—but they knew I was changed. They knew the blood lust would manifest itself eventually.

And they just . . .

They went on acting like nothing had happened. Crowley, they're lucky I didn't start devouring people as soon as I hit puberty. I don't think my father ever would have mentioned it, even if he'd caught me draining the maid. *"Basil, change into some new things for dinner. You'll upset your stepmother."*

Though he'd much prefer to catch me *disrobing* the maid. . . . (Definitely more disappointed in my queerness than my undeadness.)

My father never acknowledges that I'm a vampire—besides my flammability—and I know he'll never send me away because of it.

But my mother?

She would have killed me.

She would have faced me, what I am, and done what was right.

My mother never would have let a vampire into Watford. She *didn't*.

I end my walk at the door to her tomb. At the stone in the wall that marks it.

She was the youngest person ever to lead Watford—and one of three headmasters in history to die defending it. She's kept here, in a place of honour, part of the school's foundation.

My mother came back.

She came back *for me*.

What does it mean that she couldn't find me?

Maybe ghosts can't see through coffins.

Maybe she couldn't see me because I'm not fully alive. Will I get to see *her* when Simon finally finishes me?

He will . . . Finish me.

Snow will do the right thing.

I stay in the Catacombs until I'm done feeding. Until I'm done raging. Until I can't stand staring at that photograph of myself anymore. (Chubby, lucky bag of blood.)

Until I'm done crying.

You'd think that's something you'd lose in the change—tears. But I still piss, and I still cry. I still lose water.

(I don't really know how it all works, being a vampire; my family won't let me near a magickal doctor—and it's not like I get colds or need vaccinations.)

The flowers I've laid outside my mother's tomb have wilted. I cast *"April showers!"* and they bloom again. It takes more magic than I can afford right now—flowers and food take life—and I slump forward against the wall.

When I'm tired lately, I can't keep my head up. And my left leg isn't quite right since the numpties; it goes numb. I stomp it into the stone floor, and some feeling shoots up my heel.

If my mother came back through the Veil, that means she hasn't completely moved on. She isn't here—she can't see me—but she isn't in the next place. Her soul is stuck in the in-between.

How am I supposed to help?

Find this Nicodemus? Is he the one who sent the vampires?

I've always been told that the Humdrum sent the vampires. Even Fiona thinks the Humdrum sent the vampires. The Humdrum sends everything else to Watford. . . .

My leg's so numb when I get to our tower, I have to lead with my right and drag my left behind me, all the way up the stairs.

Bunce is gone from our room. Snow's in bed, and the windows are open. He's showered. Snow uses the soap the school provides—he smells like a hospital when he's clean.

I don't bother rinsing my face or changing. Just strip to my undershirt and pants, and climb in my bed. I feel like death. Death not even warmed over.

As soon as I'm settled—eyes closed, willing myself not to

cry again—Snow clears his throat. Awake, then. I won't cry.

"I'll help you," he says—so softly, only a vampire could hear him.

"Help me what?"

"I'll help you find whatever killed your mother."

"Why?"

He rolls over to face my bed. I can just see him in the dark. He can't see me.

He shrugs. "Because they attacked Watford."

I roll away.

"Because she was your mother," he says. "And they killed her in front of you. And that's—that's wrong."

# 41

## LUCY

The Veil is closing, pulling us all back—but it can't get its grip on me.

I don't think there's enough of me left. Imagine that, not having enough life in you to be properly dead. Not enough to break through and not enough to drag back.

I'd rather stay here.

I'd rather keep speaking to you, even if you can't hear. Even if I can't see you. (There was a moment when I thought I could; there was a moment when I thought you *heard.*)

I stay. And I drift. I slip through floors that won't hold me. I blow through walls that don't stop me. The whole world is grey, and full of shadows.

I tell them my story.

# BOOK THREE

# 42

## SIMON

Baz is already mostly dressed when I wake up.

He's standing at the windows—he's closed them, even though it's already too hot in here—and he's tying his tie in the reflection.

He has long hair for a bloke. When he plays football, it falls in his eyes and on his cheeks. But he slicks it straight back after a shower, so he always looks like a gangster first thing in the morning—or a black-and-white movie vampire, with that widow's peak of his.

I've wondered whether Baz gets away with being a vampire by looking so much like one. Like, it would be too much to call him out for it—a little too on the nose. (Baz has a long thin nose. The kind that starts too high on someone's head and practically gets in the way of their eyebrows. Sometimes when I'm looking at him, I want to reach out and yank it down half an inch. Not that that would work.) (His nose is also a little bent towards the bottom—I did that.)

I don't know where we stand this morning.

I mean, I promised to help him find out what happened to his mum. Are we supposed to start that right now? Or is it the sort of promise that's going to come back to haunt me years from now, just when I've forgotten about it?

And, no matter what, we're still enemies, right? He still wants to kill me?

He probably won't try to kill me until I've helped him with his mum—I guess that's a comforting thought.

Baz gives the knot in his tie one last tug, then turns to me, putting on his jacket. "You're not getting off."

I sit up. "What?"

"You're not going to pretend that last night was a dream or that you didn't mean what you said. You're helping me avenge my mother's death."

"Nobody said anything about *avenging*." I throw back my blankets and stand up, shaking my hair out with both hands. (It gets matted when I sleep.) "I said that I'd help you figure out who murdered her."

"That's helping me, Snow. Because as soon as I know, I'm killing them."

"Well, I'm not helping with that part."

"You already are," Baz says, hitching his bag over his shoulder.

"What?"

"Starting now," he says, pointing at the floor. "We're starting this now. It's our first priority." He heads for the door.

I want to argue. "What—?"

Baz stops, huffs, then turns back to me.

"What about everything else?" I ask.

"What everything else?" he says. "Lessons? We can still go to our lessons."

"No," I growl. "You *know* what everything else." I think of the last seven years of my life. Of every empty threat he's made—and every full one. "You want me to work on this with you, but . . . you also want to push me down the stairs."

"Fine. I promise not to push you down the stairs until we solve this."

"I'm serious," I say. "I can't help you if you're setting me up all the time."

He sneers. "Do you think this is a setup? That I brought my mother back from the dead to fuck with you?"

"No."

"Truce," he says.

"Truce?"

"I'm fairly certain you know what 'truce' means, Snow. No aggression until we're through this."

"No aggression?"

He rolls his eyes. "No *acts* of aggression."

I grab my wand off the table that sits between our beds and walk over to him, raising it in my left hand and holding out my right. "Swear it," I say. "With magic."

He narrows his eyes at me. I see the tension in his chin.

"Fine," he says, swatting my wand away. "But I'm not letting you anywhere near me with that." He slips his own wand out of the pocket inside his jacket and holds it between us. Then he takes my hand in his—he's cold—and I pull back, out of reflex. He tightens his grip.

"Truce," Baz says, looking in my eyes.

"Truce," I say, sounding much less certain.

"Until we know the truth," he adds.

I nod.

Then he taps our joined hands. ***"An Englishman's word is his bond!"***

I feel Baz's magic sink into my hand. Someone else's magic never feels like your own—like someone else's spit never tastes like your own. (Though I guess I can only speak for Agatha's.) Baz's magic *burns*. Like heat rub. It hangs in the muscles of my hand.

We've just taken an oath. I've never taken an oath before. Baz could still break it—he could still turn on me—but his hand would cramp up, and he'd lose his voice for a few weeks. Maybe that's part of his plan.

We're both staring at our joined hands. I can still feel his magic.

"We can talk about this after our lessons," Baz says. "Back here."

His grip loosens, and I yank my hand back. "Fine."

I get to breakfast late, and Penelope hasn't set any kippers or toast aside for me.

She says she doesn't feel like talking, and I don't feel like talking either, even though I have so much I need to tell her.

Agatha still isn't sitting with us. I don't even see her this morning—I wonder if she's off somewhere with Baz. I should have added that to the truce: *And also you have to leave my girlfriend alone.*

Ex-girlfriend, I guess. Anyway. "Have you heard any more from your mum?" I ask Penny.

"No," she says. "Is Baz going to turn me in?"

"No. Is the Mage back?"

"I haven't seen him."

She eats half as much of her breakfast as usual, and I eat twice as much, just to keep my mouth busy. I leave early for my Greek lesson because I feel like I've let Penny down—I can't take her side against the Mage. For what it's worth, I could never take his side against her, either.

When I get to the classroom, Baz is already there. Ignoring me. He ignores me all morning. I see him in the hallway a few times, whispering with Dev and Niall.

When it's time to meet back in our room, I tell Penny that

I'm skipping tea to study, and run across the courtyard to get back to Mummers House.

I get as far as the stairs before I start wondering whether the meeting is a trap—which is just paranoid. Baz doesn't have to *lure* me to our room; I'm there every night.

It's not like the time he tried to feed me to the chimera. That time, he asked me to meet him in the Wavering Wood. He said he had information for me, about my parents, and that it was too dangerous to risk saying it on school grounds.

I knew he was lying.

I told myself I was going to the Wood just to see what he was up to and beat him into the ground. But part of me still thought that maybe he really *did* know something about my parents—I mean, *someone* must know who they are. And even if Baz was just going to use what he knew against me, it would still be something.

It was fucking beautiful when the chimera noticed Baz first, hiding in the trees, and went after him instead of me. I should have let the monster have a go at him. It would have served Baz right. . . .

Then there was the time when we were sixth years, and he left me a note in Agatha's handwriting, telling me to wait for her under the yew tree after dark. It was freezing, and of course she didn't show up, and I was stuck outside all night until the drawbridge was lowered the next morning. My heat spell wouldn't work, and the snow devils kept throwing chestnuts at my head. I thought about smashing them, but they're a protected magickal species. (Global warming.) I kept expecting something worse to show up. Why would Baz torture me with snow devils? They're just half-sentient snowballs with eyebrows and hands. They're not even *dark*. But nothing else came, which meant Baz's evil plan fell apart—or that his evil plan was to freeze me only half to death on the night before a big exam.

Then last year, he told me Miss Possibelf wanted to see me, and when I got to her office, he'd trapped a polecat in there. Miss Possibelf was sure I must be responsible—even though she really likes me.

I retaliated by putting the polecat in his wardrobe, which wasn't much of a retaliation because we share a room.

I'm at our door now. Still trying to decide whether this is a trap. I decide it doesn't matter—because even if I knew for sure that it *was* a trap, I'd still go in.

When I open the door, Baz is wheeling an old-fashioned chalkboard in front of our beds.

"Where did that come from?" I ask.

"A classroom."

"Yeah, but how did it get up here?"

"It flew."

"No," I say, "seriously."

He rolls his eyes. "I **Up, up and away**-ed it. It wasn't much work."

"Why?"

"Because we're solving a mystery, Snow. I like to organize my thoughts."

"Is this how you normally plot my downfall?"

"Yes. With multicoloured pieces of chalk. Stop complaining." He opens up his book bag and takes out a few apples and things wrapped in greaseproof paper. "Eat," he says, throwing one at me.

It's a bacon roll. He's also got a pot of tea.

"What's all this?" I say.

"Tea, obviously. I know you can't function unless you're stuffing yourself."

I unwrap the roll and decide to take a bite. "Thanks."

"Don't thank me," he says. "It sounds wrong."

"Not as wrong as you bringing me bacon butties."

"Fine, you're welcome—when's Bunce getting here?"

"Why would she?"

"Because you do everything together, don't you? When you said you'd help, I was counting on you bringing your smarter half."

"Penelope doesn't know anything about this," I say.

"She doesn't know about the Visiting?"

"No."

"Why not? I thought you told her everything."

"It just . . . seemed like your business."

"It *is* my business," Baz says.

"Right. So I didn't tell her. Now, where do we start?"

His face falls into a pout. "I was counting on Bunce to tell us where to start."

"Let's start with what we know," I say. That's where Penelope always starts.

"Right." Baz actually seems nervous. He's tapping the chalk against his trouser leg, leaving white smudges. *Nicodemus,* he writes on the chalkboard in neat slanted script.

"That's what we don't know," I say. "Unless you've come up with something."

He shakes his head. "No. I've never heard of him. I did a cursory check in the library during lunch—but I'm not likely to find anything in *A Child's Garden of Verses.*"

Most of the magickal books have been removed from the Watford library. The Mage wants us to focus on Normal books so that we stay close to the language.

Before the Mage's reforms, Watford was so protective of traditional spells that they'd teach those instead of newer spells that worked better. There were even initiatives to make Victorian books and culture more popular with the Normals, just to breathe some new life into old spells.

*"Language evolves,"* the Mage says. *"So must we."*

Baz looks back at the chalkboard again. His hair is dry now and falling in loose locks over his cheeks; he tucks a piece behind his ear, then writes a date on the chalkboard:

*12 August 2002.*

I start to ask what happened that day, then I realize.

"You were only 5," I say. "Do you remember anything?"

He looks at me, then back at the board. "Some."

# 43

## BAZ

Some. I don't remember how the day started or any of the normal parts.

I remember only a few things about that whole year: A trip to the zoo. The day my father shaved his moustache and I didn't recognize him.

I remember going to the nursery, in general.

That we got digestives and milk every day. The rabbit mural on the ceiling. A little girl who bit me. I remember that there were trains, and I liked the green one. That there were babies, and sometimes, if one was crying, the miss would let me stand over the cradle and say, "It's okay, little puff, you'll be all right." Because that's what my mum would say to me when I cried.

I don't think there were that many of us there. Just the children of faculty. Two rooms. I was still in with the babies.

I don't specifically remember going there on the twelfth of August. But I do remember when the vampires broke down the door.

Vampires—we—are unusually strong when we're on the hunt. A heavy oak door carved with bunnies and badgers . . . that wouldn't be a barrier for a team of us.

I can't tell you how many vampires came to the nursery that day. It seemed like dozens, but that can't be right, because I was the only child who was bitten. I remember that one of them, a man, picked me up like I was a puppy—by the back of my dungarees. The bib came up and choked me for a second.

The way I remember it, my mother was right behind them, there almost immediately. I could hear her shouting spells before I saw her. I saw her blue fire before I saw her face.

My mother could summon fire under her breath. She could burn for hours without tiring.

She shot streams of fire over the children's heads; the air was alive with it.

I remember people scrambling. I remember watching one of the vampires light up like a Roman candle. I remember the look on my mother's face when she saw me, a flash of agony before the man holding me sank his teeth into my neck.

And then *pain*.

And then nothing . . .

I must have passed out.

When I woke up, I was in my mother's quarters, and Father and Fiona were casting healing spells over me.

When I woke up, my mother was gone.

# 44

## SIMON

Baz lifts his hand to the board and writes *Vampires,* and then, *On a mission from the Humdrum,* and then, *one fatality.*

I don't know how he can do this—talk about vampires without acknowledging that he is one. Pretending that I don't already know. That he doesn't know I already know.

"Well, not just one fatality," I say. "There were also the vampires, weren't there? Did your mother kill them all? How many?"

"It's impossible to say." He folds his arms. "There were no remains." He turns back to the chalkboard. "There *are* no remains, in that sort of death—just ashes."

"So the Humdrum sends vampires to Watford—"

"The first breach in school history," he says.

"And the last," I add.

"Well, it's got a lot harder, hasn't it?" Baz says. "That's one thing we can give your Mage—this school's as tight as a drum. He'd hide Watford behind the Veil if he could."

"Have there been *any* vampire attacks since then?"

Baz shrugs. "I don't think vampires normally attack magicians. My father says they're like bears."

*They.*

"How?" I ask.

"Well, they hunt where it's easiest for them, among the Normals, and they don't attack magicians unless they're starving or rabid. It's too much fuss."

"What else does your father tell you about vampires?"

Baz's voice is ice: "The subject rarely comes up."

"Well, I'm just saying"—I square my shoulders and speak deliberately—"it would help in this specific situation if we *knew* how vampires worked."

His lip curls. "Pretty sure they drink blood and turn into bats, Snow."

"I meant culturally, all right?"

"Right, you're a fiend for culture."

"Do you want my help or not?"

He sighs and writes *Vampires: Food for thought* on the board.

I shove the last bite of roll into my mouth. "Can vampires really turn into bats?"

"Why don't you ask one. Moving on: What else do we know?"

I get off the bed and wipe my hands on my trousers, then take a bound copy of *The Record* off my desk. "I looked up the coverage of the attack—" I open the book to the right place and hold it out to him. His mother's official portrait takes up half the page. There's also a photo of the nursery, burned and blackened, and the headline:

# VAMPIRES IN THE NURSERY

**Natasha Grimm-Pitch dies defending Watford from dark creatures.**

**Are any of our children safe?**

"I've never seen this," Baz says, taking the book. He sits in my chair and starts reading the story out loud:

*"The attack took place only days before the autumn term began. Imagine the carnage that would have occurred on a typical Watford day. . . .*

*"Mistress Mary, the nursery manager, said that one of the beasts attacked Grimm-Pitch from behind, clamping its fangs onto her neck after she neatly decapitated another who was threatening her very own son. 'She was like Fury herself,' Mary said. 'Like something out of a film. The monster bit her, and she choked out a **Tyger, tyger, burning bright**—then they both went up in flames. . . .'"*

Baz stops reading. He looks rattled. "I didn't know that," he says, more to the book than to me. "I didn't know she'd been bitten."

"What's **Tiger, tiger**—?" I stop. I don't trust myself to say new spells out loud.

"It's an immolating spell," he says. "It was popular with assassins . . . and spurned lovers."

"So she killed herself? Intentionally?"

He closes his eyes, and his head hangs forward over the book. I feel like I should do something to comfort him, but there's no way to be comforted by your worst enemy.

Except . . . Hell, I'm *not* his worst enemy, am I? Hell and horrors.

I'm still standing next to him, and I bump my hand against his shoulder—sort of a comforting bump—and reach for the book. I pick up reading out loud where he left off:

*"Her son, 5-year-old Tyrannus Basilton, was shaken, but unharmed. His father, Malcolm Grimm, has taken the boy to the family home in Hampshire to recover.*

*"The Coven is convened in an emergency meeting as of this*

*writing to discuss the attack on Watford; the escalation of the dark creature problem; and the appointment of an interim headmaster.*

*"There have been calls to close the school until our struggles with the dark creatures are sorted—and even suggestions that we join the Americans and Scandinavians in mainstreaming our children into Normal schools.*

"There are more articles about that," I say, "about what to do with Watford. I've read a few months' worth. Lots of meetings and debates and editorials. Until the Mage took over in February."

Baz is staring past me into nothing. His hair is in his eyes, his arms are folded, and he's holding his own elbows. I try the comforting thing again—actually resting my hand on his shoulder this time. "It's okay," I say.

He laughs. A dry bark. "That might be the one thing it *isn't*. Okay."

"No. I mean, it's okay that you're not okay. Whatever you're feeling is okay."

He stands up, shaking off my hand. "Is that what your friends tell you every time you blow up another chunk of school grounds? Because they're lying to you. It isn't okay. And it won't be. So far, it's only ever been a sign of more bad things to come. *You* won't be okay, will you, Snow?"

I feel a wave of red shoot up my back and shoulders, and I clamp down on it, deliberately walking away from him. "This isn't about me."

"I wouldn't think so," he snarls, "but I've been wrong before. It's always about you around here."

I drop the book on my desk and make for the door. I should have known this wouldn't work. He's such an unforgivable twat, even when he's being completely pathetic.

*

"I thought you were studying," Penelope says.

She's got her laptop out on a dining table and papers spread around her. There's a pot of tea, but I'm sure it's gone cold.

I lay my hand on the teapot and cast, **"Some like it hot!"** I hear the tea bubbling, and a hairline crack shoots down from the lid. "I was helping Baz with something," I say, "but now I'm done. For good."

She wrinkles her nose at the cracked teapot as I pour myself a cup. I can tell what she's thinking—*Now, that shouldn't happen*—then she jerks her head up and wrinkles her nose at me. "You were helping Baz with something?"

"Yes. It was a mistake." I sit and gulp down some tea. It burns my tongue.

"Why were you helping *Baz* with something?"

"Long story."

"I have nothing but time, Simon."

That's when we hear the first scream. I stand up, knocking the table over and breaking the teapot more conclusively.

Kids are running into the dining hall from the courtyard. They're all screaming. I catch a first year running past me, practically lifting her by the arm. "What is it?"

"Dragon!" she cries. "The Humdrum sent a dragon!"

My sword is in my hand, and I'm already running for the door. I know Penny's right behind me.

The courtyard outside is empty, but there are scorch marks on the fountain and a stripe of blackened earth. And I can feel the Humdrum in the air—the empty sucking feeling, the dry itch of him. Most Watford students recognize that feeling by now; it's as good as a siren.

I keep running through the first and second gates, and a wave of heat hits me in the archway as I'm about to step onto the drawbridge. A wall of hot breath. I hold my arm in front of my face and feel Penny grab the back of my shirt. She reaches her ring hand over my shoulder. *"U can't touch this!"*

"What's that?" I shout at her.

"Barrier spell. It won't work unless the dragon knows the song."

"How would the dragon know that song?"

"I'm doing my best, Simon!"

"I can't even see it!" I shout. "Can you?"

I can't see it, but I can hear it, I think. Flapping. A river of fire pours onto the Lawn and I look up—it's diving towards us. It looks like a red T. rex with yellow cat eyes and big rubbery red wings.

Penny's still casting spells over my shoulder to try to ground it.

"What'll we do with it on the ground?" I ask.

"Not get bombed with fire!"

I try to remember the last time I fought a dragon, but I was 11 then, and I'm pretty sure I just blew it up. *Come closer,* I think at the monster, *so I can blow you up.*

The dragon twists in the air without firing on us, and I think for a minute that one of Penny's spells is working. Then I see its target—a group of kids, maybe third years, crouching under the yew tree.

Miss Possibelf is with them, and I see her casting spells at the dragon with her walking stick. I run towards the tree, pulling my wand out of my back pocket and shouting as loud as I can at the dragon. *"Your attention, please!"*

I throw the weight of my magic into it.

The dragons stops mid-zoom to look at me, hanging in the air for a moment like it's been paused. Then it rears its head back and thrusts forward in my direction.

"Oh, blast," Penelope says. She's a few feet away. She reaches out to the school—not the dragon—and yells, **"There's nothing to see here!"**

"What are you doing?" I scream, breaking right to lead the dragon away from the buildings.

"Your attention spell worked on everyone!" Penny says. "They're all coming out to watch! **There's nothing to see here!**" she shouts again at the gates. **"As you were!"**

I glance back and see kids standing on the drawbridge and running to the edge of the ramparts. The dragon is diving again, and I decide to run at it. A ribbon of fire shoots over my head. I drop at the last moment and roll away—its teeth scrape at the ground beside me.

It pulls up, snorting in what I think is frustration, then lunges towards me, snapping its jaws. I swing my sword at its neck, and the blade catches and sticks. The dragon heaves up again, and I go with it, holding on to my sword and using the momentum to swing onto the beast's head, my knees tucked behind its jaw.

This is better. Now I can just throttle it.

The dragon's trying to swing me loose—and I'm trying to get my sword out of its hide, so that I can stab it again—when I hear Baz calling my name. I look up and see him running along the ramparts.

He must have cast some spell on his voice to make it carry. (I wonder if it's a **Hear ye, hear ye**—I've never managed that.) "Simon," he's shouting, "don't hurt it!"

Don't hurt it? Sod that. I go back to yanking on my blade.

"Simon!" Baz cries out again. "Wait! They're not dark creatures!" He gets to the end of the ramparts, but instead of stopping, he leaps up on top of the wall, then out over the moat—just takes a running jump off the building! And doesn't fall! He floats out over the moat and lands on the other side. It's the prettiest thing I've ever seen.

The dragon must think so, too, because it stops struggling with me and follows Baz with its head.

Its wings are beating less furiously. It almost lolls in the air, dipping in Baz's direction and snuffling little puffs of fire.

Baz runs towards us, then stands with his legs apart, his wand in the air.

"Baz!" I yell. "No! You're flammable!"

"So is everything!" he shouts back at me.

*"Baz!"*

But he's already pointing at the dragon and casting a spell:

***"Ladybird, ladybird, fly away home, your house is on fire, and your children are gone."***

The first line is a common spell for pests and mice and things like that. But Baz keeps going. He's trying to cast the whole nursery rhyme. Like he's Houdini himself.

***"Ladybird, ladybird, fly away home, your house is on fire and your children shall burn. All except one, and her name is Nan, and she hid under the porridge pan."***

There's nothing in our world more powerful than nursery rhymes—the poems that people learn as kids, then get stuck in their brains forever. A powerful mage can turn back an army with "Humpty Dumpty."

***"Ladybird, ladybird, fly away home, your house is on fire, and your children shall burn."***

The dragon isn't flying away home, but it's fascinated by Baz. It lands in front of him and cocks its head. One breath of fire now, that's all it would take to obliterate him.

Baz stands his ground:

***"All but one, and that's little John, and he lies under the grindle stone."***

I slide off the beast's neck, yanking my sword out with my body weight as I fall.

*"Ladybird, ladybird, fly away home, your house is on fire, and your children shall burn."*

I wonder why no one is helping him—then I look around and see every student and teacher in the school standing in the windows or out on the ramparts. All still paying attention, like I told them to. Even Penny has given in. Or maybe she's as gobsmacked as I am. Baz keeps going.

*"All except one, and her name is Aileen, and she hid under a soup tureen."*

The dragon looks back over its shoulder, and I think maybe it's thinking about hoofing it. But then it stamps, frustrated, and spreads its wings wide.

Baz lifts his voice louder. There's sweat on his forehead and along his hairline, and his hand is trembling.

I want to help, but chances are, I'd just spoil his spell. I think about taking a whack at the dragon while it's distracted, but Baz told me to stop. I move slowly until I'm standing behind him.

The dragon shakes its head and starts to turn again. I'm beginning to think it really wants to go. That it *wants* the spell to work.

*"Ladybird, ladybird, fly away home, your house is on fire, and your children shall burn."*

Baz's whole arm is shaking now.

I put my hand on his shoulder to steady him. And then I do something I've never done before—something I probably wouldn't try with anyone I was scared of hurting.

I *push.*

I take some of the magic that's always trying to get out of me, and I just push it into Baz.

His arm straightens like a rod, and his voice hitches louder—
*"away home!"*—midsentence.

The dragon's wings shudder, and it lurches back.

I push a little more magic. I worry that it's too much, but
Baz doesn't fall or crumple. His shoulder is rock hard and
steady under my palm.

*"Ladybird, ladybird, fly away home!"* he booms. The
dragon's wings are flapping frantically, and it's jerking itself
back into the air, like a plane taking off backwards.

I stop pushing and close my eyes, letting Baz draw on my
magic as he needs it. I don't want to overdo it and set him off
like a grenade in my hand.

When I open my eyes again, the dragon is a red spot
on the sky, and there's applause ringing out from the
ramparts.

*"As you were!"* Baz shouts, pointing his wand at the
school. The crowds immediately start to scatter. Then Baz
steps away from my hand and faces me.

He's looking at me like I'm a complete freak. (Which we
both already knew was true.) His right brow is arched so high,
it looks like it's broken free of his eye.

"Why did you help me?" I ask.

"Truce," Baz says, still alarmed. Then he shakes his head,
just like the dragon did when it was trying to throw off his
spell. "Anyway, I wasn't helping you." He brings his hand up
to rub the back of his neck. "I was helping the dragon. You
would have killed her."

"It was attacking the school."

"Not because she wanted to. Dragons don't attack unless
they're being threatened. And dragons don't even live in this
part of England."

Penelope runs into me like a freight train. She grabs my

hand and puts it on her shoulder. "Show me," she says. "Turn on the juice."

I pull my hand back. "What?"

She grabs it again. "I saw what just happened." She puts my hand on her shoulder. "When did you learn to do that?"

"Stop," I say, and I try to say it meaningfully, looking around at everyone who can hear us. The Lawn is full of kids, all inspecting the scorch marks and generally acting like people who almost just died but didn't. "I was just giving him moral support."

"Excellent work, gentlemen." Miss Possibelf is standing beside us; I didn't even see her walk up. "I've seldom seen such a strong and nuanced nursery rhyme, Mr. Pitch—and never a situation that so desperately required it."

Baz bows humbly. Perfectly. His hair falls forward.

"Mr. Snow," she goes on, turning to me, "perhaps you'll provide a report for the headmaster upon his return. And you can work on moderation this week in Elocution."

I dip my head. "Yes, miss."

"As you were," she says without any magic.

Penelope puts my hand on her shoulder again. I pull it away.

When I turn back to the castle, I see Agatha, the only one still watching us from the ramparts.

# 45

## SIMON

"You got Visited! And you didn't tell me!"

Penelope is standing with her hands on her hips, and I'm pretty sure she'd be casting a world of hurt at me if Baz hadn't taken away her wand.

"You told *him*?" She swings her hand at Baz. "But you didn't tell *me*?"

"It was *his* mum," I say.

"Yeah," she says, "but he wasn't even here."

"I was going to tell you, Penny, but then he came back, and everything got complicated."

"We're telling you now," Baz says.

"'We'?" she says. "Since when are you two a 'we'?"

"We're not a 'we'!" I half shout.

Baz throws his hands up in the air and falls back on his bed. "You people are impossible."

"And since *when*," Penny says to me, "are you a power outlet that other magicians can just plug in to?"

"I don't know," I say. "I've never tried it before."

"Try it again now," she says, flopping down on my bed next to me.

"Penny, no, I don't want to hurt you."

She puts my hand on her shoulder. "Simon, imagine what we could do with your power and my spells. We could finish the Humdrum off by dinner—and then take on hunger and world peace."

"Imagine what the Mage will do when he realizes he has a nuclear power generator in his backyard," Baz croons from his bed.

I swallow and look at the wall. Penny's hand drops. I have to admit that I'm not eager to tell the Mage—or anybody—what I did today. It's bad enough that I can't control my power. I don't want it pulled completely out of my hands.

Penny's hand covers mine on the bed. "Was it a special spell?" she asks softly.

"No," I say. "I just . . . pushed."

"Show me."

Baz raises himself up on one elbow to watch. I lock eyes with Penny.

"I trust you," she says.

"That doesn't mean I won't hurt you."

Penny shrugs. "Pain is temporary."

"That doesn't mean I won't *damage* you."

She shrugs again. "Come on. We have to figure out how this works."

"We never *have* to," I say. "You just always *want* to."

She squeezes my hand. "*Simon.*"

I can see she's made up her mind; she won't leave me alone until I do this. I try to remember how it felt out on the Lawn. Like I was opening, unwinding—just a little. Just barely letting go . . .

I give the very smallest *push*.

"Great snakes!" Penny says, snatching her hand away from

me and jumping off the bed. "Fuck a nine-toed *troll*, Simon." She's shaking her hand, and there are tears in her eyes. "Stevie Nicks and Gracie Slick! *Fuck!*"

I'm on my feet. "Sorry! Penny, I'm sorry, let me see!"

Baz drops back onto his bed, cackling.

Penelope holds out her arm. It looks red and mottled. "I'm so sorry," I say, gently taking her wrist. "Should we go to the nurse?"

"I don't think so," she says. "I think it's passing." Her arm is quivering. Baz gets off his bed to take a look.

"Did it feel like I cast a spell on you?" I ask.

"No," they both say at once.

"It was more like a shock," Penelope says, then looks up at Baz. "What about for you?"

He gets out his wand. "I don't know. I was focusing on the dragon."

"Did it hurt?" she asks him.

"Maybe you didn't see what you think you saw," Baz says. "Maybe Snow really *was* just giving me moral support."

"Right. And maybe you're the most gifted mage in five generations."

"Maybe I *am*," he says, tapping his ivory wand against her arm. ***"Get well soon!"***

"How did *that* feel?" I ask her.

"Better," she says reluctantly, pulling her arm away from us. She frowns at Baz—"Hot."

He grins, hitching up that eyebrow again.

"I meant temperature-wise," she says. "Your magic feels like a grease-burn, Basil."

Baz waves his wand in a shrug and turns to the chalkboard. "Runs in the family."

Like I said, everyone's magic feels different. Penelope's

magic feels thick and makes your mouth taste like sage. I quite like it.

"So . . . ," she says, following him to the chalkboard. "You got a Visiting. An actual Visiting—Natasha Grimm-Pitch was *here*."

Baz glances back over his shoulder. "You sound impressed, Bunce."

"I am," Penelope says. "Your mother was a hero. She developed a spell for gnomeatic fever. And she was the youngest headmaster in Watford history."

Baz is looking at Penny like they've never met.

"*And,*" Penny goes on, "she defended your father in three duels before he accepted her proposal."

"That sounds barbaric," I say.

"It was traditional," Baz says.

"It was brilliant," Penny says. "I've read the minutes."

"Where?" Baz asks her.

"We have them in our library at home," she says. "My dad loves marriage rites. Any sort of family magic, actually. He and my mother are bound together in five dimensions."

"That's lovely," Baz says, and I'm terrified because I think he means it.

"I'm going to make time stop when I propose to Micah," she says.

"The little American? With the thick glasses?"

"Not so little anymore."

"Interesting." Baz rubs his chin. "My mother hung the moon."

"She was a legend," Penelope beams.

"I thought your parents hated the Pitches," I say.

They both look at me like I've just stuck my hand in the soup bowl.

"That's politics," Penelope says. "We're talking about *magic*."

"Obviously," I say. "What was I thinking."

"Obviously," Baz says. "You weren't."

"What's happening right now?" I say. "What are we even doing?"

Penelope folds her arms and squints at the chalkboard. "We," she declares, "are finding out who killed Natasha Grimm-Pitch."

"The legend," Baz says.

Penelope gives him a soft look, the kind she usually saves for me. "So she can rest in peace."

# 46

## BAZ

Penelope Bunce is a fierce magician, I don't mind saying.

Well, I don't mind saying, now that she's standing momentarily on my side of things.

No wonder Snow follows her around like a congenitally stupid dog on a very short leash. I'm fairly certain we don't know anything now that we didn't know before, but Bunce is so sharp and confident that every minute with her in the room feels like progress.

Also she fixed our window, and now it doesn't creak.

I can tell she still finds me both loathsome and distasteful, but Rome wasn't built on mutual admiration. She's got a fine mind for magickal history—her house must be teeming with forbidden books—and half her opinions would get her thrown in a dungeon if her name were Pitch instead of Bunce.

(There must be mundanity in her blood somewhere; Bunce is the least magickal name in the Realm. And you should see her father, *Professor Bunce.* He's a book full of footnotes brought to life. He's a jacket made of elbow patches. He taught a special unit on the Humdrum last term, and I don't think I ever managed to follow him to the end of a sentence.)

Snow and Bunce send me down to get dinner—because

I'm the one who has an in with Cook Pritchard; she's a distant cousin—and when I come back, Bunce has a piece of green chalk, and she's adding notes to my notes in small, cramped handwriting on the blackboard.

> *Nicodemus —Check library —Ask Mum? (Any risk?) — Ask the Mage? No. —Google? Yes! (Can't hurt, Simon.)*

Even her notes are addressed to Snow. They're like Ant and Dec, the pair of them. Joined at the hip. Hmm . . . I wonder if Wellbelove will be coming aboard, too.

"Simon's right about the vampires," Bunce says without turning away from the chalkboard.

The dinner tray tilts in my hands. I stoop a bit to correct it. "What?"

"The vampires," she says, turning around and putting her hands on her hips. Her skirt is covered with chalk dust.

Snow puts down a book and comes to take the jug of milk off the tray. He lifts it towards his mouth, and I kick his shin.

"Anathema!" he says.

"I'm not trying to hurt you; I'm trying to protect you from your own disgusting manners. The room won't blame me this time, you oaf. There are glasses right here."

He sets the milk down on the table between our beds, then takes the drinking glasses and the handkerchief full of sandwiches. "Cook Pritchard just *gave* you all this?" He unwraps a stack of brownies.

"She likes me," I say.

"I thought she liked *me*," he says. "I saved her from a kitchen skink!"

"Yes, well she likes me for who I am."

"*Vampires,*" Penelope says. "Are you even listening?"

I sneer. Out of habit. "Put a sandwich in it, Bunce."

"How can we guess who sent the vampires or what the vampires even wanted," she prattles on, "if we don't know anything about vampires?"

"Vampires want blood," Snow says through a maw full of roast beef.

"But they can get that anywhere," she says. "They can get it easily. In Soho. After midnight." She picks up a sandwich and sits on Snow's bed, crossing her legs. I could see right up her skirt if I felt like it—and if I tipped my head a bit. "I can't think of a more difficult place for a vampire to get blood," she says, "than Watford, in the middle of the day."

She's got a point there.

"So why even try it?" she asks.

"Well, the term hadn't started yet," I say, picking up an apple, "so no one was on guard."

"Yeah, but it's *Watford*." She shakes her long hair. "Even back then, there was a wall of wards against dark creatures."

"It doesn't have to make sense," Snow says. "The Humdrum sent the vampires. Just like that dragon today. *It* didn't want to be here either."

I wasn't sure Snow realized that, or believed me when I told him. I thought he was going to murder that dragon hen in cold blood in front of the whole school.

Well, not in cold blood—it *was* attacking us. But slaying a dragon is dark stuff, too dark even for my family. You don't slay a dragon unless you're trying to open a doorway to hell.

"But if Headmistress Grimm-Pitch was talking about the Humdrum," Bunce says, "why would she throw that on Baz's shoulders—does she expect him to kill the Humdrum? And what about this Nicodemus?"

Snow frowns. "We should stop thinking of it as an isolated attack."

"It's the only vampire attack in the history of the school," I argue.

"Yeah," he says, "but all sorts of other stuff was going on back then. The Mage said the dark creatures thought we were getting weak—they were making a serious move on our realm."

"When did he say that?" Penny asks.

"It's in *The Record*," Snow says. "The Mage gave a speech to the Coven—even before the Watford invasion." He sticks what's left of his sandwich in his mouth and reaches around Penny for a book. His jacket and jumper are on the floor, and his white shirt tugs out of his trousers on one side.

He finds the right page soon enough, holding it out to us. I stand above them, not prepared to actually sit on Snow's bed.

It's the front page of *The Record*. The Mage's speech is printed in full, and there's a large chart with dates and bold-faced atrocities—all the attacks on magickind over a fifty-year period. **OUR DOMINION IN DANGER?** the headline asks.

"Wait a minute. . . ." Bunce takes the book from him and hands him her sandwich to hold; he takes a bite. "There's nothing about the Humdrum." She flips ahead to the story about my mother's death, then scans it with her finger. "No Humdrum here either."

She closes the book and taps the cover with her ring. ***"Fine-tooth comb—Humdrum!"*** The book opens, and the pages start rifling forward. They pick up speed towards the end; then the book slams shut on her lap.

"No mentions," Penny says.

"That doesn't make sense," I say. "The Humdrum existed

then. The first dead spot appeared in the late '90s. Near Stonehenge. We've studied it in Magickal History."

"I know," she says. "My mother was pregnant with me when it happened. She and Dad visited the site." Bunce takes what's left of her sandwich back from Snow and takes a bite. She looks up at me, chewing suspiciously. "I wonder how they knew . . ."

"Who?" I ask. "What?"

"I wonder how they figured out that it was the Humdrum behind everything," Bunce says, "behind the dark creature attacks and the dead spots? How would they know it was him before they knew how he felt? That's how we identify him now. That *feeling*."

"Did you feel the Humdrum?" Snow asks. "That day in the nursery?"

"I was a bit distracted," I say.

"What did they tell you?" Bunce asks.

"What did who tell me?"

"Your family. After your mother died."

"They didn't tell me anything. What was there to say?"

"Did they tell you it was vampires?"

"They didn't have to tell me that. I was there."

"Do you remember?" she asks. "Did you see the vampires?"

"Yes." I set the apple back on the tray.

Snow clears his throat. "Baz, when *did* you first hear that it was the Humdrum who sent the vampires?"

They're imagining my father sitting me down in a leather club chair and saying, *"Basilton, there's something I need to tell you. . . ."*

He's never said those words.

Nobody *tells* anyone anything in my family. You just know. You learn to know.

No one had to tell me that we talk about Mother, but we don't talk about Mother's death.

No one had to tell me I was a vampire:

I remembered being bitten, I grew up with the same horror stories everyone else did—then I woke up one day craving blood. And no one had to *tell* me not to take it from another person.

"I learned it in school," I say. "Same as you." They both look surprised.

"What happened to the vampires?" Snow asks. "Not the ones your mother killed—the others."

"The Mage drove most of them out of England," I say. "I think it's the only time my family has co-operated with his raids."

"Mum says the war started with the vampire raids," Bunce says.

"Which war?" Snow asks.

"All of them," she says. She leans over Snow's lap to reach the brownies.

I take a sandwich and the apple, and stand up. "I need some air."

I wait until I'm down in the Catacombs to tuck in. I don't really like eating in front of people.

# 47

## SIMON

Penny is back at the chalkboard, making notes.

> *Talk to Dad at Xms break. OK to wait that long? Ask him to send notes?*

"Why *all* of them?" I ask.

"Hmm?"

"Why all the wars? Why did they *all* start with the vampire raids?"

"The war with the dark things started there," she says. "That should be obvious. I mean, mages and vampires have never got on—we need Normals alive, and they need them dead. But invading Watford, that was an act of war. And it was the first real attack by the Humdrum, too."

"What about the war with the Old Families?"

"Well, the Mage's reforms started then," she says.

"I wish there were just one war," I say. "And one enemy that I could get my head around."

"Wow," Penny says, finally turning away from the board, "what are you going to do with yourself now that you don't have Baz?"

"I still have Baz."

"Not as an enemy."

"We're just having a truce," I say.

"A magic-sharing truce."

"Penny." I frown and lie back on my bed. I'm knackered.

I feel her climbing up next to me. "Try again," she says, taking my hand.

"No."

"Why did you try with Baz?"

"I didn't," I say. "I just wanted to help him, and I didn't know how. So I put my hand on him and *thought* about helping him."

"It was pretty extraordinary."

"Do you think everyone could tell?"

"No . . . Maybe. I don't know. *I* couldn't tell, not for certain—and I was the closest. But I saw him stand straighter when you touched him. And then the spell started working. There's no way that Baz is powerful enough to chant back a dragon. . . ." She squeezes my hand. "Try again."

I squeeze hers back. "No. I'll hurt you."

"You didn't hurt Baz."

"Maybe I *did*—he'd never admit it."

"Maybe it didn't hurt him," she says, "because he's already dead."

"Baz isn't dead."

"Well he's not alive."

"I . . . I think he is," I say. "He has magic. That's life."

"Morgan's tooth—imagine if you *could* do it again. If you could actually control your power, Simon."

"Baz was the one controlling my power."

"It was like you were focused for the first time—directed. You were using him like a wand."

I close my eyes. "I wasn't using him."

# 48

## BAZ

When I come back, Bunce is gone. I can tell she's been sitting on my bed again—it smells like her. Like blood and chocolate and kitchen herbs. I'll snap at her about it tomorrow.

Snow has showered, the room is humid from it, but our papers and dinner things are still scattered on the table and the floor. It's like having two slovenly roommates.

The chalkboard is in order, though, completely filled with Bunce's tight-fisted handwriting and pushed against the wall.

I take my jacket off and spell it clean, hanging it in my wardrobe. My tie's tucked in the pocket. I pull it out and loop it around the hanger.

I ate my sandwich down in the basement, washing it down with a few rats. I need to go hunting in the Wood again; the rats are getting few and far between in the Catacombs, even though I try not to take the females.

It's a pain to hunt in the Wood. I have to do it during the day because the Mage brings the drawbridge up at dusk, and I can't **Float like a butterfly** over the moat every night like I did today; I don't have the magic.

I look over my shoulder at Snow—a long, blanketed lump on his bed.

*He* has the magic.

He could do anything.

I'm still humming with his magic, and it's been hours since he pulled his hand away. He's thrown spells at me before, but this was different. This was like being struck by benevolent lightning. I felt scorched clean. Bottomless . . .

No, that's not right, not bottomless. *Centreless.* Like I was bigger on the inside. Like I could cast any spell—back up any promise.

At first it was as if Snow was giving magic to me. Sending it to me. But then the magic was just *there.* It was mine, in that moment, everything that was his.

All right. I have to stop thinking about it like this. Like it was a gift. Snow would never have opened himself up to me if there hadn't been a dragon overhead. . . .

I wonder if I could *take* the magic from him if I tried, but the thought turns my stomach.

I change in the bathroom and brush my teeth, and when I come out, I see that Snow is sitting up in his bed.

"Baz?"

"What." I sit on my own bed, on top of the covers.

"I . . . can you come here?"

"No."

"I can come over there, then."

I cross my legs and arms. "You may not."

Snow huffs, exasperated. *Good,* I think.

"Just. Come here," he says. "Okay? I have to try something."

"Can you even hear how ridiculous you sound?"

He gets up. It's dark in our room, but the moon is out, and I can always see him better than he sees me. He's wearing grey flannel pyjama bottoms, school-issued, and his gold cross. His skin is as grey as mine in this light, and shining like a pearl.

"You can't sit on my bed," I say as he sits on my bed. "And neither can Bunce. My bed reeks of intensity and brownies."

"Here," he says, holding out his hand.

"What do you *want* from me, Snow?"

"Nothing," he says. And he means it, the actual bastard. "We have to try again."

"Why?"

"So that we know that it wasn't a fluke," he says.

"It *was* a fluke. You were fighting a dragon, and I was helping you—it was a fluke squared."

"Merlin, Baz, don't you want to know?"

"Whether I can tap into you like a generator?"

"It wasn't like that," he says. "I let you do it."

"Are you going to let me do it again?"

"No."

"Then it doesn't matter if it was a fluke!"

Snow's still sitting on my bed. "All right," he says. "Maybe."

"Maybe what?"

"Maybe I'd do it again," he says. "If it were a situation like today—if there were lives at risk, and this might be a solution, an option other than, you know, *going off.*"

"What if I turned it against you?"

"My magic?"

"Yes," I say. "What if I took your magic, cast it against you, and settled Baz versus Simon, once and for all."

Snow's mouth is hanging slightly open. His tongue shines black in the dark. "Why are you such a villain?" He sounds disgusted. "Why have you *already* thought of that?"

"I thought of it when I was still rhyming at the dragon," I say. "Didn't you?"

"*No.*"

"This is why I'm going to beat you," I say.

"We're on a truce," Snow says.

"I can still *think* antagonistically. I'm thinking violent thoughts at you constantly."

He grabs my hand. I want to pull it away, but I don't want to look scared—and also I *don't* want to pull it away. Bloody Snow. I'm thinking violent thoughts at him right now.

"I'm going to try now," he says.

"Fine."

"Should you be casting a spell?"

"I don't know," I say. "This is your experiment."

"Don't, then," he says. "Not right away. But tell me if it hurts."

"It didn't hurt before," I mutter.

"It didn't?"

"No."

"What *did* it feel like?"

"Stop talking about feelings," I say, shaking his hand. "Hit me. Or charge me. Whatever it is you want to do."

Snow licks his bottom lip and closes his eyes halfway. Is this how he looked this afternoon? *Crowley.*

I feel his magic.

At first it's a buzz in my fingertips, then a rush of static up my arm. I try not to squirm.

"Okay?" he asks. His voice is soft.

"Fine. What are you doing?"

"I don't know," he murmurs. "Opening? I guess?"

The static in my arm settles into a heavy thrum, like electrical sparks catching into flames. The discomfort goes away, even though the licking, flaming feeling gets stronger. This I know what to do with: This is fire.

"Still okay?" he asks.

"Grand," I say.

"What does that mean—does that mean you could use it?"

I laugh, and it comes out more good-natured than I mean it to. "Snow. I think I could cast a sonnet right now."

"Show me," he says.

I'm so full of power, I feel like I can see without opening my eyes. Like I could go nova if I wanted to and have my own galaxy. Is this what it's like to be Simon Snow? To have infinity in your chest pocket?

I speak clearly: *"Twinkle, twinkle little star!"*

By the time I get to the end of the next phrase, the room around us is gone, and the stars feel close enough to touch.

*"Up above the world so high!"*

Simon grabs my other hand, and my chest opens wider. "Merlin and Morgana," he says. "Are we in space?"

"I don't know," I say.

"Is that a spell?" he asks.

"I don't know."

We both look around us. I don't *think* we're in space; I can breathe just fine. And I don't feel like floating away—though I am teetering on the edge of hysterical. So much power. So many stars. My mouth tastes like smoke. "Are you holding back at all?" I ask him.

"Not consciously," Snow says. "Is it too much?"

"No. It's like you completed the circuit," I say, gripping his other hand. "I feel kind of drunk, though."

"Drunk on power?" he asks.

I giggle. "Shit, Snow. Stop talking. This is embarrassing."

"Do you want me to pull back?"

"No. I want to look at the stars."

"I'm pulling back," he says.

And then he does. It feels like the tide going out—if the

tide were made of heroin and fire.

I shake my head. I don't let go of Snow's hands.

"All right?" he asks.

"Yeah. You?"

"Fine."

Now we're just sitting on my bed, holding hands, Simon Snow and I. I can't look at his eyes, so I stare at his cross.

"Your mother . . . ," he says. "When she came back, she said that thing about stars. *'He said we'd be stars.'*"

"I think that's a coincidence," I say.

"Yeah." Simon nods. "Do you have any of it left? Like, did it stay with you? My magic?"

"Residually?" I ask.

"Yeah."

I shake my head. "No. A feeling. A hum. Not power."

"Can you do it on your end?"

"What do you mean?"

"We're still touching," he says. "Try to tap into it."

I close my eyes and try to be open, try to be a vacuum or a black hole. Nothing happens. I try to pull at Snow, then. To suck at him with my own magic . . . Still nothing.

I open my eyes. "No. I can't take it from you. I've never heard of a magician taking someone else's magic. Can you imagine? If there were a spell for that? We'd tear each other apart."

"We're already tearing each other apart."

"I can't take it," I say again.

"Do you think it hurt you, my magic?"

"I don't think so."

"So we could do it again."

"We just did, Snow."

He looks uncharacteristically thoughtful. I wonder if he's forgotten that he's holding my hands. Or if he's forgotten what it *means* to hold hands. Or if he's forgotten who I am entirely.

I think again about pulling my hands away—but Snow could light fires in my palms at this point, and I wouldn't pull away. It feels like he has.

"Baz," he says, and it's not unprecedented for him to say my name, but I know he avoids it. "This is stupid. If we're going to be working together, you can't keep pretending that I don't know."

"Don't know what," I say, yanking my hands back.

"Don't know about you. What you are."

"Get off my bed, Snow."

"It won't change anything—"

"Won't it?"

"Well, it *would* make things easier," he says. "How can we discuss what we know about vampires when you won't even admit that you are one?"

*"Get off my bed."*

Snow stands up, but doesn't stand down. "I *know*. I've known since our fifth year. How're we supposed to help you if you're still keeping all these secrets? Like, why did you start school late this term? And what happened to you? And why are you limping?"

"That's none of your business," I hiss. "None of it."

"You're right, but you said you wanted my help. So you made it my business."

"I'll tell you whatever I think is relevant."

"We're supposed to find out who sent blood-sucking vampires to kill your mother, and you *are* a blood-sucking vampire. You don't think that's relevant?"

As if I can just admit that. Out loud. On the record. As if every other magician wouldn't gladly light me up if they knew it to be true.

As if Snow himself hasn't been trying to expose me every day for seven years.

I clamp my jaw shut.

I should leave. Go back to the Catacombs. But Snow's magic has wiped me out—I'm not sure I could stand now. So I just close my eyes.

"I'm done with you today," I say. "I've been struck by lightning twice in the last twelve hours, and now I'm just done."

# 49

## SIMON

Agatha wants to talk to me after our Magic Words lesson.

She hasn't said a word to me since we broke up—she hardly even looks at me—so when she approaches me now, my initial response is to look at the floor and try to walk around her. She has to grab my sleeve to get my attention, which is awkward for both of us.

"Simon," she says. "Could I talk to you?"

She looks so nervous; she's biting her bottom lip. I have to admit, my first thought is that Agatha misses me. That she wants to get back together.

I'll say yes, of course. I won't even make her ask. We can go right back to how we were. Maybe I'll even tell her what's going on with Baz—maybe she can help.

Then I think about Agatha being in the close quarters of our room, close enough that Baz can smell her pulse—and decide that I won't tell her about everything, not right away.

But I will take her back.

This has all been such shit. Ignoring each other. Sitting apart. Acting like enemies when all we've ever been is friends.

I'll take her back. Just in time for Christmas.

I've been thinking a lot about Christmas lately. I always spend it with the Wellbeloves. I have since I first came to Watford.

I think at first it must have been a philanthropic thing for her dad, Dr. Wellbelove. That's exactly the sort of thing he'd do—open the house up on Christmas to orphans.

It's how Agatha and I got to be friends. I'm not sure she ever would have talked to me if she hadn't been trapped with me in her house every year for two weeks.

It's not that Agatha's stuck up—

Well . . . She is a bit stuck up. I think she likes being prettier than everyone else and having better clothes and being luckier.

I can't blame her for that.

But also, she's just not that social. Especially at school. She used to be really involved in dance, before Watford, and she's still all caught up in horses, and I think she's closer to her summer Normal friends than anybody here.

Agatha's not like Penny. She doesn't naturally care about magickal politics. And she's not like me, she doesn't *have* to care.

I don't think Agatha cares that much about magic, full stop. The last time we talked about the future, she was thinking about becoming a veterinarian.

Dr. Wellbelove is all about Normal–magickal equality, and how it doesn't serve mages to think of ourselves as better than Normals. ("I get what Welby's saying," Penelope's mum will say, "but we can do everything the Normals can do, *plus* magic. How is that not better?")

Her dad's never pressured Agatha to choose a magickal career. I think she could probably even date a Normal, if she wanted. (Her mum might mind that; Normals aren't allowed at the club.)

Anyway, I love being at the Wellbeloves, so long as they're not throwing a posh dinner or dragging me through event season. Everything in their house is brand new and top of the line. They have a TV that takes up an entire wall, with giant speakers hidden behind paintings of horses, and all their couches are made of leather.

Agatha's mum's always out, and her dad's usually at the clinic. (He's a Normal doctor, too, but most of his patients are mages. He specializes in acute abNormal ailments.) They've got a maid-type person, Helen, who cooks for Agatha and drives her around. But nobody treats Helen like a maid. She dresses in regular clothes, not any uniform, and she's obsessed with *Doctor Who*.

They're all good to me, Helen included. Agatha's mum gives me nice clothes for Christmas, and her dad talks to me about my future like I'm not going to die in a ball of fire.

I just really like them. And I like Christmas. And I've been thinking about how weird it's going to be to sit around the dinner table, talking to Agatha's parents, knowing that we're broke up.

Agatha and I stay in the Magic Words classroom after everyone else leaves.

She's still biting her lip.

"Agatha . . . ," I say.

"It's about Christmas," she says.

She pushes her hair behind her ears. She has perfectly straight hair that parts in the middle and naturally frames her face. (Penny says it's a spell. Agatha says it is *not*. Penny says beauty spells are nothing to be *ashamed* of.)

"My dad wants you to know that of course you're still

welcome at our house for Christmas," Agatha says.

"Oh," I say. "Good."

"But I think we both know how uncomfortable that would be," she goes on. She looks very uncomfortable, just saying it. "For both of us."

"Right," I say. It would be uncomfortable, I guess.

"It would ruin Christmas," she says.

I stop myself before I can say, *"Would it? Would it really, Agatha? It's a big house, and I'll stay in the TV room the whole time."*

"Right," I say instead.

"So I told him that you were probably going to stay with the Bunces."

Agatha knows I can't stay with the Bunces. Penelope's mum can only take about two or three days of me before she starts treating me like a Great Dane who can't help knocking things over with its tail.

The Bunces' house isn't small, but it's full of people—and stacks and stacks of stuff. Books, papers, toys, dishes. There's no way not to be underfoot. You'd have to be incorporeal not to knock anything over.

"Right," I say to Agatha. "Okay."

She looks at the floor. "I'm sure my parents will still send gifts."

"I'll send them a card."

"That would be nice," she says. "Thank you." She pulls her satchel up over her shoulder and takes a step away from me— then stops and flips her hair out of her face. (It's just a gesture; her hair is never in her face.) "Simon. It was amazing how you beat that dragon. You saved its life."

I shrug. "Yeah, well, Baz did it, didn't he? I would've slit its throat if I could have figured out how."

"My dad says the Humdrum sent it."

I shrug again.

"Merry Christmas, Simon," Agatha says. Then she walks past me out the door.

# 50

## SIMON

"You should really just let me stay in your room," Penelope says. "It would make things easier."

"*No*," Baz and I say at once.

"Where would you sleep," I ask, "the bathtub?"

The chalkboard is still taking up the open area at the end of our beds, and there are stacks of books around it now. Every useful book in the Watford library has made its way to our room, thanks to Baz and Penelope—and not a one of them properly checked out, I'm sure.

We've been working here every night, though we don't have much but a mess to show for it.

"I don't mind sleeping in the bath," Penny says. "I could spell it squishy."

"No," Baz says. "It's bad enough sharing a bathroom with Snow."

"Penny, you have a perfectly good room," I say, ignoring the jab.

"Simon, a perfectly good room wouldn't have Trixie in it."

"That's your roommate?" Baz asks. "The pixie?"

"Yes," Penelope says.

He curls his lips up and down at the same time. "Imagine

you're a pixie," he says. "I know it's distasteful, but imagine—you're a *pixie*, and you have a daughter, and you name her *Trixie. Trixie the pixie.*"

"I think it's kind of cute," I say.

"You think *Trixie's* kind of cute," Penny says.

"Trixie *is* cute." I shrug.

"Snow," Baz says. "I've just eaten."

I roll my eyes. He probably thinks pixies are a lesser species. Half-sentient, like gnomes and Internet trolls.

"It's like being a fairy named Mary," he goes on.

"Or a vampire named Gampire," I say.

"Gampire isn't even a proper name, Snow. You're terrible at this game."

"In Trixie's defence," Penelope says, and you can tell it pains her to say it, "the pixies probably don't go around calling themselves 'pixies.' I mean, you could be a human named Newman or a boy named Roy, and no one would think twice."

"I'll bet your room is covered in pixie dust," Baz says, shuddering.

"*Don't* get her started," I say. "Good-night, Penny."

"Fine," she says, climbing to her feet and picking up the book she was reading. It's a bound copy of *The Record;* we've all taken to reading them straight through, looking for clues. We're becoming experts in decade-old current events.

It's all so weird. . . .

Not just to be working with Baz, but to have him around all the time when I'm hanging out with Penny.

He still won't talk to us outside of the room.

Baz says it would confuse his minions to see him consorting with the enemy. He actually called them that—"my minions." Maybe he was taking the piss. . . .

I can't always tell when Baz is mocking me. He's got a cruel mouth. It looks like he's sneering even when he's happy about something. Actually, I don't know if he ever *is* happy. It's like he's got two emotions—pissed off and sadistically amused.

(And plotting, is that an emotion? If so, three.)

(And disgusted. Four.)

Anyway, Penelope and I still don't tell Baz everything. We never talk about the Mage, for example—it turns immediately into a fight if we do. Plus Penny doesn't want Baz to know that her family might be on the outs with the Mage. (Even though Baz'd probably sympathize.)

Penny keeps reminding me that Baz is still my enemy. That when the truce ends, he could use everything he's learned against me.

But I'm not sure *I'm* the one who needs reminding. Half the time we're together, I'm just sitting on my bed reading while Penelope and Baz are comparing their Top 10 favourite spells of the 1800s or debating the magickal worth of *Hamlet* versus *Macbeth*.

The other day, he walked her over to the Cloisters on his way to the Catacombs. When he came back, he reported that there weren't any clues about how she gets into Mummers House. The next day, she told me he didn't acknowledge at all that he was on his way to suck blood out of rodents.

"You going my way?" she says to him now, from the doorway.

"No, I'm in for the night," he says.

So fucking weird.

"See you guys at breakfast," Penny says, closing the door behind her.

If Baz isn't going hunting tonight, I may as well take a shower and go to sleep. We tend to fight more viciously when it's just the two of us.

I'm getting my pyjamas together when he speaks up:

"So what's your plan next week? For the holidays?"

I feel my jaw tighten. "Probably go home with Penny for a few days, then spend the rest of it here."

"Not celebrating round the Wellbelove family hearth?"

I slam my wardrobe shut. We haven't talked about this yet. Me and Baz. About Agatha.

I don't know if the pair of them're talking. Or meeting. Agatha doesn't even come to dinner anymore. I think she eats in her room.

"Nope," I say, walking past his bed.

"Snow," he says.

"What."

"You should come to Hampshire."

I stop and look at him. "What? *Why?*"

Baz clears his throat and folds his arms, lifting his chin to emphasize how much he looks down on me.

"Because you've sworn to help me find my mother's killer."

"I *am* helping you."

"Well, you'll be more help to me there than you are here. The library at home is far too big for me to cover myself. And I have a car there—we could actually investigate. You don't even have the Internet here."

"You're suggesting I go home with you."

"Yes."

"For Christmas."

"Yes."

"With your family."

Baz rolls his eyes. "Well, it's not like you have any family of your own."

"You're mad." I move again towards the bathroom.

"How is it mad?" he demands. "I could use your help, and

there's nothing here for you—you'd think you'd appreciate the company."

I stop at the door and turn back again. "Your family *hates* me."

"Yes, and? So do I."

"They want to kill me," I say.

"They won't kill you—you'll be a guest. I'll even cast the spell if you want. **Be our guest.**"

"I can't stay in your house. Are you kidding me?"

"Snow, we've lived in the same room for seven years. How can you have a problem with this?"

"You're mad!" I say, closing the door.

Completely off his nut.

"Your mum doesn't *trust* me?" I say.

We're walking down the hall, and Penelope immediately starts shushing me with her hand. "She *does* trust you," she says. "She trusts you completely. She knows that you're honest and forthright, and that if you hear something you shouldn't, you'll go right to the Mage with it."

"I wouldn't!"

"You might, Simon."

"Penny!"

"*Shhhhh.*"

"*Penny,*" I try again, more quietly, "I'd never do anything to get your mother in trouble with the Mage. And I can't imagine she's done anything that *would* get her in trouble with the Mage."

"She's sent his Men away again," Penny says. "Premal says the Mage himself is coming to the house next time."

"Then I should be there," I say. "He'd never hurt her in front of me."

Penny stops in her tracks. "Simon. Do you really think the Mage would hurt my mother at all?"

I stop, too. "No. Of course he wouldn't."

She leans in. "Mum's filing an appeal with the Coven; she thinks this will work itself out. But you *know* I need to research the Watford Tragedy while I'm home, and there's no way Mum will let you into our library with everything that's happening. She calls you Mini-Mage."

"Why doesn't she like me?"

"She likes you," Penny says, rolling her eyes. "It's him she doesn't like."

"Your mother does not like me, Penny."

"She just thinks you attract trouble. And you do, Simon. Possibly literally."

"Yeah, but I can't help it."

Penelope starts walking again. "You are preaching to the head of the choir."

It's not that I mind being alone at Watford—I don't mind it *much*. But nobody's here on Christmas Day. I'll have to break in to the kitchen to eat. I guess I could ask Cook Pritchard for the key. . . .

We get to my next lesson, and I intentionally slam my shoulder into the wall next to the door. (People who tell you that slamming and bashing into things won't make you feel better haven't slammed or bashed enough.) "Is that what we're calling it now?" I ask. "'*The Watford Tragedy*'?"

It takes Penny a second to backtrack in our conversation. "It's what they called it at the time," she says. "What does it matter what we call it?"

"Nothing. Just. We're doing this because somebody died. Baz's mum died. 'The Watford Tragedy' makes it sound like it happened to people far away who don't matter to us."

"Tell the Mage you're staying here for Christmas," she says. "He'll want to spend it with you."

That makes me laugh.

"What?" Penny asks.

"Can you imagine?" I say. "Christmas with the Mage?"

"Singing carols," she giggles.

"Pulling crackers."

"Watching the Queen's speech."

"Think of the *gifts*," I say, laughing. "He'd probably wrap up a curse for me just to see if I could break it."

"Blindfold you, drop you in the Hell of the Wood, and tell you to come home with dinner."

"Ha!" I grin. "Just like in our third year."

Penny pokes my arm, and I slide away, along the wall. "Talk to him," she says. "He's a mad git, but he cares about you."

Baz is one of the last students to leave for break. He takes his time packing his leather trunk. He's got most of our notes in there. . . . He still hasn't decided whether to talk to his parents about all this, but he's going to find out what he can. "Someone has to know something about Nicodemus."

I'm lying on my bed, trying to think about how nice it will be to have the room to myself—and trying not to watch him. I clear my throat. "Be careful, yeah? I mean, we don't know who this Nicodemus is, and if he's dangerous, we don't want him to twig that we're looking for him."

"I'll talk only to people I trust," Baz says.

"Yeah, but that's it, isn't it—we don't *know* who to trust."

"Do you trust Penelope?"

"Yes."

"Do you trust her mother?"

"I trust her not to be evil."

"Well, I trust my family. It doesn't matter whether you do."

"I'm just telling you to be careful," I say.

"Stop showing concern for my well-being, Snow. It's making me ill at ease." He closes the lid of his trunk and snaps the latches. Then he looks at me, frowning, and decides something. I'm familiar with that look. I put my hand over the hilt of my sword.

"Snow . . . ," he says.

"What."

"I feel like I should tell you something. In the interest of our truce."

I look over at him, waiting.

"That day you saw Wellbelove and me in the Wood . . ."

I close my eyes. "How can this possibly be in the interest of our truce?"

He keeps going: "That day you saw me with Wellbelove in the Wood—it's not what you think."

I open my eyes. "You weren't trying to pull my girlfriend?"

"No."

"Sod off," I say. "You've been trying to get between me and Agatha since the day she chose me over you."

"She never chose you over me."

"Get over yourself, Baz."

He looks pained; that's a new one. "No," he goes on. "What I'm saying is—I've never been an option for Wellbelove."

I push my head back into my pillow. "I shouldn't have thought so, but apparently, I was wrong. Look, you've got a clear shot at her now. She's done with me."

"She *interrupted* me," he says. "That day in the Wood."

I ignore him.

"She interrupted my *dinner*. She saw me. I was asking her not to tell anyone."

"And you had to hold her hands for that?"

"I only did that bit to piss you off. I knew you were watching."

"Well, it worked," I say.

"You're not listening." He's looking very pained now. "I'm not *ever* going to come between you and Wellbelove. I was always just trying to piss you off."

"Are you saying you flirted with Agatha just to hurt me?"

"*Yes.*"

"You never cared about her?"

"*No.*"

I grit my teeth. "And you think I want to hear that?"

"Well, obviously. Now you can make up with her and have the best Christmas ever."

"You're such an arse!" I say, jumping to my feet and charging at him.

"Anathema!" he shouts, and I hear him, but I almost plant my fist in his jaw anyway.

I stop just short. "Does she know?"

He shrugs.

"You're *such* an arse."

"It was just flirting," Baz says. "It's not like I tried to feed her to a chimera."

"Yeah, but she *likes* you," I say. "I think she likes you better than me."

He tilts his head and shrugs again. "Why wouldn't she?"

"Fuck you, Baz. Seriously." I'm standing so close, I'm practically spitting in his face. "She was carrying around your bloody handkerchief, that whole time you were gone. Since last year."

"What handkerchief?"

I go to the drawer where the handkerchief is shoved in

with my wand and a few other things, then I wave it in his face. "This one."

Baz pulls the fabric out of my hand, and I pull it right back because I don't want him to have it. I don't want him to have anything right now.

"Look," he says. "I'll stop. I'll leave Wellbelove alone from now on. She doesn't matter to me."

"That makes it worse!"

"Then I *won't* stop!" he says, like he's the one who should be angry. "Is that better? I'll damned well marry her, and we'll have the best-looking kids in the history of magic, and we'll name them all Simon just to get under your skin."

"Just go!" I shout. "*Seriously.* If I have to look at you anymore, I won't even care about the Anathema. If I get kicked out of Watford, at least I'll finally be done with you!"

# 51

## BAZ

I was trying to do Snow a favour.

A favour that doesn't serve my interests at all—*at all*.

I bloody well should marry Wellbelove. My father would love it.

Marry her. Give her the keys to whatever she wants keys to. Then find a thousand men who look exactly like Simon bloody Snow and break each of their hearts a different way.

Wellbelove isn't very powerful, but she's gorgeous. And she's got a great seat; she and my stepmother could go riding.

Then my father could stop wringing his hands about the Pitch name dying with me. (Even though the Pitch line *already* died with me; I'm fairly certain vampires can't have babies.) (Crowley, could you imagine vampire babies? What a nightmare.) (And why doesn't Aunt Fiona pass on *her* bloody name? If my mother gave me hers, Fiona can surely provide the world with a few more Pitches.)

I think if I got married, to a girl from a good family, my father wouldn't even care that I'm queer. Or who fathered his grandchildren. If the idea of passing on my mother's name that way didn't turn my stomach, I'd consider it.

Snow would probably find a whole new way to hate me if

he knew I thought this coldly about love and sex and marriage. About his perfect Agatha.

But what does it even *matter* if my intentions are never good? My road to hell isn't paved with good intentions—or bad—it's just my road.

Go ahead, Snow. Forgive your girlfriend. I'm not standing in your way. Go stand on bloody hilltops together and watch the sun set in each other's hair—I'm done being a nuisance. *I'm done. Truce.*

I didn't expect to mend any fences with all this . . . *co-operating*. I didn't expect to convince or convert Snow. But I thought we were making progress. Like, maybe when this was all over, he and I would still be standing on either side of the trench, but we wouldn't be spitting at each other. We wouldn't be spoiling for the fight.

I know Simon and I will always be enemies. . . .

But I thought maybe we'd get to a point where we didn't want to be.

# 52

## SIMON

With Penny (and Baz) gone, I spend a lot of time walking around the school grounds. I decide to look for the nursery. . . .

Baz thinks the Weeping Tower swallowed it after his mum died. Penny says that can happen sometimes when a magician is tied to a building, especially if they've cast blood magic there. When their blood is spilled, it hurts the building, too. The place forms sort of a cyst around it.

I think about what might happen if I died in Mummers House—after all the times I've spilled my blood to let our room recognize me.

This is one reason Penny doesn't like blood oaths and spells. *"If you're as good as your word, words should be good enough."*

I'm quoting her again. I've been having conversations with her in my head all day. Sometimes Baz joins the imaginary conversation, too—usually to tell me I'm a twat . . . though he never uses that word, even in my head. Too vulgar.

I'm rattling around the Weeping Tower that way, talking to myself and poking my nose in corners when something out the window catches my eye. I see a line of goats moving through the snow across the drawbridge. A figure that must be Ebb trails behind them.

Ebb. *Ebb* . . .

Ebb's been at Watford since she was 11—and she's at least 30 or 40 now. She must have been here when Headmistress Pitch died. Ebb never left.

The goats are back in their barn by the time I get out there. I knock at the door—I don't want to give Ebb a shock; she lives out here with the goats.

I know that's strange, but honestly, it's hard to imagine Ebb living around other people. Other staff members. She can do as she likes in the barn. The goats don't mind.

"Hiya, Ebb!" I say, knocking some more. "It's me, Simon."

The door opens and one of the goats peeks its muzzle out before Ebb herself appears. "Simon!" she says, holding the door wide and waving me in. "What're you doing here? I thought everybody had gone home."

"I just came by to say Happy Christmas," I say, following her into the barn. It's warmer inside, but not by much. No wonder Ebb's dressed like she is—her ratty Watford jumper layered over another jumper, with a long striped school scarf and a mess of a knit hat. "Snakes alive, Ebb, it's cold as a witch's wit in here."

"It's not so bad," she says. "Come on, I'll build up the fire."

We walk through the goats to the back of the barn, which serves as Ebb's sitting room. She's got a little table and a rug back here—and a TV set, the only one at Watford, as far as I know. Everything's set up around a potbelly stove that isn't connected to any wall or chimney.

That's the best part of visiting Ebb—she doesn't care at all about wasting magic. Half the things that come out of her mouth are spells, but I've never seen her magic-thin or exhausted.

The stove is magicked, I'm sure. And she probably uses magic to watch football matches.

*"Why doesn't she put in a magickal shower?"* Agatha asked, the last time she visited Ebb with me—which must have been years ago. I don't know where Ebb washes up. Maybe she just **Clean as a whistle**s every morning.

(I had the same idea when I was 13, but Penny gave me a lecture about whistles not being very clean, actually, and **Clean as a whistle** only taking care of the dirt you can see.)

Ebb feeds some branches into the stove and pokes at the fire. "Well, Happy Christmas yourself," she says. "You caught me just in time. Going home tomorrow."

"To see your family?" I ask.

Ebb's from East London. She nods.

"Do you need someone to watch over the goats?"

"Nah, I'll let them wander the grounds. What about you? Off to Agatha's?"

"No," I say. "I thought I'd stay here. My last year and all, trying to soak up as much Watford as I can."

"You can always come back, Simon—I did. You want some coffee? 'Fraid all I've got out here is coffee. No, wait, I've got some Rich Tea biscuits. Let's eat 'em before they go soft."

I turn over a bucket and sit close to the fire. Ebb fusses at the cupboards she's nailed to the back of the barn. She's got shelves hanging there, too, crammed with dusty ceramic animals.

When I was a second year, I gave Ebb a little breakable goat for Christmas; I'd found it over the summer at a car boot sale. She fussed over it so much that I brought her bric-a-brac every Christmas for a few years. Goats and sheep and donkeys.

I'm feeling shamefully empty-handed when Ebb hands me a chipped mug of coffee and a stack of biscuits.

"I'm not sure what I'd do around here," I say. "I don't think Watford needs two goatherds." One of the smaller goats has wandered over and is nuzzling at my knee. I hold out a biscuit in my palm, and it takes it.

Ebb smiles and settles into her easy chair. "We'd find something for you. It's not like there was an opening when Mistress Pitch brought me on."

"Baz's mum," I say, scratching the goat's ears. Getting Ebb to talk about all this might be easier than I thought.

"The same," she says. "Now, *there* was a powerful magician."

"Did you know her well?"

Ebb takes a bite of biscuit. "Well, she taught Magic Words when I was in school," she says, puffing crumbs out onto her dirty scarf. "And she was the headmistress. So I guess I knew her that way. We certainly didn't move in the same circles, you understand—but after my brother Nicky passed, my family didn't move in any circles at all."

Ebb's brother died when she was in school. She talks about him a lot, even though it gets her all worked up and morose every time. This is one reason Penny never took to Ebb. *"She's so melancholy. Even the goats seem bummed out."*

The goats seem fine to me. A few are poking around Ebb's chair, and the little beggar has settled down at my feet.

"I was afraid to leave Watford," Ebb goes on, "and Mistress Pitch told me I didn't have to. Looking back, she was probably worried I'd get up to my own brand of trouble. I always had more power than sense. I was a powder keg—Nicky and I both were. Mistress Pitch did a service to magic when she took me in and told me not to worry about what was next. Power doesn't have to be a burden, she said. If it's too heavy 'round your neck, keep it somewhere else. In a drawer. Under your bed. *'Let it go, Ebeneza,'* she said. *'You were born with it, but it doesn't have to be your destiny.'* Which is never what my da told me . . . I wonder if Mistress Pitch would have been so forgiving if I was one of her own."

I'm giggling and trying not to spit out wet biscuit.

"What?" she says. "This is supposed to be an inspirational story."

"Your name is Ebeneza?"

"It's a perfectly good name! Very traditional." She laughs, too, and shoves an entire biscuit into her mouth, washing it down with coffee.

"She sounds good," I say. "Baz's mum."

"Well, yeah. I mean, she was fierce as a lion. And darker than most people were comfortable with—all the Pitches are—and she fought the reforms with her own teeth and nails. But she loved Watford. She loved magic."

"Ebb . . . how *did* your brother die?" I've never asked her that before. I've never wanted to upset Ebb any more than she already was.

She immediately shifts forward in her chair and looks away from me. "Well, that's not something we talk about. I'm not to talk about him at all—they buried his name when we couldn't bury his body, even struck him from the Book—but he was my twin brother. Doesn't feel right to pretend he never was."

"I didn't know he was your twin."

"Yeah. Partner in crime."

"You must miss him."

"I *do* miss him." She sniffs. "I haven't talked to him since the day he crossed over—no matter what people say."

"Of course not," I say. "He's dead."

"I *know* what they say."

"Honestly, Ebb. I've never heard anyone talk about your brother but you."

She stares at me for a second, her back stiff; then she seems to remember herself and turns to the fire, slouching again.

"Sorry, Simon. I just . . . I think people thought I was going to go with him. That I wouldn't be able to live without him. Nicky wanted me to go."

"He wanted you to kill yourself, too?"

"He wanted me to go with him to . . ." She looks around, anxiously, and her voice drops to a whisper. "To the vampires. Nicky said he'd be waiting for me—that he'd always be waiting for me."

The biscuit I'm holding snaps. "To the vampires?"

"Does no one really talk about him? About me?"

"No, Ebb." *To the vampires?* Ebb's brother went *to the vampires?*

She looks lost. "They never mention him, even after all he done . . . I guess that's what happens when they strike you from the Book. I was there for it. Mistress Pitch let me keep the words."

She holds up her staff—and even though it's just Ebb, I'm spooked enough that I startle. The goat resting at my feet jumps and scutters away. Ebb doesn't notice. She's as melancholy as I've ever seen her. There are tears running in clean streaks down her filthy cheeks.

She waves the staff over the fire, and the words spill out into the flames, but don't burn:

*Nicodemus Petty.*

I'm so shocked, I almost reach out and grab them. Nicodemus! Nicodemus who went to the vampires!

"Nicky," Ebb whispers. "The only magician ever to *choose* death with the vampires." She wipes her eyes with her sleeve. "Sorry, Simon. I shouldn't speak of him—but I can't help but *think* of him this time of year. The holidays. Out there on his own."

"He's still *alive*?"

That was the wrong question, or maybe I'm being too

intense: Ebb wipes away a new fall of tears.

"He's still out there," she says. "I think I'd know if he were gone. I could always feel it, before, when he was in trouble."

"Where is he?" I ask. I feel like I must sound too urgent, too desperate to know.

Ebb turns back to the fire. "I told you, I haven't talked to him since the day he left. I swear it."

"I believe you," I say. "I'm so sorry. You must . . . You must miss him."

"Like I'd miss my own heart," Ebb says. She nudges her staff into the fire and takes back each letter one by one.

"Was he with them?" I ask. "The vampires who killed Baz's mum?"

Ebb's chin jerks up. "No," she says defensively. "I asked Mistress Mary myself—before she passed. She swore to me that Nicky wasn't there that day. He'd never do such a thing. Nicky didn't want to kill people. He just wanted to live forever."

"Were you here?" I ask. "When it happened?"

Her face falls further than I thought possible. "I was out with the goats. I couldn't help her."

"What happened to the nursery?" I push, worried that in a minute Ebb'll be crying too much to answer any more questions. "Where did it go?"

"It hid itself away," she says, sniffing hard. "It was warded to protect the children, and it failed. So the wards hid it. Pulled it into the walls and the floor. I found it in the basement once. Then in the heart of the Weeping Tower. And then it was gone."

I should probably ask Ebb more questions. Penny wouldn't stop now. Baz would have his wand out, demanding to know *everything*.

But instead I just sit with Ebb and stare into the fire.

Sometimes I see her wipe her eyes with the end of her scarf. Like she's wiping dirt back onto her face.

"I'm sorry," I say. "I didn't mean to bring up so many painful subjects. There's so much about Watford I don't know. . . ."

"What do any of us know about Watford?" Ebb sighs. "Even the Wood nymphs can't remember a time before the White Chapel."

"I'm sorry," I say.

Ebb leans towards me and lays her arm around my shoulders. She does that sometimes. When I was a kid, I loved it. I'd sit extra close to her, so that I'd be easier to reach.

"Pish," she says. "You didn't bring it up. It's always on my mind. In a way, it's good to talk about it. To get some of it out of my heart, even for a minute."

I stand, and she follows me to the door, then pats me heartily on the back. "Happy Christmas, Simon," she says, giving her cheeks another wipe. "If you get lonely," she says, "you can call me. Send up a flare, yeah? I'll feel it."

Saw me in half, Ebb must be as powerful as the Mage— *send up a flare?*

"I'll be fine," I say. "Thanks, Ebb. Happy Christmas."

She opens the door for me, and I try not to seem like I'm in a hurry to say good-bye—but as soon as she closes it, I start running towards my house. I clomp snow all the way up to our turret—then dig out the cash I keep at the bottom of my wardrobe. It isn't much, but it'll get me to Hampshire, I think.

I try to hitch to the train station, but no one picks me up. It's fine. I keep running. I get to the station and buy my ticket and a sandwich.

I'm on a train, an hour away from Watford and an hour from Winchester, when I realize that I probably could have just borrowed a phone from somebody and called.

# 53

## BAZ

I like to practise violin in the library. My brothers and sisters aren't allowed in here yet, and there's a wall of lead-paned windows that look out on the gardens.

I like to practise violin, full stop. I'm good at it. And it distracts all the parts of my brain that just get in my way. I can think more cleanly when I'm playing.

My grandfather played, too. He could cast spells with his bow.

I forgot my violin here when I left for school—I wasn't in my right mind—and I'm a bit stiff now from the lack of practice. I'm working on a Kishi Bashi song that my stepmother, Daphne, calls "needlessly morose."

"Basilton . . . *Mr. Pitch.*"

I let the instrument drop from my chin and turn. Vera is standing at the door. "I'm sorry to interrupt. But your friend is here to see you."

"I'm not expecting anyone."

"It's a friend from school," she says. "He's wearing your uniform."

I set the violin down and straighten my shirt.

I guess it could be Niall. He comes over sometimes.

Though usually he'd text first . . . Not usually—always. And he wouldn't be in uniform. Nobody would; we're on break.

I pick up the pace, practically trotting through the parlour and dining room, wand in hand. Daphne's at the table with her laptop. She looks up curiously. I slow down.

When I get to the foyer, Simon Snow is standing there like a lost dog.

Or an amnesia victim.

He's wearing his Watford coat and heavy leather boots, and he's covered in snow and muck. Vera must have told him to stay on the rug, because he's standing right in the middle of it.

His hair is a mess, and his face is flushed, and he looks like he might go off right there, without any provocation.

I stop at the arched entrance to the foyer, tuck my wand in my sleeve, and slip my hands into my pockets. "Snow."

He jerks his head up. "*Baz.*"

"I'm trying to imagine what you're doing at my door. . . . Did you roll down a very steep hill and land here?"

"*Baz* . . . ," he says again. And I wait for him to get it out. "You're—you're wearing jeans."

I tilt my head. "I am. And you're wearing half the countryside."

"I had to walk from the road."

"Did you?"

"The taxi driver was afraid to come down your drive. He thinks your house is haunted."

"It is."

He swallows. Snow has the longest neck and the showiest swallow I've ever seen. His chin juts out and his Adam's apple catches—it's a whole scene.

"Well," I say, pointedly lifting my eyebrows. "It was good of you to stop by—"

Snow lets out a stymied growl and steps forward, off the rug, then steps back. "I came to talk to you."

I nod. "All right."

"It's . . ."

"All right," I say again, this time cutting him some slack. I don't actually want him to get so frustrated that he leaves. (I never want Snow to leave.) "But you can't come in the house like that. How did you even *get* like that?"

"I told you. I walked from the main road."

"You could have cast a spell to stay clean."

He frowns at me. Snow never casts spells on himself—or anyone else—if he can help it. I slip my wand out my cuff and point it at him. He flinches but doesn't tell me to stop. I ***"Clean as a whistle!"*** his boots. The mud whirls off, and I open the front door, sweeping the mess outside with my wand.

When I close the door, Snow is taking off his sodden coat. He's wearing his school trousers and red jumper, and his legs and hair are still wet. I lift my wand again. "I'm fine," he says, stopping me.

"You'll have to take off your boots," I say. "They're still dripping."

He crouches to unlace them, wet wool trousers straining ridiculously over his thighs. . . .

And then Simon Snow is standing in my foyer in his red-stockinged feet.

All the blood I've got in me rises to my ears and cheeks.

"Come on, Snow. Let's . . . talk."

# 54

## SIMON

I follow Baz from one giant room to the other. His house isn't a castle, I don't think, but near enough.

We walk through a dining room that looks like something off *Downton Abbey,* and there's a woman at the table, working on a flash silver laptop.

She clears her throat, and Baz stops to introduce me. "Mother, you remember my roommate, Simon Snow."

She must have already recognized me, but she still looks shocked, which reminds me to ask myself what the bleeding hell I think I'm doing here. In the House of fucking Pitch.

Which I should have thought through on the train, or in the taxi, or even walking the five miles from the main road to Baz's front door.

*I never think.*

"Snow," Baz says. "You've met my stepmother, Daphne Grimm."

"It's nice to see you, Mrs. Grimm," I say.

She's still looking shocked. "And you, Mr. Snow. Are you here on official business?"

I don't know what she means; I never have official business.

Baz is shaking his head, trying to cut off whatever that look is on her face. "He's just here to visit, Mother. We have a project we're working on together—a school project. And you don't have to call him that. You can just call him Simon."

"*You* don't call me Simon," I mumble.

"We'll be up in my room," Baz says, ignoring me.

His stepmum clears her throat. "I'll send for you when dinner's ready."

"Thank you," Baz says, and he's on the move again, leading me up a staircase so grand, there are statues built into it—naked women holding circles of light. I can't tell if they're electric light or magickal, but it makes sense to have lights built into your stairs when everything in your house is either dark wood or dark red, and the windows are so far away that the middle of the house feels like the bottom of the ocean.

I try to keep up with him. I still can't believe he's wearing jeans. I guess he wouldn't wear his uniform when he's not at school, but I'd always imagined Baz lounging around in suits and waistcoats—with, like, silk scarves hanging around his neck.

I mean . . . they do look like really expensive jeans. Dark. And snug from his waist to his ankles without looking tight.

I wonder for a moment if he's leading me into a trap. He didn't know I was coming, but don't houses like this just *come* with built-in traps? He's probably going to pull a black-tasselled cord and drop me into the dungeon—as soon as I finish telling him what I know.

We get to a long hallway, and Baz opens a tall arched door into a bedroom. His bedroom.

It's another vampire joke: The walls have red fabric panels, and his bed is monstrous and decorated with gargoyles. (There are *gargoyles*. On his *bed*.)

He shuts the door behind me and sits on a chest at the foot of the bed. There are gargoyles on that, too.

"All right, Snow," he says, "what the hell are you doing here?"

"You invited me," I say. So lame. So eternally lame.

"Is that why you're here? For Christmas?"

"No. I'm here because I have something to tell you—but you *did* invite me."

He shakes his head like I'm an idiot. "Just tell me. Is it about my mother?"

"I found out who Nicodemus is."

That gets his attention. He stands up again. "*Who?*"

"He's Ebb's brother."

"Ebb your girlfriend?"

"Ebb the goatherd."

"She doesn't have a brother."

"She does," I say. "A twin. He was stricken from the Book when he became a *vampire.*"

I swear Baz's face gets even whiter.

"Ebb's brother was Turned? They struck him from the Book for that?"

"No, he joined up with the vampires himself. Voluntarily."

"What?" Baz sneers. "That isn't actually how it works, Snow."

I step into his space. "How *does* it work, Baz?"

"You don't fucking *join up.*"

"This Nicodemus did. He tried to get Ebb to go with him."

"Ebb. The *goatherd.* Has a brother named Nicodemus that nobody's ever heard of—"

"I told you—we haven't heard about him, because he's *stricken.* That's why Ebb lives at Watford. Your mum gave her a job, so she wouldn't join her brother. They're both bloody superheroes, I guess, and everybody was afraid they'd team up and be supervampires."

"Ebb knew my mother?"

"Yeah. Your mum gave Ebb her job."

Baz is just standing there like he wants to punch something—or suck it dry.

"Well, where is he now?" he asks. "This Nicodemus?"

"Ebb doesn't know. She's not supposed to talk to him. She's not supposed to talk about him, even."

Baz sneers again, then reminds me that he actually *is* a super-vampire—a supervillain: "Doesn't know, does she? Well," he says, "we'll see about that."

I put my hand on his chest. I don't have to step any closer to reach him. "No," I say firmly. "Ebb doesn't know where Nicodemus is. We're not talking to her again."

Baz swallows and licks his grey-pink lower lip. "I'll talk to the goatherd if I want to, Snow."

"Not if you want my help." I keep my hand on his chest because I feel like he still needs to be held back, but I can't believe he's letting me do it.

His hand flies up and closes over my wrist. (As if he's read my mind.) (Is that a vampire thing?) "Fine," he says, shoving my wrist down. "Then how *do* we find Nicodemus?"

"I haven't thought it through that far. I came here as soon as I left Ebb's."

"Well, what does Penelope think?"

"I haven't talked to her yet."

"Where is she?"

"I don't know—I told you, I haven't talked to her. I came straight here."

Baz seems confused. "You came straight here?"

"Would you rather I waited to tell you after Christmas break?"

He narrows his eyes and licks his lips again. I put my hands on my hips, just to have something to do with them. "What about you?" I ask. "Have you made any progress?"

He looks away. "No. I mean, I've been reading a lot of books about vampires."

I stop myself from saying, *"Self-help?"* "What have you found out?" I ask instead.

"That they're dead and evil and like to kill babies."

"Huh," I say. "Did it say anything about salt and vinegar crisps?" Baz eats them on his bed when he thinks I'm asleep, then brushes the crumbs between our beds.

He glares at me, then moves away, walking towards his desk. "No one knows anything about the vampires," he says, fiddling with a pen. "Not really. Maybe I should just go talk to them."

There's a knock at his door, and it swings open.

"You're supposed to knock!" Baz snaps before the girl even steps inside. It's his sister, I think. She's too young for Watford yet. She looks like his stepmother, dark-haired and pretty, but not like Baz and his mother—they're drawn in bolder lines than this.

"I did knock," she says.

"Well, you're supposed to wait for me to say 'come in.'"

"Mum says you have to come down for dinner."

"Fine," he says.

She stands there.

"We'll be down soon," he says. "Go away."

The girl rolls her eyes and lets the door close. Baz goes back to thinking and fiddling with the pen.

"Well," I say, "I'd better head back. Send a message if you hear more. You can try to call, but I don't think there's anyone answering the school phone over break."

"What?" He scowls up at me.

"I said, send a message if—"

"You're not leaving now."

"I told you everything I know."

"Snow, you came in on the last train, then you walked for an hour. You haven't eaten all day, and your hair's still wet—you're not going anywhere tonight."

"Well, I can't stay *here*."

"You haven't burst into flames yet."

"Baz, listen—"

He cuts me off with a hand. "No."

# 55

## BAZ

Snow was a wreck at dinner.

Which I might have enjoyed if I wasn't so desperate for him to stay.

Everything on his plate seemed to confuse him, and he alternated between staring at his food miserably and hoovering it up because he was clearly ravenous.

Daphne went out of her way to make him feel comfortable, and the children just stared at him. Even they've heard of the Mage's Heir.

Father seems to think I have some dark plan at work. (I guess I do have a dark plan, but this time it has nothing to do with disabling Snow.) He—Father—pulled me aside after dinner and asked if I wanted him to call in the Families for assistance.

"No," I said. "Please don't. Snow's just here for a school project."

Father practically winked.

I've thought about telling him. That Mother came back for me. But what if he asks why she didn't come back to him? What if he takes it to the Families? They'd never understand why I was working with Snow and Bunce. And right now, Snow and Bunce seem like the best allies I could have. They're relentless once they set their minds to something. Completely trustworthy, with no sense of self-preservation. I've watched these two uncover plots and beat back monsters time and again.

Snow is still eating dinner. Daphne keeps offering extra helpings, out of politeness, and Snow keeps accepting them.

I've never actually sat at a table *with* Snow before. I let myself watch him, and let myself enjoy it, at least for a few minutes. I keep doing that, since this all started—indulging myself. (What's that they say about having dessert first if you're on the *Titanic*?)

Snow's table manners are atrocious—it's like watching a wild dog eat. A wild dog you'd like to slip the tongue.

After dinner, we go to the library and I show him what I've found on vampires. He keeps moving away from me, and I pretend not to notice. We should probably call Bunce and see what she thinks of all this—I'll suggest it tomorrow.

There's nothing in our library about any Nicodemus. I've already searched, but I do it again. I stand at the door and cast, ***"Fine-tooth comb—Nicodemus Petty!"*** None of the books come flying out of the shelves.

We *do* find a few mentions of the Petty family, so we read those. They're an old East End family, and a big one, and every few generations, they turn out a powerhouse like Ebb. If Snow hadn't come along, Ebb might be the most powerful magician in our world—and to think she wastes it all on goats and moping.

"Do you think it would have made it into *The Record*?" Snow asks. "When Nicodemus crossed over?"

"I don't know," I say. "Maybe not. They probably wanted to keep it hush-hush, and it doesn't seem like he hurt anybody."

"What's the point of becoming a vampire," Snow says, "if

you're not planning to hurt anybody?"

"What's the point of becoming a vampire?" I ask.

"You tell me."

I swallow my temper and then swallow it again, and keep looking through a book.

Snow sits down across from me at the small table, pulling up a quilted chair. "No," he says. "I'm being serious. Why would Nicodemus have done it?"

"You're asking me to pose a theory?"

He nods.

"To become stronger," I say. "Physically."

"How much stronger?" Snow asks.

I shrug. "You'd have to ask him. I wouldn't know how to compare." Because I don't remember being normal.

"What else?" he asks.

"To enhance himself . . . his senses."

"Like, to see better?"

"In the dark," I say. "And hear more. And smell more sharply."

"To live forever?"

I shake my head. "I don't think so. I don't think it works like that. But he wouldn't ever . . . be sick."

Snow lowers his eyebrows. "When you look at it that way, why doesn't everyone cross over?"

"Because it's *death*," I say.

"It clearly isn't."

"They say your soul dies."

"That's tosh," he says.

"How would *you* know, Snow?"

"*Observation.*"

"Observation," I say. "You can't *observe* a soul."

"You can over time," he says. "I think I'd know—"

"It's *death*," I say, "because you need to eat life to stay alive."

"That's everyone," he says. "That's eating."

"It's death," I say, refusing to raise my voice, "because when you're hungry, you can't stop thinking about eating other people."

Snow sits back. His mouth is open—because no one ever taught him to close it. He pushes at his bottom lip with his tongue. I think about licking blood from it.

"It's death," I say, looking back down at my book, "because you look at other people, living people, and they seem really far away. They seem like something else. The way that birds seem like something else. And they're full of something you don't have. You could take it from them, but it still won't be yours. They're full, and . . . you're hungry. You're not alive. You're just hungry."

"You have to be alive to be hungry," Snow says. "You have to be alive to change."

"Maybe *you* should write a book about vampires," I say.

"Maybe I should. Apparently, I'm the world's leading expert."

When I look up, Snow's staring right at me.

I can feel the cross around his neck, like static in my salivary glands, but it's never been less discouraging. I could knock him over right now. (Kiss him? Kill him? Improvise?)

"You should ask your parents," Snow says.

"Whether I'm *alive*?" Fuck. I didn't mean to say it like that. To concede, even a little.

Snow closes his mouth. Swallows. That's where I'd bite him, right in the throat.

"I *meant*," he says, "you should ask them if they remember Nicodemus. Maybe they know where he is."

"I'm not asking my parents about the only magician to run off to join the vampires. Are you a *complete* moron?"

"Oh," he says. "I guess I didn't think about it that way."

"You didn't think—" I say. And then—"Oh. Oh, oh, *oh*."

# SIMON

Baz is running up the steps again, so I'm running behind him. We haven't seen anyone else since dinner. This house is so big, it could absorb a mob and still seem empty.

We're in a different wing now. Another long hallway. Baz stops in front of a door and starts casting disarming spells. "So predictably paranoid," he mutters.

"What're we doing?" I ask.

"Looking for Nicodemus."

"You think he might live here?"

"No," he says. "But—"

The door opens, and we're in another creepy goth bedroom. This one is like Goth Through the Ages, because on top of the gargoyles, there are posters of '80s and '90s rock stars wearing lots of black eyeliner. And somebody's even written *Never Mind the Bollocks* in yellow spray paint on one wall, ruining the antique black-and-white wallpaper.

"Whose room is this?" I ask.

Baz is crouching next to a bookshelf. "My aunt Fiona's."

I step back into the doorway. "What are we doing here?"

"Looking for something . . ." A second later, he pulls out a big purple scrapbook with *Remember the Magic* embossed on the front in gold. "Aha!" he says. "I'm pretty sure Fiona went to school with Ebb. I've heard her talk about her.

Disparagingly, I promise you. She never mentioned Ebb's brother, though. . . ."

Baz is flipping through the pages. I crouch down next to him. "What is that?"

"It's a memory book," he says. "They used to give them out at Watford before the Mage took over. At your leavers ball. It's got class pictures from every year and little stories. . . ." He holds the book open to a page full of photos. It makes me wish I had something like it—I don't have any pictures of myself or my friends. Agatha has a few, I think.

Baz has turned to the back of the book, and he's poring over a big class picture, squinting.

Underneath the picture, someone has taped in a few snapshots. "Look," I say, pointing at a photo of a girl sitting against a tree—the yew tree. She's got mad dark hair with a blond streak, and she's grinning with her nose crunched up and her tongue between her teeth. There's a rawboned boy sitting next to her with his arm slung around her shoulders. "Ebb," I say. Because the straight blond hair is the same. And the cliff's-edge cheekbones. But I've never seen Ebb looking so cocksure of herself—and I can't imagine her smirking like that. Under the picture, someone's written *Me and Nickels*, and dotted the *i* with a heart.

*"Fiona!"* Baz says, snapping the book closed.

I take it from him and open it again, settling down on the floor and leaning against the bed. There are a few pages for each year Fiona was in school—with big class photos and blank pages where you can put other pictures and certificates. It's not hard to spot Fiona in each posed class photo—that white streak must be natural—and then to find Ebb and Nicodemus, always standing next to each other, looking almost exactly alike, but completely different. Ebb looks like Ebb, gentle and unsure, in every picture. Nicodemus looks like he's about to hatch a plan. Even as a first year.

I find another snapshot of Nicodemus and Baz's aunt, this time posing in old-fashioned costumes. "Did you know Watford used to have a drama society?" I ask.

"Watford had a lot of things before the Mage." Baz takes the book from me and puts it back on the shelf. "Come on."

"Where are we going?"

"Now? To bed. Tomorrow? London."

I must be tired, because neither of those statements makes sense to me.

"Come on," Baz says. "I'll show you to your room."

My room turns out to be the creepiest one yet:

There's a dragon painted on the archway around the door, and its face is charmed to glow and follow you in the dark.

Plus there's something under the bed.

I don't know exactly *what*, but it moans and clicks and makes the bedposts shake. I end up at Baz's door, telling him I'm going back to Watford.

"What?" He's half asleep when he comes to the door. And flushed—he must have gone hunting after I went to bed. Or maybe they keep kennels for him on the grounds.

"I'm leaving," I say. "That room is haunted."

"The whole house is haunted, I told you."

"I'm leaving."

"Come on, Snow, you can sleep on my couch. The wraiths don't hang out in here."

"Why not?"

"I creep them out."

"You creep *me* out," I mutter, and he throws one of his pillows into my face. (It smells like him.)

I realize, as I'm settling in on his couch, that I don't mean it. About him creeping me out.

I used to mean it. I usually do.

But he's the most familiar thing in this house, and I fall asleep better, listening to Baz breathe, than I have since winter break started.

# 56

## FIONA

All right, Natasha, I know I shouldn't have told him anything.

You wouldn't have done.

Swans right into my flat, looking for trouble. *Being* trouble, every bloody moment he's alive.

"Tell me about Nicodemus," he says, like he already knows everything he needs to.

He knows he's my favourite; that's the problem. He would be, even if you'd had a litter of pups. Cocky as Mick Jagger, that one. And smart as a horsewhip.

"Who's been talking to you about Nicodemus?" I ask.

He sits at my grotty little table and starts drinking my tea, dunking the last of my lavender shortbread in it. "Nobody," he says. *Liar.* "I've just heard that he's like me."

"A scheming brat?

"You know what I mean, Fiona."

"Nice suit, Basil, where are you headed?"

"Dancing."

He's all kitted out in his finest. Spencer Hart, if I'm not wrong. Like he's here to collect his BAFTA.

I sit across from him. "He's nothing like you," I say.

"You should have told me," he says. "That I wasn't the only one."

"He chose it. He crossed over."

"What does it matter whether I chose it, Fiona? The result is the same."

"Not hardly," I tell him. "He left our world. *Left*. Said he was going to evolve."

He said he was going to be more than magic.

*"You're powerful enough now, Nicky."*

*"What do we say about 'enough,' Miss Pitch?"*

*His school tie tucked into his jacket pocket. That cruel, cool smile.*

"He betrayed us, Basil." I feel the old anger—the old everything—rising up in my throat.

"And he was stricken," my nephew says.

"Because he was a betrayer," I say.

"Because he was a vampire," Baz says, and I can't help it—that word still makes me recoil.

It wasn't supposed to be *me*, Natasha. Telling this boy how to make his way in the world. I'm no good at this. Look at me. Thirty-seven years old, rolling my own joints in my dressing gown, eating bikkies for breakfast whenever I manage to get up—I'm a disgrace.

What would *you* say to him if you were here?

No . . . Never mind. I know what you'd say—and you're *wrong*.

That's one way I've bettered you. I was weak enough to give your son a chance. And look at him now—he may be dead, but he isn't lost. He's dark as pitch and sharp as a blade, and he's full of your magic. He's a bonfire. He'd make you proud, Tasha.

"You're not going to be stricken, Basil," I tell him. "Is that what this is about? No one knows about you, and even if they find out—which they won't—they'll know we can't spare you. The Families are finally ready to strike back at the Mage. It's all happening."

He licks his bottom lip and looks out my little window. The sun's still out, and I know it bothers him, even if he won't complain. I unhook the curtain, and my kitchen falls into shadow.

"Is he still alive?" Baz asks. "Nicodemus?"

"I think so. In a matter of speaking. I haven't heard any different."

"*Would* you have heard?"

There's a pack of fags on the table. I light one with my wand and take a few good drags, tapping the ash out on my saucer. "You know that the Families use my London connections. . . ."

"What does that mean, Fiona?"

"I talk to people here who no one else wants to. Undesirables. I'm not worried about getting my hands dirty now and then."

Then, sister, he cocks one of your eyebrows at me.

I spit out some smoke. "Pfft. Not like that, you perv."

"So Nicodemus is an undesirable," he says.

"We're not permitted to talk about him. It's mage law."

"Would you cut *me* off so easily?"

"Oh, fuck, Baz, you know I wouldn't. What are you on about?"

"I can't help but be curious." He leans towards me over the table. "Is he alive? Does he hunt? Has he aged? Has he Turned anyone?"

"Nicodemus Petty doesn't have any answers for you, boyo." I'm jabbing my cigarette at him, so I put it out before I accidentally torch him. "He's a two-bit gangster—a third-tier thug in a Guy Ritchie movie. He thought he was going to be the über-mage, but he ended up shooting dice in the back room of some vampire bar in Covent Garden. He threw his whole life away, and hurt everyone who loved him—*and there's nothing you can learn from him, Basil.* Other than how to be a shitty vampire."

Baz's eyebrow is still raised. He drinks the rest of my tea. "Fine," he says. "You've made your point."

"Good. Go home and study."

"I'm on break."

"Go home and figure out how to take down the Mage."

"I told you. I'm going dancing."

I look at his suit again and his shiny black shoes. "Basil. Have you met a bloke?"

He smiles, and he's made of trouble. We should have dropped him in the Thames in a bag of stones. We should have left him out for the fairies.

"Something like that."

# 57

## AGATHA

I'm sitting at Penelope's counter, spreading pink icing on another gingerbread lady.

"Why do the gingerbread girls have to wear pink?" Penny asks.

"Why should the gingerbread girls feel like they shouldn't wear pink?" I say. "I like pink."

"Only because you've been conditioned to like it by Barbies and gendered Lego."

"Lay off, Penny. I've never played with Lego."

Hanging out with Penny is actually going better than I thought. When she cornered me in the courtyard before we left for break, I thought she was going to chew me out for abandoning Simon.

"Hey," she said, "I heard that Simon isn't coming over for Christmas."

"Because we're not dating anymore, Penelope. Happy?"

"Generally," she said, "but not because you broke up."

It's impossible to end a conversation with Penny. You can be rude, you can ignore her—she's unshakable.

"Agatha," she said, "do you honestly think I want to *be* with Simon?"

I think Penny wants to be the most important person in Simon's life, so is that a yes or a no? "I don't know, Penelope. But I know you didn't want *me* to be with him."

"Because you both seemed miserable!"

"That wasn't any of your business!"

"Of course it was!" she said. "You're my *friends.*"

I rolled my eyes at her, very obviously, but she kept going.

"This isn't what I wanted to talk to you about," she said briskly. "I heard Simon isn't coming to your house for Christmas. And he can't come to my house because my mum's pissed off at the Mage, but I thought maybe you and I could still get together and make biscuits and exchange gifts."

We always do this, every year, the three of us. "Without Simon?"

"Right, like I said, my mum's got a bee in her bonnet about Simon."

"But we never hang out without Simon," I said.

"Only because he's always around," Penny said. "Just because you guys broke up doesn't mean we're not still friends, you and me."

"We're friends?"

"Nicks and Slick, I hope so," Penny said. "I only have three friends. If *we're* not friends, I'm down to two."

"What're you girls doing?" Penny's mum comes into the kitchen, carrying her laptop, like she can't put it down long enough to make herself a cup of tea. Her hair is pulled up in a messy dark bun, and she's wearing the same cardigan and joggers she was wearing when I got here yesterday. My mother wouldn't leave her bedroom looking like that.

Professor Bunce teaches History of the Middle Ages at a Normal university, and she's a magickal historian. She's published a whole shelf full of mage books, but she doesn't make any money doing it. There aren't enough magicians to support magickal arts and sciences as careers. My father does well as a magickal physician because he's one of a few with the right training, and everyone needs a doctor. Penny's dad used to teach linguistics at a local university, but now he works full-time for the Coven, researching the Humdrum. He even has his own staff of investigators who work in the lab with him upstairs. I've been here almost two days, and I haven't seen him yet.

"He only comes out for tea and sandwiches," Penny said when I asked her about it. She has a few younger siblings, too; I recognize them from Watford. There's one camped out in the living room right now, watching three months' worth of *Eastenders*—and at least one more upstairs attached to the Internet. They're all frightfully independent. I don't even think they have mealtimes. They just wander in and out of the kitchen for bowls of cereal and cheese toasties.

"We're making gingerbread," Penny says in answer to her mother. "For Simon."

"Let it rest, Penelope," her mum says, setting her laptop on the island and checking out our biscuits. "You'll see Simon in a week or two—I'm sure he'll still recognize you. Oh, Agatha, honestly, do the gingerbread girls *have* to be wearing pink?"

"I like pink," I say.

"It's good to see you girls spending time together," she says. "It's good to have a life that passes the Bechdel test."

"Because our house is just teeming with *your* women friends," Penny mutters.

"I don't have friends," her mum says. "I have colleagues. And children." She picks up one of my pink gingerbread girls and takes a bite.

"Well, I'm not avoiding other girls," Penny says. "I'm avoiding other *people.*"

"And I have plenty of girlfriends," I say. "I wish I could go to school with them." Not for the first time today, I think that I'm wasting a day with my real friends, my Normal friends, just to make nice with Penelope.

"Well, you'll get to be with them next year, at uni," her mum says to me. "What are you going to study, Agatha?"

I shrug. I don't know yet. I shouldn't have to know—I'm only 18. I'm not *destined* for anything. And my parents don't treat me like I have to rise to greatness. If Penny doesn't cure cancer and find the fairies, I think her mum will be vaguely disappointed.

Professor Bunce frowns. "Hmm. I'm sure you'll sort it out." The kettle clicks, and she pours her tea. "You girls want a fresh cup?" Penny holds hers out, and her mum takes mine, too. "I had girlfriends when I was your age; I had a best friend, Lucy. . . ." She laughs, like she's remembering something. "We were thick as thieves."

"Are you still friends?" I ask.

She sets our mugs down and looks up at me, like she's only been half paying attention to our conversation until now. "I would be," she said, "if she turned up. She left for America a few years after school. We didn't really see each other after Watford, anyway."

"Why not?" Penny asks.

"I didn't like her boyfriend," her mum says.

"Why?" Penny says. God, Penny's parents must have heard that question a hundred thousand times by now.

"I thought he was too controlling."

"Is that why she left for America?"

"I think she left when they broke up." Professor Bunce

looks like she's deciding what to say next. "Actually . . . Lucy was dating the Mage."

"The Mage had a *girlfriend*?" Penny asks.

"Well, we didn't call him the Mage then," her mum says. "We called him Davy."

"The Mage had a *girlfriend*," Penny says again, goggling. "And a *name*. Mum, I didn't know you went to school with the Mage!"

Professor Bunce takes a gulp of tea and shrugs.

"What was he like?" Penny asks.

"The same as he is now," her mum says. "But younger."

"Was he handsome?" I ask.

She makes a face. "I don't know—do you think he's handsome now?"

"Ugh, no," Penny says, at the same time as I say, "Yes."

"He *was* handsome," Professor Bunce admits, "and charismatic in his way. He had Lucy wrapped around his little finger. She thought he was a visionary."

"Mum, you have to admit," Penny says, "he really was a visionary."

Professor Bunce makes a face again. "He always had to have everything his way, even back then. Everything was black-and-white with Davy, always. And if Lucy didn't agree—well, Lucy always agreed. She lost herself in him."

"Davy," Penelope says. "So weird."

"What was Lucy like?" I ask.

Penny's mum smiles. "Brilliant. She was *powerful*." Her eyes light up at that word. "And strong. She played rugby, I remember, with the boys. I had to mend her collarbone once out on the field—it was mad. She was a country girl, with broad shoulders and yellow hair, and she had the bluest eyes—"

Penny's dad wanders into the kitchen.

"Dad!" Penny says. "*Now* can we talk?"

The other Professor Bunce fumbles towards the kettle and turns it on. Penny's mum turns it off and takes it to the sink to add water, and he kisses her forehead. "Cheers, love."

"*Dad,*" Penny says.

"Yeah . . ." He's rummaging in the fridge. He's a smallish man, shorter than Penny's mum. With sandy blond-grey hair and a big squishy nose. He's got unfashionable, round, wire-rimmed glasses tucked up on his head. Everyone in Penny's family wears unfashionable glasses.

The gossip about Penny's dad is that he's not even half as powerful as her mum; my mum says he only got into Watford because his father used to teach there. Penny's mum is such a power snob, it's hard to imagine her married to a dud.

"Dad, remember? I needed to talk to you."

He's stacking food in his arms: Two yoghurts. An orange. A packet of prawn crackers. He grabs a gingerbread girl and notices me. "Oh, hello, Agatha."

"Hello, Professor Bunce."

"Martin," he says, already leaving. "Call me Martin."

"*Dad.*"

"Yeah, come on up, Penny—bring my tea, would you?"

She waits for his tea, then snatches a couple more gingerbread people—they're eating them faster than I can decorate them—and follows him upstairs.

"Why did they break up?" I ask Professor Bunce after Penny and her dad have cleared out.

She's staring at her laptop, holding her tea, forgotten, halfway up to her mouth. "Hmmm?"

"Lucy and Davy," I say.

"Oh. I don't know," she says. "We'd lost touch by then. I imagine she finally realized he was a git and had to cross the ocean to get away from him. Can you imagine having *the Mage* for an ex? He's everywhere."

"How did you find out that she left?"

Professor Bunce looks sad. "Her mother told me."

"I wonder why the Mage has never dated anyone else. . . ."

"Who knows," she says, shaking it off and looking back at her computer. "Maybe he has secret Normal girlfriends."

"Or maybe he really loved Lucy," I say, "and never got over her."

"Maybe," Professor Bunce says. She's not paying attention. She types for a few seconds, then looks up at me. "You just reminded me of something I haven't thought of in years. Wait here." She walks out of the kitchen, and I figure she probably won't be back. The Bunces do that sometimes.

But she does come back, holding out a photograph. "Martin took this."

It's three Watford students, two girls and a boy, sitting in the grass—by the football pitch, I think. The girls are wearing trousers. (Mum says nobody wore school skirts in the '90s.) One of them is pretty obviously Penelope's mum. With her hair down and wild, she looks a lot like Penny. Same wide forehead. Same smirk. (I wish Penny were down here, so I could tease her about that.) And the boy is obviously the Mage—different with his hair longer and loose, and with no silly moustache. (The Mage has the worst moustache.)

But the girl in the middle is a stranger.

She's lovely.

Shoulder-length yellow-blond hair, curly and thick. With rosy cheeks, and eyes so big and blue, you can see the colour in the photo. She's smiling warmly, holding Penelope's mum's hand, and leaning into the boy, who has his arm around her.

The Mage really was dead handsome. Better looking than either of the girls. And he looks softer here than I've ever seen him, smiling out one side of his mouth, with an almost sheepish look in his eyes.

"Lucy and I never really fought," Professor Bunce says. "I'd fight, and Lucy would just try to change the subject. It was never a fight at the end, either. I think she stopped talking to me because she got tired of defending Davy to me. He was so intense by the time we left school—radicalized, ready to charge the palace and set up a guillotine."

I realize that Professor Bunce is talking to herself now, and to the photo, more than she is to me.

"And he never *shut up*," she says, setting the photo on the counter. "I still don't know how she could stand him."

She looks up at me and narrows her eyes. "Agatha, I know I'm being indiscreet—but nothing we say in this kitchen leaves the kitchen, understood?"

"Oh, of course," I say. "And don't worry about it—my mother complains about the Mage, too."

"She does?"

"He never comes to her parties, and when he does, he's wearing his uniform, and it's usually caked with mud, and then he leaves early. It gives her a migraine."

Professor Bunce laughs.

Her mobile rings. She takes it out of her pocket. "This is Mitali." She looks back at her computer and clicks at the touchpad. "Let me check." She picks up the laptop, balancing it against her stomach, propping the phone between her ear and shoulder, and walks out of the room.

She leaves the photo on the counter. After a moment, I pick it up.

I look at the three of them again. They look so happy—it's hard to believe none of them are on speaking terms now.

I look at Lucy, at the colour in her cheeks and her blue-sky eyes, and slip the photo into my pocket.

# 58

## LUCY

I wish you could have known him when he was young.

He was handsome, of course. He's still handsome. Now he's handsome in a way that everyone sees. . . .

Then it was just me.

I *did* feel sorry for him; I guess that's how it started. He was always talking, and no one was ever listening.

I liked to listen. I liked his ideas—he was right about so many things. He still is.

"How goes the Revolution, Davy?"

"Don't tease, Lucy. I don't like teasing."

"I know. But I do."

He was sitting alone under the yew tree, so I sat down next to him. When we first started talking, I'd meet him here so that no one would see us together—so no one would see me with daft old Davy.

Now I liked to meet him under the yew tree because it was almost like being alone together.

"You've been quiet lately," I said.

"There's nothing more to say. Nobody's listening."

"I'm listening."

"I brought my grievances before the Coven," he said.

"They laughed at me."

"I'm sure they didn't laugh, Davy—"

"You don't have to laugh out loud to mock someone. They treated me like a child."

"Well, you are a child. We both are."

He looked directly into my eyes. There's something about Davy's eyes. They're half magic. I could never look away.

"No, Lucy. We're not."

After that meeting with the Coven, Davy was always in the library, or bent over a book in the dining hall, dripping gravy over some four-hundred-year-old text.

Sometimes I'd sit with him, and sometimes he'd talk to me.

"Lucy, did you know that Watford used to have its own oracle? That's the room at the top of the Chapel with the window that looks out over the school walls. The oracles worked there. They were as important as the headmasters."

"When did that end?"

"Nineteen fourteen. It was an austerity measure. The idea was that oracles would donate their services as needed after that."

"I don't know any oracles," I said.

"Well, it was the Watford oracle who trained other oracles. It's a dead profession now. The library still has a whole wing for their prophecies—"

"Since when do you care about crystal balls and tarot cards?"

"I don't care about children playing with tools they don't understand, but this . . ." His eyes glittered. "Did you know that the potato famine was prophesied?"

"I did not."

"And the Holocaust."

"*Really?* When?"

"In 1511. And did you know that there's only one vision that every oracle has had since the beginning of Watford?"

"I didn't even know there *were* oracles thirty seconds ago."

"That there's a great Mage coming."

"Like the children's song," I said. "*And one will come to end us, / and one will bring his fall, / let the greatest power of powers reign, / may it save us all.*"

"Yes."

"My grandmother used to talk about the Greatest Mage."

"There are dozens of prophecies," Davy said. "All about one mage, the Chosen One."

"How do you know they're all about the same person?" I ask. "And how do you know he—or she—hasn't come and gone already."

"Do you really think we'd miss someone who saved our whole people? Someone who fixed our world?"

"Does it say what they'll fix?"

"It says there will be a threat, that we'll be dark and divided—that magic itself will be in danger, and that there will be a mage who has power no one else has ever dreamt of, a magician who draws his power from the centre of the earth. '*He walks like an ordinary man, but his power is like no other.*' One of the oracles describes him as 'a vessel'—large and strong enough to hold all of magic itself."

Davy was getting more and more excited as he talked. His eyes were shining, and his words were tripping over each other. He gestured towards the stack of books as if their very presence made the prophecies irrefutable.

I felt my chin pull back. "You don't . . ."

"What?" Davy asked.

"Well, you don't think . . ."

"What, Lucy? What don't I think?"

"Well . . . that *you're* the Greatest Mage? . . ."

He scoffed. "Me? No. Don't be a fool. I'm more powerful than any of these cretins"—he glanced around the library—"but I have the sort of power you can imagine."

I tried to laugh. "Right. So . . ."

"So?"

"So why is this so important to you?"

"Because the Greatest Mage of all is *coming*, Lucy. And he's coming at the hour of our greatest need. When the mages are *'scrabbling with clawed hands at each others' throats'*—when *'the head of our great beast has lost its way.'* That's soon. That's now. We should all care about this! We should be getting ready!"

# 59

## PENELOPE

I like my dad's lab. In the attic. No one's allowed to clean up here, not even his assistants. It's a complete mess, but Dad knows where everything is, so if you move a book from one pile to the next, he goes a little mental.

One whole wall is a map of Great Britain—the holes in the magickal atmosphere haven't spread across the water yet, but they've grown over the years. Dad uses pins and string to map the perimeter of each hole, then uses different colours of string to show how the holes have grown. Little flags record the date of measurement. A few of the big holes have merged over the years—there's almost no magic left in Cheshire anymore.

Dad's assistants are out on a surveying mission now. He's just hired someone new, a magickal anthropologist, to study the effects of the voids on magickal creatures. He'd like to study how the holes affect Normals, but he can't get the funding.

I walk over to the map. There are two holes in London—a big one in Kensington and a smaller one in Trafalgar Square. I hate to think about what would happen if the Humdrum attacked near our house in Hounslow. Plenty of magickal families have had to move, and sometimes it weakens them. Your magic settles in a place. It supports you.

I sit at one of the tall tables. Dad likes to stand while he works, so all the tables are tall. He's already got a book open, and he's copying numbers into a ledger. He uses a computer, too, but he still keeps all his records by hand.

"I'm working on a project for school," I say. "And I was looking through some old copies of *The Record*. . . ."

"Mmm-hmmm."

"And I was reading about the Watford Tragedy."

Dad looks up. "Yes?"

"Do you remember when it happened?"

"Of course." He goes back to his ledger. "Your mother and I were still at uni. You were just a little girl. . . ."

Mum and Dad got married just after Watford and started having kids right away, even though they were still in school and Mum wanted a career. Dad says Mum wanted *everything, immediately*.

"It must have been terrible," I say.

"It was. No one had ever attacked Watford before—and poor Natasha Grimm-Pitch."

"Did you know her?"

"Not personally. She was older than us. Her sister was a few years below me at school—Fiona—but I didn't know her either. The Pitches always kept to their own sort."

"So you didn't like her? Natasha Grimm-Pitch?"

"I didn't like her politics," he says. "She thought low-powered magicians should give up their wands."

Low-powered magicians. Like my dad.

"Why *did* the vampires attack Watford?" I ask. "They'd never done it before."

"The Humdrum sent them," Dad says.

"But it doesn't say that"—I lean towards him, across the table—"in the initial news stories, right after the attack. It just says it was vampires."

He looks up at me again, interested. "That's right." He nods. "We *didn't* know at first. We just thought the dark creatures were taking advantage of how disorganized we were. It was a different time. Everything was looser. The World of Mages was more like a . . . club. Or a society. There was no line of defence. There were even werewolf attacks back then—in London proper, can you imagine?"

"So no one knew the Humdrum was behind the attack on Watford?"

"Not for a while," he says. "We didn't know the Humdrum was an entity at first."

"What do you mean?"

"Well, when the holes started appearing—"

"In 1998."

"Yes," he says, "that's when we first recorded them. Seventeen years ago. We thought they might be a natural phenomenon, or maybe even the result of pollution. Like the holes in the ozone layer. It was Dr. Manning who first coined the term, I remember. He visited the hole in Lancashire and described it as '*an insidious humdrum, a mundanity that creeps into your very soul.*'" Dad smiles. He likes a well-turned phrase. "I started my research not long after that."

"When did you guys realize that the Humdrum was a 'he'?"

"We still don't know it's a 'he.'"

"You know what I mean—when did you realize it was a thing with intention? That it was attacking us?"

"There wasn't one day," he says. "I mean, everything sort of shifted in 2008. I personally think that the Humdrum got more powerful around that time. We'd been tracking these small holes, like bubbles in the magickal atmosphere—and they suddenly mushroomed, like a cancer metastasizing. Around the same time, the dark world went mad. I suppose it was when the dark creatures started coming for Simon directly that we knew there was malice there—and intelligence—not just natural disaster. And then there was the feeling. The holes, the attacks . . . there's a distinct feeling." His eyes focus on me, and his mouth tightens.

After the Humdrum kidnapped Simon and me last year, Dad wanted to know every detail. I told him most of it—everything about the Humdrum, even what he looks like. Dad thinks the Humdrum took Simon's form to mock him.

I rest my elbows on the counter. "Why do you think the Humdrum hates Simon so much?"

"Well." He wrinkles his nose. "The Humdrum seems to hate *magic*. And Simon does have more of it than anyone— maybe anything—else."

"It's weird that the Humdrum isn't its real name," I say. "I mean, that it didn't come with that name or name itself. . . ."

"Do you think a dark creature would choose the name 'the Insidious Humdrum'?"

"I've never thought about it," I say. "It's just always been there."

Dad sighs and pushes up his glasses. "That breaks my heart, to think that you can't remember a world without the Humdrum. I worry that your generation will just acclimate to it. That you won't see the necessity of fighting back."

"I think I'll see, Dad. The foul thing kidnapped me—and it keeps trying to kill my best friend."

He frowns and keeps looking at me. "You know, Penelope . . .

There's a team of Americans coming in a few weeks. I think I finally got their attention when we visited this summer."

Dad met with as many other magickal scientists as he could while we visited Micah. There was a magickal geologist who took a real interest in Dad's work.

The American mages are much less organized than we are. They live all over the country and mostly do their own thing. But there's more money there. Dad's been trying to convince other international scientists that the Humdrum is a threat to the entire magickal world, not just the British one.

"I'd love it if you could come along on a few of our surveys," he says. "You could meet Dr. Schelling; he has his own lab in Cleveland."

I see what he's doing—this is how my dad is going to keep me safe from the Humdrum. By hiding me in Ohio.

"Maybe," I say. "If I can get out of lessons."

"I'll write you a note."

"Can Simon come, too?"

He presses his lips together and pushes up his glasses again. "I'm not sure I can write a note for Simon," he says, picking up his pen. "What did you say your school project is about?"

"The Watford Tragedy."

"Tell me if you turn anything up that sheds light on the Humdrum. I've always wondered whether anyone felt his presence there."

His head's back in his work now. So I hop off the chair and start to leave. I stop at the door. "Hey, Dad, one more thing— did you ever know a magician named Nicodemus?"

He looks up, and his face doesn't move at all—so I can tell he's purposely not reacting. "I can't say that I have," he says. "Why?"

It's not like my dad to lie to me.

It's not like me to lie to him. "It's just a name I saw in *The Record*, and I didn't recognize it."

"Hmm," he says. "I don't—I don't think he's anyone important."

# 60

## SIMON

We wait until after midnight to go looking for the vampires. Baz's aunt wouldn't tell him exactly where they hang out, but he thinks he can find them, and he says they should be done hunting by midnight. . . .

Which freaks me right out. To think of all those murders happening. While we wait.

If the vampires are hunting Normals every night, why don't we do something about it? The Coven must know it's happening. I mean, if Baz's aunt knows, the Coven *must* know.

I decide Baz isn't the right person to talk to about this right now.

We have time to kill after we leave his aunt's, so we go to a library—the big one—and then to the reading room at the British Museum, where Baz steals at least a half dozen books.

"You can't do that," I argue.

"It's research."

"It's *treason*."

"Are you going to tell the Queen?"

When the museums all close, we walk around a park, then find a place where I can eat a curry while he looks through his stolen books.

"You should eat something," I say.

He raises an eyebrow at me.

"Oh, piss off." I wonder if this is why he's never had a girlfriend. Because he'd take her on dates to the library, then insist on sitting there creepily while she ate dinner alone.

I've finished my curry and two orders of samosas, and I'm watching him read—I swear he sucks on his fangs when he's thinking—when he snaps the book shut with one hand and stands up.

"Come on, Snow. Let's go find a vampire."

"Thanks"—I wipe my mouth on my sleeve—"but I'm already over the limit."

Baz is already walking out the door.

"Hey," I say, trying to catch up. When he ignores me, I grab his arm.

He frowns. "You can't just grab people when you want their attention."

"I said 'Hey.'"

"Still."

"I've been thinking," I say, "if we're going to do this, you have to start calling me by my name."

I don't know why this seems important. Just—if we're going to walk into a vampire den together, it seems like we need to get past some of this stuff and actually *be* allies.

"Snow *is* your name," Baz says. "Possibly. Who named you, anyway?"

I look away. It was written on my arm—*Simon Snow*. Whoever left me at the home must have written it. Maybe it was my mother.

"You have to call me *Simon*," I say. "You've called me that before."

He opens his car door and gets in, as if he didn't hear

me—but I know that he did.

"Fine," Baz says. "Get in the car, Simon."

I do.

It took us almost two hours to find this place—Baz sniffed it out; it was like walking around Covent Garden with a bloodhound.

"Is this it?" I ask. "Are they here?"

He straightens his collar and cuffs. We're standing outside an old building full of flats, with a row of names next to the doorway and a brass slot for letters. "Stay close," he whispers, and raps at the door with the back of his fist.

A large man opens the door. He sees Baz, then opens it a bit wider. Another man, standing behind a long bar in the centre of the room, looks over and nods. The doorman motions with his head for us to come in.

I follow Baz into a deep, low-ceilinged room with no overhead lights. The bar runs down the middle, and ornate, private booths line the walls on either side, each booth lit by a hanging yellow lamp.

Everyone sitting along the aisles turns to look at us. A woman near the door drops her glass, and the man next to her catches it.

They don't look like vampires.

*Are* they all vampires?

They just look rich. And . . . grey. But they don't look beautiful or thin or cheekboney like they do in the films.

It's Baz they're checking out, not me. He's got to be scared, or at least nervous, but he doesn't look it. I swear he gets less ruffled the more that he's threatened. (When I'm the one threatening him, that's infuriating. But it's kind of cool now.)

Every one of them must be so jealous of him. He's everything they are, plus magic. Plus he looks the part, like he was born to be some sort of dark king.

Baz stops at the first booth. "Nicodemus," he says, and he doesn't even make it a question.

A man with grey hair and skin, and a shimmering grey suit meets Baz's eyes and nods towards the back of the room—then looks at me and sneers. I wonder if it's my cross or my scent that's getting to him. Or maybe he knows who I am. The Mage's Heir. (The Mage kills vampires; he doesn't think it's murder.) (Why hasn't the Mage killed *these* vampires?)

I follow Baz through the room, wishing I'd worn all the posh gear he tried to push on me before we left Hampshire. I'm wearing my Watford trousers and one of his Scandinavian jumpers—and I only took the jumper because he said my Watford uniform made me look 12.

Baz is walking so slow, I keep kicking the back of his heels. It's like he wants everyone here to get their fill of him. (Maybe he's also trying to hide his limp.) The room gets darker, the deeper we go. I scan the booths for Nicodemus, but I'm not sure I'd recognize him, even if there were enough light. Does he still look like a mean, boy version of Ebb?

We reach the back wall, and I'm ready to turn around, but Baz continues through a doorway I didn't even see. I follow him down a free-standing spiral staircase with a loose rail. By the time we get to the bottom, I'm dizzy.

Then we're in the basement, I think. It's like a cavern—much larger than the room above us, with an even lower ceiling, and dim blue lights set into the floor, like at the cinema.

It's hard to tell how many of them are down here, because I can't really see, but I feel like I'm in a room full of people. There's electronic music playing, but it's so soft, it sounds like it's coming from far away.

Baz stands at the bottom of the stairs with one hand in his trouser pocket, scanning the room like he's looking for a friend.

They could just set on us now, if they wanted—the vampires—and tear us to pieces. We're hopelessly outnumbered, and we wouldn't have time to cast any good spells. I don't even have my wand on me, though they don't know that. (Baz knows. He couldn't believe I left it at Watford.) (I was in a hurry!)

I could take on some of them with my sword, but probably not all.

I could *go off*. And then, who knows what would happen?

Baz starts walking. The clothes are less posh down here. Are these the down-on-their-luck vampires? How do vampires get down on their luck? Even though we're in the basement, everything and everyone is clean. I don't know what I was expecting. Bloodstains? Blood cocktails? It looks like most people down here are drinking gin. I see bottles of Bombay Sapphire on the tables. Someone makes eye contact with me and holds it, so I let my magic come to my skin—I just think about it overflowing. He looks away.

We're so deep into the cavern now, I've lost track of where the door is. Baz pulls on someone's sleeve—a man almost twice his size. "Nicodemus," Baz says, still not asking questions. The man flicks his head behind him, and Baz lets go.

We walk on, till we get to a row of pool tables.

Baz stops. He pulls a pack of fags from inside his jacket, then lights one with his wand. Everyone standing at the table jolts back. Baz takes a deep breath—the end of the cigarette glows red—and blows the smoke out over the table.

I didn't know he smoked.

"Nicodemus," Baz says, still puffing out smoke.

Then I see him—Ebb. A rougher, rangier Ebb. With his blond hair slicked back. He's wearing a suit, too, but it looks cheap, and there are popped stitches on the sleeve.

He smiles at Baz and eyes him up and down. "Well . . . look at you. Aren't you living the dream."

Baz inhales again, then languidly meets Nicodemus's stare. "My name is Tyrannus Basilton Pitch. And I'm here to talk to you about my mother."

"Of course you are, Mr. Pitch." Nicodemus is practically whispering. "Of course you are."

Nicodemus grins again, and I see the gaps in his smile; his eyeteeth are missing. His tongue is pushing at one of the holes.

The other men who were at the table with him have backed away, leaving the three of us alone now in the dark.

"What do you want from me?" Nicodemus asks.

"I want to know who killed my mother."

"You know who killed her." His tongue pushes into the gap, worrying his gum. "Everyone knows. And everyone knows what your mother did to them who were there."

Baz brings the cigarette up to his mouth, breathes in, then drops his hand, flicking ashes on the floor. "Tell me the rest," he says. "Tell me who was responsible."

Nicodemus laughs. "Or what? Are you going to bite me?" He glances down at the cigarette. "Am I supposed to think you're your mother's son? Going to set us all alight? You haven't killed yourself yet, Mr. Pitch. I don't think you'll choose today."

Baz looks around the room. Like he's thinking about how many vampires he could take with him.

"Tell him the rest," I snarl. "Or *I'll* kill you."

Nicodemus looks over Baz's shoulder at me, and his grin

sours. "You think you're so invincible," he says. "With all your power. Like nothing can beat you."

"Nothing has yet," I say.

He laughs again. It's nothing like Ebb's laugh—Nicodemus laughs like nothing matters; Ebb laughs like everything does.

"Fine," he says. "I'll tell you. Some of it." He lays his cue on the table. "Vampires can't just walk into Watford. We can't go anywhere uninvited. Except home. Someone came to me—a few weeks before the raid—wanting me to broker a deal. That's what I do to get by. Make deals, introduce people. Not a lot of work out there for a vampire who can't bite nor a magician without a wand."

His tongue slides compulsively between his teeth. "The pay was good," he says. "But I said no. My sister lives at Watford. I'd never send death to her door, not unless she wanted it." He turns his jack-o'-lantern smile on Baz again. "I wonder if *you* were part of the plan, Mr. Pitch. Hard to believe the magicians have allowed it. . . . Why *do* they keep allowing it? What are they hoping to *do* with you?"

"Who was it?" Baz says. I don't think he's blinked since we walked in here. "Who came to you? Was it the Humdrum?"

"The Humdrum? Yeah, it was the bogeyman, Mr. Pitch. It was the monster under your bed."

"Was it. The Humdrum," Baz says again.

Nicodemus shakes his head, still smiling. "It was one of you," he says. "But his name isn't worth my life. Maybe you'll kill me if I don't tell—but I'll die for certain if I do."

Baz rests the fag between his lips and slips his wand out his sleeve into his palm. "I could make you tell."

"That would be illegal," Nicodemus says. He's right.

Compulsion spells are forbidden.

"And dangerous," he says. Right again.

"What would the Coven do if you cast a forbidden spell, Tyrannus Basilton?" Nicodemus smirks. "Do you think they would be forgiving of one such as you?"

"I should kill you right here," Baz says, his chest pushing forward. "I don't think anyone would stop me. Or miss you."

I put my hand on Baz's shoulder. "Let's go."

"He hasn't *told* us anything," Baz hisses at me.

"I've told you enough," Nicodemus says.

"Come on," I say, pulling Baz back.

"Yeah, go now," Nicodemus says to Baz. "Go with your mate. You'll find your way back here someday."

Baz tosses his cigarette onto the pool table, and Nicodemus jumps back, losing his composure for the first time. He flails out for his drink and pours it over the fag. Baz is already striding away.

I look at Nicodemus. "Your sister misses you," I say.

Then I turn back to Baz and shuffle to catch up. He waits for me at the top of the stairs. (You'd think I was his best friend—I guess that's what he wants them to think.) Then he's cool as ice, cutting through the room upstairs to the door.

When we get outside, nighttime London is so bright, it hurts my eyes.

We find the car, his father's Jaguar, and Baz has it started before I've even opened the passenger door. As soon as I'm inside, he jerks out of the parking spot and guns it, driving as fast as he can down the busy street. He rides up on a taxi, then wrenches the car into the next lane.

"Hey," I say.

"Shut up, Snow."

"Look—"

**"Shut up!"** He says it with magic, but he's not holding his wand, so it doesn't go anywhere. Then he grabs his wand, and I thinks he's going to curse me, but instead he points it at a bus. **"Make way for the king!"** The bus changes lanes, but there's another car just ahead of it. Baz points at it and casts the spell again. It's a stupid waste of magic.

"You're gonna keel over before we get out of the West End."

He ignores me, points his wand ahead of him, and hits the gas. The next time he casts the spell, I put my hand on his biceps and push some magic into him. **"Make way!"** he says. The cars ahead of him cut to the left and the right. It's like the whole road is parting for him—I've never seen anything like it.

I've never *felt* anything like it.

I close my eyes at every red light and wish for green. Baz pushes the pedal into the floor.

We're flying.

The magic holds as long as I touch Baz's arm.

I feel clean.

I feel like a current.

I don't know how Baz feels. His face is stone, and when we get out of London, tears start to fall from his eyes. He doesn't wipe them or blink them away, so they streak down his cheeks and cling to his jaw.

Once we're in the countryside, he doesn't need my magic to clear the way anymore, and I let go of him. He keeps turning onto smaller and smaller roads until we're driving along some woods, gravel kicking up beneath us and banging on the bottom of the car.

Baz pulls off the road suddenly and hits the brakes, fishtailing halfway into a ditch, then gets out of the car like he's just parallel-parked it, and walks towards the trees.

I open my door and start to follow him, then go back to turn off the car and grab the keys. I run along his footprints in the snow, past the tree line, until I lose his trail in the darkness.

"Baz!" I shout. "Baz!"

I keep moving, nearly tripping on a branch. Then I do trip. *"Baz!"* I see a blaze of light—fire—ahead of me, deeper in the trees.

"Fuck off, Snow!" I hear him yell.

I run towards the light and his voice. "Baz?"

There's another shot of fire. It catches on a branch and takes hold—illuminating Baz, sitting under the tree, his head in his arms.

"What are you doing?" I say. "Put it out."

He doesn't answer me. He's shaking.

"Baz, it's all right. We'll just get the name from someone else. This isn't over. We're going to do what your mother asked us to."

He swings his wand and practically howls, spraying fire all around us. *"This* is what my mother would want for me, you idiot."

I drop to my knees in front of him. "What are you even talking about?"

He sneers at me, baring his teeth—all of them. His canines are as sharp as a wolf's. "My mother died killing vampires," he says. "And when they bit her, she killed herself. It's the last thing she did. If she knew what I am . . . She would never have let me live."

"That's not true," I say. "She loved you. She called you her 'rosebud boy.'"

"She loved what I *was*!" he shouts. "I'm not that boy anymore. I'm one of them now."

"You're not."

"Haven't you been trying to prove I'm a monster since we were kids? Crowley, you have your proof now. Go tell the Mage—tell everyone you were right!" His face is dancing with firelight. I feel the heat at my back. "I'm a vampire, Snow! Are you happy?"

"You're not," I say, and I don't know why I say it, and I don't know why I'm crying all of a sudden.

Baz looks surprised. And irritated. "What?"

"You've never even bitten anyone," I say.

"Fuck. *Off.*"

"No!"

He drops his head in his arms again. "Seriously. Go. This fire isn't for you."

I grab his wrists and pull. "That's right," I say, "it can't be. You always said you'd make sure there was an audience when you finished me off." I pull on him. *"Come on."*

Baz doesn't fight me, just slumps forward. A cloud of sparks settles near him, and I growl at them, blowing them out.

I lift up his chin. "Baz."

"Go away, Snow."

"You're not a monster," I say. His face is cold as a corpse in my hand. "I was wrong. All those years. You're a bully. And a snob. And a complete arsehole. But you're not one of them."

Baz tries to jerk his face away, but I hold it fast. He opens his eyes, and they're pools of grey and black and pain. I can't stand it. I growl again. The fire blows back.

"This is what I deserve," he says.

I shake my head. "Well, it isn't what I deserve."

"Then *go*."

I see the fire flickering in his eyes, which means it must be all around us.

"I won't," I say. "I've never turned my back on you. And I'm not starting now."

# 61

## BAZ

That's it. I'm going to have to spell this imbecile away from me. My last deed will be to save Simon Snow's life, and my whole family will be ashamed.

He's holding on to my face, expecting me to stay alive just because he's told me to—because he's Simon bloody Snow, and he gets whatever he wants if he growls loud enough.

I think I might kiss him before I send him flying.

(Can I get him away from me without breaking any of his bones? What spell will keep him away, so he doesn't come running back into the fire?)

I think I might kiss him. He's right here. And his lips are hanging open (mouth breather) and his eyes are alive, alive, alive.

*You're so alive, Simon Snow.*

*You got my share of it.*

He shakes his head, and he's saying something, and I think I might kiss him.

Because I've never kissed anyone before. (I was afraid I might bite.) And I've never wanted to kiss anyone but him. (I won't bite. I won't hurt him.)

I just want to kiss him, then go.

"Simon . . . ," I say.

And then *he* kisses *me*.

## SIMON

I just want him to shut up and stop talking like this. I just want him to get up and follow me out of here. I just want to be back at Watford in our room, knowing he's there, and that he isn't hurting anyone, and no one is hurting him.

## BAZ

Is this is a good kiss? I don't know.

Snow's mouth is hot. Everything is hot.

He's pushing me, so I push back.

His cross is rattling in my tongue and jaw. His pulse is beating in my throat. And his mouth is killing everything I'm trying to think.

*Simon Snow.*

## SIMON

Baz's mouth is colder than Agatha's.

*Because he's a boy,* I think, and then: *No, because he's a monster.*

He's not a monster. He's just a villain.
He's not a villain. He's just a boy.
*I'm kissing a boy.*
I'm kissing Baz.
He's so cold, and the world is so hot.

## BAZ

I am going to die kissing Simon Snow.
Aleister Crowley, I'm living a charmed life.

## SIMON

If Baz thinks I'm ever letting him go, he's wrong. I like him like this. Under my thumb. Under my hands. Not off plotting and scheming and talking to vampires.

*I've got you now,* I think. *I've finally got you where I want you.*

## BAZ

Snow has done this before.

He's doing this nice thing with his chin. Moving it up and down. Tilting his head. Pushing me back even farther.

I don't try to mimic him. I just let him go.

I'm going to die kissing Simon Snow. . . .
*Simon Snow is going to die kissing me.*

# SIMON

Baz grabs my shoulders and pushes me off him.

It only works because I'm not expecting it.

He reaches into his sleeve and pulls out his wand, then points over my shoulder, screaming, ***"Make a wish!"*** There's fire all around us now, slithering closer through the grass.

Baz's spell lands, and one of the trees goes out, then quickly catches fire again. Baz takes a breath, and I put both hands on his chest, letting him take what he wants from me. ***"Make a wish!"*** he shouts, and his voice is thunder.

The fire dies in one breath—more like it was sucked in than blown out. My ears pop, and smoke pours out of the trees.

I look at Baz.

Was that it? Did he just need me to kiss him to snap out of his suicidal funk?

He drops his wand and reaches up to my jumper (his jumper), then pulls it down at the neck. With his other hand, he tears open my shirt collar, popping the top button, and grabs at my cross, eyeing the chain. He gives the cross a good yank—the chain snaps—and he tosses it away.

Then Baz looks at me like he always looks at me when he's about to attack.

# BAZ

Simon Snow is still going to die kissing me.

Just not today.

# 62

## SIMON

I end up sitting on the ground next to Baz, facing him. Kissing him. He took me by the shoulders a while ago, on either side of my collar, and he won't let go.

I'm not sure what we're doing, to be perfectly honest—but nothing's on fire anymore. And I feel like maybe we've solved *something*. Even though this is probably just a new problem.

For a minute, I think about Agatha, and I feel like a bounder, but then I remember that we're not together anymore, so it's not cheating. And then I think about whether this, what's happening right now, means that I'm gay. But Baz and I are hidden in the trees, and no one can see us, and I decide I don't have to answer that last question right now. I don't have to do anything but hold on to Baz; I *have* to do that.

I've still got my hands on his cheeks, and his cheeks aren't so cold anymore, not where I've been touching them. And when I suck on his lips, they go almost pink. For a few seconds, anyway.

I wonder how long he's wanted this.

I wonder how long *I've* wanted it.

I'd say that I didn't—that the possibility just now occurred to me for the first time. But if that's true, then why is there a list in my head of all the things I've always wanted to do to Baz. Like this:

I push my hand up into his hair. It's smooth and slips through my fingers. I clench my fist in it, and he jams his face forward into mine—then just as suddenly snatches his head away.

"Sorry," I say. (I'm out of breath. It's embarrassing.)

Baz lets go of my jumper and shakes his head, holding on to his forehead. "No. It's . . . Where's your cross?"

I feel for it on the ground around us. When I find it, I hold it up between our faces.

"Put it back on," he says.

"Why? Are you gonna bite me?"

"No. Have I ever bitten you?"

"No. You've never kissed me before either."

"*You* kissed *me,* Snow."

I shrug. "So? *Are* you going to bite me?"

Baz is getting to his feet. "No . . . I'd just rather think less about it. I need to drink. It's been—" He looks around, but it's too dark to see anything. "—too long." He glances back at me, then sheepishly away. "Look, I have to . . . hunt. Will you wait?"

"I'll go with you," I say.

"Crowley," he says, "you will not."

I jump up. "Can it be anything?"

"What?"

"Anything with blood, yeah?"

"What?" he says again. "Yeah."

I take his hand. "Call something. There must be hunting spells."

"There are," he says, lowering his eyebrows. "But they only work at close range."

I squeeze his hand.

He takes out his wand, watching me like I'm being an extra-special idiot. ***"Doe!"*** he says, pointing his wand into the trees. ***"A deer!"*** My magic shimmers around us.

No more than a minute later, a doe steps through the blackened branches.

Baz shivers. "You have to stop doing that."

"What?"

"Godlike displays of magic."

"Why?" I say. "It's cool."

"It's terrifying."

I grin at him. "It's cool."

"Don't watch," he says, walking towards the deer.

I keep smiling at him.

He looks back at me. "Don't watch."

## BAZ

I lead the doe into the trees, where it's too dark for Snow to see us. When I'm done with it, I drop the body into a ravine.

I can't remember the last time I drank so deep.

When I get back, Snow's still sitting in the circle of ash. I know he can't see me; I call out, so I don't startle him. "It's me, Snow."

"You called me Simon before."

I can see it in his eyes when he finally discerns me walking towards him. I light a flame in my hand. (Not *in* my hand— floating above it.) "No, I didn't."

"You did."

"Let's get back to the car," I say. "The neighbours are already going to think we had some sort of dark ritual here."

"I'm not sure we *didn't*," he says, following me.

Snow's quiet when we get to the car. And I'm quiet because I genuinely have no idea how to proceed. How do you pick up from, *"I have to stop kissing you, so I can go drink some blood."*

"You're a vampire," Snow says finally. (I guess *that's* how you pick up.)

I don't answer.

"You really are," he says.

I start the engine.

"I mean, I *knew* it—I've known for years. But you really are. . . ." He touches my cheek. "You're warmer now."

"It's the blood," I say.

"Would you be heavier? If I lifted you?"

"I imagine. I just emptied a deer." I glance over at him; he still looks like something I want to eat. "Don't try."

"How does it work?" he asks.

"I don't know. . . . Magic, blood magic. Virus, magickal virus. I don't know."

"How often do you have to drink?"

"Every night, to feel good. Every few nights, to stay sane."

"Have you ever bitten anyone?"

"No. I'm not a murderer."

"Does it have to be fatal every time? The biting? Couldn't you just drink *some* of a person's blood, then walk away?"

"I can't believe you're asking me this, Snow. You, who can't walk away from half a sandwich."

"So you don't know?"

"I've never tried. I'm not . . . that. My father would kill me if I touched a person." (I think he really would, if I bit a person. He probably should, anyway.)

"Hey," Snow says, wrinkling his forehead at me, "don't."

"What?"

"Think. Whatever you're thinking. Stop."

I exhale, frustrated. "Why doesn't this all *bother* you?"

"What?"

"I'm a *vampire*."

"Well, it used to bother me," he says. "Back when I thought you were going to drain me dry some night— or turn me into a zombie. But the last few days have been properly educational, haven't they?"

"So now that you know I'm a vampire, for certain, you don't care?"

"Now that I know that you just sneak around, drinking household pets and legal game, yeah, I'm not too bothered. It's not like I'm a militant vegetarian."

"And you still don't believe that I'm dead."

He shakes his head once, firmly. "I do not believe that you're dead."

We're at my driveway now, and I turn in. "Sunlight burns me," I say.

He shrugs. "Me, too."

"You're an idiot, Snow."

"You called me Simon before."

"No, I didn't."

# SIMON

I'm not sure why I'm so happy. Nothing's changed.

*Has* anything changed?

The kissing. That's new. The wanting to kiss.

The looking at Baz and thinking about the way his hair falls in a lazy wave over his forehead . . .

Yeah, nope. I've thought about that before.

Baz is a vampire; that's not news.

Baz is apparently the world's most reluctant, least blood-sucking vampire—which is a bit of a surprise.

And also apparently the best-looking. (Now that I've seen a few.)

*I want to kiss a bloke.* That *is* a change, but not one I'm prepared to think about right now.

. . . *Again.* I want to kiss him again.

We park the car in an old barn that's been converted into a garage, then go into the house through the kitchen door. Quietly. So we don't wake anyone. "Are you hungry?" Baz asks.

"Yeah."

He pokes around in the refrigerator. Just your typical teenage vampire, getting a midnight snack.

He shoves a casserole dish into my arms, then grabs some forks. "Milk?" he asks. "Coke?"

"Milk," I say. I'm grinning, I can't stop grinning. He puts the carton on top of the casserole, grabs some cloth napkins from the drawer, then heads back up to his room. It's a struggle to keep up.

I wish I knew what he was thinking. . . .

## BAZ

I don't know what I'm thinking.

# SIMON

When we get up to his room, Baz turns on a lamp—the shade is dark red, so it doesn't give out much light—and sits on the floor at the end of his bed, even though the room is full of comfortable things to sit on.

I sit down next to him, and he takes the casserole dish from me and casts a quick, *"You're getting warmer!"*—then opens the lid. It's shepherd's pie.

"Do you *need* to eat?" I ask. "Or do you just like it?"

"I need it," he says, scooping up a bite, avoiding my eyes, "just not as much as other people do."

"How do you know that you're not immortal?"

He hands me a fork. "No more questions."

We finish the shepherd's pie, eating out of the bowl on Baz's lap. He chews with his hand over his mouth. I try to remember whether I've ever seen him eat before. . . . I finish the milk. He doesn't want any.

When we're done, he sets the dishes outside his door, then starts a fire in the fireplace with his wand.

I crawl over to sit next to him. "You're a pyro," I say.

He shrugs, staring into the fire.

"You're not thinking about burning the house down, are you?"

"No, Snow. I don't have a death wish. I wish I did—it would make everything easier."

"Please stop talking like that."

He doesn't say anything for a moment. And then he turns to me, abruptly. "Is that why you kissed me? To keep me from killing myself?"

I shake my head. "Not exactly. I mean, I *did* want to keep you from killing yourself."

"Why, then?" he asks.

"Why did I kiss you?"

"Yeah."

"I guess I wanted to," I say, shrugging.

"Since when?"

I shrug again, and it pisses him off. He wedges another log into the fire.

"Did you want me to?" I ask.

"No," he says. "Why would I want that? Why would that thought even occur to me? *'Hey, you know what would fix this miserable situation with the vampires and my mother and the war and the decline of magic? Snogging my halfwit roommate. The one who will probably fuck my life for good someday. That's a plan.'*"

"You don't have to be such a prat," I say. "We're on the same side here."

"For the moment," Baz says. "You'll help me find out who killed my mother, I'll kill whoever it is, and then you'll make sure I get thrown in a tower for it. You've already won—as soon as you tell the Mage I'm a vampire, he'll pull out my fangs and snap my wand. I'll end up in Covent Garden, licking Nicodemus's heels. And that's if I'm *lucky.*"

Does Baz really think I'd do that? Now? "Those vampires were in awe of you," I say. "They wanted to put a crown on your head."

"Are you suggesting I cross over?"

"No. I'm just saying, you were amazing today."

"You're not listening to me at all, are you?"

"*I am,*" I say. "But you're wrong. Nothing's going back to normal after this. How could it?"

"Because we're friends now?"

"Because we're more than that."

Baz picks up a poker and jabs at the fire. "One kiss, and you think the world is upside down."

"Two kisses," I say. And I take him by the back of his neck.

# BAZ

I don't know what time it is.

The darkness has changed colour in the room, like the sun is sneaking up on us. We're lying on our backs next to the fire, what's left of it, holding hands.

Snow sighs and squeezes my hand—and when I yelp, he frowns and holds it up between us: There's a cross-shaped burn on my palm from when I yanked his necklace off last night. (His cross is on the other side of the room now; Snow took care of it himself this time.)

He brings my palm to his mouth and kisses it.

"I didn't think you were gay," I say. Quietly.

He shrugs. Half of Snow's sentences are shrugs.

"What does that mean?" I whisper.

"I don't know," he says, closing his eyes. "I guess I've never thought much about what I am. I've got a lot on my plate."

That makes me laugh. A juvenile snorty laugh. Snow starts laughing with me. "A lot on your plate?" I repeat.

"Are *you* gay?" he asks, looking over at me, still laughing.

"Yeah," I say. "Completely."

"So you do this all the time?"

I roll my eyes. "No."

"Then how do you know you're gay?"

"I just do. How do you *not* know?"

"Dunno," he says. He laces his fingers in mine and holds my hand loosely. "I try not to think."

"About being gay?"

"About anything. I make lists of things not to think about."

"Why?"

"Because," he says, "it hurts to think about things that you can't have or help. S'better not to think about it."

I rub my thumb back and forth on the back of his hand. "Am I on your list?"

He laughs again and shakes his head; his hair brushes against mine. "Fat chance." He sounds sleepy. "Trying not to think about you . . . S'like trying not to think about an elephant that's standing on my chest."

I think about that.

About Snow thinking about me.

I grin. "I can't decide whether that's a compliment. . . ."

"Me neither," he says.

"So you don't *think*," I say.

"S'pointless."

I raise myself up on one elbow and look down on him. "I don't understand you. You're the most powerful magician alive—who's ever lived, probably. You can have anything you want. How is it pointless for you to think about that?"

Snow pushes up on both elbows and lets his head fall in my direction. "Because it doesn't matter. In the end, I just do what's expected of me. When the Humdrum comes after me, I fight him. When he sends dragons, I kill them. When you trick me into meeting a chimera, I go off. I don't get to choose or plan. I just take it as it comes. And someday, something will catch me unawares or be too big to fight, but I'll fight anyway.

I'll fight until I can't anymore—what is there to *think* about?"

Simon drops back onto the floor. I reach out and very carefully push his curls back off his forehead. He closes his eyes.

"I always thought you were going to kill me," I say.

"Me, too," he says. "I tried not to think about it."

I wind my fingers in his hair. It's thicker than mine, and curlier, and it shines golden in the firelight. There's a mole on his cheek that I've wanted to kiss since I was 12. I do.

"For a long time," I say.

"Hmmm?" He opens one eye.

"I've wanted to do this for a long time. Almost since we met . . ."

Snow closes his eyes again and smiles like he's trying not to.

I smile, too, only because he isn't watching. "I thought it was going to kill me."

# 63

## AGATHA

Penelope wakes me up by pulling the covers down. I yank them back up.

"Wake up, Agatha. We have to go."

"I'll go later. I'm sleeping."

"No, we have to go. Now. Come on."

I'm lying at the end of her bed. We slept this way, and she kept kicking me in the back.

"Go *away*, Penelope."

"I'm trying. But I need you to drive me."

I open my eyes. "Drive you where?"

"I can't tell you. Yet. But I will."

"Somewhere in London?"

"No."

"Penny, it's Christmas Eve. I have to go home."

"I know!" She's already dressed. She's got her hair pulled back in a giant frizzy ponytail that would probably be nice and wavy if she'd put any product in it at all. *Anything.* Hand lotion. Shaving cream. "And you *can* go home, Agatha. But first I need you to drive me to the country."

"Why?"

"It's a surprise," she says.

"No."

"An adventure?"

"I'm going home."

Penny sighs. "We have to go help Simon."

I close my eyes and roll away from her.

"Agatha? Come on . . . Is that a yes or a no? If it's a no, can I take your Volvo?"

# 64

## BAZ

I wake up at least an hour before Snow.

It's hard not to watch him sleep.

I've done it before—excessively—but that's when I thought I was never going to get any more than that. That's when creeping on Snow felt like my life's consolation prize.

I'm still not sure what's happening between us. We kissed last night. And this morning. A lot. Does that mean we get to do it today? He's not even sure that he's gay. (Which is moronic. But Snow is a moron. So.)

He's lying on my couch, and I'm sitting at the end, next to his legs. He rolls into the cushions, burying his face. "You don't get to watch me sleep now," he says, "just because we're snogging."

"Just because we snogged," I correct him. "And I'm not watching you; I'm trying to figure out how to wake you up without you pulling a sword on me."

"I'm up," he says, dragging one of the cushions down over his head.

"Come on. Bunce is on her way."

He lifts the pillow up. "What? Why?"

"I told her we have new information—she has some, too. We're having a briefing."

He sits up. "So she's just coming here?"

"Yes."

"To your Gothic mansion?"

"It's not Gothic; it's Victorian."

Snow rubs his hair. "Is this a trap? Are you luring us all here to kill us?" He seems genuinely suspicious.

"How did I *lure* you? You hitchhiked to my door."

"After you invited me," he snaps.

"Yes. You caught me. I'm a villain." I stand. "I'll see you in the library when you've cleaned up." I try not to look like I'm stomping away from him—I wait till I leave the room, then stomp down the stairs.

I don't know what I expected. For Snow to open his eyes and see me there, then pull me into one of his expert kisses and say, *"Good morning, darling"*?

Simon Snow is never going to call me "darling."

Though he did just say we were snogging. . . .

We don't have a chalkboard in the house, but my stepmother has a giant whiteboard in the kitchen that she uses to keep track of all my siblings' lessons and sport. I take a photo of it with my mobile, then erase the board and lift it off the wall.

My 7-year-old sister watches me do it. "I'm telling Mum," she says.

"If you do, I'll stop up all the chimneys, so Father Christmas can't get in."

"There are too many chimneys," she counters.

"Not for me," I say. "I'm willing to put the time in."

"He'll just come to the door."

"Don't be an idiot, Mordelia, Father Christmas never comes to the door. And if he did, I'd tell him he had the wrong house." I'm carefully manoeuvring the whiteboard through the kitchen door.

"I'm telling Mum!" she shouts after me.

I prop the board up in the library, and I'm making columns—*Everything we know* and *Everything we still don't*—when Snow walks into the room. I ignore him.

"It's not that I think you'll betray us," he says.

I make a noise that I'm afraid sounds a lot like "harrumph."

Simon hassles his curls with one hand. "It's just . . . Well, it's still weird between us, isn't it?"

I continue ignoring him.

"I mean . . . you haven't said . . . that things are different now for you. *I've* said that I'm not going to kill you."

"No, you haven't," I say.

"It must have been implied."

"No."

"Um, all right." He clears his throat. "Baz. I'm not going to kill you. I'm not going to fight you at all, am I?"

"Good," I say, stepping back from the whiteboard and admiring my columns. "That will make things much easier."

"What things?"

"Crowley, I don't know. Whatever the Families cook up for me. Probably I'll be the one they ask to poison your Ribena, now that you trust me. What I *can* promise, Snow, is to weep over your corpse."

"Or not," he says.

"Fine, I'll weep in privacy when the day arrives."

"No," he insists, "I'm serious. *Or not.*"

I look over my shoulder at him. "What are you trying to say?"

"That we don't have to fight."

"You realize that your mentor has raided my house twice this month."

"Yeah—I mean, no, I didn't realize that—but the point is, *I* didn't raid your house. What if," he says, stepping closer, "I help you find out who killed your mum, then you help me fight the Humdrum, and we just forget about the rest?"

"*'The rest,'*" I say, turning around. "Way to oversimplify a decade of corruption and abuse of power."

"Are you talking about the Mage?"

"Yes."

He looks pained. "I wish you wouldn't."

"How can I not talk about the Mage when I'm talking to *the Mage's Heir*?"

"Is that how you think of me?"

"Isn't that how you think of yourself? Oh, right. I forgot— you don't think at all."

Simon groans and rakes at his hair. "Jesus Christ. Do you *ever not* go for the lowest blow? Like, do you ever think, 'Maybe I shouldn't say the *most* cruel thing just now?'"

"I'm trying to be efficient."

He leans against the shelf where I've set the whiteboard. "It's vicious."

"You should talk, Snow. You always go for the kill shot."

"When I'm fighting. We're not fighting."

"We're always fighting," I say, going back to the board.

I'm facing the board; he's standing next to me, facing the room. He leans towards me a bit, without looking at me, and bumps his arm against mine, ruining the word I'm writing. "Or *not*," he says.

I erase the word and start over. I'm working on the *Everything we still don't* list. I'm tempted to write: *everything important* and also: *whether Simon Snow is actually gay.* And: *whether I'll live forever.*

"I'll help you find out who killed your mother," he says again, like he's laying out a plan. "And you'll help me stop the Humdrum—that's a shared goal, yeah?—and then we'll worry about the rest later."

"Is this how you get what you want? By just repeating it until it comes true?"

"Isn't that how you cast a spell?"

My chalk hand drops, and I turn to him, exasperated. "Simon—"

"A-ha!" he shouts, springing up and pointing. It scares the hell out of me. I've seen him kill a dog with less effort. (He said the dog was *were;* I think it was just excited.) "You did it again!"

"Did what?" I say, slapping his hand away from my face.

He sticks his other hand in my face, pointing. "Called me Simon."

"What would you prefer—Chosen One?"

His hand dips. "I prefer Simon, actually. I . . . I like it."

I swallow, and it must be obvious how nervous I am, because he looks down at my neck. "Simon," I say, and swallow again, "you're being idiotic."

"Because I like this better than fighting?"

"There is no 'this'!" I protest.

"You slept in my arms," he says.

"Fitfully."

He lets his hand fall, and I catch it. Because I'm weak. Because I'm a constant disappointment to myself. Because he's standing right there with his tawny skin and his moles and his morning breath.

"Simon," I say.

He squeezes my hand.

"It's not that I don't prefer *this*. It's that . . ." I sigh. "I can't even imagine it. My family objects to everything the Mage stands for."

"I know," he says emphatically. "But I actually think we

have bigger problems than that. If we find out who killed your mum, and then we go after the Humdrum together—maybe we can help everyone see that we're better off uniting, and then—"

"And then the whole World of Mages will see how much better it is to work together, and we'll sing a song about cooperation."

"I was thinking we'd stop cursing each other," he says, "and locking each other up in towers."

"Potato, potahto."

He pulls at my arm and I fall forward a bit. Or maybe I'm swooning—it's not beneath me. (Snow is. Beneath me. Always. By at least three inches.)

"How can you be like this?" I whisper. "How can you even trust me, after everything?"

"I'm not sure I do trust you," he whispers back. He reaches out with his other hand and touches my stomach. I feel it drop to the floor. (My stomach, that is.) "But . . ." He shrugs.

He's rubbing my stomach, and I close my eyes—because it feels good. (So good.) And also because I want him to kiss me again.

Snow kissed me last night until my mouth was sore. He kissed me so much, I was worried I'd Turn him with all my saliva. He held himself up on all fours above me and made me reach up for his mouth—and I did. I would again. I'd cross every line for him.

I'm in love with him.

And he likes this better than fighting.

# 65

## SIMON

If Penelope were here, I'd tell her she's wrong about me. She thinks I solve everything with my sword. But apparently, I can also solve things with my mouth—because, so far, every time I lean into Baz, he shuts up and closes his eyes.

If Penelope were here, she'd make me explain myself.

Thank magic she isn't here yet.

I've just pushed my fingers between Baz's shirt buttons; his skin is room temperature.

Then someone clears her throat. Baz stands up straight, which means his mouth jerks away from mine. I step away so quickly, I'm not sure I didn't teleport.

His maid or nanny or whatever she is, is standing in the archway. She's wearing a black dress and a white apron. "Mr. Pitch," she says, and she must get paid to pretend she doesn't notice anything around here, because she doesn't even flinch. Boys kissing is probably mild—she's probably walked into interrogations and goat sacrifices. "You have guests," she says. "Two young ladies."

"Thank you, Vera," Baz says without a hint of apology. "Send them in." He straightens his shirt and smooths down his hair.

"Girls?" I say. "More than one?"

"Agatha," Baz says over my shoulder, "welcome. Hello, Bunce."

I spin around. Penelope and Agatha are standing in the library door; they must not have waited for the maid to come back for them. Penny's already eyeing the library bookshelves lustfully. Agatha's looking at me.

"What are you doing here?" I say.

"Baz called us," Penny says. She walks into the room and hands me a plate of gingerbread biscuits covered in clingfilm.

"What are *you* doing here?" Agatha asks me.

"Agatha was staying with me," Penny explains, "and she had her car, so—"

"Please come in, Agatha," Baz invites. "Could I get you both something to drink?"

"I'll have tea," Penny says.

"Excellent," he says, striding past Agatha out the door.

"What is this?" Agatha says. "Penelope wouldn't even tell me where we were going. What are you *doing* here, Simon?"

I frown at Penny.

She unwraps the plate of gingerbread and takes one. "I didn't know what I was allowed to say! And I didn't think she'd drive me if I told her where we were going. You two need to get over this, Simon. If you can make peace with Baz, you can make peace with Agatha."

"Temporary peace," Baz says, already back with tea and a plate of fruit. He must have used magic.

"I'll pour," Penny says.

"Temporary peace?" Agatha asks. Penny hands her a cup of tea. "Are you all *possessed*?" She hands the tea back. "I'm not drinking this."

Baz looks at me. "Your call, Snow. Do you trust her?"

Agatha's fuming. "Does he trust *me*?"

"Of course," I say. And it's true, to some extent, anyway. I trust Agatha not to be evil. I don't trust her alone with Baz—though I guess I should rethink all that, in light of recent information. "Agatha, um—"

"We're trying to figure out who killed Baz's mother," Penelope cuts in.

"The Humdrum killed her," Agatha says.

Penny holds her teacup up, gesturing with it. "Not according to her, he didn't."

Agatha looks confused. And a little pissed off.

I look to Baz. It seems like he should be the one to tell this part, as much of it as he wants to, but he's back at his whiteboard, filling out the *Everything we know* column—*ghosts, Visitings, vampires*. Penny jumps up as soon as Baz adds *Nicodemus* to the list.

I take her place on the couch next to Agatha.

"When did this all start?" Agatha asks me.

"When the Veil thinned," I say. "Natasha Grimm-Pitch came through to find Baz and found me instead. She wants him to find her murderer. When Baz came back, I told him I'd help him figure it out."

Agatha's eyebrows are almost touching in the middle, and her nose is wrinkled. "Why?"

"Because it seemed like the right thing to do."

"It *did*?"

I shrug. "Yeah. I mean—it was an attack on Watford. A murder."

"What did the Mage say about all this?"

"He didn't. Exactly." I look down at my lap, scratching the hair above my neck. "Penny and Baz don't think we should tell him."

"Penny *and Baz* think?"

"It's Baz's mum," I say, "so I feel like I should respect his wishes on this."

"But Baz hates you!"

I nod. "I know. We're sort of . . . on a truce?"

"Simon, listen to yourself—a *truce*?"

"You went to a vampire bar!" Penny shouts from across the room. Baz must be catching her up. "What a pair of splendid morons you are! Did you take photos?"

"Vampires don't show up in photos," I say.

"That's mirrors, you dolt," Baz says.

"You can't see yourself in the mirror?"

Baz ignores me and goes back to telling Penny about Nicodemus.

"But . . ." Agatha is staring at the two of them. "Baz is dark. He's *evil.*"

"I thought you never believed that," I say.

"I absolutely believed it," she says. "You told us he was a *vampire*, Simon. Wait—" She turns to him, then back to me. "—did he just now admit that he *is* a vampire?"

I pull at the hair on my neck. I can tell I'm making an idiotic face. "I'm not sure it's that simple. . . ."

"That Baz is a vampire?"

"No, he's definitely a vampire," I say. "I guess it is that simple. But you can't tell anyone, Agatha."

"Simon, *you've* already told everyone. You've been telling everyone since we were third years."

"Yeah, but nobody believed me."

"*I* believed you."

"'One of you'?" Penelope says loudly. "What does Nicodemus mean by that? That it was another mage who let the vampires in? Or one of you Pitches, someone in your family—"

"It wouldn't have been someone in my family," Baz protests. "Never."

"Your relatives are famous betrayers," Penny argues. "There was a time in the 1700s when they weren't even allowed to sign contracts."

"Yes, but we never betray *each other*."

Baz keeps telling Penny about Nicodemus. And Ebb. "Simon's the one who broke it all open," he says, "without even opening a book."

"Typical," Penny says.

Baz doesn't tell her the way Nicodemus threatened him or taunted him. He doesn't tell her much about Fiona. He doesn't say how fucking cool he was at the bar, or how he lost it completely as soon as he walked out. How I kissed him to save his life—and then kissed him just because I wanted to. (I'm just now realizing that maybe I could have saved his life some other way. . . . )

"So you're staying here?" Agatha says. To me.

"No, I just came to tell Baz about Nicodemus, and then I didn't have a ride home."

"Who's Nicodemus again?"

"The person who knows who the traitor is," Penny answers, then turns to me. "I can't believe you guys just walked away from him, knowing he has all the answers! If he'd told you who tried to hire him, we'd be done now."

"We couldn't compel him," I say. "And we couldn't beat it out of him—we were surrounded by vampires."

Penelope folds her arms. "I guess."

"The ethics on you, Bunce," Baz says.

"What did *you* find out, Penny?" I ask.

"Not much, in comparison." She leans back against a bookshelf and crosses her ankles. "I talked to my dad about the Humdrum. He confirmed that nobody blamed the

Humdrum for the Watford Tragedy until years later. They just thought it was another vampire attack. Hey, Agatha, are you caught up yet? Maybe we could talk to *your* parents—your dad might remember something—"

"I'm not caught up," Agatha says.

"Well, catch up," Penny says. "It's all on the whiteboard. I've got to say, it's good to have you back."

"I'm not sure I am back," Agatha mutters. Only I hear her.

"It's been really good," I tell her. "Actually. Working with Baz instead of fighting with him."

"Is that why you were looking for him?" she asks. "That night on the ramparts? Because of a Visiting?"

"Sort of . . ."

Penny and Baz keep adding notes to the board. They're fighting over the dry-erase marker. I feel like I should stay sitting with Agatha, and answer her questions, but she doesn't say any more. And she still won't drink any tea.

Penny drills Baz until she finds out about Fiona's school memory book, then she wants to see it. Then Penny and Agatha spend an hour poring over the pictures.

Baz's stepmum brings us sandwiches. When she walks in, Baz and Penny move to block the whiteboard—Baz, looking cool; Penny, looking like she has a terrible secret.

I try to convince them that it's stupid to have all our notes out in the open, and that we should erase the whiteboard now, but they're both addicted to the thing.

Then Baz's dad comes home from work. He still seems confounded by my presence, but he's thrilled to meet Penny and Agatha—even though I know he doesn't get along with their parents. Maybe he just has nice manners. Baz keeps rolling his eyes.

By late afternoon, we're all cream-crackered, and we

haven't made any real progress. Even Penny has abandoned the whiteboard.

I'm still sitting next to Agatha on the couch. Baz is sitting in a stuffed chair, across from us; I think Agatha and I are both watching him, but he rarely looks our way.

Penelope slumps down onto the arm of Baz's chair. I see his nostrils twitch, but he doesn't pull away. I guess he's gone this long without eating anyone, so I'm not going to be bothered about it.

"We have to go back to Nicodemus," Penny says. "It's what Headmistress Grimm-Pitch told us to do."

"We can't compel him," I say, "and he's not gonna tell us anything."

"Maybe you guys didn't ask *nicely* enough," she says, waggling her eyebrows.

"Corking idea, Penelope," Baz says. "We'll have you *seduce* him."

"*No,*" I say.

"I was thinking Agatha . . . ," Penny says.

"I'm not even here," Agatha says. "When you're all put on trial before the Coven, I wasn't here."

"We haven't broken any laws," I object.

"Oh, like that matters," she says.

"Hear, hear," Baz agrees. "You know, I've always expected to be tried unfairly before the Coven someday, but I never thought I'd be in such good company."

"Nobody's *seducing* a vampire," I say.

Baz frowns at me.

"Unless," I say, "we could convince your aunt—"

"*No.*"

"I don't know how you're going to get this vampire to confess to murder," Agatha says flatly, "when you can't even get Baz to tell you where he was for two months."

"He was ill," Penny says. She turns to Baz. "Weren't you? You said you were ill. You certainly *looked* ill."

"He wasn't ill," Agatha says. "Dev said he was missing."

Baz's lip curls. "Dev told you that?"

"I told you your relatives are betrayers," Penny says.

Baz sneers some more. "He only told Agatha because he has a dirty crush on her."

"See," Penny says, "I *told* you we could use Agatha to seduce people."

"You said you were ill," I say to Baz.

He looks at me, narrows his eyes into a glare, then looks away. "I *was* ill," he says, crossing one leg over the other and smoothing out his dark trousers. "But I was also missing."

"Where were you?" I demand.

He meets my eyes again, still glaring, "I really don't think this is relevant—"

"Everything is relevant," Penny says.

"I—" He clears his throat and looks down at his knees. "—was kidnapped."

I sit up. "Kidnapped?"

"Kidnapped," he repeats, then clears his throat again. "By numpties."

"Numpties?" Penny says. "Was it an accident? Did they mistake you for a hot water bottle?"

"They put a bag over my head while I was leaving the club, actually."

Agatha sits up. "You were kidnapped at *the club*?"

"Why didn't you tell anyone?" I ask.

"Well, I tried," he says. "I guess nobody heard me shouting from inside the coffin."

I'm still holding a sandwich. I drop it. "The numpties kept

you in a coffin? For two months?"

"Six weeks," he mutters. "And I think they thought they were doing me a favor, with the coffin. . . ."

Penny shoves his shoulder. "Basil. Why didn't you tell *us*?"

"Why didn't I tell you?" He's glaring at her now. "Think about it: Who would pay numpties to kidnap the heir to the House of Pitch? Who has it out for my family right now? Who's raided my house twice in the last month—who threw my cousin in a tower?"

"Not the Mage," I say.

"Of course the Mage!" Baz has got both his hands in his pockets, and he's leaning forward over his crossed legs, his elbows flaring out. "He thought he could terrify my parents, so they'd co-operate with his latest campaign. It must drive him mad to see me at school and know I got away from him! Why didn't I tell you? *'Hey, Simon, your Jedi master is out to get me, do we still have a truce?'*"

"How did you get away?" I ask.

"Fiona found me. She's fearless."

"That's why you were so thin," I say. "And pale. And why you're still limping. Did they hurt you?"

He sits back, looking down at his lap. "Not intentionally, I don't think. They did something to my leg when they caught me, and it didn't get a chance to heal."

"You should go see my dad," Agatha says.

"Is he a vampire doctor now?"

"Was there a ransom?" Penny asks.

"Yeah," Baz says. "My family wouldn't pay it. Pitches don't negotiate for hostages."

"If I'm ever kidnapped at the club," Agatha says, "tell my parents to pay the ransom."

"My aunt found me with a souped-up finding spell," Baz

says. "She canvassed most of London."

"I would have helped," I say. "It wouldn't have taken six weeks with me helping."

Baz is scornful. "You never would have helped my family."

"I would! It was driving me mental not knowing where you were. I thought you were going to jump out from every corner."

"It wasn't the Mage . . . ," Penny says. Thoughtfully.

"*This* is why I didn't tell you lot," Baz says. "I knew you wouldn't believe me. You're so convinced that the Mage is a hero—"

"No," Penny cuts him off. "It wasn't *the Mage*, Baz—it was the murderer!"

"I thought it was numpties . . . ," Agatha says.

"It was the same person who sent vampires after your mother!" Penny says, jumping to her feet. "They knew that the Veil was lifting, and that there was a good chance your mum would come back to talk to you. It was a classic Visit—a dangerous secret, a crime against justice. The traitor was worried that Natasha Pitch might come back, and *knew* that she'd come back to you. So he—or she, I guess—hid you. This used to happen all the time! There's a family in Scotland who lost a different family member every twenty years because the murderer kept killing the person most likely to avenge the previous deaths. No one wanted a ransom for you, Baz—they just wanted you tucked away until the Visitings were over."

Baz looks at her. Licks his lips. "Not the Mage?" he asks.

"The *murderer*," Penny says—looking all too pleased about it, considering that murderer is still at large.

"If that's true," Agatha says, "then we need to tell the Mage about all of this. Immediately."

# 66

## PENELOPE

All right, fine. It was probably a mistake to bring Agatha.

But it had gone on too long, all this tension between her and Simon. I didn't want them to go all year without sorting it out.

And I thought maybe a good mystery might distract her from—well, from everything else. I should have remembered that Agatha doesn't appreciate a good mystery.

And also that she's the world's worst snitch.

"We *have* to tell the Mage," she says, crossing her arms and then her legs. "You all know it."

She's doing her best not to look at either of the boys. . . . I also should have thought through their whole love-triangle dynamic before I dragged Agatha to Baz's house. But their whole love-triangle dynamic is so persistently stupid, you can't blame me for blocking it out.

"Agatha," I say, "we're just starting to make some progress here."

"Towards what?" she asks. "Infiltrating the numpties?"

"We could just talk to them," Simon offers. "Can numpties talk?"

"Barely," Baz says. "And what are we going to ask

them—'*Lose something?*'"

"We're going to ask who hired them to kidnap you," I say.

"They might not feel co-operative," Baz says. "My aunt did kill a few of them."

Simon looks horrified. "Your aunt murdered numpties?"

"In self-defence!"

"Did they attack her?"

"In *my* self-defence," Baz says. "Are you really taking their side? They held me hostage for six weeks."

"Your aunt should have asked for help!"

"If you'd have been there, Snow, *all* the numpties would be dead."

"Maybe." Simon sticks his chin out. "But it wouldn't have taken six weeks."

"So we'll interrogate the remaining numpties," I say.

"We will not," Agatha says. "We'll tell the Mage and let him handle this—it's his job to handle it. We're talking about kidnapping! And murder!"

"Look here, Wellbelove," Baz says. "We're not going to the Mage. We've all already agreed."

"Well, *I* didn't agree." Agatha looks furious, and also fed up, and also I think she was supposed to be home two hours ago.

Simon puts his hand on her shoulder. "Baz, she's right. A lot has changed. We know about Nicodemus now, and we've connected your mum's murder to your kidnapping—"

"No," I say. "We're not going to the Mage."

Simon looks surprised. "Penny, come on. Why not?"

"Because Baz is right, Simon. The Mage isn't in any mood to help the Pitch family right now. And he's right that we all already agreed not to involve the Mage."

Agatha huffs.

"I know you didn't agree, Agatha," I say. "But you also don't have to be part of this."

She huffs again.

"I mean, you don't have to be part of this *from now on*. I'm sorry I dragged you here."

"I need to get home," she says. "It's Christmas Eve."

I look at my watch. "Damn. My mum's going to hit the roof. We've got to go. We'll regroup on Boxing Day, yeah?"

The boys nod, both of them staring at the floor.

There's not much to gather up. Baz goes to get our coats. I'm disappointed that we didn't get to see more of his house—or even dig into the library. I went to the bathroom a few times, but it's just down the hall, and it seems like a modern addition. (There's a Japanese toilet in there with comforting music and a seat warmer.)

Agatha pulls on a soft white hat and a matching scarf. "Come on, Simon, didn't you bring a coat?"

Simon is still sitting on one of the couches, thinking too hard about something. Probably about killing numpties. He looks up. "What?"

"Come on," Agatha says. "We have to go."

"Go where?"

"We came to get you," she says.

He still looks confused. "To take me back to Watford?"

Agatha furrows her brow. (She's going to have a vicious wrinkle there someday, and I'm going to laugh about it.) "Just . . . come on," she says. "It's Christmas Eve. My parents will be glad to see you."

Simon smiles like somebody just handed him a huge present. Baz is standing behind him, grimacing. (Irritating love-triangle dynamic.) I think Simon is right; you really can see Baz's fangs sometimes through his cheeks.

Baz clears his throat, and Simon looks back over his shoulder.

"I . . . ," Simon says. "Well, actually, I feel like maybe I should keep working on this numpties thing."

Merry Morgana, does Simon actually realize that getting back together with Agatha would be a terrible idea?

"*Simon.*" Agatha is staring hard at him, but I'm not sure what she means by it. I don't think *she* wants to get back together either. She's probably just tired, and tired of ignoring each other.

Maybe she feels like a jerk about leaving him at Pitch Manor on Christmas Eve. I know I do. The vibe here is very, *Let's kill a virgin and write a great Led Zeppelin album.* (Though the library is lovely, and Baz's stepmum seems very nice.) (I wonder, *is* Simon still a virgin . . . ) (Surely not.) (Maybe?)

"But I thought—" Simon says.

"Come on," Agatha insists. "If you don't come, who'll eat all the leftovers and make sure we watch *Doctor Who*?"

Simon glances back at Baz. Baz still looks pissed off. I wonder if there's an Agatha clause in the truce. Maybe she's a no-fly zone.

But that's not fair: Agatha isn't just Simon's not-at-all-suited-for-him ex-girlfriend; she's also one of his only friends. And she *will* be, even after this truce has ended.

"Come on, Simon," I say. "We'll regroup after Christmas."

"Right . . ." He turns to me. "*Right.* I'll get my jacket."

# 67

## BAZ

I'm holding my violin, not playing it, when my father comes back to the library.

"The Magelings are gone," he says.

I nod. He walks into the room and sits on the long horse-hair couch, where Simon spent most of the afternoon. Father's dressed for dinner. We dress for dinner on Sundays and holidays, and tonight he's wearing a black suit with a red sheen. His hair went white when my mother died, but it looks like mine—thick, with a bit of wave and a stark widow's peak. It's nice to see that my hairline probably won't recede completely.

Everyone says I favour my mother in appearance—we're from the Egyptian branch of the Pitch family—but I consciously mimic the way my father carries himself: the way you can never see what's happening behind his eyes. I've practised that in front of the mirror. (*Of course* I can see myself in the mirror; Simon Snow is a fool.)

Currently I'm pretending that I don't care that Snow left. I'm pretending I don't even notice he's gone.

I'm not sure why it surprised me when he left—I'd been reminding him for the last twenty-four hours that we weren't friends, kisses notwithstanding. So I shouldn't be shocked and dismayed that he left with the two people who actually are his friends. . . . With the one person he's always wanted, as long as I've known him.

Father clears his throat and crosses his legs idly. "Are you in over your head, Basilton?"

No one ever calls me Tyrannus. My mother insisted on it because it's a family name, but my father hates it.

"No," I say.

"Is this part of some mad scheme of your aunt's?" He sounds bored. He picks at his trouser leg, pulling the crease straight.

"No," I say blandly. "It's a school project, actually. I thought I'd play nice for once, see where it gets me."

He raises an eyebrow. It's so quiet in the library, I can hear his watch tick.

"Because it would be a bad time to make a move," he says, "independently. The Families have their own plan."

"With a role for me?"

"Not yet. I'd like you to finish school first. I'd like you to recover. I was talking to your mother—she thought you might like to speak to someone . . . About your situation."

He calls Daphne my mother. I don't mind.

"A doctor?" I say.

"More of a counsellor."

"A *psychologist*?" That didn't come out bored. I settle my face. Clear my throat. "Father," I say more calmly, "I can't imagine what part of my situation could be discussed with a Normal therapist."

"Your mother . . . She mentioned that you're already accustomed to speaking about your condition carefully. You could avoid specifics."

"I'm fine," I say.

"Your mother—"

"I'll consider it."

He stands. Gracefully. Shoots his cuffs. "Dinner will be ready soon," he says. "You should change."

"Of course, Father."

Daphne bought me a grey suit for the holidays—but I'm stuck in grey every day at school, and I'm already grey enough. So I put on a dark green one that I picked out myself. Greenish black with a bit of silver. I'm just knotting a blood-pink tie when Mordelia opens my bedroom door.

"Knock," I say to her in the mirror.

"Your—"

"Leave. And knock. I'm ignoring you until you do."

She groans and leaves, slamming the bedroom door behind her, then bangs on it. I'd despair if she were a Pitch. She doesn't behave as if she has an ounce of Grimm in her either; my stepmother's blood is thin as gruel.

"Come in," I say.

Mordelia opens the door and leans in. "Your friend's back."

I turn from the mirror. "What?"

"The Chosen One."

"Simon?"

She nods. I push past her out the door, muttering, "Don't call him that," then run down the stairs. If he's here, something must be wrong. Maybe they were attacked on the road. . . . I slow down when I get to the dining room.

Simon is standing in the foyer, covered in snow and muck. Again.

I put my hands in my pocket. "Déjà vu, Snow."

He runs his hand through his hair, smearing it with mud. "There's still no good way to get from the road to your house."

"And you still can't remember a basic weatherization spell. Where are the girls?"

"Halfway to London by now."

"Why aren't you with them?"

He shrugs.

I walk down the last steps into the foyer and take out my wand.

He holds up his hand. "I'd prefer to just take a shower and change, if you don't mind."

"Why'd you come back?" I say—softly, just in case Mordelia is lurking around.

"I can leave if I'm not welcome."

"That's not what I meant."

"I thought you'd be happy that I came back."

I step closer to him, and my voice drops to a menace. "Why? So we can tumble around and kiss and pretend to be happy boyfriends?"

He shakes his head, like he's at his limit, then rolls his eyes mightily. "Yeah . . . I guess so. *Yes.* Let's do that, okay?"

I fold my arms. "Take off your shoes. I'll find you something to wear. You'll make us late to dinner."

Simon looks stunning in a grey suit.

# SIMON

I came back because I was afraid of what might happen if I didn't.

Baz might just pretend that nothing had *ever* happened between us. He'd make me feel like I dreamt this whole thing—like I was a maniac and a moron for believing he'd ever felt something for me.

I was already feeling like a maniac and a moron in the car with Penny and Agatha.

Agatha was on a *rant*. Which almost never happens. (It usually only happens when we're stranded or kidnapped or stuck at the bottom of a well that's rapidly filling with water.) But she was clearly fed up with the both of us.

"What were you thinking?" she demanded of me. "Those are the *Pitches*. He is a *vampire*."

"That's never stopped you from cavorting with him in the Wavering Wood," Penny said to her.

"That happened *once*," Agatha said. "And it was an adolescent crush."

"It was?" I said.

"I was only hoping for a kiss—I wasn't conspiring against the Mage!"

"You were?" I couldn't even figure out who I was jealous over in this situation. Both of them, I guess.

"We aren't conspiring against the Mage!" Penny argued. "We're conspiring . . . apart from him."

"As far as I can tell," Agatha said, "you don't know *what* you're doing."

I worried that she was right.

Everything was turned upside down: co-operating with Baz, keeping secrets from the Mage. What would Agatha say if she knew about the kissing?

*"You're not even gay, Simon."*

I rubbed my palms into my eyes.

"The prophecy doesn't actually say that Simon has to listen to the Mage," Penny was going on. "It says that he's here for the *World* of Mages. That includes Baz's mum—" She glanced back at me. "Simon, are you okay?"

"Headache," I said.

*"You're not even gay,"* she'd say, *"and he's not even alive."*

"Do you want me to try and shrink it?" Penny offered, leaning back between the bucket seats.

"My head?"

"Your headache."

"Merlin, no. I'll be fine."

*"You're not even gay, and he's not even alive, and that isn't even the* worst *part of this idea—what will the Mage say?"*

"It isn't your job to solve murders," Agatha said. "You're not the police."

"Now, *there's* an interesting concept," Penny said. "Magickal law enforcement. I'd like magickal social programmes, as well. Plus a department of health and wellness."

"The Mage's Men are the police," Agatha said.

"The Mage's Men are some sort of personal army."

"You're talking about your brother!" Agatha shouted, pulling herself forward over the steering wheel.

"I know!" Penny shouted back. "We're in desperate need of reforms!"

"But the Mage is the Great Reformer!"

"Oh, anyone can call themselves that. Besides, Agatha, I know you think the Mage is a tax-happy interloper with a chip on his shoulder about the aristocracy. I've heard you say so."

"My mother thinks that," Agatha said. "He's still *the Mage*."

"Stop," I choked out. "Pull over."

Penny turned back to me. "Are you okay? Are you going to be sick?"

"No," I said. "I just need to get out. Please."

Agatha yanked the car over to the side of the road, kicking up a cloud of dust and gravel, then turned in her seat to look at me. "What's wrong, Simon?"

"I need to go back."

"Why?"

I put my hand on the door handle. "I . . . forgot something."

"Surely it can wait," she said.

"It can't."

"Then I'll drive you back."

"*No.*"

"Simon," Penny said seriously, "what's this about?"

I opened the door. "I need to go back and make sure that Baz is okay."

"Baz is fine," Agatha insisted as I climbed out.

"He's not fine! We just found out that he was in a coffin for six weeks."

They were leaning into each other between the front seats, turned completely around to shout at me.

Penny: "He's fine *now!*"

Agatha: "Get back in the car!"

I put my hand on the door and bent over so I could see them. "He shouldn't be alone right now."

"He isn't!" they both said.

"I should keep an eye on him." I stood up again.

"We'll drive you back," Agatha said.

"No. No. You'll be late for Christmas Eve. Go." I shut the door, turned around, and immediately started to run.

I didn't think rich people actually ate this way. At a long table covered with red and gold cloth. Thick napkins tied with poinsonsettias. Platters with heavy silver lids.

It wouldn't surprise me if rich people really *don't* live like this—but that the Pitches do it, just to make a scene. If this is Christmas Eve, what do they have planned for tomorrow?

"Sorry we're late, Mother," Baz says, pulling out a chair.

"What a nice surprise, Mr. Snow," his dad says. He's smiling, but in a way that makes me regret my decision to come back.

"Thank you, sir. I hope I'm not intruding."

Baz's stepmum smiles, too. "Of course not." I can't tell if she means it or is just being polite.

"I invited him," Baz says to his father. "It's not like he has anywhere else to go at Christmas." I can't tell if Baz is actually being rude to me or doing it for show. I can't read any of their faces—even the baby just looks bored.

I thought there might be extended family here for the holidays, miscellaneous Grimms and Pitches, but it's just Baz's parents and his siblings. There's the older girl, Mordelia, then two other little girls, maybe twins—I'm not sure how old, old enough to sit up by themselves and gnaw on turkey legs—and a baby in a fancy carved high chair tapping a rattle onto his (her?) tray.

They all look like Baz's stepmum: dark hair, but not black like Baz's, with round cheeks and those Billie Piper mouths that don't quite close over their front teeth. They don't look dangerous enough to be Baz's siblings—or his father's children. Penny says the Grimms are less political and less deadly than the Pitches, but Baz's dad looks like a pit viper wearing a pin-striped suit; even his snow-white hair is scary.

"Stuffing?" Baz asks, handing me a platter. It seems like their servants have the day off. (I've counted at least four since I've been here: Vera, two women cleaning, and a man out front shovelling the walks.)

I take a big scoop of chestnut stuffing and notice that there's almost nothing on Baz's plate. The platters and boats go around twice, and he just passes them to me—I wonder if he has an eating disorder.

I eat enough for both of us. The food here is even better than at Watford.

"Did you ever believe in Father Christmas?" Baz asks. He's laying out blankets and pillows for me on his couch. His stepmother brought them up after Baz explained that I didn't want to sleep in the guest room. *"He's afraid of the wraiths,"* he told her.

That made his little sisters giggle. They were eager to get to bed, so that Father Christmas could get here. *"Did you tell Father Christmas that you'd be here?"* Mordelia asked me. *"So that he can send your presents?"*

*"I didn't,"* I told her. *"I should have."*

"I don't think so," I tell Baz now. "I mean, sometimes the home would get somebody to dress up like Father Christmas and hand out crap gifts, but I don't remember believing in him. What about you?"

"I believed in him," Baz says. "And then, the year after my mother died, he didn't come. . . ." He throws me a pillow and walks over to a tall wooden chest of drawers. "I thought I'd been very, very bad. But now I think my dad was probably just depressed and forgot about Christmas. Fiona showed up later that day with a giant stuffed Paddington."

"The bear?"

"There's nothing wrong with Paddington Bear. Here." He's holding out some pyjamas, his pyjamas. I take them. Then he sits at the end of his bed and leans against one of the posts. "So . . . you came back."

I sit next to him. "Yeah."

He's still wearing his dark green suit. He slicked his hair back for dinner—I wish he wouldn't do that. It looks better when it's loose and falling around his face.

"We can go talk to the numpties tomorrow," he says.

"On Christmas Day? Do numpties celebrate Christmas?"

"I don't know." He cocks his head. "I didn't really get to know them. According to the books, they don't do much but eat and try to stay warm."

"What do numpties eat?" I ask.

"Rubble," he says, "as far as anyone can tell . . . maybe they just chew on it."

"Do you think Penny is right? That it was your mother's murderer who hired the numpties?"

Baz shrugs. "It would make sense—and Bunce is *usually* right."

"You're sure you can handle going back there?"

He looks at his knees. "I'd rather talk to the numpties than go back to Nicodemus, and those are our only two leads."

"I still wish we had a motive . . . ," I say. "Why would someone want to hurt your mother?"

"I'm not sure they *did* want to," Baz says. "What if the target was the nursery, not my mother? There was no way of knowing that she'd be the one who came. Maybe the vampires wanted to take the children—maybe they wanted to Turn us all." He's rubbing his hand along the top of his thigh. His legs are longer than mine; that's where all his height is.

"I'm not a very good boyfriend," I say.

Baz's hand settles on his trouser leg and tugs. He sits up straighter. "I understand, Snow. Trust me. I'm not planning our next mini-break—I'm not even going to tell anyone about us."

"No," I say, turning slightly towards him. "That's not what I mean. I mean . . . I've always been a terrible boyfriend. That's why Agatha broke up with me. I basically just did what I thought she wanted me to, but I always got it wrong, and I never put her first. I never once felt like I was getting it right in three years."

"Then why did you stay together?"

"Well, I wasn't going to break up with *Agatha*. It wasn't *her* fault."

He's smoothing his hand along his leg again. I like everything about Baz in this suit.

"I'm just saying," I say, turning a bit more, "that I don't know how to be your boyfriend. And I don't think you'd want that from me."

"Fine," he says. "Understood."

"And I know that you think we're doomed—Romeo-and-Juliet style."

"Completely," he says to his knees.

"And I don't think I'm gay," I say. "I mean, maybe I am, at least partly, the part that seems to be demanding the most attention right now. . . ."

"No one cares whether you're gay," Baz says coldly.

I'm sitting sideways now, facing his profile. His eyes are narrow, and his mouth is a straight line.

"What I'm saying is . . ." My voice fades out. I suck at this. "I like to look at you."

His eyes shoot over to me, and he lowers his eyebrows but doesn't turn his head.

"I like this," I go on. "All of this that we've been doing."

He ignores me.

"I like *you*," I say. "And I don't even care that you don't like me—I'm used to it, I wouldn't know what to do if you did. But I like *you*, Baz. I like *this*. I like helping you. I like knowing that you're okay. When you didn't come back to school this autumn, when you were missing . . . I thought I was going to lose my mind."

"You thought I was plotting against you," he says.

"Yeah," I say. "And I missed you."

He shakes his head. "There's something wrong with you—"

"*I know*. But I still want this, if you'll let me have it."

Baz finally turns to look at me. "What's *this*, Snow?"

"*This*," I say. "I want to be your boyfriend. Your terrible boyfriend."

He cocks an eyebrow and stares at me, like figuring out what's wrong with me is something he'll never have enough time for.

There's a soft knock at the door.

Baz stands up, straightening his suit, and walks to the door. He opens it and leans over, picking up a tray, then brings it back to his bed. There's a pitcher of milk and a heavily laden plate from dinner.

"Who's that from?" I ask.

"My stepmother."

"Why didn't you just eat at dinner?"

"I don't like eating in front of people."

"Why not?"

"Why do you ask so many questions?"

"Is it anorexia?"

"No, Snow, it's not anorexia—do you even know what that means?" He sits on the far side of his bed and takes the napkin off the tray, shaking it unfolded. "My fangs pop when I eat," he says. "It's noticeable."

I crawl across the bed to sit next to him. "I didn't notice the other night, when you ate in front of me."

"Well, you're not very observant, are you."

"Or maybe it's not as noticeable as you think."

Baz looks up at me, and his cheeks look fuller than normal. He smiles then, and I see them—long white fangs, trying to push out over both his lips.

"*Wicked,*" I whisper, trying to look closer. He pushes me back, but not far. "Open your mouth again," I say. "Let me see."

He sighs and pulls back his lips. His fangs are *huge.* And they look so sharp. "Where do they even come from? Like, where do they go when you're not using them?"

"I don't know." He sounds kind of like he's wearing braces.

"Can I touch them?"

"No. They're sharp. And toxic."

"I can't believe there's a part of your body that grows when you need it. You're like a mutant."

"I'm a vampire," Baz says, "and can you *hear* yourself?"

I sit back. "Yeah."

I expect him to look aggravated, and he does, but he's also kind of smiling. Around his fangs.

I hand him his plate—turkey, stuffing, bacon, lashings of gravy. He takes it.

"Are you still hungry, Snow?"

"I could eat."

"Come on, then." He hands me the fork and keeps the spoon for himself. The turkey's so tender, the spoon works fine. He takes a huge bite, and I see the full length of his fangs. "Wicked," I say again.

Baz shakes his head. "You're an idiot," he says with his mouth extra full. He looks down at his plate. "But you can have . . . *this.* If you want it."

I do.

# 68

## AGATHA

It's a three-hour drive back to London. Penelope casts, **"Time flies!"**—but neither of us are having any fun, so it doesn't work.

I've half a mind to drive straight to Watford to tell the Mage everything, but my parents were expecting me ages ago—and, honestly, I don't relish the thought of talking to the Mage by myself. He's not exactly approachable. He's always dressed like Peter Pan, and he carries a sword. Like, all the time. Once he showed up at our door in the middle of the night with his ear in his hand. Dad had to sew it back on.

I've known the Mage since before I was in school; he and Dad have been on the Coven together forever. But I'm not sure the Mage even knows my name. I've never heard him say it. He never really speaks to me.

Penny says he's sexist, but the fact is that the Mage hardly talks to anyone at Watford. Not even Simon. I don't get why he wants to be headmaster—does he even like kids?

Maybe that's why Lucy broke it off with him.

Or maybe he's such a prat *because* she broke up with him, and he never got over it.

I still have that photo in my handbag. I hope Penny's

mum doesn't realize I stole it. I *really* hope she doesn't tell my parents.

I went through a shoplifting phase when I was 14 and got grounded for an entire summer when my parents found my stash of unopened eyeliners and nail varnish.

*"We would buy you cosmetics,"* my father said.

*"You didn't use magic?"* my mother asked. *"You just took it?"* And then she said, *"Oh, Agatha, purple varnish. How common."*

Penny only lets me ignore her for twenty minutes or so before she bursts. "I thought you'd want to be included, Agatha!"

"You didn't," I say.

"I did! I could tell you missed Simon. I could tell you were sad. Are you really saying you'd rather we just left you out and ignored you for the rest of the year?"

"No!"

"Then what, Agatha? What do you want?"

"I want to be friends," I say, "but I don't want to be, like, comrades-in-arms. I don't want to have secret meetings! I just want to hang out! Like, make biscuits and watch telly. Do normal friend stuff!"

"We're supposed to watch telly while Simon fights the Humdrum? And Baz gets kidnapped by numpties?"

"No!" I lean forward, squeezing the steering wheel. "In the scenario I'm describing, none of that would be happening!"

"But it *is* happening."

"Well, then, yeah, I think I would rather just stay home. Because I can't actually do anything to help. When have we ever been any help, Penelope? Like, *real* help. We're just . . . witnesses. And hostages. And, like, future collateral damage. If we were in a movie, one of us would have to die while

Simon watched. That's all we're good for."

"Speak for yourself!" she shouts.

"I will!" I shout back.

But neither of us speaks for the rest of the trip.

I drop Penny off at her house, and she's still so pissed off that she slams the car door. I'm *really* late, but my parents are busy getting ready for their party, and hardly notice when I walk in.

They do a travelling party every Christmas Eve. It starts at one house, then moves on to the next house, then the next . . . until everyone's so trolleyed, they have to spell the cars to drive them home.

Simon and I are always expected to say hello when the guests get here; then we hide in the lounge and watch telly and eat hors d'oeuvres until we fall asleep by the fire.

Except for once, four years ago, when we snuck out on Christmas Eve to track werewolves through Soho. They'd stolen some key—or maybe a gem, I can't bloody remember. I've never been colder in my life! We nearly died outside Liberty, and then, after it was finally over, Penny made us stay out and collect werewolf fur, so that she could make these grotesque premenstrual talismans. I gave mine to the cat. Wait—the moonstone. That's what it was, the werewolves stole *the moonstone*. What a load of rubbish. Thank magic we were back before my parents got home.

(Should I tell Mum now? What I know? What Simon is up to?) (No. Simon will be fine. Simon is always fine. And Penny will love bragging to me about their adventures with the numpties. Maybe Baz is their new third wheel. Have fun hanging out with a vampire, Simon! Good job making your life even more stupid and dangerous.)

"I think you can come along with us tonight," my mother says. She and Helen, our housekeeper, are getting things set up. Our house is first on the party circuit this year. "Since you don't have Simon to entertain."

"*Mum.*"

"Don't whine, Agatha," my father says, plucking a crab claw from a platter. He's on the phone with a patient. "No, no, I'm listening, Balthazar, but it all sounds quite normal. No, I don't mean Normal—I mean normal."

I sigh and follow my mother into the kitchen. "But I'm not dressed for a party."

"Then get dressed."

"Mum, I'm knackered."

She's leaning into the refrigerator. "You'll get your second wind. Is Simon coming round tomorrow, then?"

I frown and fidget with a tray of prawn cocktails. "I don't think so. . . ."

I already told her that Simon was spending Christmas at Watford, but somehow Mum got it in her head that he would still stop by here on Christmas Day. It's tradition, I suppose.

Maybe I should feel guilty for disinviting him, but I don't— I tried to take it back tonight.

Mum stands up, holding a sparkling tiered jelly. "I think it's good that he's spending the holidays with the Mage," she says. "As far as I can tell, the Mage usually spends Christmas alone at Watford. He told me once that the holidays were too auspicious to waste on festivities."

"What does that mean?" I ask.

"Oh, who knows," she says, handing the jelly off to Helen. "I hope Simon doesn't end up *fasting by moonlight*. We'll have to stuff him with sweetmeats tomorrow."

"Auspicious . . . ," I say. "Why is the Mage such a weirdo?"

"Hush, Agatha. Don't be treasonous."

"I'm not, I'm just saying—was he always like this?"

"I wouldn't know," she says. "We certainly never travelled in the same circles. I can't even remember him from school."

I reach for a prawn, but Helen takes the tray away. "Do you remember Professor Bunce?" I ask Mum. "From school?"

"Which one?"

"Either."

"Martin and Mitali were a few years behind me," Mum says. She's getting out another pudding—a huge stacked trifle. "But don't they have a son even older than you? They started popping them out awfully early—that's the Bunce influence, I think. I went to Watford with a *litter* of Bunces, not a one of them powerful enough to be there. That happens, you know, in big families: The magic gets watered down."

My mother is obsessed with power—who's got it, who doesn't. *She* doesn't. At least not much. She blames her own mother for marrying down. *"My father couldn't light a match in a rainstorm."*

I'm adequate, magickally speaking. I'm no Simon. Or Baz. Or Penelope. But I get through my lessons just fine.

I know that's why my parents never had more kids after me; they didn't want my magic to be diluted—even though Dad says it's an old wives' tale that siblings split magic.

I also know my parents are hoping I'll marry someone more powerful than I am, to get the family back on course.

Before I started dating Simon, I had a secret Normal boyfriend—Sacha. If my mother had known, she would have locked me in a tower. (She probably would have taken away my horse.) I wonder what Sacha is doing these days. . . .

"So, you wouldn't have known their friends?" I ask.

"Professor Bunce mentioned someone named Lucy, she showed us a photo—"

"Lucy Day?"

"I'm not sure. . . ."

"Lucy McKenna?"

"She was Professor Bunce's best friend," I say. "Butterscotch blond, hair down to her waist. Sort of a boho nouveau look."

"Darling," Mum says, helping Helen lift the trifle, "that was everyone in the '90s."

"She looked like Baby Spice," I say. "But with big shoulders."

"Oh, Lucy *Salisbury*. Hell's spells, I haven't thought of her in years." Mum stops in front of the fridge and puts her hands on her hips.

"Did you know her?" I ask.

"*Of* her, yes. She was five or six years younger, but her family went to the club. Darling, you know Lady Salisbury. She plays Black Maria with me. She'll be here tonight."

I do know Lady Salisbury. She's probably my grandmother's age, but she hangs out with my mother's set. She tells bawdy jokes and always encourages everyone to eat more cake.

"Would she tell me about her daughter?"

"Dear magic, Agatha, no. What a thing to ask. Everyone knows her daughter was a scandal. And her son was a dud!"

"What kind of scandal?"

"Lucy ran off, just a few years out of Watford. She was the Salisburys' pride and joy, then she ran off with some man. I heard it was a Normal. Maybe even an American. Ruth— Lady Salisbury—broke down at a charity do, a lawn-bowling tournament for stutterers—and confessed to Natalie Braine that she was worried there might be a child involved. *An illegitimate child.* That's the last Ruth's ever spoken of it. And no one's seen Lucy, not in our realm, since school."

"Lucy disappeared?" I say.

"Worse," Mum says. "She ran away. From magic. Can you *imagine*?"

"Yes," I say, then, "no."

My mother brushes nonexistent crumbs from her hands. "Get changed, darling—the guests will be here any minute."

I start to walk out of the kitchen, and Mum hands me a stack of hand-embroidered napkins to give to Helen on my way through the dining room. I hand them to Helen without saying anything. I'm too busy thinking. . . .

"I knew Lucy Salisbury," Helen says. "We went to school together."

It's quite like Helen to wait until my mother isn't in the room to speak to me. My mother prefers a more formal relationship, but Helen has always treated me like family. (Not close family, more like a niece; I think she prefers Simon.)

"Lucy was a few years older," Helen says. "All the girls in my year went mad when we heard she'd run away. We thought it was so romantic. And terrifying!"

"Did she really run away?"

"That's what we heard. Met a man and took off—for California."

"California!"

"I used to think of her," Helen says, "with that long, blond hair, lying out on the sand."

I climb into bed without changing into my party clothes and pull out the stolen photo, holding it up above me.

Lucy Salisbury ran away from magic.

She was dating the most powerful living Mage, the guy who was about to take over the world—and she just ran away.

Professor Bunce said Lucy was a powerful magician in her

own right. She could have been the First Lady of magic. Or maybe she could have ruled beside the Mage. *And she walked away.*

*Was* there a baby? Did she take the baby with her?

Maybe she's raising him in the Normal world. Maybe that's the gift Lucy Salisbury gave herself and her child—not to have to grow up with all this shit. Not to have the Mage as his dad, and a world at war for its inheritance.

That kid got off.

And Simon got stuck with it instead.

# 69

## LUCY

I was happy.

I loved him.

And he was always more good than bad.

He's still more good than bad, I think. It just goes to show how much of both a person can hold.

We were together by the time we left Watford. Davy had a cottage he'd inherited from his grandmother, and I followed him there. I lied to my parents—they never liked Davy.

He spent most his time reading in those days, and writing letters and pamphlets that he'd send to magickal scholars.

He never felt like seeing friends or just going out. I remember we went to London once to have dinner with Mitali and Martin, to meet their little boy—I wore a long peasant skirt, and I'd spelled flowers into my hair, and I was so happy to see them. To see Mitali.

At first it was good. We were drinking red wine, and I was curled up in a big Papasan chair. And Davy started talking to Mitali about the Coven—she was campaigning for a seat.

"You won't change anything," he said. "Nothing will change."

"I know you think so," she said. "I've read your papers."

"Have you?" That perked him up. He leaned forward in his chair, dangling his wineglass between his knees. "Then you know that the only answer is revolution."

"I know that things will only get better if good people fight for what's important."

"And you think the Coven cares about 'good people' and 'what's important'? You think Natasha Grimm-Pitch cares about your idealism?"

"No," Mitali said. "But if I'm on the Coven, I'll have as many votes as she does."

Davy laughed. "The names on the Coven haven't changed in two hundred years. Only the faces. They might as well carve 'Pitch' onto the headmaster's chair at Watford. All they care about, all any of them care about, is protecting their own power."

Mitali wasn't cowed. In her wide-legged jeans and her wine-coloured velvet jacket, her hair falling to her shoulder blades in messy dark curls, *she's* the one who looked like a radical. "They're protecting all our power," she said. "The whole World of Mages."

"Are they?" Davy said. "Ask Natasha Grimm-Pitch about suicide rates among low-magicians. Ask your Coven what they're doing to fight pixie sticks and every other magickal disease that doesn't affect their own sons and daughters."

"How is a revolution going to help the pixies?" Mitali huffed. "How is throwing aside centuries of tradition and institutional knowledge going to help any of us?"

"We'll build better traditions!" Davy shouted. I don't think he realized he was shouting.

"We'll write new rules in blood?"

"If need be! Yes! Yes, Mitali—does that frighten you?"

We left shortly after that. I said I had a headache.

Davy was still flushed from the wine, but he wouldn't let me drive. He didn't notice me casting **Stay the course** on him from the passenger seat.

We never went back to London after that.

We rarely left the cottage. We didn't have a phone, or a television. I bought chickens from the farmer down the road and spelled them not to wander away. I wrote long letters to my mother. All fiction. Davy stayed inside most days with his books.

I called them *his* books, but they were all stolen from Watford. He'd go back and take more whenever he needed them. He was so powerful, he could make himself nearly invisible.

Sometimes Davy would go away for a few days to meet with other magickal activists. But he always came back more dispirited than when he'd left.

He gave up on a revolution. No one read his papers.

He gave up on everything except the Greatest Mage. I think Davy must have been the greatest Greatest Mage scholar in the history of magic. He knew every prophecy by heart. He wrote them on the stone walls of our cottage, and diagrammed their sentences.

When I brought him his meals, he might ask for my opinion. What did I think *this* metaphor meant? Had I ever considered *that* interpretation?

I remember a morning when I interrupted him to bring him eggs and oatmeal. Crowley, we ate so much oatmeal—which I was also feeding to the chickens.

You can extend food with magic, you can make food out of pillows and candles. You can call birds down from the sky and deer in from the fields. But sometimes, there's nothing.

Sometimes, there was just nothing.

"Lucy," he said. His eyes were lit from inside. He'd been up all night.

"Good morning, Davy. Eat something."

"Lucy, I think I cracked it." He wrapped his arm around my hips and pulled me closer to his chair—and I loved him then.

"What if the oracles kept having the same visions because they weren't prophecies at all? What if they were instructions? *Lucy*—what if they're meant to guide us to change, not foretell it? Here we are, just waiting to be saved, but the prophecies tell us how to save ourselves!"

"How?"

"With the Greatest Mage."

He left again. He came back with more books.

He came back with pots of oil and blood that wasn't red. I'm not sure when he slept—not with me.

I went for long walks in the fields. I thought about writing letters to Mitali, but I knew she'd fly here on a broom if I told her the truth, and I wasn't ready to go.

I never wanted to leave Davy.

So much of this is his fault—I *want* you to be angry with him. But I never asked to leave. I never asked him to let me go.

I thought . . . I thought that whatever was coming would be better if I was there with him. I thought it helped him to be tied to me. Like a kite with a string. I thought that as long as I was there, he'd never get carried away completely.

He killed both my chickens.

He crawled into our bed one night, smelling of mud and burnt plastic, and lifted my hair to kiss the back of my neck. "Lucy."

I rolled over to see him. He was smiling. He looked young, like someone had wiped the bitterness from his face with a warm cloth.

"I've got it," he said, kissing my cheeks, then my forehead. "The Great Mage, Lucy. We can bring him."

I laughed—I was so happy just to see him happy. I was so happy to have his attention. "How, Davy?"

"Just like this."

I shook my head. I didn't understand.

He pushed me onto my back, kissing along my neck. "The two of us. We'll make him."

He kept kissing my neck down into my nightshirt.

"Are you talking about a baby, Davy?"

He pulled his head up and grinned. "Who better than us?" he said. "To raise our saviour?"

# BOOK FOUR

# 70

## NICODEMUS

She won't talk to me. Hasn't since. Because it's against the rules.

She wasn't so concerned with the rules when we were kids. Made our own rules, didn't we. We was so brute, who was gonna stop us?

I'll never forget the time Ebeneza spelled the drawbridge down so the three of us could go into town and get pissed. The look on the headmistress's face when she caught her own sister sneaking back in legless! (Fiona never could hold her cider.) Mistress Pitch was steaming—standing on the Lawn in her dressing gown and nine months up the duff.

Ebb lost her wand—her staff—for a week because she was the one who snuck us out. Then the next night, Ebb spelled the bridge down with *my* wand. (We could always use each other's pieces.) Gutty as fuck, she was.

Course we got caught again.

Getting away with it wasn't the point.

The point was that we were young and free and full of magic. What was Mistress Pitch going to do? Toss out her own sister and the two strongest magicians at Watford?

They weren't going to toss out Ebeneza; they were too

worried she'd go rogue on them. Too worried she'd realize she could do more with all that magic than stick the desks to the ceilings—or call every shaggy dog in the county to Watford, like she was the Pied Piper.

I realized. What Ebb could do. What I could do.

I get to our street and cut down the alley, then let myself into the back garden. The gate creaks. I'm a few minutes early—Ebb'll be inside still. I make my way over to the willow tree and sit down on Mum's bench.

Wish I could have a fag.

Gave 'em up when I crossed over—almost twenty years ago. But that Pitch brat blew smoke in my face, and now I've got a taste for it again.

Fi and I used to roll our own, on menthol papers.

Ebeneza wouldn't have any of it. Said tobacco gunked up her magic.

"Your sister's trynta stay pure," Fiona would tease. "Like an athlete. Like Princess Di."

We used to give Ebb hell over being a virgin. Hell, she's probably still a virgin. (Does feeling up other girls even count?)

The back door opens, and I look up. But it ain't Ebb. Just somebody—no one I recognize—stepping out for a smoke. I close my eyes and inhale. This vampire nose is good for something.

Ebb'll come out soon, and she'll walk out into the garden and lean against the gate. And she won't talk to me. That's the agreement. That's the rule.

She'll just talk.

She'll tell the wind how she's doing. She'll catch the Christmas moon up on all the family goings-on. Sometimes she might do magic—not for me. Just for the sake of it.

Anything alive comes out to say hello to Ebb, even in the dead of winter. Last year, a deer pranced up the alley, caszh as anything, and rested its head in Ebeneza's hands. I knifed and drained it as soon as Ebb went back in. I think she knew that I would—maybe it was a gift. Maybe she was trying to keep *me* pure for a day.

Anyway, I had to haul the deer's body a mile before I found a bin big enough for it.

Ebb'll come out soon. And she'll talk. And I'll listen. I don't talk at all—don't think Ebb would want that. It would be too much like a conversation. Too close to breaking the rules.

Plus, what would I say? I've got nothing to report that she wants to hear. No news that won't turn her stomach. All Ebeneza really wants to know is that I'm still here. Such as I am.

Mostly my sister talks about the school. The grounds. The goats. The kids. That dryad she's been mooning over since sixth year. She doesn't talk about the Mage. Ebb's never been one for politics. I expect she stays out of his way—though she told me once that they got into a royal dust-up when one of his merwolves ate one of her goats.

I've never seen the merwolves, only heard about them from Ebb. It's the only animal I've ever known her not to like. She says they try to throw themselves up on the drawbridge. That the bridge shakes while the children and goats are crossing it. One of the wolves actually made it out once—dragged itself around the Lawn, snarling, until Ebb came and cast it back into the water. *"I spell them to sleep now when the bridge is down,"* she told me. *"They sink to the bottom of the moat."*

Whoever it was who came out for a fag finishes it and goes back in, slamming the screen door shut.

❖

I was early. But now Ebeneza's late. Real late.

The noise has stopped inside the house. The kids'll be in bed. Ebb says all our brothers and our little sister have kittens these days. I never thought about having any of my own before I crossed over. I think about it now. Me and Fi. Coupla sprogs. Her family woulda had a fit if she settled down with me. Guess she was never gonna settle down with no one. . . . I know where Fi is now. Our paths would cross if I let them. Don't fancy *she* wants to hear anything I have to say either.

Ebb's late.

Maybe she forgot.

Not like her to forget. Never has, in all these years.

Can't call her. Don't even know if she has a mobile these days.

I stand, and pace a bit under the tree. Normally, Ebb casts a spell so that no one sees me.

I'm antsy. I creep up closer to the house. If anyone's up, I should be able to hear them. The house is dark. One of the kitchen windows is cracked, but I can't smell dinner. Ebb says she helps Mum with the cooking now. Roasted gammon, it'll be. And bread and butter pudding. Ebb usually brings me out a plate.

I go up the back steps and peek inside the window in the door. The kitchen is empty. I can't hear anything.

I twist the knob, not expecting it to turn, but it does, and the door gives. I step forward gingerly, not sure whether I'll be allowed—but the house accepts me, and I stand there for a moment feeling right sorry for myself in my mum's kitchen.

I smell the child before I see her. . . .

She's hiding behind the doorway, peeking out at me. "Is that you, Aunty?"

"Aunty?" I say. "Do I look like somebody's aunty?"

"I thought you were my Aunt Ebb. You look like her."

She's a little blond one in a red plaid nightgown. Must be my sister Lavinia's. Vinnie wasn't much older than this herself last time I saw her.

"I'm family," I say. "I come to talk to Ebb—why don't you go get her for me? She won't be mad." Not at the girl, anyway.

"Aunty Ebb's gone," the chick says. "She left with the Mage. Grandmum's still crying. We can't even have Christmas."

"The Mage?" I say.

"Himself," the girl says. "I heard everybody say it. Mum says Aunty Ebb was arrested."

"Arrested! For what?"

"I don't know. I guess she broke a rule."

I stare at the child. She stares back. Then I turn for the door.

"Where are you going?" she calls after me.

"To find your aunty."

# 71

## SIMON

I wake up feeling hungry.

And not until I'm awake do I realize that it's not *me* who's hungry.

The air is dry. And itching. Pulling at my skin—pulling with needles, pricking at me.

I sit up and shake my head. The feeling doesn't go away. I take a deep breath and then it's inside my lungs, too. Like sand. Like ground glass.

*The Humdrum.*

I look over at Baz's bed—the sheets and blankets are cast aside. He's not there. I stumble to my feet and out of the room, standing in the blood-dark hallway. *"Baz,"* I whisper.

No one answers.

I follow the bad feeling down the hallway, down the stairs, to the front door of the manor—the night sky and the snow are so bright, there's light streaming into the foyer. I open the door and run out into the snow.

The feeling is stronger out here. Worse. Almost like I'm standing inside one of the Humdrum's dead spots. But when I reach for my magic, it's still there: It rises to the surface of my skin and hums in my fingertips. It pools in my mouth.

I try to force it down again.

I follow the itchy feeling forward. (I should go back inside. I should put on shoes.) I find myself running towards the private forest that sweeps along the side of the Pitches' house like a curtain.

I'm wearing Baz's red-and-gold-striped pyjamas, and they're wet to my thighs. The hungry feeling gets stronger with every step. It sucks at me. I feel my magic slipping out, sliding around my skin. A tree branch drags against me and catches fire.

I keep pushing forward.

I don't know where I'm going—I've never been in this forest before. Plus there's no space between the trees. I'm not on a path, there isn't a clearing.

When I hear him laughing, I stop so abruptly that my magic sloshes forward, spilling up over the sides of me.

He's right there, leaning against one of trees.

Him. The Insidious Humdrum.

Me.

"Hello," he says, tossing his ball in the air. He catches it, frowns at me for a second, then tucks the ball into the pocket of his jeans.

"You can talk," I say.

"I can now. I can do all sorts of things now." He looks up into the tree and reaches for one of the slimmest branches; his hand passes through it. He grimaces and tries again. This time his hand closes around the twig, and he snaps it off. Then he looks back up at me and grins, like I should be proud of him.

"Why do you look like me?" I ask. This still feels like the most important question.

"This is just what I look like." He laughs. "Why wouldn't I look like you?"

"But you're not me."

"No." The Humdrum frowns. "Look at you. You're different every time I see you. But I always look just like this." The twig is still in his hands. He breaks it in two, then drops it and steps towards me. "You can do all sorts of things I can't do."

I step back. Into a tangle of branches. "Why are you here—what do you want from me?"

"Nothing," he says. "Nothing, nothing, nothing. But what does *he* want from you? That's the real question."

I hear someone groan. There's something moving in the trees. . . . I wish I could see better, and as soon as I wish it, my magic gets brighter—I'm glowing. The Humdrum laughs again.

"*Simon?*" someone calls. I think it's Baz, but he sounds wrong. Like he's out of breath or in pain.

"Baz? Are you okay?"

"No, no . . . *Simon!*"

Then I see Baz ahead of me, twenty feet or so, leaning against a tree. The Humdrum is above us now, sitting on a low branch, watching. Baz's head hangs low.

I rush forward. "Baz!"

He lifts his face, and it's wrong, too. Twisted. His eyes are dilated and black, and his mouth is full of white knives—his lips have retracted to make room for them.

I should back away, but instead I squeeze between the trees to try to get to him. It's Baz who backs away from me. "Something's wrong," he says. "I'm hungry."

"Baz, you're always hungry."

"No. It's different." He shakes his head and shoulders like an animal. "I saw you in the forest," he says. "Just now. But you were young—you looked like you did the very first time I saw you." His words are slurred. Like he's shoving them through his teeth. "I thought for a minute that you were *dead*. I thought it was a Visiting."

"It wasn't me." I take a step towards him. "You saw the Humdrum."

"You touched me," he says. "I leaned down and you put your hand on my face."

"It isn't me," I say.

"And then you pushed it into me." He stumbles backwards, staying a step away from me. "Like you do, Simon. But it wasn't magic this time. It was a void. You pushed a void into me, and everything else left to make room."

"Baz, stop. Let me help you."

He keeps shaking his head. He reminds me for a moment of the red dragon, swinging her head back and forth.

"It's easy with creatures," the Humdrum says. He's standing behind Baz now. He reaches out and presses a hand onto Baz's hunched spine. "I just take what I got and give it to them."

Baz whines and unfolds until his back is arched.

"*What*?" I demand. "What do you give them?"

The Humdrum shrugs. "Nothing. I give them some of my nothing."

Baz lifts his face to me, all pupil and fang. He takes a step forward. "Get away, Simon. I'm hungry."

"I give them some of my nothing," the Humdrum says again, "and then they're drawn to the biggest of all somethings—*you*. And then you give me more nothing. It's a great game."

Baz keeps coming for me. I stand my ground.

"Get away, Simon! I'm hungry!"

"What are you hungry for, Baz?"

"For you!" he shouts. "For magic, for blood, for magic—for everything. *For you. For magic.*"

He's shaking his head so fast, it blurs.

There's a tree between us, and Baz rips it from the ground and tosses it aside.

"Wicked," the Humdrum says. "I've never tried it with one of these before."

Baz ploughs into me like a steel gryphon. I catch him in my arms and roll to the ground.

He's much stronger than I am—but I'm made of magic right now, so there's no crushing me. We thrash around on the ground. I hold his head in both my hands, pushing his jaw away.

"I'm so hungry," he whines. "And you're so full."

"You can have it," I say, trying to look in his eyes. "Baz. You know you can have it."

I push on his chin and grab at his hair, holding him back— but I let my magic go.

I let it flow into him from my every pore. Baz sobs and abruptly stops fighting. It feels like I'm pouring water into an empty well.

It goes.

And it goes.

Baz's body sags against mine.

"Wow . . ." the Humdrum says. "That's even better than fighting." He feels close. I look up, and he's standing right over us, rock solid in the moonlight. "When did you learn to do that? It's like you turned on a tap."

"Did you take his magic?" I shout at the Humdrum.

"Did I take his magic?" he repeats, like it's a hilarious question. "No. I don't take anything. I'm just what's left when you're done." He grins, like the cat with the canary, and it's an expression I've never seen on my own face.

"Simon!" Baz is shouting beneath me. I look down—he's glowing now, too. His fangs are gone, but he still looks like he's in pain. He's squeezing my triceps. "Enough!"

I let go of him and roll away. But the magic is still pouring out of me, through me. It *is* like a tap. I concentrate on turning it off. When it feels like the magic's staying inside me again—when I stop glowing—I get up on my hands and knees. "Baz?"

"Here," he says.

I move towards his voice. "Are you okay?"

"I think so." He's lying on the ground. "I just feel a bit . . . burnt."

"Are you on fire?"

"No," he says. "No. Burnt on the inside."

I look around, but I don't see the Humdrum. Or hear him. Or feel him sucking at my breath.

"Is he gone?" Baz asks.

"Seems like it." I collapse next to him.

"Are you okay?"

"I'm fine."

Baz gropes for me with his arm, and when he feels me, he wraps his arm around my neck and shoulders, weakly pulling me towards him. I move closer until my head falls on his chest.

"Are you okay?" he asks again.

"Yeah. You?"

"Tip-top." Baz coughs, and I push my face into his chest. "What *was* that?" he asks.

"The Humdrum."

"Simon, are *you* the Insidious Humdrum?"

"*No.*"

"Are you sure?"

## BAZ

I feel burnt out.

Incinerated.

That kid—it *was* Simon—emptied me somehow. Like he pressed my magic out or down. . . .

And then Simon filled me up again with fire.

I feel like a phoenix rebirthed itself in my lower intestines.

Simon's hiding his face in my chest, and I hold him tighter.

It *was* Simon. Like seeing him again for the very first time. Crap jeans and dirty T-shirt. That rawness in his skin, that hunger in his eyes. When I saw him step out from between the pines tonight, I wanted to kick him in the knees—it was definitely Simon.

Simon—the grown one—is trembling, so I wrap my other arm around him, too. My arms feel hollow, but Simon feels solid through.

Simon Snow is the Humdrum.

Or . . . the Humdrum is Simon Snow.


## SIMON

*"Did I take his magic? No. I don't take anything. I'm just what's left when you're done."*

I'm lying on Baz, and he has both arms around me. And I keep trying to shake the Humdrum's face out of my head. (To shake my face off his head.)

*"I give them some of my nothing . . . and then you give me more nothing."*

I sit up and rub my eyes. "Do you still need to hunt?"

"No," Baz says. "I was finishing up when he found me."

I move into a crouch, then stand, holding out my hand to him. "Did he say anything? Before he attacked you?"

Baz takes my hand and pulls himself up. He doesn't let go. "He said, *'You'll do.'*"

I close my eyes, and my head drops forward. "He used you. He used you against me."

"Everyone does," Baz says softly. I feel his arm slide, slowly, gently, back around my waist.

I slouch into him. "I'm sorry."

## BAZ

If Simon Snow is the Humdrum . . . that makes him a villain. A supervillain.

Can I be in love with a supervillain?

## SIMON

Baz is shaking, and I think he might be crying—which would make sense, after what just happened. I open my eyes and lift up my chin.

He's not crying—he's laughing.

He's laughing so hard, he's falling against me.

"What's wrong with you?" I ask. "Are you in shock?"

"You're the Humdrum."

"I'm not," I say, trying to push him back by the shoulders.

"I'm dead, not blind, Snow. You're the *Humdrum*."

"That wasn't me! Why are you laughing?"

Baz keeps laughing, but he's also giving me a sneery grin. "I'm laughing because you're the Chosen One," he says giddily. "But you're also the greatest threat to magic. You're a bad guy!"

"Baz. I swear. That wasn't me."

"Looks like you. Sounds like you. Tosses that infernal red ball in the air like you." He holds me tighter.

"I think I'd know if I were the Insidious Humdrum," I say.

"I wouldn't give you that much credit, Simon. You're exceedingly thick. And criminally good-looking—have I mentioned that?"

"No."

He leans in like he's going to bite me, then kisses me instead.

It's so good.

It's been so good every time.

I pull away. "I'm not the Humdrum! But why does thinking so make you want to kiss me?"

"Everything makes me want to kiss you. Haven't you worked that out yet? Crowley, you're thick." He kisses me again. And he's laughing again.

"I'm not the Humdrum," I repeat, when I get the chance. "I'd know if I were."

"What you are is a fucking tragedy, Simon Snow. You literally couldn't be a bigger mess."

He tries to kiss me, but I hold back—"And you like that?"

"I love it," he says.

"Why?"

"Because we match."

✿

We make our way out of the forest. Baz knows the way.

It really is stocked with deer just for him. It doesn't creep me out at all to know that—apparently I can get used to anything.

Apparently he can, too.

"That thing," I try again. "It isn't me."

"Maybe it's you in the past," he says. "Maybe you're a time traveller."

"But wouldn't I remember it? If he's me when I was a kid?"

"I don't know how time travel works," Baz says. "It's not magic."

"You're not limping," I say.

He looks down and shakes out his leg. "It feels better," he says. "Crowley, Snow, you've healed me. I wonder if I'm still a vampire?"

I raise my eyebrows, and he laughs. "Calm down, miracle boy, I'm still a vampire—you still smell like bacon and homemade cinnamon buns."

"How can I smell like bacon *and* homemade cinnamon buns?"

"You smell like something I'd gladly eat." Baz stops and holds an arm out in front of me. "Wait. Do you feel that?"

I stop, too. It's faint, but it's there. That parched feeling. That scratch in the back of my throat.

"The Humdrum," Baz says. "Is he back?"

There's shouting ahead of us, somebody calling Baz's name.

I hold my hand above my hip, trying to call my blade. It doesn't come. I can't feel my magic anywhere.

Baz has his wand tucked into his pyjamas (of course he does).

He whips it out and tries to cast a spell. Nothing happens. He tries again.

"It's a dead spot," I whisper. "It's one of the Humdrum's dead spots."

*"Basilton!"* Baz's stepmother is screaming and running towards us. She's wearing her nightgown, and her hair is down. *"Malcolm, he's here!"*

"The Humdrum . . ." Baz looks over at me, as pale as I've ever seen him, his face chalky and white in the moonlight. "Snow. Run."

"What?"

"Go," he says. "You did this."

# 72

## SIMON

I could probably walk to London.

If I were wearing shoes.

And if there weren't all this snow. . . .

When Baz told me to go, when he blamed the dead spot on me, I wanted to argue. But his parents were running towards us, and they were panicking, and I couldn't tell what was happening. Had the hole swallowed up their entire house? Their whole estate?

I turned to run back into the forest—but it was on fire. From me. From my magic. And I couldn't do anything to stop it, because now I didn't have any.

"Go!" Baz said again, so I did. I ran.

I got to the drive, and my feet were going numb from cold, but I kept running. Down the long, long drive. To the road. Away from him.

I'm still running.

My magic comes back to me all at once and sends me to the ground, shaking. If only I had my wand. Or a mobile . . .

I could hitchhike—would anyone pick me up? Would anyone be driving down this road, in middle-of-nowhere Hampshire in the middle of the night? On Christmas Eve?

(Father Christmas isn't real—the Tooth Fairy is.)

I'm kneeling in the snow at the side of the road. *I can do this*, I think. *I've done this before. I just have to want it. I have to need it.*

I think about getting away, about getting to Penny, I think about my magic filling me up and shooting out my shoulders. And then I feel them tearing through Baz's pyjamas—

Wide, bony wings.

There are no feathers this time; I must have been thinking about the dragon. These wings are red and leathery with grey spikes at the hinges. They spread out as soon as I think about them, and pull me up out of the snow.

I tear off the remains of my flannel shirt, and I don't think about how to fly; I just think about where I want to go—***Up. Away.***—and it happens. It's colder up here, so I think about being warm, and my skin starts to flicker with heat.

Baz's house is below me now, in the distance. The fire I started is still burning; I watch the smoke pouring out of the forest, and try to move closer—but I can't. I'm made of magic, and there's no magic there anymore.

I hover in the sky.

I think about putting out the fire. The clouds are full of freezing rain—so I *think* about pushing them towards the forest, and they go.

And then I think of Baz telling me to go, so I do.

And then I stop thinking.

# 73

## PENELOPE

My little sister, Priya, was the one to get the door. She was waiting up for Father Christmas—and doing a hell of a job, too; she made it until four in the morning. I think she outlasted Mum and Dad.

Priya heard the knocking and thought that it was Father Christmas himself. We don't have a fireplace; she must have thought he had to come through the front door.

When she opened the door, Simon fell in, and she shrieked.

I don't blame her. He looked like Satan incarnate. Massive red-and-black wings. A red tail with a black spade at the end. He'd cast some sort of spell on himself that made him glow yellow and orange, and he was covered in snow and debris, and wearing the filthiest, *fanciest* pyjama bottoms.

Mum and Dad heard Priya scream and came thumping down the stairs. Mum screamed, too. And then Dad shouted, and then apparently he had to keep Mum from throwing curses—she thought Simon was possessed or enchanted or that he'd gone full Lucifer.

The rest of us came running down the stairs then (except for Premal, who didn't come home, even for Christmas)—and

I saw Simon and ran to him. It didn't occur to me to be scared of him.

That snapped Mum and Dad back to normal.

Mum started casting warming spells, and Dad got a bowl of hot water and a cloth to clean Simon up. We ended up putting him in the shower. He was so exhausted, he could hardly stand. He couldn't even tell us where he'd been. I assumed he'd made it back to Baz's house, but I didn't want my parents to know that we'd left Simon on the road in the middle of the countryside on Christmas Eve.

I helped my mum and dad give him a shower, and nobody cared that I was seeing him naked. Then we put him in some of Mum's trackies, and she tried to tuck his tail down one leg.

I kept casting, ***"Nonsense!"*** until Mum told me to shut up.

"It's not working, Penny."

"But it worked last time."

"Maybe it's not a spell," Dad said. "Maybe he transformed."

"Maybe he evolved," Priya said from the bathroom doorway, "like a Pokémon."

"Go to bed, Priya," Dad said.

"I'm waiting for Father Christmas!"

"Go to bed!" Mum shouted.

Mum was casting spells, too. ***"As you were!"*** and ***"Back to start!"***

"Careful, Mitali," Dad said. "You'll turn him into a baby."

But none of Mum's spells touched Simon. She tried casting spells in Hindi, too. (She doesn't speak Hindi, but my great-grandmother did.) Nothing worked.

They put Simon in my bed, and Dad thought they should call the Mage, but Mum said they should wait to see what Simon wanted them to do.

(Simon seemed conscious, but he wasn't saying anything.

And he wouldn't make eye contact.)

My parents were still arguing about it after they left my room and shut the door. "Go to bed, Priya!" my father shouted.

I climbed onto the bed next to Simon and laid my ring hand over his red wings.

*"Nonsense!"* I whispered.

*"Nonsense!"*

# 74

## SIMON

I wake up on Christmas morning in Penelope's bed.

She's sitting next to me, staring at me.

"What?" I say.

"Thank magic! I was worried you'd never speak again."

"Why?"

"Because you weren't talking at all last night. For heaven's snakes, Simon, what happened to you?"

"I . . ." I'm lying on my stomach. I try to roll onto my back, but can't—the wings must still be there. Just thinking about them makes them spread out again, and they knock Penny over.

"Simon!"

"Sorry!" I say, trying to pull them back. "Sorry."

Penny takes the edge of one wing and rubs it between her thumb and forefinger. "Are these permanent?"

"I don't know," I say. "Not intentionally."

"We coated you in spells yesterday, and none of them did anything."

"Who's we?"

"Me, my parents. Do you even remember coming here?"

"Sort of . . . I remember flying. I didn't recognize London.

From above. So I had to go to the Eye, then sort of half-fly down the streets to find your house. I've only ever come here before on the Tube."

"I wonder if anyone saw you."

"I don't know. I tried to think about being invisible—"

"You what?"

I close my eyes now and think about the wings. I think about how I don't need them anymore. I feel the magic welling up in me. (The magic is always welling up in me lately. Always coming up the back of my throat.) I think about how I don't want to fly, then I think about pulling the wings back into my back.

When I open my eyes again, Penny is staring at me, her hand empty where the wing had been. She looks spooked. "What did you just do?"

"Got rid of the wings."

"What about the tail?"

I reach down and feel a ropy, leathery tail. "Jesus." I think hard about getting rid of it, and it zips through my hand, scratching my palm on its way back into my body.

"Why did you even *have* a tail?" Penny asks.

"I don't know," I answer, sitting up. "I must have been thinking about that dragon."

"Simon . . ." She's shaking her head. "What *happened* last night?"

"The Humdrum," I say. "He attacked me at Baz's house. He tried to use Baz against me."

"He created the biggest hole in Great Britain!"

"What?"

"My dad got the call this morning. All of Hampshire is gone."

"*What?*"

"Dad and the team are there now, but the Pitches told them

they can't come on their land. They're calling it an act of war."

"By the Humdrum?"

"By *the Mage*," she says. "They say he's controlling the Humdrum—maybe even that the Mage *is* the Humdrum. The Old Families have convened a Council of War, no one knows where. Mum says the Mage is looking for you, but she'll be damned if she tells him you're here. Unless you *want* her to tell him. Do you want her to tell him?"

"I don't know, I guess so. . . . Why would the Pitches blame the Mage for this?"

Penny bites her lip and looks down. "I think because of *you*, Simon. Everyone is saying that you went to the Pitches' on Christmas Eve and did some dark ritual to kill their magic."

"I was fighting the Humdrum! I mean, I was trying. The Humdrum did something to Baz—he sent him after me like he does the dark creatures."

"So you fought *Baz*?"

"No! I gave him my magic, so he could fight the Humdrum off. It was like a spell. The Humdrum was *there*, Penny, looking like me again—and he talked to me this time. In my voice. He watched us. And then . . . then he just disappeared. What if he stole the magic at Baz's house out of spite? Because I beat him?"

Penny keeps biting her lip. "I still don't understand why you had a tail. . . ."

"I—I needed to get out of there." I've got my hands in my hair. I try to remember it, clearly, how it happened. "When Baz was himself again, we walked out of the forest right into a dead spot. His parents were freaking out, and Baz told me to go. So . . . I did. I didn't have any other way to get here."

"So you flew."

"Yeah."

She looks more worried than I've ever seen her outside of a kidnapping situation. "What spell did you cast, Simon?"

"Penny . . . It was just like last time. I didn't cast any spell. I just—I did what I needed to do."

She's watching herself wring her hands in her lap.

"Penny?"

"Yeah?" She doesn't look up.

"What should I do?

She sighs. "I don't know, Simon. Maybe Agatha's right." She finally meets my eyes. "Maybe it is time to talk to the Mage."

Penny decides we should eat lunch first. Late lunch. I've been sacked out most of the day.

Her parents are gone, and there's nothing in the fridge but a raw turkey. Penny doesn't trust herself to spell it cooked, so we eat cereal and toast and Christmas sweets.

Her little sister wanders in. "You're the reason that Father Christmas didn't come," she says to me. "You scared him off."

"Father Christmas will come, Priya," Penny says. There are five kids in their family: Premal, Penny, Pacey, Priya, and Pip. (Penny says her mother should be charged for child cruelty, and her father for neglect.)

"Father Christmas is a lie," Pacey calls from the living room. "So is God."

I don't know Pacey well. He's at Watford, year five, but he and Penny don't get on. Penny and her siblings all argue constantly. I'm not sure they know how to communicate any other way.

I still feel terrible: cold and wet, even though I'm perfectly dry and wearing some of Pacey's clothes. (I woke up in ladies' trackie bottoms.) And even though I couldn't feel that weird dragon tail when I had it, now that it's gone, it kind of aches. My Weetabix keep lurching up my throat, and I swallow them down hard.

I'm trying not to worry or think about what I should do next. Penny's right—we'll go to the Mage. The Mage will tell us.

When someone knocks at the door, I think it must be him. Priya goes for it, and Penny stops her. I stand up and summon my blade, just to be safe.

It's Baz.

Standing on Penny's doorstep, wearing that greenish black suit again and smelling faintly of smoke. His hand is in his pocket, and his eyes are narrow. He tilts up his chin. "Let me in, Bunce. There's no time for pleasantries."

"Don't you have to be invited in?" she says.

He sneers, and she waves him in. "Come on."

Baz shoves past her and looks around the living room. "Where's your dad's office?"

"My dad isn't here—he's at your house. And what makes you think I'd let you in his office? Why are you even here?"

"I'm here," Baz says, looking over at me, then looking me up and down, "because we have an agreement."

Penelope steps between us. "If you make a single move towards Simon—even a gesture—in my house, I will slaughter your whole family, Basilton. I'll kill them so hard, they won't even be able to find the Veil. Simon didn't do this."

He sneers at her some more. "That's where you're wrong— show me your father's office. Are there maps? I'm assuming there are maps."

We both stare at him. Me, because I can't help it. Penny, in shock.

"Truce!" he says. "Come on, we're still on truce. Make haste!"

I nod. "Come on, Penny. Take us up."

She sighs and unfolds her arms. "Fine, but you can't touch anything up there. Either of you."

We follow her up the stairs. Baz knocks against me with his shoulder and elbow. "All right, Snow?" he asks softly.

"Yeah. You?"

"Fine," he says.

"Your magic?" I whisper.

"Fine."

He touches my back so lightly, I'm not sure it's not an accident.

We take the last step up into the attic, where Penny's dad works. I've never been up here before—the whole *room* is maps. Maps on the walls, covered with string and pins. Maps spread out on high tables, held in place by empty tea mugs. One entire wall is a blackboard, filled with numbers and sentence fragments.

"Lovely," Baz says. "You come by it honestly, Bunce."

He walks around the room until he finds what he's looking for. "There," he says. "Already labelled." I step up behind him. It's a map of the South East with a red string around Hampshire. The flag on the pin says, CHRISTMAS EVE 2015.

"Last night, the Humdrum attacked Simon—and the biggest hole in Britain opened up." He glances back at us. "When did the dragon attack Watford? What day?"

I shrug.

"It was after our Magic Words exam," Penny says. "The middle of November."

"Right . . ." Baz walks around the room, reading the flags. He stops in front of a map of Scotland. "There," he says. "November fifteenth. The Isle of Skye."

"Are you saying that the Humdrum is linked to the holes?" Penny asks. "Because we already knew that."

"I'm getting there, Bunce. . . . Now, when did the holes first appear?"

"Do we really have to do this by Socratic method?"

Baz frowns at her.

Penny sighs. "Nobody really knows. We didn't start documenting the holes until 1998, but there were small ones all over the country by then—"

He nods quickly, cutting her off. "And when were you born, Simon? You'd think I'd know, but I can't remember you ever celebrating your birthday."

I shrug again. Then clear my throat. "I don't know. I mean . . . Nobody knows. They just guessed when they found me."

"But you're probably eighteen now. Maybe nineteen?"

"They put 1997 on my papers."

Baz nods. "Good—1997, shortly before the holes were discovered. And when did you realize you were a magician?"

Penny's paying attention now. She and I have never talked about this. I don't like to talk about this.

"I didn't realize it," I say. "The Mage told me."

Baz is pinning me to the wall with his eyes. "But how did the Mage know? How did he find you?"

I clear my throat. "I went off." They both know what that means. But I didn't, not at 11. I woke up in the middle of the night, during a vicious nightmare—I'd gone to bed hungry, and in my dream, my stomach was on fire. I woke up, breathless, and magic was pouring out of me. Blasting out. The children's home was burnt to the ground, and everyone in it woke up streets away. Unharmed, but still, *streets away*. (Once I watched a show about tornadoes in America, and they showed furniture that had been picked up and set in a yard miles away without breaking. It was like that.)

"You lit up the magickal atmosphere like a Christmas tree," Baz says.

"Like a carpet bomb," Penny chimes in. "My mum actually threw up when it happened."

"*When?*" Baz says. "When did it happen?"

"August," I say. I know he already knows this. "The year we started school."

"August," Baz says, "2008." He walks around the room. "Here," he says, pointing at a dead spot on the map. "And here." He points at another.

Penny and I stare at the map.

Then she steps forward. She points at a string circle. "And in Newcastle . . . ," she says softly. "And a bunch of tiny ones on the coast. The holes changed that year. My dad says they metastasized."

"But—but I wasn't any of those places!" I sputter. "I've *never* been at the site of a new dead spot before last night."

Baz turns to me. "I don't think you have to be there. To make it happen."

"Simon," Penny asks, "when did you go off on the chimera?"

"Our fifth year," Baz says. "Spring 2013."

"Here," Penny says, pointing. "And a big one over there."

"Are you saying I'm the Humdrum?" I step away from them. "*Because I'm not the Humdrum.*"

Baz meets my eyes. "I know. I know you're not. But Simon, listen. The Humdrum *told* us—he said he doesn't take the magic, that he's 'what's left when you're done.'"

"I don't even know what that means, Baz!" I feel like I might go off right now. My fingertips are buzzing.

"It means, the Humdrum doesn't take the magic, Simon—you do."

Penny gasps. "*Simon*. The first time you went off, you were eleven years old—"

"Exactly," Baz says. "Probably wearing a shitty T-shirt and cast-off jeans—and bouncing that bloody ball."

They're looking at each other now. "Simon went off," Penny says, "and he sucked up so much magic—"

Baz nods eagerly.

"—he tore a hole in the magickal atmosphere!" Penny says.

"A Simon-shaped hole . . . ," Baz agrees.

I hold my head in both hands, but it still doesn't make sense. "Are you saying I created an evil twin?"

"More of an impression," Baz says.

"Or an echo," Penny says, still awestruck.

Baz tries to explain it again: "It's like you tore so much magic out at once, you left fingerprints. . . . Whole-being prints."

"But—," I say.

"But . . ." Penny shakes her head. "Why didn't the magickal atmosphere just accommodate Simon the way it accommodates every powerful magician? It's a balanced system."

"So is the earth," Baz says, "but if you clear-cut a forest, the ecosystem doesn't just bounce back."

"This doesn't make sense!" I say. "Even if I did tear a me-shaped hole, how did it come alive? And why is it a monster?"

"*Is* it alive?" Penny asks.

"And is it a monster?" Baz wonders.

"We're talking about the Insidious Humdrum!" I shout.

"We're talking about a *hole*," Baz says calmly. "Think about it. What do holes want?"

"To be filled?" I guess. I know I'm not keeping up.

"Crowley, no," he says. "To *grow*. Everything wants to

grow. If you were a hole, all you'd want is to get bigger."

"That's it, Baz!" Penny throws her arms around him. "You're a genius!"

He shoves her off after a second. "Careful. I'm also a vampire."

I slump against one of the walls; a few pins fall to the floor. "I still don't get it."

"Simon," Penny says, "you're too powerful. You use too much magic at once. The magickal atmosphere can't take it— it just collapses when you go off."

"Theoretically," Baz says.

"Theoretically," she agrees.

"But . . . ," I say. There must be more "but's." "Why does the Humdrum keep trying to kill me? Why send every dark creature in the UK after me?"

"He isn't trying to kill you," Baz says. "He's trying to get you to go off."

"And use more magic," Penny says.

Baz holds his hand up to the maps behind him. "To make a bigger hole."

I stare at them.

They stare at me.

They still seem so proud of themselves—and excited—as if they're not staring at the greatest threat the magickal world has ever known.

"We have to tell the Mage," I say.

Baz's face falls. "Over my dead body."

# 75

## BAZ

"If this is true," Snow says, "if even a little bit of it is true—we can't keep it a secret. We have to go to the Mage."

I knew this was coming.

I knew this would be his solution.

I've known from the beginning that Simon would go running for the Mage when things got serious.

"The fuck we do," I say. "We have to go to the numpties."

*The numpties*," Snow says. As if he can't believe what I'm saying. "You just told me that I'm destroying the World of Mages, and now you want to go numpty hunting?"

"We have an agreement," I remind him. I try to sound urgent, not desperate.

Snow looks at me funny—like maybe I'm talking about how we're boyfriends now. As if that even matters anymore.

I sigh bitterly. "Not that agreement, you twit—you promised to help me find my mother's killer."

"I *will* help you find your mother's killer," Snow says, "after we figure out how to stop this." His head falls back. "Maybe. I mean. If I'm still alive then, if the Mage doesn't decide the answer is just ending me."

"*Simon,*" Bunce admonishes.

"He'll have to get in line," I say, "once my family finds out what's happening—once the whole World of Mages finds out. The Old Families already think you and the Mage are scheming to take their magic. The person who takes you out will be given a crown."

"*Baz,*" Penny says. "I suppose you think it will be you," Snow says, narrowing his eyes.

"We have a truce," I say, my voice rising. "The shit has already hit the fan, and if we don't solve my mother's murder now, we never will. And you promised, Simon. *I promised.*"

"There are more important things to worry about right now!" Snow shouts at me.

"Nothing is more important than my mother!"

# 76

## BAZ

I only remember where the numpties live because Fiona said, *"Christ, what a mess, and right under Blackfriars Bridge—this city has gone straight to hell,"* when she was dragging me to her car.

It doesn't take long to get to Blackfriars from Hounslow. It's Christmas Day, and there's no one out. I park the car and clear a path in the snow to the head of the bridge.

I'm starting to feel a bit panicky.

I know I shouldn't have come alone, but anyone I could have asked for help would have dragged me back to the matter at hand—the fact that my family is now magickally homeless. Even Fiona wouldn't have listened to me today.

Simon and Penny are back to saving the day. Or destroying it. Maybe both. That's all right; I always knew where I stood with Simon—just below the rest of the world. And far, far below the Mage.

All right. It's all right.

I'm afraid—but that's reasonable. You try going back to the place where you were kept in a coffin until you couldn't remember what light looked like.

But I'm in a better position than I was last time. I'm

conscious, for one. I have my wand. And my wits about me.

The door to the numpties' lair is easy to find—it's basically just a hole in the pilings. I slide down some mud, and my stomach churns at the smell. Wet paper and decay. I'm in the right place.

It's too dark down here even for me to see, so I hold my hand and start a fire in my palm, illuminating a circle of nothing around me.

I let the flames grow larger . . . and see a lot more nothing. I'm in a chamber full of debris. Hunks of pavement. Large stones. None of it's familiar; I was unconscious when I was brought here and mostly unconscious when I left. I don't even really know what the numpties look like.

I clear my throat. Nothing happens.

I clear it again. "My name is Basilton Pitch," I call out loudly. "I'm here to ask you a question."

One of the big rocky things starts to tremble. I hold the fire in its direction. And my wand.

The big rocky thing opens like a Transformer into a bigger rocky thing that seems to be wearing a giant oatmeal-coloured jumper. *"You,"* it rumbles in a voice like roadworks.

It's a familiar rumble. I feel the walls closing in on me, and my mouth tastes like stale blood. (Blood's thicker when it stales; it clots.)

*"You,"* the thing says. *"You killed some of us."*

"Well, you kidnapped me," I say. "Remember?"

*"Didn't kill you,"* it says. There are more of the things now, *ca-runch*ing around me. I don't see where they're coming from, but there does seem to be less debris lying around. I try to make out their faces—everything about them is yellow-grey on yellow-grey. They're like piles of wet cement.

"You were well on your way to killing me," I say, "but that's not why I'm here. I came to talk to you."

I'm surrounded by them now. It's like standing inside a stone circle.

*"Don't like talk,"* one rattles out. It might be the one in the jumper again. Or it might be this one, right next to me, wearing an electric blanket, the plug dragging behind it on the ground.

*"Too cold to talk,"* another growls. *"Time to rest."*

That's right, I forgot. Numpties hibernate. I must have woken them. "You can rest," I say. "I'll leave you. Just tell me this one thing. . . ."

They rumble to themselves.

"Who sent you after me?"

The numpties don't answer. I feel like they're moving closer to me, even though I can't see it happening.

"Who sent you to take me?" I shout. I'm holding my wand in the air, my arm coiled back behind my shoulder. Maybe I should already be casting spells at this point, but killing them won't bring me answers. And what if they fight back?

Are they already fighting back?

It suddenly feels like I'm squeezing between stone walls. They're closing in on me, pinching around my left arm . . . around the fire in my hand . . . *the fire.*

"If you crush me," I yell, "my fire will go out!"

The crunching stops; I think they're standing still. They seem to settle in sloppy slabs around me, around my hand. How long do they think I can stand like this? (And why don't they just move somewhere tropical?)

"Tell me," I order. "Who sent you to take me?"

*"Won't say,"* one of them answers. It's like listening

to rocks being broken into gravel.

"Why not?"

The wall behind me lurches closer. *"Told us not to."*

I stand straighter. "Well, I'm telling you otherwise."

*"Kept us warm,"* the biggest one says.

"You don't look warm."

*"Kept us warm for a while,"* it says.

*"Told us not to talk,"* grumbles another.

*"Don't like talk."*

I let the fire in my hand go out, and they make a noise like ten thousand teeth grinding.

*"More fire,"* I hear. *"More firrrre."*

"I'll give you more fire when you answer my question!" They're vibrating. I'm not sure whether it's from anger or impatience or something else. "Who sent you? Who paid you to take me?"

*"Warmed us,"* I hear.

"Who?"

*"One of you."*

*"Magic ones."*

"Which one of us? Was it a man? What did he look like?"

*"Like a man. Soft."*

*"Warm."*

*"Wet spot on the pavement."*

*"Green."*

"Green?" I say.

The largest numpty unfolds, then crunches down into a pile right in front of me, forcing the others away. *"Your headstone!"*

*"One of you."*

*"Warm."*

*"Take the vampire brat,"* the big one grinds, *"keep him in the dark, give him blood."*

*"Hold him till the cold comes and stays."*

*"Fire. Warm. You promised."*

They're pressing closer again. *"You promised."*

I restart the fire in my hand, but instead of backing off, they crush closer to it; I can't even see my wrist.

"Get back!" I yell. My left arm is sucking away from my shoulder, and my wand arm is pressed up against my ear. ***"Back off!"***

"Cast **Paper beats rock,**" someone shouts. Not a numpty—a man!

"What?!"

"**Paper beats rock**—do it."

I call out, ***"Paper beats rock!"*** And then a specific kind of chaos erupts:

There's someone hopping on top of the numpties, slapping them with sheets of newspaper like he's playing whack-a-mole. They try to heave away, but when he thumps them, they go still. Actually still. The pressure around me stops.

I look up and see none other than Nicodemus himself standing on top of the biggest numpty, catching his breath.

"What the fuck are you doing here?" I ask him, my mouth surely hanging open.

He sneers. "I came to save you from numpties."

"Did you just put them to sleep with *The Guardian*?"

"I did. Why didn't you?"

Nicodemus is wearing a cheap blazer over a white T-shirt, black jeans with a wallet chain, and ancient steel-toed Doc Martens. It's clear what my ridiculous aunt saw in him.

He reaches down and takes my wrist, pointing my wand at the rock wall that's trapping my other arm. **"Have a break, have a Kit-Kat,"** he says.

"What?"

"Say it."

"Why?"

He pinches my wrist.

**_"Have a break, have a Kit-Kat!"_** I cast, and the rock crumbles around my arms. "That shouldn't work," I say, shaking my hand free.

The numpties don't wake up, despite me breaking pieces off them.

"Stop complaining," Nicodemus says, "and come on. The newspapers won't hold them forever."

He's holding out his arm, so I take it, even though he smells like sour blood and cider. He hauls me up until I'm standing on the numpties, too.

We hop from one to the next, then onto the ground. "This way," Nicodemus says, switching on a big flashlight.

I follow him up the mud pathway and out into the daylight. As soon as we're above ground, I push him away from me.

"Watch it," he says. "I just saved your life!"

"You just ruined my plan—they were about to tell me who kidnapped me!"

"They already told you," he snarls. "It was the Mage!"

The Mage. The green man. The headstone. *The Mage?*

Nicodemus curls his lip, so I can see his missing eyeteeth. "It was the Mage who had you kidnapped," he says. He keeps moving forward, and I keep stepping back. "And the Mage who let the vampires into Watford."

"What?" I stumble in the snow, and catch myself.

"He made a deal with them," Nicodemus says, inches from my face. "If they attacked Watford and gave everyone a good scare, he'd let them live in London, unbothered. He wanted me to make the deal, but I wouldn't, so he found someone else."

"The Mage sent vampires to kill my mother?"

"I tried to warn her, but she wouldn't believe Merlin's oath coming from me." Nicodemus shrugs. "For what it's worth, I don't think the Mage meant for your mum to die—but I don't think he minded much. Made everything else easier, didn't it?"

I take another step back. "Why are you telling me this now? Why not before? And why are you even here—did you follow me?" I whip my head around, looking for more vampires. Is this a trap?

"I couldn't tell you," Nicodemus says. "He would have killed me! But now it doesn't matter what he does. He went and arrested my sister, didn't he? Your Mage. He's got Ebeneza now. And I need your help getting her back."

It was the Mage. It was the Mage all along.

I mean, I always thought it was him, but I never really *thought* it was *him*. How could he? He's *the Mage*. How could he just—?

I make a noise like Snow, a growl that starts in my stomach and triggers my fangs. Then I turn and run for my car.

Nicodemus runs after me. He grabs my arm. "Wait! I'm coming with you!"

"You're not coming with me."

"I told you—he has my sister!"

"What do I care?"

"I'm going to help you fight."

"I don't want your help, you monster."

"Too bad," he says, yanking me. "You'll have it!"

We're interrupted by desperate yelping: A Normal is out walking his dog, a cross-eyed Cavalier spaniel, and it's taken an interest in Nicodemus and me, barking madly.

"Come along, Della." The Normal pulls on her chain, and the dog nearly chokes herself jumping at us. *Bark, bark, bark.*

I could swear it's saying, *"Baz! Baz! Baz!"*

I turn away from Nicodemus and look more closely at the spaniel. "Are you saying my name?"

"Baz!" the dog barks. "Thank magic! It's me, Penelope!"

"Bunce?" It does sound like her. In a yelpy, canine way. "Who turned you into a dog?"

"Am I a dog?" she yaps. "The spell's never worked that way before. Baz, you have to come get me!" The Normal is leaning over to pick up his dog, as if I'm a threat to her.

I am. I grab the dog and hold it up to my face.

"Hey, now," the Normal says. Nicodemus hisses at him, and the man lets go of the dog's chain.

"Bunce, what are you talking about?"

"Baz, we can't let Simon face the Mage alone—I have a really bad feeling about it. I need you to come get me!"

Simon. Alone with the Mage. With my mother's murderer.

"I'm coming." I shove the animal under my arm and look up at the Normal. "I need to borrow your dog."

"You can't just—"

I hold up my wand. ***"There's nothing to see here!"*** The Normal looks at us, then down at his hands, then gets a cigarette out of his pocket.

I start running towards my car.

Nicodemus is right behind me. "I'm coming with you!"

I keep running. He grabs at my arm again, and I whirl around, starting a fire in that palm. He jumps back.

The Bunce spaniel yelps at him.

"I have to save my sister," he says. "And you could use my

help. You know I can't get in on my own."

I tilt up my chin. "I *could* use your help. And if what you're saying is true, Ebb certainly could. But I'll be damned to hell twice over before I let a vampire into Watford. Even a gelded one."

# 77

## AGATHA

"Oh, thank magic," Mum says. She's standing in my doorway in her dressing gown.

I lift my head up from my pillow. "What?" I fell asleep in my clothes, on top of the blankets. I don't know what time it is.

"Mitali Bunce just called. Simon and Penelope have run off to who knows where, and I thought you might be with them."

"No—they've run off?"

"She hopes they've just run off, that they weren't taken." Mum's voice breaks. "After last night."

"Mum, what's wrong?"

"There's been another attack," she says. "That horrible Humdrum—he attacked the *Pitches*. Ate everything. It's such a shame. It was the grandest estate in magic."

"But Simon—," I say.

"What dear? Did he tell you something?"

They've gone to find the numpties. I'm sure of it. It's exactly the sort of thing they'd do. Run off to confront a pack of ogres without talking to their parents or asking for help . . .

I think about telling my mother. That Simon was at the Pitches' last night. That he and Penny—and *Basilton*

*Grimm-Pitch*—were plotting together.

But Mum would just ask why I hadn't told her sooner.

And then I think she'd tell me to keep my mouth shut. That no good could come of getting involved now, with the whole World of Mages on the brink of war, or possibly over it.

My dad's at an emergency Coven meeting, Mum says. And the Mage is holed up in his tower, communing with the stars or something.

I can tell she's relieved that I'm not with Simon and Penny, but also weirdly concerned. "Agatha, is everything, you know, tickety-boo with Simon?"

"Aside from the fact that he's missing?"

"You know what I mean, darling. *Between* you. The two of you."

"We're fine," I assure her.

I'm not about to tell her that we broke up. I don't even know whether Simon's alive; I'm not telling my mother about my ruined prospects until I absolutely have to.

I get some leftover party food—a Diet Coke and some soggy artichoke crostini—and go back to my room. I fell asleep last night before my parents' party, and they never woke me. They must have decided I needed the rest.

I take a bite of bread. There's nothing I can do about this. Any of it.

I don't even *really* know where Simon is. "Out chasing numpties" isn't helpful. What else do I know—that he might be with Baz? That he and Baz are friends now? That's not a clue.

I still can't believe they're *friends*.

I can believe it of Simon; he'll make friends with anyone who's willing. Anyone who doesn't mind the risks of befriending a human wrecking ball. But what's in it for Baz?

All Baz has ever wanted from Simon is his demise. Baz would do anything to get Simon out of his way.

Anything . . .

What if this is all a trick?

What if Baz is *luring* Simon to the numpties? The way he lured me into the Wood that night . . .

Well. He didn't quite lure me. I followed him. But still. But *still* . . .

Baz is a vampire.

Baz is a villain.

Baz is a *Pitch*.

My phone is on my nightstand. (I'm allowed to have one at home.) I pick it up and text Penny.

*Your mum is looking for you. Everyone's worried.*

And:

*Are you fighting numpties? Do you need help? I could get help.*

Then:

*Are you with Baz? I think it might be a trick. That he's trying to hurt Simon.*

And then:

*You could have at least left a note. That seems pretty basic.*

I throw the mobile down on the bed and pop open my Diet Coke. The photo of Lucy and Davy is stuffed under my pillow. I pull it out.

What would brave, bold Lucy Salisbury do in a hopeless situation like this?

Hot-tail it to California like a rational human being, apparently. Leave it to the heroes.

If Baz *has* turned on Simon, there's nothing I can do to help. . . .

But I can't just sit here, doing nothing, damn it! (Damn *him*.) (Damn them all.) Even when I'm not involved in their stupid drama, I'm still involved—I still have to play my part. . . .

And this is the part where I always scream for help.

My mother's on the phone when I slip out. I take the Volvo.

# 78

## BAZ

It took me a good bit to figure out that Bunce was just possessing the dog—that she wasn't trapped inside its body. I've never even heard of such a thing. I'm certain it isn't legal.

The real Bunce, terrifying mage that she is, is hiding behind a hedge in Hounslow, waiting for me.

I'm on my way to get her.

"I wouldn't have had to do this if you weren't so cagey about your mobile number!" she yaps from the back seat.

## PENELOPE

I'm hiding in our neighbour's garden. I can't go home because I know if Mum's there, she won't let me leave. And I *have* to leave—I can't let Simon face the Mage alone. He might already be at Watford. He probably just *thought* about teleporting and arrived there.

I really blew it with Simon.

He was going to let me go with him, I think, after Baz

stormed off. But then I tried to talk him down—I tried to *reason* with him.

"Maybe Baz is right," I said.

Simon was pacing around my bedroom, swinging his blade, and he stopped to shoot me a scornful look. "Seriously, Penny? Numptics?"

"No, not about the numpties—but, Simon, think it through, what's going to happen when people find out about you?"

"I don't care about people!" he growled.

I shushed him. My little brothers and sisters were still downstairs. "You care about the Mage," I said. "What's going to happen when he finds out you're stealing magic?"

*"I'm not stealing it!"* he whispered.

*"Whatever you're doing!"* I whispered back. "What's going to happen?"

"I don't know! The Mage will decide."

That's when I probably should have given up. But instead I stood in front of him and reached for his hand. He let me take it.

"Simon," I said, "maybe we should just *go.*"

He looked confused. He clenched his sword in his other hand. "Penny. That's what I'm saying. We have to go."

"No." I stepped closer to him, squeezing his hand. "I think this might be our only chance to . . . to leave."

He looked at me like I was mental.

I kept at it: "Everyone has already connected you to the Humdrum. When they figure out what's actually happening, even the people who care about you—you're a threat to everyone, Simon. To our whole world. Once they find out . . . Maybe this is our last chance to *leave.* We could just . . . *go.*"

He shook his head. "Go where, Penny?"

"Wherever we have to," I said. "Away."

## SIMON

Away. There is no away.

There's only here and Normal. Did Penelope think that would be an escape for me—to run away from magic?

I don't even think it's possible. I *am* magic. And whatever I'm doing, running away won't stop it.

"I have to fix this," I said. "It's my job to fix it."

"I don't think you can," she said.

I let go of her hand. "I have to. It's why I'm *here.*"

But maybe that's not why I'm here. Maybe I'm just here to fuck everything up. . . .

It doesn't change what I have to do next.

## PENELOPE

"I'm going to talk to the Mage," he said.

"Simon," I begged, "please don't."

But he'd already stopped listening to me. Dark red wings were unfolding from his shoulders, and that arrowlike tail wound its way down his thigh.

He looked at me with his jaw set. And then he took off.

That's when I called Baz.

He pulls up now in a burgundy sports car. I climb out from

the bushes, and Baz has already leaned over to open the car door.

There's a little cross-eyed dog in the back seat. I break my possession spell, and it yelps.

# 79

## LUCY

We snuck back into Watford on the autumn equinox.

"He'll be born at solstice," Davy said, pulling me up the hole in the floor into the old Oracle's room, at the top of the White Chapel.

"Or she," I said.

He laughed. "I suppose that's right."

I climbed onto the wood floor. "How did the Oracles get up here?"

"There used to be a ladder," he said.

The room was round, with curved stained glass windows and an intricately painted domed ceiling—a mural of men and women holding hands in a ring, looking up at a field of foiled stars and ornate black script. I could only make out some of it—*In time's womb.* Shakespeare. "How did you find this place?"

Davy shrugged. "Exploring."

He knew Watford like no one else. While the rest of us had flirted and studied, he'd roamed every inch.

I watched him draw a pattern on the floor with salt and oil and dark blue blood. (Not a pentagram—something else.) And I pulled my shawl around my shoulders and legs.

We hadn't brought anything with us. Blankets or pillows. Or mats.

Davy had a stack of notes, and he kept going back to them.

"You're sure of everything?" I asked for the twentieth time this week. He'd been more indulgent with me since I agreed to this.

I *did* agree to it.

I thought . . .

I thought Davy might do it without me. That he might find a way.

I thought that as long I was there, I could keep him from going too far.

And I thought . . . that Davy wanted a child. Underneath it all, we were talking about *a child.* He was asking me to have his child. To change our lives.

I wanted that.

"I'm sure," Davy said. "I've compared the ritual and phrases over three sources; the three accounts complete each other, and the divergence is small."

"Why hasn't anyone else tried this?" I asked.

"Oh, I think they have," he said brightly. "But *we* haven't. You said it yourself, no one has studied these rituals like I have. None of these scholars had access to each other's notes."

He'd shared some of the spells with me. *Beowulf.* The Bible. I wrapped my shawl tighter. "So there's no risk—"

"There's always risk. It's creation. It's life."

"It's a child," I said.

He stood and hopped over his designs to crouch in front of me: "Our child, Lucy, the most powerful magician the World of Mages has ever known."

✻

The room was lit by seven candles.

And Davy chanted every spell seven times.

*Why is it always seven?* I wondered, lying on my back on the cold wood floor.

I wished that we'd brought music. But there was singing outside—the students at the equinox bonfire out on the Great Lawn.

The night was turning out more solemn than I had expected. It had been a lark, sneaking into Watford, finding the hidden room. But now Davy was focused and quiet.

I wondered how we'd know whether the ritual had worked. . . .

How would we know if our baby was the most powerful mage in the world? Would he look any different? Would his eyes glow?

Davy said we couldn't talk at all during the ritual, so instead I caught his gaze. He looked happy, excited.

Because he's finally *doing* something, I thought—not just shouting at the sky.

I tried not to talk. I lay very still.

And I knew—oh, I *knew* the moment it happened that magic and luck were on our side.

There was a pull deep in my belly. Like a star had collapsed there. The world around me went white, and all my magic contracted into a tight ball in my pelvis.

When I could see again, all I could see was Davy's golden face above mine, as happy as I'd ever known him.

# 80

## AGATHA

The gates are open when I get to Watford, and there's a single set of tyre tracks in the snow. That's good; that means the Mage is here. I follow them and park the Volvo in the main courtyard right next to the Mage's Jeep. I won't get in trouble—this is an emergency.

I'm not good in emergencies. I can't wait to find the Mage and hand this off to him. I'll tell him what I know, then I'll get as far from this mess as I can.

Maybe I'll go over to Minty's house. And we can watch *Mean Girls.* And her mum will make us virgin mojitos. And we'll do gel manis—Minty's got her own machine.

Minty doesn't care about magic.

Minty won't even read fantasy novels. *"I just can't make myself care,"* she says. *"It's all so fake."*

(I tried to do manicures with Penelope once, and she got distracted, trying to come up with a way to do it magickally.)

I run through the snow to the Weeping Tower and up to the Mage's office. It's a thousand stairs, I swear. There are lifts, but I don't know the spells.

I'm worried about knocking at the Mage's door, but it's wide open, and when I walk inside, it's a catastrophe. It looks like Penny's been in here: There are books everywhere, in stacks and lying open. There are pages ripped out and taped all over one wall. (Not *taped*—stuck to the wall with spells.) (And this is exactly the sort of thing I'm sick of. Like, just use some tape. Why come up with a spell for sticking paper to the wall? Tape. Exists.) Anyway, the Mage isn't here. I suppose I could leave him a note, but how would he ever find it? And what if he doesn't come back in time? The Mage should really have a secretary, given his responsibilities. I close one of his books out of spite and lean against a window frame, trying to decide what to do next.

That's when I see the lights in the White Chapel.

## SIMON

I'm not sure how I know the way to Watford.

I'm not sure I'm really flying anymore. Or if I'm just *thinking* about being there.

I wonder if this—what I'm doing, the magic I'm using— is enough to tear a new hole, or if it's just making an old one bigger.

I wonder if they're all wrong about me, all of them.

## AGATHA

I don't like the White Chapel. Whenever we have assemblies in here, I can't get the smell of incense out of my hair.

It smells more like smoke than incense today. Smoke and

spent magic. Like a classroom after an exam.

I'm just going to find the Mage, tell him what I know, then leave.

(Minty's house might not be far enough away from this disaster. Maybe I'll go to university in Scotland. At that school where Kate went to meet William.)

The front hall of the Chapel is empty. I walk deeper in, following the smoke, which seems like an idiotic move—a Simon move—but also seems like the best way to find the Mage.

I keep going, opening doors, making my way deeper into the building. It's smokier back here. And darker. And I think I hear the Mage chanting. I'm probably interrupting some heavy magic. Maybe he's searching for Simon.

"Sir?" I call out. I don't know what else to call him—I've never heard anyone actually call the Mage "the Mage" to his face.

There's a crash like wood hitting wood. I can't tell where it's coming from, and I can't see anything. I start looking for a light switch. Some of the older Watford buildings don't have switches—you have to turn on the lights with magic. But my wand is in the car, lying on the passenger seat; it didn't fit in my coat pocket.

There's another crash. I stand very still and listen:

A metallic clanging. Someone shouting. Footsteps coming towards me—running. Panting.

Someone slams into me, pushing me aside and running past me. Then someone else catches me and pins me, my back against the wall. "I told you not to run!" he growls.

"You didn't," I say. "You didn't tell me."

He's holding my arms so tight, I think they might actually break. ***Let there be light!*** he says.

And there is.

I stare into the Mage's eyes. When he sees that it's me, he throws me aside.

"Where did she go?" he demands.

"Who, sir?"

He swings his wand around him. ***"Come out, come out, wherever you are!"*** His teeth are bared. "You know I don't have time for this. The hour is near!" He slashes with his wand. ***"Please!"*** (Slash.) ***"Please!"*** (Slash.) ***"Please!"*** (Slash.) ***"Let me, let me, let me!"***

I'm not sure what he's casting for, but the spell tugs at me, and I fall forward.

"You . . . ," the Mage says, noticing me again. His tunic is open, and he's sweating profusely. There's something blue smeared all over his chest. "What are you doing here, girl?"

"I came to tell you about Simon, sir."

"Simon!" he says wildly. "Where's Simon?" He holds up his hand. "Wait—" The Mage looks like he wants to run away, like he's listening. I take a step away from him, but he grabs my arm. "Where is Simon?"

"I don't know, sir," I say. "But I came to tell you—he was with Basilton Pitch. Last night. They told me they were going to find some numpties, but I think it's a trap! You have to help him!"

The words rush out of me. Everything I rehearsed in the car.

The Mage groans and holds his head, pacing now across the dark room, coming in and out of my sight. The light from his spell still hangs in the air around me. I take a step towards the door.

"Numpties now. Vampires. *Children*. I don't have time for this!" He growls, in frustration, and I hear something loud and heavy, like a bookcase, fall to the ground. Maybe he's distracted. I turn to run from the room, but the Mage is right there, grabbing me. "You'll have to do," he says. "You'll have to do for now."

My legs give out, and he drags me.

"You don't have much to give," he says, "but I'll take it."

# BAZ

Bunce is biting her nails. She keeps trying to cast spells on the car, but I'm already driving it as fast as it can manage, and all her spells come out nervous and tight.

She's worried that the Mage will kill Simon once he finds out that Simon is causing the Humdrum.

I'm worried she'll figure out that I want to kill the Mage first.

# PENELOPE

I don't trust Baz.

I only called him for help because he has a car.

I mean, I'd love to trust him—he's a brilliant magician and excellent company—but I can't.

I only trust four people: my parents, Micah, and Simon. I don't have any spare trust lying around, and if I did, I wouldn't give it to Tyrannus Basilton Grimm-Pitch. He's cynical, manipulative, and utterly ruthless. All he cares about is getting what he wants and protecting his own people.

And there's something in the way he looks at Simon. . . .

I don't think Baz has set aside the last seven years of hostility. He's got a mad glint in his eyes for Simon. If he gets a chance to stab him in the back, I think he might take it.

I need to get Simon away from the Mage.

And then I just need to get him *away.*

## AGATHA

I should be scared. And I am—terrified.

But I'm also thinking, *Fucking of course. Of course this is how I'm going to die! Because somebody's looking for Simon and finds me instead. I'm going to be murdered by some power-hungry maniac who doesn't even know my name.*

I don't try to fight. What's the point? But I go limp. And start to cry. Just because I knew I was going to die like this doesn't mean I'm ready for it. I wish I'd been nicer to my mum this morning. I wish I were wearing something other than leggings and Ugg boots. I always figured I'd make a more beautiful corpse.

The Mage hauls me to another room, where a trapdoor hangs open in the ceiling, light streaming down.

He points his wand at himself—*"Up, up, and away!"* You're not supposed to cast that spell on people; you can accidentally pull their lungs through their shoulders. But the spell works for him, and we start to float up through the door.

Then another spell—*"And we all fall down!"*—knocks us both to the ground. Whoever casts it falls, too. I hear her land.

"No, Davy," she says. "Let her go."

And I think it must be Lucy. Here. To save me.

## SIMON

I land on the Great Lawn at sunset and walk across the drawbridge. I see the Mage's Jeep, and Dr. Wellbelove's Volvo, and I wonder if they're here—or if they're off somewhere fighting. Actually fighting. Blades out, wands drawn. I don't even know where to look for the war if it isn't at Watford.

I'm headed for the Mage's office when I see the light at the top of the Chapel.

It's in a tower I've never seen lit before. I've never even noticed the stained glass there—it looks like a crown, or a cluster of stars.

As I'm looking, the windows blaze with light.

## AGATHA

The Mage lurches up onto his hands and knees and starts casting spells. ***"Please, please, please! Let me, let me, let me!"***

***"Hell hath no fury!"*** the woman shouts. Fire pours from her staff and hits him in the chest. I've never seen anything like that, not even from Simon. The light from the fire finally illuminates her face—it's Ebb. The goatherd.

"Run, Agatha!" she says.

But the Mage has fallen on top of me. "I can't!" I sob.

The Mage raises his wand to cast at her, and I hit his hand as hard as I can. His wand goes flying, and he rolls away from me to get it.

*"**Run for your life!**"* Ebb shouts, and I do. I scrabble to my feet and run from the room like there's a jet stream at my back.

I run through the smoke and darkness out into the light and snow, and then I keep running.

# 81

## EBB

He would have killed that girl.

I don't suppose I had a choice but to come back.

## THE MAGE

There's no time.

The Humdrum is devouring us.

And today's the day—today is a day that my magic might work. Holidays are auspicious, the solstice lingers.

Today is the day.

This is the hour.

If only Simon were here. . . .

I thought we'd done it—at great cost, yes—but I thought we'd done it, Lucy. We'd brought the Greatest Mage.

*He is the greatest mage.*

I hid him among the Normals, so that no one would know. So that no one would ask. I hid him until he was ready. Until he called me to him, just like every prophecy said he would!

I didn't know that he was broken.

I couldn't see that he was a cracked vessel.

Maybe it was too much power for a babe to hold—maybe that was my mistake.

If he were here, I could fix it. I have different spells now. (I'd been looking too far in the past; I should have realized that new power must come from new psalms.) I have a chance now, I could relieve him.

But Simon isn't here. And I can't wait for him. The Humdrum won't wait. The Pitches are on their way—

This woman will have to do. She's the brightest star in the Realm, next to Simon.

Our Simon.

I can take her power.

I just have to kill her first.

## EBB

I don't suppose I ever had the choices I thought I did.

## THE MAGE

She's all brute force and '90s clichés.

I've seen her weave spells like a master on the goats and the grounds. But in battle, Ebb's a cannon at a sword fight. No wonder Simon follows her around like a lost kid.

I'd thought about making her redundant over the years— what does Watford need with goats?—but she's powerful, and she protects the school when I'm away.

I wouldn't sacrifice her today if the fate of our world didn't hang in the balance.

# EBB

I'm out of practice.

I was never *in* practice, with spells like this. I know ten spells to turn water into whisky, and I can bring the goats in with a turn of phrase. But I never saw the point of all this.

Even when Nico and me would get in a dust-up, I'd usually settle him with **Don't worry, be happy** or **Hush little baby**.

My only chance now is to overpower Davy.

I throw, *"Head over heels!"* and *"Hit the floor!"*—spells I learned in pub brawls. The Mage does something I've never seen before—obeying the spells instead of letting them hit him.

He looks like a madman. His shirt is torn open, and he's covered in muck. Who knows what dark magic he's about—he still hasn't said what he wants from me. We're circling each other like two wolves.

"You're no match for me, Ebb," he says, then shouts, *"Resistance is futile!"*

I absorb the spell. I can do that sometimes, let a spell burn out in my magic. *"Bend over backwards!"* I shout back desperately, when I'm able.

The Mage swings back into the ground like he's made of rubber—then picks himself up, sighing.

# THE MAGE

She caught me by surprise with that one, and my head is ringing. "I'm sorry, Ebb. But I don't have time for this. I need your power—the World of Mages needs your power."

"I'm not a fighter," she says.

"I know. But I am." I step closer. "Make this sacrifice for your people."

"What do you want from me, Davy?" She's scared. I'm sorry for that. A hank of blond hair covers one of her eyes.

"Your power. I need your power."

"I'll give it to you. I don't want it."

"It doesn't work that way," I say. "I have to take it."

She steels her jaw, holding her shepherd's staff between us. ***"Helter skelter!"*** she screams—and the room goes mad.

Floorboards peel up and whirl about us like ticker tape. Every ancient window shatters.

It's a child's spell. A tantrum. For upsetting board games and scattering marbles.

The power in this woman . . .

Wasted.

I stumble forward through the chaos and sink my blade in her chest.

# EBB

I decide the Mage must be right, even though he talks like a madman.

I decide this is for the best. This is for a reason.

I hope that someone remembers to bring the nannies home.

# 82

## SIMON

As I reach the door to the White Chapel, every window explodes. It sounds like the world is ending, and it's made of glass.

I hope I'm not too late. . . .

To stop whatever needs to be stopped.

To help whoever needs to be helped.

I run into the Chapel, behind the pulpit. Then I think about the Mage, and find my way to a room at the back, with a trapdoor hanging open in the ceiling. I flutter my wings—I still have wings—and catch the edge of the opening, hauling myself up.

It's a round room, ruined now, and the Mage is kneeling in the centre, his eyes closed and his shoulders heaving. There's someone lying on the ground below him—and for a breath, I think it might be Baz. But Baz went to the numpties; I know he did.

Whoever it is on the floor, it means it's all started.

I clear my throat and rest my hand on my hip. The blade appears without the incantation. It's like the whole world is just *reacting* to me. I don't even have to *think*.

I don't have to think.

The Mage has his hands on the person's chest. There's a haze of deep magic around them, and he's chanting. It takes me a minute to recognize the song. . . .

*"Easy come, easy go. Little high, little low."*

I step forward quietly; I don't want to interrupt him in the middle of a spell. Especially if he's trying to revive someone.

*"Carry on, carry on,"* the Mage sings.

One more silent step, and I see that it's Ebb beneath him— I cry out, I can't help it.

The Mage's head turns, his lips still murmuring Queen lyrics.

"Simon!" he says, so startled that he pulls his hands away.

"Don't stop," I say, falling on my knees. "Help her."

"Simon," the Mage says again.

Blood flows out of Ebb's chest.

"Help her!" I say. "She's dying!"

"I can't," the Mage says. "But, Simon. You're here. I can still help you."

He reaches for me, his hands wet with Ebb's blood. And I know I have to tell him now. I stand jerkily, pulling away from him.

The Mage picks up his blade—it's bloody, too—and stands with me. His head is split open above his ear, bleeding down his neck and shoulder.

"You're hurt, sir. I can help."

He shakes his head, staring just past me. I think he's freaked out by my wings, but I'm not sure I can put them away right now.

"I'm fine, Simon," he says.

It's too late, I've already thought about making him better: The gash above his ear heals from the outside in, mending itself.

His hand goes to his head. His eyes widen. *"Simon."*

My chin starts to wobble, and I squeeze the hilt of my blade till the wobbling stops. I try to think about making Ebb better—I think I've been thinking about it all along—but she still lies there, bleeding.

The Mage steps closer to me, like he's stepping close to an animal. "You've come just in time," he says softly. He lifts his hand and touches my face. I feel blood trickle down my cheek. "I owe you an apology," he says. "I got so much wrong."

I look him in the eye. We're the same height. "No, sir."

"Not the power," he says. "You *are* the most powerful mage who ever lived, Simon. You're . . . a miracle." He cups my face in his wet palm. "But you're not the Chosen One."

I'm not the Chosen One.

Of course I'm not.

*I'm not the Chosen One.*

Thank magic. This is the only thing anyone has said today that makes sense. But it doesn't make a difference—

I still have to tell him.

I swallow. "Sir, I have something to tell you. Baz and Penelope—"

"They don't matter now! None of them. The Pitches and their war. As if all of *magic* doesn't hang on the precipice! As if the Great Devourer hasn't marked our door!"

*"Sir—"*

"I thought I could salvage you," he whispers. He's standing so close to me. Holding my face like a baby's. Or a dog's. "I thought I could keep my promise to take care of you. That I'd find the right text, the missing rhyme. I thought I could *fix* you. . . . But you weren't the right vessel." He nods to himself. It's like he's still looking past me. "I got this part wrong," he says. "I got you wrong."

I look down at Ebb. Then back at the Mage. "The Humdrum—," I say.

His face contorts. "You'll never be strong enough to fight him! You'll never be *enough*, Simon—it isn't your fault."

"It is!" I shake my head, and he holds my jaw firmly. "Sir, I think my power is tied to the Humdrum. I think I might be causing him!"

"Nonsense!" His spit hits my mouth. "The Humdrum was foretold—*The greatest threat the World of Mages has ever known.*' Just as the Greatest Mage was foretold."

"But Baz says—"

"You can't listen to that whelp!" He drops my face and steps back, raising his arms, waving his red sword. "Cut from the same cloth as his mother. Does anyone think that Watford was better under her care? These halls were empty! Only the most prosperous, the most privileged magicians ever learned to speak. Natasha Grimm-Pitch loved her power and wealth—she loved the past—far too much to ever allow Watford to change."

The Mage is pacing. He's talking to the floor. I've never seen him like this—he's moving too much, he's saying too much.

"Should I weep over her death?" he asks, his voice too loud. "When it means a generation of magickal children have learned how to use their power? Am I supposed to be *sorry*? I'm not sorry! What is the greater *good*?"

He rounds on me again and clamps his hand where my neck meets my chest, catching my eyes and holding them. "I'm. Not. Sorry."

Then he leans closer. His hair brushes against mine. "If I could go back, there's nothing I'd change. Nothing. Except you . . . I can't fix you, Simon." He shakes his head, growling and gritting his teeth. "I can't fix you—but I can *relieve* you. And I can fulfil the prophecy."

I don't know what to say. So I nod.

I've known all along that I was a fraud—it's such a relief to hear the Mage finally saying it. And to hear that he has a *plan*. I just want him to tell me what to do.

"Give me your magic, Simon."

I take a step back—in surprise, I think—but the Mage holds me by the neck. He presses his right hand over my heart. "I can take it. I finally found a way, but then I heard that you'd gotten there first. You can give it to me freely now, can't you? Like you gave it to the Pitch brat?" I feel every one of his fingertips against my skin. "Don't make me take it, Simon. . . ."

I look down at Ebb. Her blood is pooling around her arm and shoulder. It's just reached the tips of her blond hair.

"Think of it," the Mage murmurs. "I have control that you'll never have. Wisdom . . . Experience . . . With your power, I can obliterate the Humdrum. I can settle these quarrels once and for all—*I can finally finish what I started*."

"What you started?"

"My reforms!" he hisses. Then his head drops forward, like he's tired. "I thought it would be enough to throw them out of power. To change the rules. But they're like cockroaches, these people—they creep up on you as soon as you turn off the lights.

"I can't focus on my enemies because of the Humdrum"— he tilts his head to the right—"and I can't focus on the Humdrum because of all this *squabbling*." He tilts it to the left. "It was never supposed to be like this." He looks back up at me. "You were supposed to be the answer."

"I'm not the Greatest Mage," I say.

"You're just a child," he says, disappointed.

I close my eyes.

The Mage pinches my neck. "Give it to me."

"It could hurt you, sir."

He takes my hands roughly. "*Now*, Simon."

I open my eyes and look down at our hands. I *could* give it to him. All of it. I could give it to him, and then it would be *him*. It would be the Mage draining the world of magic or finding a way not to. . . .

I squeeze one hand and give him a bit of magic. A fistful.

The Mage clenches my fingers, and his body seizes, but he doesn't let go. "Simon!" His eyes light up. Literally. "I think this will work!"

"It *will* work," my voice says. But I'm not the one speaking—the Humdrum is standing beside us. Over Ebb's body.

The Mage goes still, his mouth dropping open. I forgot; he's never seen the Humdrum. "Simon," the Mage says. "It's you."

"It's the Humdrum," I say.

"It's you on the day I found you." His eyes are wide and soft. "My boy—"

"I'm not him," the Humdrum says. "I'm not anybody's boy."

"You're my shadow," I say to the Humdrum. I'm not afraid of him now.

"More like an exit wound," he says. "Or an exhaust trail—I've had loads of time to think about it."

"The Insidious Humdrum," the Mage whispers.

"It's a crap name," the Humdrum says, bouncing his ball. "Did you come up with it?"

The Mage turns to me and grabs both my wrists. "Now, Simon, give it to me. He's right here."

"When did you get wings?" the Humdrum asks. "I'll never have wings. Or a sword. I'll never even have a proper ball—I'd like a football."

The Mage jerks on my wrists, still staring at the Humdrum. "*Now, Simon!* We'll end this once and for all!"

"Do it," the Humdrum says. "He's right. End everything. All of the magic. *All of it.*"

The Humdrum tosses the ball to me, and I push the Mage off me to catch it.

"Simon!" the Mage says.

I tuck the red rubber ball in my suit jacket—I'm not sure when I thought up this grey suit—and I look down at the Humdrum. It's the only way.

I take the boy by his shoulders.

He laughs. "What're you gonna do—hit me? Go off on me? I'm pretty sure that won't work."

"No," I say. "I'm going to end this. I'm sorry."

"You're *sorry*?"

"I'm sorry that all the good stuff happened after I left you."

The Humdrum looks confused. I close my eyes, and then I imagine myself unlocking every door—opening every window, turning every tap—and pouring it all into him.

He doesn't flinch or pull away. And when I open my eyes again, he's still looking up at me, less confused now.

The Humdrum puts his hands over mine and gives me a small nod. His jaw is set, and his eyes are flinty. He looks like a little thug, even now.

I nod back.

I give it all to him.

I let it all go.

The Mage tries to push us apart—he's shouting at me, cursing—but I'm rooted to the centre of the earth, and the Mage's hands pass right through the Humdrum. The boy's disappearing—it's getting harder for me to keep my hands on his shoulders.

I don't think I'm hurting him. The Humdrum. He just looks tired.

He's a hole. He's what's left when I'm done.

And sometimes holes want to get bigger, but Baz was wrong—sometimes they just want to be filled.

I give him everything, and then I feel him pulling at me. Before, I was pouring the magic, but now it's being sucked out. Spilling into a vacuum.

My hands slip through the Humdrum's shoulders, but my magic keeps rushing into him.

I fall to my knees, and it rushes out faster.

My fingertips tingle. I smell fire. Sparks chase themselves over my skin.

*This isn't going off,* I think. *This is going out.*

# 83

## BAZ

I can't imagine we're not too late.

And on top of everything else, on top of *abject failure*, I'm so thirsty, I could drain a Clydesdale.

I should drain that yappy spaniel and put it out of its misery.

Maybe I should put Bunce out of hers.

We come up over a hill, and we can see the school ahead of us. I'm ready to tear through the wide-open gates, but the Jag gets stuck in the snow. Bunce and I get out and start running across the Great Lawn.

It's a shock when we see Wellbelove running towards us like a panicked rabbit from the opposite direction.

## PENELOPE

Agatha's weeping and panting—and running like she's Jessica Ennis, even through all this snow. It's too bad Watford doesn't have a track team.

She doesn't stop when she sees us, just grabs my hand and

tries to pull me with her. "Run," she says. "Penny, run—it's the Mage!"

"What's the Mage?" I grab her other hand, and she runs in place around me, spinning me in a circle.

"He's evil!" she says. "Of course he is!"

Baz tries to take her shoulder. "Is Simon here?"

Agatha pulls away from him, jogging backwards, then back towards us. "He just got here," she says. "But the Mage is evil. He's fighting the goatherd."

"Ebb?" I say.

"And he tried to hurt me. He was going to do something, take something. He wants Simon."

"Come on!" Baz yells.

"Come with us," I say to Agatha. "Come help us."

"I can't," she says, shaking her head. "I can't."

And then she runs away.

# BAZ

Wellbelove runs in one direction, and Bunce runs in the other.

There's a noise from the school—like artificial thunder, like a hurricane on a tin roof.

I chase after Penny across the drawbridge. As soon as we make it to the courtyard, it's immediately clear where Simon is: All the windows have shattered in the White Chapel. There's smoke pouring out, and the walls themselves seem to be shimmering, like heat on the horizon.

The air is thick with Simon's magic. That burning green smell.

Bunce stumbles, coughing. I take her arm and lean against her, propping her up. I'd be surprised if she could cast a cliché right now. "All right, Bunce?"

"Simon," she says.

"I know. Can you take it?"

She nods, pushing away from me and shaking her ponytail resolutely.

The miasma gets worse, the closer we get to the Chapel. Inside the building, it's unnaturally dark, like something more than light is missing. I think I feel the Humdrum's presence, the scratch and the suck of him, but my wand stays alive in my hand.

Something rolls through me—like a wave in the air, in the magic—and Bunce pitches forward again. I catch her.

"We don't have to keep going," I say.

"Yes," she says, "we do. I do."

I nod. I don't let go of her this time. We walk together towards the worst of it, to what must be the back of the Chapel, through doorways, down halls.

My stomach roils.

There's no more air, just Simon.

Bunce pushes open another door, and we both throw our arms up in front of our eyes. It's bright as fire inside.

"Up there!" Bunce shouts.

I try to look where she's pointing. The light stutters into blackness, then back again. It seems to be coming from an opening in the ceiling—twenty feet above us, at least.

Bunce holds out a hand to cast, but clutches her stomach instead.

I wrap my left arm around her, then point my wand at the trapdoor. ***"On love's light wings!"***

It's a hard spell and an old spell, and it works only if you

understand the Great Vowel Shift of the Sixteenth Century—
and if you're stupidly in love.

Bunce and I float to the opening, and I don't try to shield
us, because there's nothing that *could*.

We climb into a room too loud and strobing to describe,
then kneel in broken glass, trying to hold ourselves together.
Bunce throws up.

In the seconds when the light isn't too bright or gone
completely, I see Simon in the middle of the room, holding
on to the Humdrum like he's about to tell him something
really important.

Simon has those red wings again, and they're spread
wide.

The Mage is here, too, clawing at Simon uselessly—nothing
can move Snow when he looks like that, his shoulders hunched
forward, and his jaw pushed out.

Bunce is on all fours, trying to lift her head. "What's he
doing?" she rasps, then heaves again.

"I don't know," I say.

"Should we try to stop him?"

"Do you think we could?"

The light is getting less intense. So is the dark.

I can hardly see the Humdrum anymore, but Simon still
has something in a death grip.

The noise is changing, too—getting higher, like it's winding
up, from a roar to a whine.

When the sound stops, my ears pop, and Simon falls forward
to the ground, lit only by moonlight through the broken
windows.

He falls, and he doesn't get up.

# PENELOPE

For a moment, the only sound is Baz, howling.

Then the Mage falls on Simon's limp body.

"What have you done?" He's shaking Simon, and beating on his wings. "Give it to me!"

Simon lifts an arm to push the Mage off, and that sign of life is all it takes to unleash Baz. He moves so fast, my eyes can't focus on him until he's holding the Mage by the chest, his fangs open over the man's neck.

"No!" Simon whispers, trying to pull himself up by grabbing their legs.

The Mage points his silver-tipped wand at Baz, but Simon grabs it and holds it against his own heart. "No," he says to Baz—or maybe to the Mage. "Stop!"

The three of them twist and stumble. The Mage is covered in blood, and Baz's mouth is full of teeth.

"Give it to me!" the Mage shouts at Simon. Does he mean his wand?

"It's gone!" Simon cries, using the wand to hold himself up. "It's all gone!"

The Mage pushes his wand into Simon's chest. "Give it to me!"

Baz yanks at the Mage's hair, pulling him back.

"Stop!" Simon cries. "It's gone! It's over!"

No one is listening to him.

I hold out my ring hand and speak as loudly and clearly as I ever have, letting my magic rise up from the empty pit of my stomach—***"Simon says!"***

Simon's next words ring out, dense with magic—

*"Stop it, stop hurting me!"*

The Mage jerks away from him, then sags in Baz's arms.

Baz steps back, confused, and lets the Mage drop to the floor. Then Baz reaches for Simon, but Simon is kneeling over the Mage, grasping at his chest.

"I . . . I think he's dead. Penny! I think I killed him. Oh God," Simon sobs. "Oh Merlin. Penny!"

I'm still shaking, but I crawl across the room towards them. "It's okay, Simon."

"It's not okay—the Mage is dead. Why is he dead?"

I don't know why he's dead.

I don't know what's happening.

"Maybe that's the only way he could stop hurting you," I say.

"But I didn't mean to kill him!" Simon cries, holding the Mage up, his arms around his back.

"Technically, it was Bunce who killed him," Baz says, but he says it gently, and there are tears in his eyes.

"He's dead," Simon says. "The Mage is dead."

# 84

## LUCY

I didn't know that something was wrong; I'd never been pregnant before. And no one had ever been pregnant with you, Simon.

The books say that you'll feel butterfly wings and twitches. A quickening. I felt so much more.

I felt you humming inside me. Busy and bright. I felt flushed from my belly to my fingertips.

Davy never left my side. He cooked for me. He cast blessings over us both.

And maybe you'll think that kindness was just for the ritual's sake. But I think he cared for me. I think he cared for you. . . .

I think he wanted us both standing beside him in the bright future he was building. A new World of Mages.

Pregnant women are always tired.

They can't hold down their meals. They feel peaked and light-headed.

One day I went out to feed our new chickens, and I realized I couldn't get back to the house. I didn't have enough energy to take another step.

I dropped to my knees, then leaned slowly forward, trying to protect you. Then I felt my lights blinking out.

Davy was inside, taking a nap. When he woke up, he found me there, red and thirsty. He carried me into the house, ranting about what could have happened and why I hadn't cast for help. But my magic had gone thin—it'd been weeks since I cast a spell. When I'd tried lately, it felt like I was knocking on a hollow box. Everything that was there before just *wasn't* anymore.

Everyone's magic goes a bit wonky when they're pregnant.

I felt better the next morning.

And worse the next.

The pulling in my stomach had gotten stronger, like a crank that kept tightening. I felt like I couldn't stay in the cottage, but I couldn't make it to the door.

"He needs air," I told Davy, and he didn't argue.

He took me out to the empty garden and lay with me in the grass. I needed to feel the ground beneath me, and the air, and the sun.

"Better," I told Davy, still feeling the crank turn.

When I was alone, I talked to you.

I told you about your family. About your grandparents. The cottage. About Watford, where your father and I met.

I named you.

"Simon," I said to Davy. We knew you were a boy then.

"All right," he said. "Why?"

"It's a good name, it's a wise name."

"Is it a saviour's name?"

"If he's the Great Mage, won't his name automatically be a saviour's name, whatever we choose?"

"Good point," he said. "Simon."

"Simon Snow."

"What's that?"

"His middle name. Simon *Snow*."

"Why on earth?"

"Because I like it. And because everyone should have a silly middle name."

"What's yours?"

"Winifred."

We laughed until it was too much for me.

Everyone feels tired when they're pregnant. Everyone feels sick. And strange.

"How do you feel?" Davy would ask.

"Good," I'd say.

"How's our boy?"

"Hungry."

I never told Davy the truth—what could he have done to help me? What would he have done if I'd said:

*"I feel like an empty hallway, Davy. Like a wind tunnel. Like there's something inside of me, and it isn't just eating me, it's eating everything. But not 'eating,' that's not the right word. Consuming, sucking, devouring. How long does it take for a star to collapse? How many trillions of years?"*

Maybe I shouldn't tell you all this. It wasn't what I came back to tell you.

I don't want you to think that it was your fault.

You're the child we would have had anyway, Simon. You were ours, in every way. And none of it is your fault. We made you this powerful—like starting a fire in the middle of the forest. We made you this hungry.

✿

In the end, I just wanted to see you.

And I thought maybe—maybe when you were born, I'd get some of myself back.

I should have asked Davy to get help when my labour came on. But we couldn't risk someone finding out what we'd done.

You came on the solstice. And you came so easily, I swear you didn't want to cause me any more pain.

Your father held you up to me and covered both our faces with kisses. He was the most powerful magician in the world before you, and he cast every safeguard he knew over our heads.

I saw you.

I held you.

I wanted you.

That's what I came back to tell you. I loved you before I met you, and I loved you more the moment I held you. And I never meant to leave you so soon.

*I never would have left you.*

Simon, Simon.

My rosebud boy.

# 85

## PENELOPE

We sit there, together, I'm not sure how long. All of us past the point of sorrow and exhaustion and relief.

Then Simon takes off his suit jacket—it tears around the wings—and spreads it over the Mage's torso. He starts crying again, and Baz pulls him into his arms. Simon lets him.

"It's okay," Baz says. "It's all okay now." One arm is tight around Simon's back, and the other is smoothing his hair out of his face. "You did it, didn't you?" Baz whispers. "You defeated the Humdrum. You saved the day, you courageous fuck. You absolute nightmare."

"I gave him my magic, Baz. It's all gone."

"Who needs magic," Baz says. "I'm going to turn you into a vampire and make you live with me forever."

Simon's shoulders are heaving.

Baz keeps talking. "Think about it, Simon. Super strength. X-ray vision."

Simon lifts his head. "You don't have X-ray vision."

Baz raises an eyebrow. His hair is in his face, and his hands are bleeding.

"I killed him," Simon says.

"It's going to be okay." Baz wraps both arms around him. "It's all right, love."

Everything is starting to make sense.

# EPILOGUE

# PENELOPE

I sent a little bird to my mum. There were a bunch of them around—they'd come in through the broken windows and were fluttering around the Mage's body.

We were all pretty wrecked, Simon, Baz, and me. I fell asleep right there. Between two corpses, that's how exhausted I was.

Simon tried to help Ebb, but she was cold. Gone. He didn't cast any spells on her—not even to cover her up—and I thought he must just be as exhausted as Baz and I were, out of magic for once in his life. I didn't understand until much later that his magic was gone for good.

Baz was exhausted *and* thirsty. All the blood everywhere—Ebb's, I think—was making him mental. Finally he started feeding on the birds. Which was disturbing, but like, not half as disturbing as everything else that had happened, and neither Simon nor I tried to stop him.

Mum showed up after a while—with Premal, of all people; he'd been helping her look for me. We were asleep by then, so Mum and Premal thought we were *all* dead. When I sat up, Mum was pale as a Visitor. I think it was like she'd walked into her greatest fear for me.

Premal wept when he saw the Mage.

Mum took one look at the Mage, cast a spell to preserve his body for the investigation, then never looked at him again.

She called Dad and Dr. Wellbelove, and a few others from the Coven, then took Simon and Baz and me to their room in the tower. (Mum's the reason I can get in; she broke the ward when Dad lived in Mummers House, and now all the female Bunces can enter.) Premal brought us tea and Hobnobs, and the three of us fell asleep again.

When I woke up, I told Mum about Agatha. I thought she might still be out there in the snow.

When Baz woke up, he called his parents.

When Simon woke up, he wouldn't talk. Just drank all the tea we gave him and clung to Baz's arm.

I'm not sure what history will say about us. Will they say that Simon killed the Mage? That I did?

I hope that Baz gets credit for ending the war.

The Old Families were still raring to go when Baz went home, even though the Mage was already dead and Simon was powerless—and nobody knew it yet, but the Humdrum was gone, too.

Mum thought the Grimms and Pitches might take the opportunity to seize control of everything.

But Baz went home, the Coven reconvened, there were new elections, and the war just never happened.

Mum's the headmistress now. Officially. The Coven appointed her.

She tried to talk me into going back to Watford, to finish my diploma. And if Simon had wanted to go back, maybe I would have made the effort. But there were just too many bad memories there. Every time I try to cross the drawbridge, I get sick to my stomach. I don't know how Baz manages it.

Agatha says she's never going back. "Over my dead body," she says. "Which is how I would have ended up if I'd stayed there."

# BAZ

Today's my leaving ceremony. I'm top of our class—there was no competition after Bunce dropped out—so I have to give a speech.

I told Simon not to come. It's a bit bleak, being surrounded by magicians all the time, when you can't even feel magic.

I didn't want him to come to Watford and think about all the things he isn't anymore. Not the Mage's Heir. Not a mage at all.

He's still everything else he's always been—brave, honest, inflammably handsome (even with that fucking tail)—but I don't think he wants to hear all that.

And I find it hard to say, honestly.

It's hard for us . . . to talk . . . sometimes. Lately. I don't blame him. Life hasn't exactly kept its promises to Simon Snow. Sometimes I think I should pick fights with him, just to restore his equilibrium.

Anyway. I don't think he'd want to be here.

My mother gave the speech at her leavers day. It's in the school archives—I found it, and I'm going to read from it today. It's about magic, the gift of magic. And the responsibility.

And it's about Watford. Why my mother loved it. She

made this list of everything she'd miss. Like, the sour cherry scones and Elocution lessons, and the clover out on the Great Lawn.

I can't say that I loved Watford like my mother did.

This was always the place that was taken from her. And the place where she was taken from me. It was like going to school in occupied territory.

Still—I knew I was coming back for my last term, even without Penny and Simon. I wasn't going to be the first Pitch in recorded history to drop out of Watford.

The speeches are in the White Chapel. The stained glass has been repaired.

My aunt Fiona's sitting in the front row. She whoops when I'm introduced, and I can see my father wince.

Fiona's as cheerful lately as I've ever seen her. She didn't know what to do with herself after the Mage died. I think she wanted to kill him again. (And again.) Then the Coven made her a vampire hunter, and everything turned around. She's on some secret task force now and working undercover in Prague half the time. I'm moving into her flat when I leave school. My parents wanted me to go to Oxford with them—they're living there, in our hunting lodge—but I couldn't be that far from Simon. My father still isn't ready to admit I have a boyfriend, and it would be too exhausting, living in a place where I have to pretend I'm not a vampire *or* hopelessly queer.

By the end of my speech, Fiona's weeping and honking her nose into a handkerchief. My father isn't crying, but he's too choked up to properly speak to me after the ceremony. Just keeps clapping me on the back and saying, "Good man."

"Come on, Basil," Fiona says. "I'll take you back to Chelsea and get you sozzled. Top shelf only."

"I can't," I say. "Leavers ball tonight. I told the headmistress I'd be there."

"Can't pass up a chance to see yourself in a suit, can you."

"I suppose not."

"Ah, well. I'll get you sozzled tomorrow, then. I'll come back for you at teatime. Watch out for numpties."

That's Fiona's standard farewell for me now. I hate it.

There are a few hours before the ball, so I take a quick walk in the hills behind the walls and gather a bouquet of yellow-eyed grass and irises, then head back across the drawbridge and into the now empty Chapel.

I make my way down into the Catacombs without bothering to light a torch. It's been years since I've got lost down here.

I'm not in a hurry, so I stop to drain every rat I find on the way. This school is going to be infested when I leave.

My mother's tomb is inside Le Tombeau des Enfants. It's a stone doorway in a tunnel lined with skulls, marked by a bronze placard.

I would have been buried here with her, if I'd died that day. I mean, died properly.

I sit by the door—there's no handle or lock, it's a piece of stone wedged into the wall—and set down the flowers.

"Some of this will be familiar to you," I say, getting out my speech. "But I've added a few flourishes of my own."

A rat watches me from the corner. I decide to ignore it.

When I get to the end of the speech, my head falls back against the stone. "I know you can't hear me," I say after a minute or two. "I know you're not here. . . .

"You came back, and I missed you. And then I did the thing you wanted me to do, so you probably won't ever come back again."

I close my eyes.

"But—I just wanted to tell you that I'm going to carry on. As I am.

"No matter how much I think about it, I don't think there's any scenario where you'd want me—where you'd *allow* me—to go on like this.

"But I think it's what you would do in my circumstances. It seems like you never gave up. Ever."

I exhale roughly and stand up.

Then I turn towards the door and bow my head. I speak softly, so that none of the other bones can hear:

"I know I usually come down here to tell you I'm sorry. But I think today I want to tell you that I'm going to be all right.

"Don't let me be one of the things that keeps you from peace, Mother. I'm all right."

I wait for a few moments, just . . . just in case. Then climb out of the Catacombs, brushing the dust from my trousers.

It's an especially grim leavers ball. The few friends I have left at Watford are here with dates—or avoiding me. Dev and Niall haven't quite forgiven me for befriending Simon. Dev said I wasted their entire childhood plotting against him.

"Oh, what else were you going to do with your childhood?" I asked.

Dev didn't bother answering.

I end up standing next to the punchbowl, talking to Headmistress Bunce about Latin prefixes. It's a fascinating subject, but I don't feel like I needed to put on a black tie for it.

I think Professor Bunce is sad that Penelope's not here. I consider consoling her with the fact that Penelope probably would've skipped the ball even if she'd stayed in school, but the headmistress is already wandering off to the other side of the courtyard to check her e-mail.

"I was hoping there'd be sandwiches," someone mumbles.

I ignore him because I'm not at Watford to make friends or small talk, especially on my way out.

"Or at least cake."

I turn around and see Simon Snow standing on the other side of the punch table. Wearing a suit and tie, with his hair properly parted and slicked to one side.

He shouldn't have been able to sneak up on me like that, but he smells different these days—like something sweet and brown. No more green fire and brimstone.

"How's the party?" he asks.

"Funereal," I say. "How'd you get here?"

"Flew."

My jaw drops, and he laughs.

"No," he says. "Penny drove me. She let me off at the gates."

"Where're your wings?"

"Still there. Just invisible. Someone's already tripped over my tail."

"I've told you to tuck it in."

"It makes my trousers fit funny."

I laugh.

"Don't laugh at me," he says.

"When will I ever laugh, then?"

Snow rolls his eyes, then cuts them nervously to the side. Towards the White Chapel.

"You don't have to be here," I say.

"No," he says quickly. "I do." He clears his throat. "I don't want you to leave without me."

*

Simon Snow can't dance.

The tail isn't helping. I take the end in my left hand and wrap it around my wrist, holding it against his lower back.

"We don't have to do this," I'd said when we walked out to the stone patio where people were dancing. "No one has to know."

"Know what?" Snow asked softly. "That I'm obsessed with you? That horse left the barn a long time ago."

I press my left hand, still holding his tail, into his back and take his hand with my right. He lifts his left hand in the air, then drops it like he doesn't know what to do with it.

"Put it on my shoulder," I say. He does. I raise an eyebrow at him. "Didn't Wellbelove ever teach you to dance?"

"She tried," he says. "She said I was hopeless."

"From the mouths of babes," I say.

At least the song isn't hopeless. It's Nick Cave. "Into My Arms." One of Fiona's favourites. It's so slow, we barely have to move.

Snow's wearing an expensive suit. Black trousers, black waistcoat and tie, and a rich velvet jacket—deep blue with black lapels. It must be Dr. Wellbelove's. It's snug at the shoulders, but I can't see where Snow's wings are hidden. Someone has spelled him neat and tidy.

I stand with my own shoulders squared. Everyone is looking at us—

Everyone dancing. Everyone standing around the courtyard, drinking punch. Coach Mac and the Minotaur and Miss Possibelf, all standing with their punch glasses stalled on the way to their lips.

"They'll know," I say. "They'll talk about it."

"What?" He's a million miles away. He's always a million miles away lately.

"They'll know that we're gay."

"There go my job prospects," Simon says flatly. "What will my family say?"

I'm not sure where the joke is.

He looks at my face and huffs, exasperated. "Baz, you're actually, literally the only thing I have to lose. So as long as doing gay stuff in public doesn't make you hate me, I don't really care."

"We're just dancing," I say. "That's hardly gay stuff."

"Dancing's well gay," he says. "Even when it isn't two blokes."

I frown at him. "You have Bunce."

"To dance with?"

"No. You have Bunce to lose."

His face falls.

I tug him closer. "No. I meant, you have more than just me. You have Bunce, too."

"She'll move to America."

"Maybe," I say. "Maybe not. And, anyway, not immediately. And beyond that—America's not amnesia. She'll still be your friend. Bunce only has two and a half friends; I don't think she'll drop you."

Snow starts to say something, then shakes his head once and looks down at his feet. A few curls escape onto his forehead.

"What?" I say, squeezing his hand. I've become very familiar with his hands. Dating Simon Snow hasn't been the erotic gropefest I'd always imagined—so far, it's a lot of sitting in silence and thousand-yard stares—but we do hold hands almost all the time. Snow's like a child who's afraid of getting lost in the market.

He squeezes my hand back, but doesn't lift his head.

I decide not to push him. He's here. Against all odds. Wearing a tie, dancing. That's all something.

I start to let my head rest against his—and he jerks his head up, just missing my nose. I pull my torso back. "Crowley, Snow!"

His face is red. "It's just—" He presses on my shoulder.

"It's just what?"

"You guys don't have to do this."

"Do what?"

He squints and grits his teeth. The fairy lights strung across the courtyard catch in his hair. "Just—you—it's not—"

"Use your words, Simon."

"You don't have to do this, you and Penny. I'm not. I'm not like you. I was never—I'm a hoax."

"That's not true."

"Baz. I'm not a mage."

"You lost your power," I argue. "You sacrificed it."

His tail whips out of my hand. It tends to slash around when he's upset. "I don't think it was ever mine," he says. "I don't know how the Mage did it, but you and Penny were right all along—magicians don't give up their children. I'm a Normal."

"Snow."

"I was bad at magic because I wasn't supposed to have any! The gates wouldn't even open for me tonight. Penny had to let me in."

A couple is drifting closer to us, clearly listening—Keris and her damnable pixie. I sneer, and they drift away.

Snow's crushing my hand and shoulder. I let him, even though I'm much stronger than he is. "*Simon*. Stop. You're talking nonsense."

"Am I? You and Penny care more about magic than anyone in the World of Mages. That's what you saw in me—

*power*—and it's gone. It was never me."

"It was!" I say. "You were the most powerful mage who's ever walked. That was real."

"I was a sorry excuse for a mage, how many times did you tell me so?"

"I said that because I was jealous!"

"Well, there's nothing to be jealous of now!"

I let go of him. "Why are you saying all this?"

Simon clenches his fists, hunching in on himself, like a bull. "Because I'm tired of *waiting*."

"For what?"

"For all of you to stop feeling sorry for me!"

"I'll never stop feeling sorry for you!" It's true. He lost his magic. It will never stop breaking my heart.

"But I don't want that either!" he says through his teeth. "I don't belong with you anymore."

"Wrong," I say. I take his hand again and put my arm back around him. "The Crucible drew us together."

"The Crucible?"

"I was eleven years old, and I'd lost my mother, and my soul, and the Crucible gave me you."

"It made us roommates," he says.

I shake my head. "We were always more."

"We were enemies."

"You were the centre of my universe," I say. "Everything else spun around you."

"Because of what I was, Baz. Because of my magic."

"*No.*" I'm nearly as frustrated as he is. "Yes. I mean, Crowley, Snow—*yes*, that was part of it. Looking at you was like looking directly into the sun."

"I'll never be that again."

"No. And thank magic." I sigh forcefully. "The way you were

before . . . Simon Snow, there wasn't a day when I believed we'd both live through it."

"Through what?"

"*Life.* You were the sun, and I was crashing into you. I'd wake up every morning and think, 'This will end in flames.'"

"I did set your forest on fire—"

"But that wasn't the end."

"Baz." His face crumples, in sorrow now—not anger. "I can't keep up with you. I'm a Normal."

"Simon. You have a *tail*."

"You know what I mean."

"Look." I bring our hands between us and knock up his chin. "Look at me. I don't want to have to say this all the time. It's the sort of thing that's supposed to go poetically unsaid. . . ." He meets my eyes. "You're still Simon Snow. You're still the hero of this story—"

"This isn't a story!"

"*Everything* is a story. And you are the hero. You sacrificed everything for me."

He looks abashed, ashamed. "I didn't do it for you, exactly—"

"Fine. For me and the rest of the magickal world."

"I was just cleaning up my own *mess,* Baz. Like, no one would call you a hero for cleaning up your own vomit."

"It was brave. It was brave and selfless and clever. That's who you are, Simon. And I'm not going to get *bored* with you."

He's still looking in my eyes. Staring me down like he did that dragon, chin tilted and locked. "I'm not the Chosen One," he says.

I meet his gaze and sneer. My arm is a steel band around his waist. "I choose you," I say. "Simon Snow, I choose you."

Snow doesn't flinch or soften. For a moment, I think he's going to take a swing at me—or bash his rock-hard head against mine. Instead he shoves his face into mine and kisses me. It's still a challenge.

I shove back. I let go of his hand to hold his neck. He smashes into me, and I take it. I don't give an inch. (It's a mess, honestly, and if he cuts his lip on my teeth, it could be a disaster.)

When we break, he's panting. I press my forehead to his, and feel the tension leave his neck and back.

"You can change your mind," he says.

"I won't." I shake my head against his forehead.

"I'll always be less than you," he whispers.

"I know; it's a dream come true."

That makes him laugh a bit, pathetically. "Still," he says. "You can always change your mind."

"We both can," I say. "But I won't."

I should have known that this is what it would be like to dance with Simon Snow. Fighting in place. Mutual surrender.

He puts both arms around my neck and slumps against me. He's either forgotten that everyone's watching, or doesn't care. "Baz?" he says.

"Yeah?"

"Are you still friends with Cook Pritchard?"

"I assume."

"It's just—I really hoped there'd be sandwiches."

# AGATHA

The sun shines every day in California.

I've got a flat I share with two other girls from school. There's a little veranda, and I sit out there with Lucy when I get home from class, and we soak in it. The sun.

Lucy's my Cavalier King Charles spaniel. I found her in the snow outside Watford. I thought she might be dead, but I didn't want to stop and sort it out. I just scooped her up and kept running.

I know that Penny will never forgive me for running away that day, but I couldn't turn back. I couldn't. I've never felt more sure of how to stay alive.

I had to run.

Technically, the farthest you can get from Watford is just east of New Zealand, in the middle of the Pacific Ocean. But California *feels* farther.

I left all my old clothes at home.

I wear sundresses now, and strappy sandals that tie around my ankles.

I left my wand at home, too; my mother would faint if she knew. She keeps asking if I've met any magicians. California is very popular with the magickal set, she says. There's even a club in Palm Springs.

I don't care. I live in San Diego. My friends work in restaurants and strip mall office buildings, and I date boys who wear dark stocking caps, even on warm days. On weeknights, I study, and on weekends, we go the beach. I spend the money my parents give me on tuition and tacos.

It's. All. So. Normal.

The only magician I still talk to, other than my parents and Helen, is Penelope. She texts. I tried not texting back, but that doesn't work with her.

She tells me how Simon is doing. She told me about the trials—I thought I might have to go back to testify, but the Coven let me do it in writing.

That's the closest I've come to talking to anyone about what happened.

About what I saw.

About Ebb.

I never knew Ebb. She was Simon's friend. I always thought she was barmy—living in that shack, spending her days with goats.

But I know more about her now.

She was a powerful magician, but she didn't do what powerful magicians do. She didn't want to be in charge. She didn't want to control people. Or fight. She just wanted to live at Watford and take care of goats.

*And they wouldn't let her.*

Like, they couldn't just let her be. She died in a war she had nothing to do with. There's no opting out of the World of Mages. There's no "no, thank you."

I don't know why she came back to save my life. I'd hardly even spoken to her.

Penny says I should honour Ebb's memory by helping to build a better World of Mages. . . .

But maybe I'll honour her memory by fucking right off, the way she tried to.

She told me to *run*.

I still have the picture of the Mage and Lucy. I stuck it in the mirror on my bedroom door. And I think about her sometimes when I'm getting dressed.

She's the one who got away.

I wonder if she's still here, in California. If she's got a family now. Maybe I'll run into her at Trader Joe's. (I won't tell her that I named my dog after her.)

I think I'm going to send the photo to Simon someday.

I'm not ready to talk to Simon yet, and I'm not sure he's ready to get a photo of the Mage in the mail. . . .

But I think Simon might be the only person who really loved the Mage. I know he killed him, but he's probably the person who was saddest to see him go.

# SIMON

Even though I'm the only one here with no magic, no one is helping me carry boxes up four flights of stairs.

"You," I say to Baz, letting a box drop on the couch, "even have superstrength. You could probably do this in half as many trips."

"Yes—" He pulls the lid off his Starbucks cup, so he can lick the whipped cream directly. "—but then your Normal neighbours would start to wonder, and they're already curious about the handsome young man haunting your door day and night."

"The neighbours don't even know we're moving in. They're all at work."

"Well, they *will* wonder, once they get a look at us. We're cool and mysterious and better-looking than any couple has a right to be." He looks up at me and pulls the cup away from his mouth. "Speaking of, come here, Snow—one of your wings is showing."

I thought the wings would fade away or even fall off after I gave the Humdrum my magic. But Penny says I used my magic to make them, and just because I gave my magic away doesn't mean everything I did with it is going to come undone.

I still have the tail, too. Which Baz won't stop mocking:

"It's not even a dragon tail—you gave yourself a cartoon devil's tail."

"I'm sure I could have it removed," I say. "I could talk to Dr. Wellbelove."

"Let's not do anything hasty."

Penny's been casting **These aren't the droids you're looking for** on me every morning, so the Normals don't notice my dragon parts, but the spell never holds all day. I'm afraid they're going to pop out during a class.

"Just tell people you're in a show," Baz advised.

"What kind of show?"

"I don't know; it's what my aunt Fiona always told me to say if anyone ever noticed my fangs."

I sit in front of Baz now, on the coffee table—which I carried up by myself. He hands me his cup, and I take a sip. "What is this?"

"Pumpkin mocha breve. I created it myself."

"It's like drinking a candy bar," I say. "I thought we were going to have tea."

"Didn't Bunce buy you a kettle? You have to start figuring this stuff out, Snow. Self-sufficiency." He holds his wand over my shoulder and taps the wing. ***"There's nothing to see here!"***

"Oh, Baz, come on. You know I hate **There's nothing to see here.** Now people are going to be running into me all day."

"Beggars can't be choosers—I don't know that robot spell of Bunce's."

Penny walks out of her bedroom. "Simon, have you seen my crystal ball?"

"Should I have?"

"It's in a box marked *Careful—crystal ball*. Oh, hey, Baz.

What're you doing here?"

"I'm going to be here all the time, Bunce. I'm going to haunt your door day and night."

"Did you come to help us move in?"

He puts the lid on his drink. "Hmm. No."

Baz and I talked about getting a flat together after he was done at Watford. He went back to finish second term, but I just couldn't. I mean, I *could* have, even though I was under house arrest; Penelope's mum would have let me.

I've only been back once, for Baz's leavers ball in the spring. Maybe I'll go again someday. When it all feels further away. I'd like to visit Ebb's grave, deep in the Wood.

Agatha didn't go back to Watford either. Her parents weren't going to make her. She's going to school in California now. Penny says she has a dog. I haven't talked to her. I didn't talk to anyone for a while, except for Baz and Penelope.

There was a three-month inquiry into the Mage's death. In the end, I wasn't charged. Neither was Penny. She had no idea that I'd say what I said after her spell—and I had no idea that what I said would kill the Mage.

I thought the World of Mages would fall apart without him. But it's been seven months, and there hasn't been a war. I don't think there will be.

The Mage hasn't been replaced.

The Coven decided the World of Mages doesn't need one leader, at least right now. Dr. Wellbelove suggested that I run for the Mage's seat, and I tried not to laugh like a madman.

I think I am, though . . . a madman.

I mean, I *must* be.

I'm seeing somebody, to talk about it—a magickal psychologist in Chicago. She's, like, one of three in the world. We do our sessions over Skype. I want Baz to talk to her, too, but so far, he changes the subject every time I mention it.

His whole family has moved to one of their other houses, up north.

The magic hasn't come back to Hampshire. Or any of the other dead spots—but there haven't been any new holes since Christmas. (Dozens of new ones opened that day. I feel bad about that—those are the ones I could have helped.) Penny's dad keeps calling to reassure me that nothing's getting worse. I've even gone along on a few of his surveys. It's not a big deal for me to visit the holes, the way it is for other magicians; I don't have any magic to lose. I mean . . . it *is* a big deal for me. But for other reasons.

Penny's dad thinks the magic will come back to the dead spots eventually. He's shown me studies about plants growing in Chernobyl and about the California condor. When I told him I was going to university, he said I should study restoration ecology. "It could be very healing, Simon."

I don't know. I'm going to start with basic courses and see what sticks.

Baz is starting at the London School of Economics in a few weeks. His parents both went to Oxford, but Baz said he'd be staked before he left London.

"Would that actually work on you?" I asked him.

"What?"

"A stake?"

"I'd think a stake through the heart would kill anyone, Snow."

He *will* call me Simon now, occasionally, but only when we're being soft with each other. (All that's still happening, too. I suppose I am gay; my therapist says it's not even in the top five things I have to sort out right now.)

Anyway, Baz and I thought about getting a flat. But we both decided that after seven years together, it might be good to have different roommates. And Penny and I have always talked about having a place together.

I never really thought that would happen.

I never thought there was a path that would lead here, a fourth-floor flat with two bedrooms and a kettle and a grey-eyed vampire sitting on the couch, messing with his new phone.

I never thought there was a path that would lead to both of us alive.

When you look at it that way, it wasn't that much to give up—my magic. For Baz's life. For mine.

Sometimes I dream that I still have it. I dream about going off, and I wake up, panting, not sure if it's true.

But there's never smoke. My breath doesn't burn, my skin doesn't shimmer. I don't feel like there's a star going nova in my chest.

There's just sweat and panic and my heart racing ahead of me—and my doctor in Chicago says that's all normal for someone like me.

"A fallen supervillain?" I'll say.

And she'll smile, from a professional distance. "A trauma victim."

I don't feel like a trauma victim. I feel like a house after a fire. And sometimes like someone who died but stayed in his body. And sometimes I feel like someone *else* died, like someone else sacrificed everything, so that I can have a normal life.

With wings.

And a tail.

And vampires.

And magicians.

And a boy in my arms, instead of a girl.

And a happy ending—even if it isn't the ending I ever would have dreamt for myself, or hoped for.

A chance.

"What time is it?" Penny asks. "Is it too early for tea? There're biscuits in one of these boxes. I could magic them up for us."

Baz looks up from his phone. "The Chosen One's making us tea the Normal way," he says. "It's occupational therapy."

"I already know how to make tea," I say. "And I wish you'd stop calling me that."

"You really were the Chosen One," Penny says. "You were *chosen* to end the World of Mages. Just because you failed doesn't mean you weren't chosen."

"The whole prophecy is bollocks," I say. "*'And one will come to end us. And one will bring his fall.'* Did I also bring my own fall?"

"No," Baz says. "That was me. Obviously."

"How did you bring my fall? I stopped the Humdrum myself."

Baz looks back at his phone, bored. "*Fell* in love, didn't you?"

Penny groans, and Baz starts laughing, trying not to crack a smile.

"Enough flirting!" Penny says, flopping down into a stuffed chair her parents gave us. (Which I carried up by myself.) "I've endured enough flirting for this *lifetime*. I'm hungry, Simon. Find the biscuit box."

Baz grins, then leans over and kisses my neck. (I have a mole there; he treats it like a target.)

"Go on, then," he says. "Carry on, Simon."

# ACKNOWLEDGMENTS

Joy DeLyria and I have never met in person or talked on the phone, and sometimes we go months without emailing. But *every time* I was feeling desperately lost and stuck with this book, she'd send me an email, asking, *"How is Simon?"*

And every time, she helped me get unstuck.

Thank you, Joy, for rooting so passionately for these characters, and for being so generous with your good advice.

Thank you, too, to Leigh Bardugo and David Levithan for being good friends and good readers. (Even if one of you was so tough, you made me cry.) (It was Leigh.)

And thank you to Susie Day for really *listening* to all this dialogue and talking to me about it. And to Keris Stainton, who answered countless questions about British life. If these characters sound American — or worse — it's despite their patience.

Thank you to my husband, Kai, for his love and encouragement, and for never running out of clichés.

To Christopher Schelling, who insisted on a higher body count.

To Sara Goodman, who has given me such freedom as an author and so much support as a friend.

And to the wonderful people at St. Martin's Press, who keep surprising me with their creativity and enthusiasm.

Finally — thank you to Nicola Barr, Rachel Petty, and everyone at Macmillan's Children's Books for making me feel so welcome in the UK and for making such gorgeous books.

# AUTHOR'S NOTE

If you've read my book *Fangirl*, you know that Simon Snow began as a fictional character in that novel.

A *fictional*-fictional character. Kind of an amalgam and descendant of a hundred other fictional Chosen Ones.

In *Fangirl*, Simon is the hero of a series of children's adventure novels written by Gemma T. Leslie—and the subject of much fanfiction written by the main character, Cath.

When I finished that book, I was able to let go of Cath and her boyfriend, Levi, and their world. I felt like I was finished with their story. . . .

But I couldn't let go of Simon.

I'd written so much about him through these other voices, and I kept thinking about what I'd do with him if he were in *my* story, instead of Cath's or Gemma's.

What would *I* do with Simon Snow?

What would I do with Baz? And Agatha? And Penny?

I've read and loved so many magical Chosen One stories— how would I write my own?

That's what *Carry On* is.

It's my take on a character I couldn't get out of my

head. It's my take on this *kind* of character, and this kind of journey.

It was a way for me to give Simon and Baz, only half-imagined in *Fangirl,* the story I felt I owed them.